# ANARCHY

## DYKARIN DRAGON SHIFTERS
### BOOK 1

# EMILY TYLER

This novel is entirely a work of fiction. The characters, places and incidents portrayed in it are the work of the author's imagination. Any resemblance to actual persons, living or dead, events and locations is purely coincidental.

ISBN-13: 978-0-6483522-2-8

# Collect your FREE GIFT of the 44 page

# Dykarin Prophecy Colouring Book

Discover the magic of Taminisha's story and the characters who share her world; the good, the bad and the uniquely different.

Get to know them and learn to love them as you indulge in the calming influence of colouring in the Dykarin images brought together by Emily for your enjoyment.

**CLICK ON OR SEARCH THE LINK BELOW**

**TO COLLECT YOUR FREE PRINTABLE COPY**

**https://dioniemcnair.wixsite.com/dykarinprophecy**

# DEDICATION

To my Father

for always being there for me,

encouraging me to keep an open mind,

and to freely exercise my imagination.

# ACKNOWLEDGEMENTS

Mary Rose Gudzenovs. Formatting and digital preparation

Georgina Hatchard. Editing

Wild Dreams Publishing & Editing. Editing

SelfPubBookCovers.com/ billwyc

# THE CONTINENT OF DYKARIN

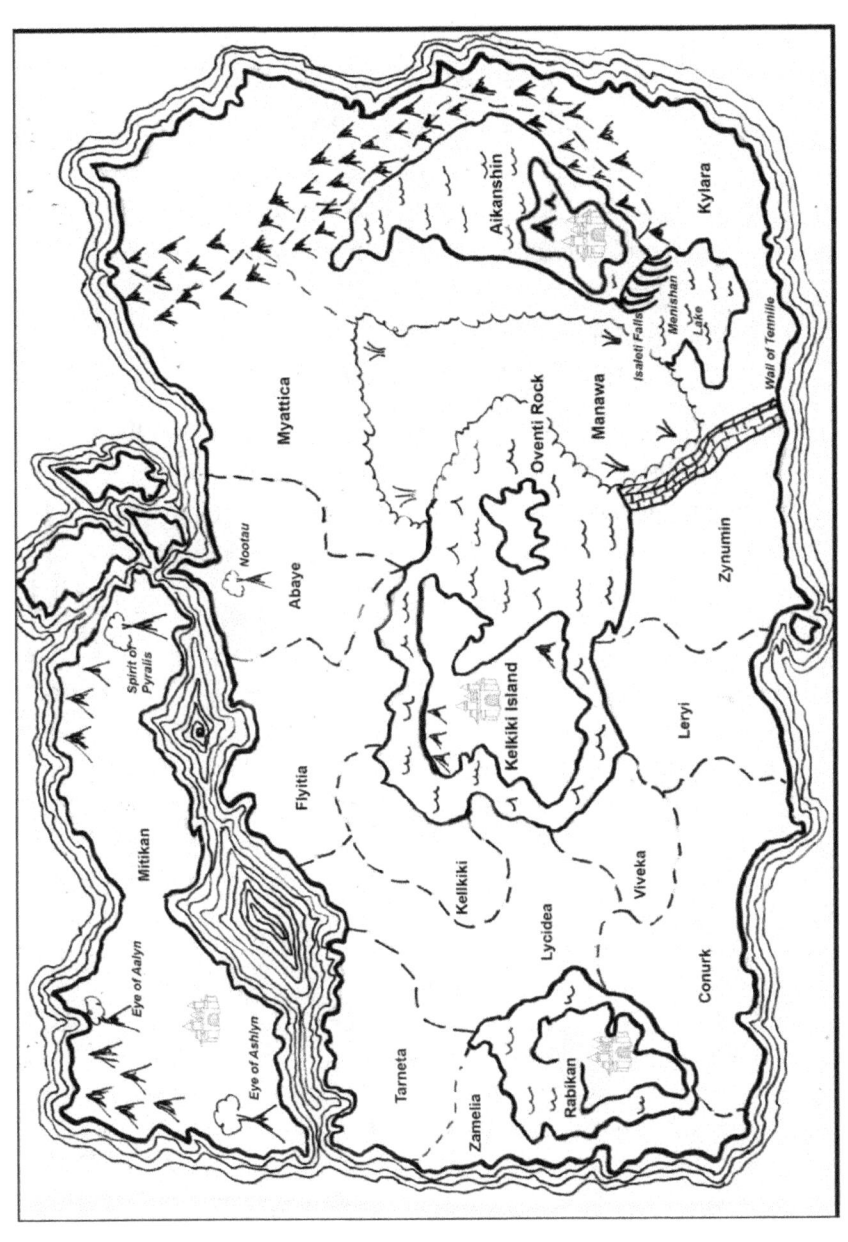

Ellkiiyn, the fire breathing, flying Dykarin dragon shape shifters, are a dying breed. The four clans, Vaprus of Aikanshin, Terraid of Rabikan, the Aqueena of Kelkiki and the Infernea of Mitikan have for centuries held a benign guardianship over the lands and fostered a peaceful existence of all species in Dykarin.

Pure Ellkiiyn bloodlines have always been highly valued, but breeding is marred with difficulties and many Ellkiiyn partner in their sachan form with other species and breed mixed blood offspring, the despised Khimaera. These creatures have minimal rights and are subject to inequality, prejudice and derision by pure blood Ellkiiyn.

# Prologue

Long before the Era of Darkness descended on Dykarin, Kokoshin, Guardian of the Vaprus Clan of Aikanshin, was killed by silver Ellkiiyn.

Kititash, his beloved soul mate was left alone to manage the realm and raise their two offspring, Shydee and Taminisha.

After a long time alone, Kititash bonded again, this time with a Terraid Ellkiiyn, Tokanin. It is a happy bonding although some Vaprus Ellkiiyn were disappointed she did not bond with another Vaprus but when the mysterious 'love call' comes it must be answered. They fail to breed.

While in Mitikan to discuss the growing problem of the Khimaera demands for equality, Kititash, her son Shydee and soul mate Rayhan are killed in a volcanic eruption. Shydee leaves behind an infant son, Jabrikan, heir apparent to the Aikanshin Guardianship. Tokanin and Taminisha care for him. Heartbroken, Tokanin becomes Regent for Jabrikan until he comes of age.

Ultimately the Khimaera's demands are denied by the Guardians of all the clans but unrest in the Mitikan Infernea simmers and grows.

Years later Tokanin bonds again, this time with Oralia, a Terraid Ellkiiyn with a drop of Fylitia blood in her veins. The Vaprus Clan are unhappy but tolerate it because Tokanin is a generous and wise leader.

Unwisely, Oralia and Tokanin breed and allow their Khimaera son to live. As Nyket grows he faces life without recognition or authority. His life is marred by prejudice and derision despite being the Regent Guardian's son. This treatment fosters a deep resentment in Nyket.

Tokanin, Regent of the Vaprus Clan of Aikanshin is dying and wants to restore the Guardianship to its rightful heir, Jabrikan. He declares his step daughter Taminisha and her soul mate Odakan joint regents for Jabrikan until he comes of age.

Already consumed with bitterness and anger his father's rejection of him for Regent drives Nyket to lead an uprising of Khimaera to secure equality for all.

# Chapter One

Potokin squeaked and wriggled against Taminisha's constraining arms. She chattered and whistled in his pointed ear to soothe his fear of Oralia's scrying chant, and the expected splash of water that would follow when Spirit revealed itself. Keen to calm him, she moved away from the speculum, the hem of her long black habilan rustling on the stone floor.

With a gentle hand, she stroked the miniature Tarki's scaly skin, but his agitation increased. With a streak of silver, he swung his head and bit down hard on Taminisha's hand, embedding razor sharp teeth into her flesh.

Taminisha tried to snatch her hand away. "Ouch. Let go, right now, you savage little beast," she said aloud in romni.

Despite the admonishment, her precious pet hung on and growled between clenched teeth.

"Let go, you undersized demon. If you do not, your Mamam will drop water on you."

The Tarki squealed in terror and withdrew his serrated fangs.

Taminisha cuddled him close and sighed in resignation as her purple blood oozed from the puncture marks in her skin to form rapidly congealing beads. *This is what I get for keeping a ferocious Tarki for a pet.*

Severely chastened Potokin settled in the crook of Taminisha's elbow, licking her blood off his lips and expressing his displeasure in a low grumble even as she moved to the window, well away from the water.

"Shhh, my pet, you are in no danger."

"Be silent, Tamin, you are destabilising the rhythm of the waters," Oralia scolded.

"Forgive me, Oralia." Taminisha hitched her habilan up and perched on the wide stone window ledge.

Below her, the realm of Aikanshin spread like a colourful painting, glowing through the light mist drifting down from the mountain. The moist silken air caressed her skin. Taminisha inhaled deeply of the waylia-scented air, its zesty floral perfume a nostalgic, but faded memory of her dead mother.

A motley group of citizens were returning from the farming paddocks. They hurried along the winding stone bridge that hung across the gushing Aikan River, keen to get home after a period of hard work.

Taminisha could see quite a number of true blood sachans from Kylara amongst the throng of mixed bloods in sachan form. She suspected the mixed blood species probably couldn't even trace their own bloodlines. The intermingling of the species was a concept she could not understand, even though most species of Dykarin accepted it as commonplace. Only the Ellkiiyn frowned on the practice.

A roar from above attracted her attention. Two Ellkiiyn soared past the castle with the lazy undulation of leathery wings. She recognised her soul mate Odakan from the iridescent flash of green and gold scales. The other, a Vaprus male, deeper purple than her, and much bigger, ignored her. He had an impressive rack of pectenites curling around his pale lavender froxcomb that bristled all the way to his tail. She waved. Odakan flicked his tail in acknowledgement.

A childish squeal drifted up from the lake below. Taminisha leaned out over the window ledge to get a better view. In the upper lake, her nephew, in Ellkiiyn form, charged through the water after Taminisha's hallegan and bodyguard, Tarlitek. She smiled. Even as Ellkiiyn, the boy had no chance of catching the Orunan shape-shifter as he powered through the water with a few sweeps of his massive tail.

Taminisha leaned further out. Potokin squeaked. She ignored his protest and broadcast in Ellkiiyn. *"You'll have to swim faster to catch, Tarlitek."*

Jabrikan hesitated in his dash through the water and looked up. *"He's too fast, and I'm only a baby."*

Taminisha chuckled to herself. *"And he's Orunan. Even I couldn't catch him."*

The child beckoned. *"Come join us, Tamin."*

Taminisha shook her head. *"I'm not allowed. I'm helping Oralia commune with Spirit."*

*"I don't like her doing her sorcery. It's scary."*

*"I know."*

Taminisha ached to transmogrify, fly down and dive into the cool waters, but she squelched her desire knowing her step father frowned on her penchant for swimming and her affinity with water. *My predilection is nothing more than they deserve for leaving me, and Shydee, in the care of an Orunan shape shifter.*

Behind her, Oralia chanted in a soft rhythmic call of unintelligible words demanding Spirit reveal the future. Calling the spirits was fraught with inherent danger and seeking the future before its time, a dice with death and madness. However, the drop of Fylitia blood running in Oralia's veins drove her to seek what the Ellkiiyn could not, and did not, want to see.

A shiver flitted across Taminisha's skin. Many were not happy when her step father joined with Oralia, even knowing she had tainted blood. Still smitten with his partner, Tokanin never said a word against her spell binding or scrying.

Most of the occupants of the castle wished he would bring a stop to it, but Taminisha would never criticize Oralia because it would upset her step father, and Tokanin had always treated her with kindness.

Despite the loss of her parents, and brother, she had a pleasant life, full of freedom and love. When Tokanin either passed to Spirit or abdicated, she would be Regent for Jabrikan and have to adapt to the responsibilities that came with such an elevation. Both she and Odakan looked forward to the challenge, but for now, she made the most of her carefree life.

Taminisha tucked a loose strand of pearls back up into her dainty rack of pectenites and smoothed her masq of purple and silver scales before she turned away from the scene below. She kept her eyes averted as Oralia sang in a high-pitched voice. Taminisha cringed against the screeching decibels as the keening invaded her head. Oralia sometimes forgot full blood Ellkiiyn had much finer hearing than she did, and her raucous sounds hurt delicate eardrums.

Despite her dislike of scrying, when Taminisha heard the waters move, she felt compelled to watch. Potokin hunched down against her breasts, covered his horny face with clawed hands and curled his tail around his plump scaly body. Taminisha did not blame him for trying to hide. *I wish I could do the same.*

Oralia stood by the scrying pool, her hands held out, with palms toward the water. Her eyes sparkled with red flecks and her long angular face seemed more pinched than usual. The beads in her pectenites trembled. Vibrations undulated through the room as the clear water in the bowl became dark and murky. Under the motion of Oralia's hands, it swayed back and forth in the white marble speculum.

"Come Spirit, come. Reveal thyself to those that ask. Come hither, fair warning or foul, come to me, I demand thee," Oralia shouted.

The water swirled and slopped back and forth, hissing loudly as gray froth fizzed on the surface. Still Oralia called.

Taminisha pressed back against the cold stone wall. Potokin trembled in her arms as eerie shadows danced around the circular tower room. She glanced out through the open window, disconcerted to see Aikanshin's glowing pastel landscape had dulled, and the mist perpetually drifting over the lake and the river had thickened into a gray fog.

Taminisha held back a scream, gulping down large breaths of air as she tried to stay silent. Sweat beaded on her forehead. She cuddled Potokin closer. *Had Oralia gone too far this time?* An ugly sensation of doom nudged at her. Taminisha resisted its presence, but it deepened, and filled the room with malevolence.

A smoky twirl of vapour rose from the speculum and wrapped gray tentacles around Oralia's lean body. Oralia threw back her head, her white blond short-cropped hair stood on end as her body trembled. The uncontrolled movement made the long-beaded earrings in her pointed ears jangle with a furious melody.

She screeched as her eyes glazed over. "Untruths, broken rules— evil grows strong within. There is no escape until the Daughter of Kylara comes. The path is set, the Clans are doomed. I am the source," she cried.

A peal of maniacal laughter bubbled from her gaping mouth, silencing her words. Oralia clutched at her hair, her face, and her breasts, but the misty tentacles tightened around her body, filling her mouth and ears, and entangling her hands until she could no longer move them. She began to spin, around and around on the spot, faster and faster, screaming louder and louder.

Taminisha shoved her pet behind the drapes, covered her ears and screamed for help.

Oralia span in a wide arc, closer and closer to Taminisha. Her dark hazel eyes were wide open, but unseeing, as they blazed with a fiery red light.

Taminisha reached out. "Oralia, be still. Take my hands, it is I, Taminisha."

Oralia did not respond. Horror was etched stark on her face. The fear reflected in her eyes, and her crimson painted lips drawn back in a snarl showing pointed teeth, terrified Taminisha. *What evil being had possessed Oralia?*

A series of thumps shook the door on its hinges, but it did not open.

"Tokanin, Nyket, anyone, help us. The Spirit has possessed Oralia!"

The battering increased and the door shuddered under the onslaught. Taminisha lunged at the door and tried to lift the latch, but it jammed.

"Taminisha, what is happening? Open the door," Tokanin shouted.

"I cannot. It's jammed."

"Stand back," Nyket, bellowed through the heavy timber.

Taminisha moved away, and with two thuds and a crack, the door burst open.

Nyket barged into the room. Tokanin hobbled in his wake, his cane cracking against the flagstones.

Nyket shoved Taminisha aside. "Mother, speak to me."

Guttural utterances burst from Oralia as she writhed on the floor unable to free herself.

Tokanin threw his cane aside, hobbled forward and slapped at the gray tentacles. "Be gone, monstrosity. Be gone from my mate."

The gray tentacles melted and dissolved.

Oralia lay still.

Tokanin eased himself to his knees, with a grunt of effort, and cradled her limp body.

"Evil comes from within, my love. We must restore the Vaprus to Aikanshin's Guardianship before this unstoppable terror rises." Oralia's voice cracked and faded. She closed her eyes and slumped against her mate's chest.

"Move out of my way, Father, I will carry Mother to her rooms," Nyket said.

Tokanin accepted Nyket's suggestion and shuffled aside.

Nyket scooped his mother from the floor and strode from the room with her cradled against his broad muscular chest.

With a curt nod, Tokanin accepted Taminisha's hand to help him rise. She retrieved his cane. He took it without a word and then staggered after his son.

Alone in the room Taminisha fought to control the nausea clenching in her gut. The ugly ambience haunting the room stalked her. She held back a whimper as she retrieved Potokin from his hiding place. Clutching him to her breasts, she hurried from the room on shaking legs. Tremors still fluttered through her long after she'd retreated to her chambers and brewed some herbal tea to calm her nerves.

She pondered Oralia's words. *Restoring the Vaprus Ellkiiyn to the Guardianship of Aikanshin was a good thing. What of the evil—did it threaten the whole of Aikanshin, or just Oralia and Tokanin? I do not understand the meaning in this evil message from Spirit.*

Taminisha shivered and swallowed the sourness in her mouth. She did not fear the physical world for she had Odakan and Tarlitek to protect her. However, how did one fight an unidentified ethereal entity? She wanted to ask Oralia the meaning, but held back; concerned her step father's soul mate would not want to relive her ordeal quite so soon.

Taminisha settled Jabrikan for sleep and walked back to the main hall. Odakan had not returned from whatever errand he'd been on earlier in the solar phasing and both Tokanin and Oralia remained closeted in their suite. She wandered up to Nyket's rooms. They were empty, and she guessed he had also stayed to comfort his mother.

Still unsettled by the strange events she retreated to her bed to wait for her soul mate's return. The lunor discs hung high in the sky when she heard him enter the room. She rolled over and watched him disrobe. It gave her immense pleasure looking at his naked sachan body. His smooth olive skin, sculptured chest, slim hips, long muscular legs and the manhood that hung loose, having no sheath to withdraw into.

He released his mahogany coloured hair from its bun and ruffled it out around his single slim pair of pectenites. He threw back the covers and slipped in beside her.

She slid into his embrace, inhaling his scent. He pulled her close, increasing her awareness of his hardness. Her nerve endings tingled. Heat flooded her nether regions and her fingers twitched and ached with the need to touch him. He kissed her. She waited for the urge to mate ripple through her. With a tender caress, she stroked his shoulders and down his chest. He kissed her again—long and hard. The urge did not come. She continued her caress down his abdomen and clasped his hardness. He growled.

"I want you, Odakan. To love me. If the urge does not come, surely we can share intimacy in the sachan way."

He pulled away and sat on the side of the bed. "If the Ellkiiyn mating urge does not come then it does not. I will not do it the sachan way. The risk is too high. I do not want you to end up like my mother."

"But, Odakan, I'm happy to take the risk."

"I am not. I will not have you suffer and die to have a child the sachan way."

She touched his back. "The chances are small. They say it is very intimate and pleasant."

"No, Taminisha. If you do not accept my edict I will go sleep in the guest room."

She clenched her jaw and stiffened her body as she put a space between them. In silent frustration, she glared at his rigid back. A painful lump clogged her throat as she fought back tears. She sighed and not for the first time acquiesced to his dictates. She sagged back onto the bed. *A simple cuddle is better than sleeping alone, I suppose.*

"All right, Odakan. Come hold me. I will take comfort in what you offer." Her voice cracked.

Her mate sighed and crawled back under the covers. She turned her back on him and he slid up behind her and wrapped his arms around her. "I love you, Taminisha. And this is why I forbid it."

"Then why does the urge not come?"

Odakan shrugged.

She lay silent, reining in her desire and hurt. When she brought her emotions under control, she spoke. "Spirit attacked Oralia during her scrying attempts."

Odakan jerked up and leaned over to see her face. "How bad? You were not hurt?"

"Oralia collapsed, but she appeared more frightened than hurt. It did not touch me."

"I will tell my uncle you are not to assist Oralia anymore."

"Tokanin will be hurt. He needs to see we support his mate and their joining."

"Not at your expense. You don't want to—do you?"

"No, Odakan."

~  ~  ~

When she woke at first light, her soul mate had already left their bed. Her head ached and her eyes burnt with the sting of unshed tears. His refusal to mate with her in the sachan way had again left her frustrated and unsettled. Others did it, and none she knew of had bred other than Odakan's late mother.

She lurched out of bed and padded up to the landing platform. The air was clear and crisp. The village stood dormant at this early hour with only a few wisps of smoke signalling life in the cottages.

She stared up toward the mist-shrouded mountain. "Spirit, badger him to change his stance. I need the intimacy."

With her pleas released to the Great Spirit, she rolled and transmogrified, stretching leathery wings wide for the solar orb's rays to soften and warm the fibrous flesh. She squinted across the empty platform, clenched her hands into fists then filled her lungs with cool air. With a tremendous huff, she spat a stream of flame across the landing platform. As the flames died, she saw the scorched vines shrivelled along the parapet. She grinned and swaggered across to inspect the damage. Satisfied with her mute statement of protest she rose into the soft pink and apricot of the solar awakening with a single flap of wings.

Below, the waters of the upper lake shimmered. She spun around and dived. The wind danced over her skin teasing its way beneath the edge of her scales. She snorted, eased her dive, tucked her wings against her back, and then splashed into the water. It swept cold and refreshing over her skin.

Taminisha closed her transparent lids over her almond shaped eyes and studied the bottom of the lake. A flash of green caught her attention. She surged forward, pumping powerful legs through the water. Three small orrtaya danced in front of her. She snapped her powerful jaws, caught one, chomped her teeth down and gulped. *Mmmm, a delicious awakening repast.*

She chased the other two and picked them off one at a time. Her hunger sated, she surfaced, rolled over and floated. The rays from the solar orb warmed her scaled belly. With slow movement of her hands, she paddled slightly against the gentle current to keep her distance from the falls. She had no desire to tumble over and end up in the dark waters of Menishin Lake and a face-to-face encounter with Tarlitek's deity, the vicious insatiable, Orunikan.

The combination of solitude and fresh air eased her restlessness and ready to face her life again she paddled to the shallows and waded ashore. With a tremendous shudder of her huge frame, she dispersed the water from her hide and flicked her purple froxcomb until it stood up along her back. She rubbed her snout plates against the pebbles then scratched her lower jaw. She glanced up at the castle. *Time I went to check on Oralia. Don't want Tokanin to think I don't care.*

With a jump and a downward thrust of her powerful wings, she launched from a standstill and soared back to the landing platform. She quite expected Odakan to be waiting to chastise her, but the platform remained empty. Before she transmogrified she licked her ekta claw, dipped it into her locket and formed a habilan. She slipped the soft stretchy garment over her head and padded down the stairs.

Nyket answered the door to Oralia's rooms. He scowled at her. The expression emphasized his long, angular features and twisted his wide mouth into a narrow line. The tattoos on his forehead distorted. "So you deigned to come."

His words cut deep as he made no effort to greet her formally, as he should.

"I thought Oralia would appreciate some time to recover. She had an awful scare."

"By Orunan scales, I wish she would desist from such barbaric practices."

"She can't, Nyket, it's in her blood."

"You would say that. Well, it isn't in mine."

"Whatever you say, Nyket. Just let me pass to visit your mother."

He stepped aside, his green eyes flashing sparks down at her. "I'll leave you to it. Enjoy."He strode down the corridor, his back stiff and his broad shoulders square.

Sympathy for Nyket flashed through her. He hated that his breeding made him a tainted Khimaera—ostracised by all pure Ellkiiyn.

She entered the room. Oralia huddled in the winged chair by the window. Rays from the solar orb poured in and bathed her in a golden glow.

Taminisha knelt beside the chair. "How are you feeling?"

Oralia looked at her. "I'm afraid of what I have done. Tokanin has taken to his sick bed and all he will say is he's made a decision."

"A decision about what?" Oralia's hand was cold and clammy when Taminisha cradled it. She almost withdrew the touch.

"The future. The message is clear. We must right the wrong or suffer the consequences."

"What wrong?"

"The Vaprus Ellkiiyn must be restored. Tokanin has outstayed his welcome as Regent Guardian," Oralia muttered.

"But Tokanin has kept his promise to my mother. If Shydee had not died, Tokanin would have already restored the Guardianship. The delay is not Tokanin's fault."

Oralia sighed. "Spirit says it's time. Go now, I need to rest."

Taminisha slipped from the room, her heart racing and every nerve ending tingling. She'd always known this time would come and she wondered how Nyket would respond if Tokanin rejected him for the role of Regent as Taminisha believed he would.

# Chapter Two

It did not surprise Taminisha when barely two awakenings later, the command came that she, and Jabrikan, present themselves in the entresol an hour before the settling of the solar orb.

She summoned her hallegan, Tarlitek.

He knocked on the door and entered, moving with a light agile step. He towered over Taminisha, his wide, muscular shoulders straining his white shirt. His shimmering cream skin and high forehead covered in a protective mask of blue green scales and an elegantly curving exoskeleton gave him a daunting countenance. Along with the Orunan reputation as being strong, cold-blooded, and ruthless, he had all the attributes needed by a hallegan. Even though she knew his mother's Myattican influence had softened his merciless killer instinct it comforted Taminisha to have him on her side.

"It is finally happening. Tokanin is to make an announcement. Can you please find Jabrikan and see him dressed in his best."

Tarlitek's fin shaped ear lobes twitched and the frills on his neck gills ruffled. "This announcement is not before time. You and Odakan are more than ready."

"Assuming he intends to confer the Guardianship on the child with us as joint regents."

"There is no other option." Tarlitek gestured as if to wipe the idea away.

"There is always Nyket. I'm worried Tokanin will nominate him as Regent."

Tarlitek grimaced showing sharp pointed incisors. "He wouldn't dare. Many are impatient to see the Vaprus restored."

"Others are eager for change that will see a tainted Khimaera rule."

"Never."Tarlitek frowned, making the spines standing up from his skull clatter as he scrunched them together. His exoskeleton flushed dark blue-green.

Taminisha shrugged. "While I have faith in Tokanin, I have concerns about others. I want you present at the announcement. Enter through the rear door, and come armed. We need to be prepared."

Dark shadows flickered in his round wide-set eyes. "Your Mamam will be cringing in her spiritual resting place."

"I know, Tarlitek. If only one had a crystal ball..." She bit down on her tongue. *Only one solar phasing ago I criticized Oralia for wanting to know, and now I do the same.* She pushed the thought aside. "Go now, and ready my nephew. We will see this change out together."

When Tarlitek left, Taminisha rummaged through her wardrobe undecided what to wear. In the end, she chose a lavender habilan and a royal purple tunic over the top. She wore her long black hair loose, wound a string of her late mother's purple gemstones around her pectenites, and hooked matching earrings in her lobes. With this new stage of life about to begin Taminisha worried about her preparedness to be Regent. She stroked Potokin. "Stay here, my pet. I will return soon."

The Tarki glanced up at her from eyes heavy with sleep then tucked his head back under his back leg.

The late solar orb rays streamed in through the stained-glass windows, throwing a kaleidoscope of colours across the crowded room. The air in the lower chamber hung heavy with a burden of scents—pungent firnit fronds and a spicy tang drifting from the kitchen: male sweat and soil from unwiped boots. The zesty essence of agitated Ellkiiyn overlay the strong aromas and stifled the breath in her nostrils.

Taminisha wrinkled her nose as she elbowed her way through the Ellkiiyn clumped together in loosely formed groups. Their presence inundated the spacious main chamber. Nobody interfered with her passage to the stairs of the entresol.

She applied pressure against her nephew's shoulder to propel him forward. "Climb faster, Jabrikan, your Grandpapa does not tolerate tardiness."

The child squirmed under her guidance, but increased his pace with short, spindly legs making hard work of the oversized steps.

*"I want to go swimming with Tarlitek. You said I could."*

Despite the fact she had spoken aloud in romni, the child had broadcast in Ellkiiyn. Such bad etiquette to not reply in like. "Mind your manners, Jabrikan, and stick to romni."

The child sighed.

"I know this is frustrating for you, but I haven't broken my promise. You can go later. First, you have to listen to your Grandpapa. What he has to say is very important."

He pushed his rosebud mouth out into a pout and squinted his yellow eyes in an effort to transform his cute babyish face into the mutinous expression he turned on her. She ignored it and gestured for him to precede her. When they reached the entresol, he slumped into one of the seats by the throne.

Taminisha smiled as her nephew kicked his booted feet back and forth against the chair legs. This child had brought her so much joy, and consolation, in the six years since her Shydee's death. Even Jabrikan's current fractious display could not tarnish her exhilaration. Finally, as the only surviving, male, Vaprus Ellkiiyn, Jabrikan would become the Guardian Apparent—its rightful Guardians would rule Aikanshin once again.

Ignoring the child squirming on the seat, she strode across the room and flung open the wrought iron gates that barred entry to outsiders via the floor to ceiling arches. She stared out over her home and wished Tokanin's declaration over. With her position as Regent secured and Odakan by her side, she could relax and look forward to the future. Edginess had gripped Aikanshin since her mother, Kititash, had taken the hand of the Spirit, along with her son, Shydee, the Heir Apparent and his soul mate. Their deaths left the realm under the Regent Guardianship of her second mate, Tokanin until Shydee's infant son came of age.

Latent tensions and resentment smouldered amongst the full blood Ellkiiyn of Aikanshin at their continued rule by a Terraid interloper and his conditional acceptance had deteriorated when Tokanin had joined with a Khimaera, and they bred a tainted son. The righteous full bloods were scandalised and took their resentment out on the ever-increasing population of scorned mixed bloods—the Khimaeras.

Tokanin's announcement should soothe those frictions, if not extinguish them, and alleviate the angst that a Khimaera would come to rule. Taminisha's heart beat erratically, ignited by expectation and underlying fear of what might occur. She flinched as the growl of pectenite horns heralded Tokanin's arrival.

An expectant hush spread through the crowd on the floor below. Tokanin, Regent of Aikanshin, leaned heavily on his cane, his shambling steps taken with arduous concentration.

Taminisha groaned inwardly at how gaunt and drawn her step father had become. He seemed as if he laboured under a great weight. Once a robust, slightly tubby male, he had become barely more than a shell of who he used to be.

Oralia followed in his wake. The mincing gait she set to match her mate's slow progress merely accentuated her sensuality. Few would notice the repeated tugging at her beads, and the constant twisting of her habilan into small scrolls, as indicating her anxiety.

Taminisha stood, and stepped forward. She held out her hands and Tokanin took them in his. Taminisha almost flinched away from the dry looseness of his skin, but forced herself to grasp his flesh and lean forward. Their pectenites clicked faintly as they touched.

"Greetings, Taminisha. Your time has come."

"Tokanin, I pay my respects."

Tokanin let go of her hands. "I thank you. Be seated."

Taminisha retreated to her seat, struggling against the urge to wipe her hands on her habilan. She sat perfectly still as Odakan stepped up in front of his uncle. He placed his hands on the old man's shoulders and leaned forward. Again, the faint click as their pectenites touched.

"Greetings, Odakan."

"Uncle Tokanin, I offer my loyalty and respect."

"Thank you, nephew. I have never had cause to doubt you. Come, stand by my side."

Odakan stepped around the old man and took his place two paces behind his uncle.

Taminisha settled deeper into her chair as everyone took his or her rightful place for this momentous proclamation. Her pulse raced as she panted in small tight breaths and clutched the arms of her chair with clammy hands. A sliding glance over those present chilled her blood; Nyket was the only one missing from this elite gathering.

Nyket's absence didn't surprise Taminisha. A sliver of sympathy glanced through her. No one could expect him to be present, and suffer in silence the humiliation of his father not only restoring the Guardianship of Aikanshin to the Vaprus Ellkiiyn through Jabrikan but then installing Taminisha as Regent until her nephew came of age.

Nyket had made no secret he wanted to become Regent for Jabrikan until the child came of age knowing it would give him years of unmitigated power. He refused to acknowledge his installation to Regent would be ferociously opposed by the Vaprus Ellkiiyn not only because he was Terraid not Vaprus but because the one drop of Fylitia blood running in his veins made him Khimaera and not entitled to rule.

She glanced at Odakan. He shook his head to indicate he did not know what had become of Nyket.

Taminisha perched on the edge of her seat. Even though she already knew the outcome of this symposium, expectation and uncertainty clamped her chest. The same qualms held all the Ellkiiyn gathered in the hall below, silent.

She startled at a touch on her back, but immediately relaxed when her hallegan stepped up beside her. He squeezed slightly on her shoulder as an offering of reassurance. It almost helped. She watched her step father. *Get on with it.*

The smell of age, and sickness, emanated from Tokanin as Oralia helped him take his place on the throne.

For a moment, Taminisha felt sympathy for her, but it died almost as it formed. Oralia didn't need her sympathy, nor would she want it.

"Citizens of Aikanshin, I am old, sick, and well beyond leading the Vaprus clan in these troubled times. My final tasks as Regent Guardian are not erroneous. A blessing on my nephew, Odakan, and his union of the heart to, Taminisha."

Approval spluttered through the crowd gathered below.

"I also announce, Jabrikan, as Guardian Apparent."

Another splutter of approval and a smattering of applause halted his next words.

When the clatter fell silent, he continued. "Joint Regents, Odakan and Taminisha, will guide Aikanshin until Jabrikan reaches maturity."

A disjointed hum of commentary came from the lower chamber. An occasional grunt, or exclamation, punctuated the conversation.

Tokanin frowned down at the gathering. "Are there those who wish to object? If so, you best speak up. I will not allow furtive dissension to undermine this realm as I lie waiting for Spirit to take me."

Taminisha sat immobile, unable to still the tremors inside. Surely, the population would accept her and Odakan as Regents. She had pure Vaprus Ellkiiyn bloodlines. She watched those below. No one spoke. No one moved. The silence stretched interminably. Unease crawled over Taminisha's skin, the hair on her nape springing upright. The silence hung, heavy and treacherous. *Why don't they speak? By the Great Spirit Ellkii, just get on with it.*

The screech of an Ellkiiyn battle call shattered the baleful hush. A gust of wind brought scudding flotsam and jetsam through the open archway. A rasp of claws on stone rent the quiet into discordant chunks threaded with hollers of welcome, and howls of fury.

The green bulk of Nyket, as Ellkiiyn, filled the space to claustrophobic capacity. He extended the golden yellow frill around his neck and huffed hot air across the room. He narrowed his overly round eyes almost hiding the red glare as he focussed on his father.

Taminisha's heart jumped fitfully, unease squeezed her stomach, and sweat beaded on her forehead. A precipice of trepidation gaped at her, the inevitability of destruction reached out with clawed fingers.

She glanced at Jabrikan and wished she could save him from the conflict to come. She clutched at Tarlitek's large hand with its webbed fingers. He leaned in close.

"Take the child; this is not for his eyes." She squeezed his hand tighter. "If this goes badly I charge you to see him safe."

"But you…"

"The boy, Tarlitek, promise me."

Tarlitek nodded. With just a small draft of air, he left with a squirming Jabrikan tucked under his arm.

"Transmogrify, Nyket. To appear as Ellkiiyn in such a situation is uncouth, and your disarray is not befitting your standing."

"*Standing?* What standing, Father? I am a Khimaera."

Taminisha stared at Nyket. She'd never seen him as Ellkiiyn, and now she understood why he never transmogrified in company. The contamination of Fylitia blood became more obvious as Ellkiiyn. The crooked scales, the short misshapen pectenites and his eyes, red in colour, but more rounded more sachan.

"Transmogrify!" Tokanin bellowed.

With a flap of leathery wings and scrape of claws, Nyket rolled across the floor then rose to his feet. In sachan form, his mixed blood barely showed with just a few misshapen scales corrupting the masq on his face. His facial tattoos disguised the shape of his eyes and brows.

Nyket snatched up his newly formed habilen, and pulled it over his naked sachan body as he regained his balance. He advanced toward his father until he stood in the middle of the floor, legs wide and chest thrust out. Contempt hardened the angular planes of his rangy features.

"So, Father, you deign to give away my inheritance while you kept me otherwise occupied on a false errand."

Odakan rose to his feet with lithe fluidity, placing his hand with deliberate precision on the hilt of his sword. He stood unmoving; his eyes flickered with red sparks.

Tokanin pushed himself to his feet, breathing hard. He teetered on the spot, grabbed the arm of the throne, and cranked his body upright. He glared at his son. "If you are wise, Nyket, you will tamp down your greed, and jealousy, and fall silent. Aikanshin is not yours to inherit. This you have always known. You are Terraid, not Vaprus."

"But that is not why you deny me the Regency. I know all too well. Tainted Khimaeras cannot rule, command those of full blood, or mate with them. If you had your way, Father, we would not be allowed to mate at all."

"You judge harshly, Nyket," Oralia cried. "It is not your father's fault—it is the law of the Dykarin Ellkiiyn Clans. For millenniums past, it has been the law."

The audience in the lower chamber mumbled, and tittered, around a muted growl of dissent.

Odakan glared down at them his eyes flaring red. "Clear the room.

Go, all of you. This is not a matter for such as you."

Grumbles billowed forth, punctuated by jeers and catcalls, sharp with resentment. Never the less they went.

Nyket suddenly appeared very alone as he confronted his parents from the middle of the floor.

Taminisha waited with bated breath for those present to squash Nyket's challenge.

A crunch of boots echoed across the entresol.

Taminisha flinched and glanced over her shoulder. Her heart thudded to the bottom of her chest and her stomach stung with tendrils of fear.

Devinkin came from behind Oralia, and stationed himself at his nephew's side.

Taminisha shivered as her perception fractured and faltered. The fact Oralia's own brother intended to betray her changed the balance of power. *But he is also a Khimaera.*

"You are my *parents.* You are the parents of a tainted son, and you *never* thought to change the law? *Never* thought to follow Byneti's example in Mitikan. Never thought to give your own son a small sign of respect?"

If the air in the room had been ice, it would have exploded into slicing shards.

Tokanin shook his head. "No, son. I did not see the advantages. You were never to rule Aikanshin, tainted Khimaera or not. Besides, the law is the law."

"Then, Father, I intend to help you see the advantages." Nyket sneered, the ugly expression scrunching his prominent nose into wrinkles. "There are so many just like me, you are already defeated. Aikanshin is mine." His mouth opened in a snarl showing elongated eye teeth as he charged forward.

Devinkin lunged low, his sword caught Odakan in the legs before he could manage to draw his weapon. He crashed to the stone floor with a tortured grunt of expressed air.

22

Disbelief held Taminisha paralysed then with a click her brain comprehended, and reacted to, what had just happened. Taminisha cried out as she leapt from her chair and lunged at Nyket. "Stop this, Brother. Stop this madness."

He shoved her aside. She turned to Odakan.

He gestured for her to flee as he scrambled to his feet, slicing his weapon over his head.

Devinkin danced out of reach, grinning.

Odakan advanced.

Devinkin lunged across the space and drove his blade through the air with his full weight.

Odakan grunted once, dropped to his knees then rolled away. Before Devinkin could attack again, Odakan used the throne for leverage to climb to his feet.

Ignoring the combatants Nyket faced his father.

Tokanin lurched forward, flailing his cane above his head.

Taminisha leaned aside keeping the throne between her and Nyket. "Desist. We can make changes. We will make changes when I am Regent. In the name of the Great Spirit, stop."

Her futile shouts splintered against the clang of metal on metal, grunts, and explosions of air behind the force of the slashes between Odakan and Devinkin.

Tokanin staggered into the fray, beating his cane across his son's shoulders.

Nyket twisted and swiped down with his blade in response to his father's attack. The cane exploded into a shower of splinters. With barely a change in momentum the blade cut an arc through the air. The finely honed blade became embedded in Tokanin's shoulder.

The old man yelped, toppled, and slammed to the floor. He scrabbled away leaving a wide swipe of blood on the stone.

Oralia shrank back from the vicious attack and her features collapsed into a gray haggard mask.

Nyket closed in on his father.

Taminisha cringed away, her gaze fixated on her embattled soul mate. Gravely injured, Odakan laboured to swing his weapon back and forth, barely keeping his attacker at bay.

Devinkin smacked his sword down. The blade bit into Odakan's neck.

Odakan clutched his throat as his green blood spurted over his chest. He looked at Taminisha and broadcast. *"I love you."* His legs sagged, and he crumpled to the floor. With a sigh, he stilled.

The wrench as her soul mate's heart stopped beating snatched her breath away, and ripped a jagged chasm right through her. She howled. Blood pounded in her head, her vision clouded and the urge to kill stabbed through her.

Nyket advanced on Tokanin, his sword raised to strike.

"Stop this senseless, fruitless killing, Nyket. It does not matter if you are tainted. Stop, we can make it right." Oralia's shriek severed the madness gripping the room.

Nyket ground to a standstill. "You lie, Mother. You and Father never had any intention of putting it 'right'."

"I do not lie." With her gaze fixed on her son, Oralia dropped down beside her mate. She ripped off her over robe and pressed it against the gaping flesh weeping copious streams of blood. The cloth immediately stained green.

Oralia stood, her hands held wide. "Nyket, I love you. We chose to give you life. My only child." Tears poured down her cheeks. "It never mattered to us that your blood was not pure."

"I am Khimaera, destined to a life of deprivation, and it's entirely your fault." Nyket struck with the speed of an enraged Tarki. He cuffed his mother's arms in a clawed grip.

"I'm sorry. *So*, sorry. I loved you the moment you hatched. Please forgive me if I've hurt you by letting you live."

"You bitch, so selfish," he shouted, showering flecks of foam into her face. He shook her. "Despite your platitudes you choose to deny me. It was all about you—never me."

Oralia whimpered. "My son, we gave you a good life, everything we could, except for inheritance."

Taminisha quailed at Nyket's rage.

He thrust his mother back and forth with savage strength.

Oralia's head snapped side to side; the violent motion dislodged the strings of jewels entwined in her pectenites. The glittering strands hit the stone floor and disintegrated, sending a myriad of gems flicking and jumping across the flagstones. "You're our son," Oralia wailed.

"I am, but what kind of son? Not Ellkiiyn, not pure—contaminated, shunned, scorned."

"Nyket..."

He jostled her again. "I should never have been bred. Never."

"Should it matter what you are to others? We love you. It's just a drop of Fylitia blood."

"Just a drop," he howled. "If it is such a trifling fault, why not bring equality to Aikanshin—for your very own son?" With a violent shove, he tried to put her from him.

She clung to him. They twirled in an ugly dance for dominance, and balance. Oralia stumbled backward, her feet tangled around each other, her arms flailed.

Taminisha crouched further behind the throne as one of Oralia's pectenites snapped from her head and bounced across the floor. Taminisha recoiled as it touched the toe of her shoe.

Oralia screamed as the impetus from Nyket's thrust propelled her into the air. With a twisted arc, her body travelled half way across the room. A thud, a yelp, and a grunt of air forced from her lungs, hung in the silence that entombed them. The whole world stilled as she wobbled on the window ledge, then with a stuttering slide, disappeared from view.

Tokanin hauled himself to his feet and lurched to the window. He leaned so far out he hovered, teetered then heaved himself back into the room. "Oralia, my love, transmogrify, fly."

No scream of terror, no flap of leathery wings, and thankfully, no cry of triumph from Nyket.

Taminisha choked back sobs as she searched through her confusion for the best option. *I should flee. I cannot stop this. Must save myself for Jabrikan's sake.*

Tokanin moved away from the window. His mouth contorted in the flabby haggardness of his face. His eyes, staring, empty, and unfocussed. "My love is dead. Dead, at the hands of my son. An unforgivable sin."

"I shall seek no forgiveness, for despite you, despite being a tainted Khimaera, I *shall* rule Aikanshin. I will rule all the Ellkiiyn Clans. It's unfortunate for you not to be here to see your mixed blood son rule."

Tokanin cried out once as Nyket ran his blade through his father's chest.

Taminisha scrambled away until her back pressed against the wall unable to look away from the horror—the standoff between the proud dying father and the arrogant, ruthless, and bitter son.

Nyket withdrew his blade before slamming it again into his father's ribs. Blood spurted. Tokanin inspected his wounds, and then looked up at his son. He clutched himself, but blood poured out between his fingers. "The true nature of Khimaeras has brought us to this."

Nyket gave a short, harsh, bark of laughter. "No, Father—the true nature of discrimination has."

Tokanin's feet slid out from under him, smearing his blood across the floor. He gave an almost imperceptible shake of his head. Tears streamed down his face. "I should have killed you the moment you were born, but your mother begged me to spare you. By the Great Spirit what have we done?"

Nyket bounded forward his sword raised to strike again, but his father already lay dead. He turned, and eyed Taminisha.

# Chapter Three

Taminisha sidled toward the door, but Devinkin stood between her and escape. Bile rose and burned her throat.

As Nyket loomed over her, she scrunched, and rolled away.

He pounced, and grabbed her leg.

She shrieked, kicking out blindly with her other foot.

"Your time has come," Nyket roared as he towered over her.

Taminisha crawled away. Nyket brought his sword down in an arc that caught her thigh in a searing slash. She howled. The sweat of terror prickled along her skin.

He yanked the blade away and swung it up again.

She dragged herself closer to Tokanin's body. The floor was slippery with blood. With trembling fingers, she fumbled under the hem of her gown for the dagger she'd strapped to her leg.

Nyket advanced, with the slow stealth of a hunting Felitza.

With the small, inadequate dagger gripped tightly in her hand, she clambered to her feet, and faced her step brother. *I'll kill you, Brother for what you have done.* She didn't feel the pain of her wounds, her entire focus on Nyket. She jabbed her finger in his face. "You are evil, Brother."

He scowled and shrugged. "You knew this was inevitable. Once I thought we might have mated, but father forbade it because he knew I couldn't complete the Ellkiiyn mating dance. However, it shouldn't have mattered. You could have birthed our child the sachan way if need be."

Taminisha shuddered. Nausea exploded in her gut and she swallowed hard on the saliva filling her mouth. The urge to flee whipped over her, but she stood her ground on trembling legs.

Nyket grimaced. "I'm sorry; we would have been good together. Things have changed and now I must eliminate you, and the true heir. You, and the child, are all that stands in my way of becoming Guardian."

"You are not Vaprus. You have no right to rule Aikanshin and as a tainted Khimaera t*hey* will not allow you to rule anything."

Nyket smirked. "*They* will have no choice. Mixed blood Khimaeras already outnumber full blood Ellkiiyn, two to one. Everyone is seething with long held resentment. All they need is a leader—a Khimaera strong enough to rise up, and conquer."

He brought his sword down. Taminisha wrenched her body sideways, but the blade caught her shoulder, slicing into her flesh. Dark purple blood welled up from the gash. Pain seared through her neck and arm. She gulped, swallowed and clenched her teeth against the excruciating burn. Hobbling on her injured leg, she slashed the dagger through the air between them. Her thrusts were well off target as she struggled to keep her balance with her damaged arm held close to her chest.

Nyket laughed at her struggles.

Devinkin came to stand next to him a cruel sneer etched on his features. Side by side, the two mixed bloods stalked her across the room, slow and deliberate.

With desperate lunges to keep them at a distance, Taminisha retreated to the balcony. As they closed in, she backed further away. With Jabrikan safe, she had only herself to save for nothing would now change the outcome of this coup. Fiery regret roiled through her that Tokanin had refused to change the laws discriminating against those with mixed blood. Such a change might have saved them from such murderous rage.

Even though the old guard of full bloods would never have allowed Nyket to ascend as Regent, equality in other areas would have soothed his humiliation. It had bothered Taminisha to see the angst and chagrin her step brother continuously felt, but she could not reconcile his hurt against the weight of his murderous rampage.

Nothing remained for her to draw strength from, and she reeled in a yawning vacuum of meaninglessness. Odakan's death had left her more alone than she'd ever been before. She hesitated, and then leapt forward, hurdling the balustrade into nothingness.

"Devinkin, come, she flies," Nyket bellowed.

The force of her abrupt downward momentum ripped the dagger from her hand. Below, the silver ribbon of the river mapped the valley before it fell away into the oblivion of the falls. The serrated face of the cliffs cradling the lower lake loomed darker, and more rugged, as she dropped.

With an agonising gyration of her wounded body, Taminisha twisted and rolled in transmogrification. Her body heated and writhed, then with a flap of leathery wings, she became airborne. One wing smarted from the wound inflicted on her sachan body, while one leg hung almost useless, but it didn't matter, for as Ellkiiyn, she was stronger than her foes.

She soared, and then swooped close to the castle, spitting forth a fiery blast that roared with ferociousness into the balcony opening.

Nyket and Devinkin ran and ducked to escape the blast.

By the time she surged past, looped back around, and advanced on the castle again, Devinkin had transmogrified. Her heart missed a beat and a lump of iciness settled in her stomach. *So you can transmogrify. Great Ellkii, now I'm in trouble.* Nausea bubbled up as she faced her bigger stronger opponent. Terror spiked through her. *Great Spirit, may he lose his transmogrification quickly.*

She plunged downward, and blasted flame again.

Devinkin flapped giant wings and rose above the fire. He circled, and zigzagged toward her.

Taminisha thrashed her wings, and rose directly above him. She spat sizzling flames that seared right along his scaly back causing his golden froxcomb to erupt into smoking tatters.

He screeched. Then exhaled. Several thin strands of smoke spurted out.

*Ha, he can't do fire.* She bellowed with triumph, but it died in her throat as Nyket loomed up in front of her—a large, dishevelled Ellkiiyn. Despite the shabby scales and small, deformed pectenites protruding from his head he made a formidable opponent.

Nyket's mouth opened. A great gaping cavern filled with a slavering tongue and jagged teeth dripping with foul smelling saliva.

Taminisha pulled away, diving down.

Nyket clamped onto the end of her tail, sinking his teeth deep into her flesh. He shook her.

She squealed in agony. Her back cracked, her tail twisted, and her head flicked from side to side. She roared in fury, and clawed at him with her uninjured back leg.

Devinkin dived at her from the side, and before she could pull away, he buried his fangs into the soft flesh of her neck.

Her vision blurred and her neck went numb. She could barely hold herself in the air with the weight of the two attackers hanging from her injured body. With a great puff, she howled, letting forth a burst of searing flame. With violent gyrations, she jerked her aching body vigorously.

Neither foe let go.

Desperate to free herself, she dived straight for the rocks, tugging the two Khimaeras with her.

They held on, shaking her as the three of them plummeted.

Seconds from colliding with the rocks, and certain death, Taminisha twisted, and took off vertically along the lakeshore. Suddenly lighter, she flicked her tail and risked a quick glance down.

Nyket had released his hold. He tumbled toward the lake in his sachan form.

With renewed strength, Taminisha wrenched her neck into tortuous twists and turns.

Devinkin sank his fangs deeper, strengthening his hold.

The pain spread down her back and up into her head. Blood dripped down her breast. She strived to make her arms obey; petrified Devinkin had broken her back. With sheer determination, she thrashed her head to and fro then batted at him with a sluggish swipe of weakened feet. One of her back claws caught his underbelly.

He bellowed.

Encouraged by his hurt she threw her whole body weight to one side. With a simultaneous movement, she jerked her foot down, relishing in the jolt of flesh ripping apart.

Green scales popped from his hide and fell, like rain, into the lake.

She yanked harder.

Devinkin released his grip as he opened his mouth to yelp.

With a savage tug, she broke free of his tenuous hold. With powerful swipes, she flapped her wings, but only one responded. Cumbersome with injury, her bulky body spun in ever decreasing circles, closer and closer to the cliffs.

Below her, Devinkin made a clumsy landing, already transmogrifying back to sachan form.

In a last desperate effort to save herself, she stretched her wings wide to catch the drafts and control her descent. Barely in command of her limbs, Taminisha curled her legs, and arms, tight around her body to cushion her landing.

The cliff loomed up. Waves flicked and splashed on the rocky shore. She cringed inside, anticipating the impact. Unable to save herself she closed her eyes and hoped for the best. Once down, there would be no hope of taking off from the dangerous shore of the lake. *Is this to be my undignified end?*

Every bone crunched in protest, as she slammed onto the rocks. Flesh tore, scales popped and her wounds bled profusely. Taminisha winced inwardly, and without warning, transmogrified. She lay naked on the rocks in her sachan form, helpless to defend herself from those who hunted her.

In the distance, she could hear Devinkin and Nyket calling to each other as they scoured the shore, coming closer and closer.

The serious injuries they had inflicted on her Ellkiiyn body became life threatening in her sachan form. In a desperate effort to minimise the damage Taminisha tried to transmogrify back to Ellkiiyn, but other than a rush of misery, nothing happened. *They'll find me soon. Cannot protect myself. Will not survive.*

Tiny wavelets lapped at her feet, so icy cold it sent chilling ripples over her bare skin. She shivered. Without the precious Ellkiiyn heat that came with transmogrification, her wounded body began to shut down against the cold. She didn't fight her slide toward death for already she could hear them coming along the shoreline. With a sigh, she sagged onto the stones, and waited for the end.

"There, by the water, in sachan form, thank the Spirit. She's ours now," Nyket shouted.

"I see her. Nyket, hurry before she can change. The wounds we inflicted will kill her in her sachan form," Devinkin yelled.

The rocks rattled and crunched under their feet. Their heavy breathing sounded laboured, punctuated by grunts as they forced their damaged bodies to move at a faster pace.

Taminisha's breath gushed in and out of her lungs and her heartbeat raced so fast she thought her heart would explode. Petrified Taminisha tried again to prise her body from the stones, levering one leg under her, but her knee collapsed, and she sprawled on her back. "Great Ellkii, help me." *Must get up. Cannot let them find me.*

As her body settled back on the stones. The rattle of their approach stopped and Taminisha heard a sound she couldn't identify.

A deep guttural grunt throbbed across the water and bounced off the cliffs.

"Devinkin, what's that racket?" Nyket hollered.

To Taminisha it seemed to be coming from the castle, and yet, from under the surface of the lake. The two 'whoop whoop' cries grew louder, one deeper, the other higher, growing sharper and more discordant as if they would collide in a crescendo of noise.

"It's the... Oh Spirit, it's Orunikan. He comes for her." Devinkin's voice squeaked high and tremulous.

Taminisha's blood gushed through her veins in an icy stream. Sweat beaded on her skin even as chills trembled through her. She swallowed convulsively. Whimpers bubbled out through clenched teeth as she protectively curled in on herself.

The most terrifying creature in all Dykarin, the taker of the dead—the evil ones refused by Spirit. If Orunikan had come for her, there would be no escape. *I am neither dead nor evil, yet I'm about to be consumed. Will Spirit still take me?* She hiccupped small sobs into silence.

"Back up, Nyket, back up, he will see her dead," Devinkin yelled.

The two 'whoop whoop' noises had blended into one ear-splitting song, right over her head. Violent shudders rattled through her aching body as she waited to die.

A sudden gush and hiss of water burst from the lake. The small wavelets transformed into to sweeping breakers of iciness that raced up her legs and over her hips. She shivered as a multitude of tiny bumps rose on her skin.

"Run, Devinkin, run. It is he," Nyket bellowed.

Taminisha scrunched her eyes shut, afraid to look. An extra cold shadow crossed her body as foul smelling water showered her skin. She cowered tightly against the hardness of the rocks. The anticipation of razor sharp teeth ripping into her flesh held her immobile.

A gurgling rumble bounced across her, the gnash of teeth grated on taut nerves and a trumpeting roar echoed in her head.

Devinkin screamed.

Taminisha opened her eyes just a slit.

Just above her, twisted a huge neck, green and scaly, decorated with ribbons of dark weed that dangled and flapped. The flattened triangular-shaped head swayed, while the gaping mouth had line upon line of pointed, spear-like teeth. The large droplet shaped eyes were deep set in the side of the head, and just below them were four frilled slits. The eyes burned with a green glow, and from the mouth, an eerie light illuminated the gaping throat. From just behind its eyes, two great horns rose up and wound around the skull in a wide curve.

Sickness twisted her gut as she gagged on the smell.

The head swayed over her, then retreated.

Taminisha peeped out of narrowed eyes.

A short distance away Devinkin crouched on the rocks. 'Help me, Nyket; help me for Spirit's sake. Do not leave me to die."

The huge head swayed past the crouching Khimaera, and then returned, with nostrils close to the rocks. Orunikan swung his head back and forth over Devinkin.

Nyket continued to retreat.

The great water monster snorted, expelling froth and snot all over the naked crouching Khimaera. Fragile, white flesh quivering against the rocks. With lightning speed Orunikan snatched him up, crunching down hard with massive jaws. Devinkin's scream became a gurgle. Orunikan snorted again. He swiped his massive head left and right before he threw Devinkin's broken body into the air, then as it fell caught it in his cavernous mouth, and gulped it down whole.

Orunikan snorted and scanned the shore. He eyed Nyket as he

retreated, ducking and hunching as he scrabbled over the rocks. Orunikan sprang forward. His pointed teeth caught Nyket's shoulder.

Nyket yowled and lunged away. His flesh ripped apart as he pulled free.

Orunikan roared, and pounced. Missed.

Nyket leapt over a rock, regained his balance then collapsed into a shallow cleft in the cliff face.

Orunikan bellowed then spat a mouthful of muck all over Nyket as he huddled just out of reach. Orunikan swayed back and forth in front of the hole several times before swinging his great head away.

Taminisha couldn't take her gaze from the monstrosity as it loomed in her direction. She clutched her rykala locket. The iktver chain shivered along her skin with the tremble of her hand. *Please Great Spirit make it swift. Protect, Jabrikan.* She pressed down against the stones, choking back her sobs. Her gut clenched, awash with a searing burn. Cold sweat beaded on her skin mixing with the blood seeping from her wounds.

Orunikan came closer. The monster put his nostrils next to her skin and sniffed, then snorted, splattering cold globs of snot all over her.

She held herself still, even as her stomach churned in disgust, and fear.

One huge eye glared down at her.

Fixated by the slimy orb, Taminisha lay motionless, her blood pounding in her ears.

Orunikan blinked a milky lid over his eye and inhaled her scent again.

In that moment of hesitation, she saw intelligence highlighted in that one gleaming eye. The knowing faded before she could interpret it, leaving a dead, cold eyeball that didn't even reflect her image. She clutched her throat. The world spun and black spots whirled in her vision. With small huffs, she dragged minute breaths of air into her constricted lungs. Whimpers slipped out. *I'm not ready to die. Great Spirit Ellkii, please spare me.*

The monster's head swivelled on the thick muscular neck. Slimy skin oozed liquid and the rays of the solar orb glistened on the scales. Rubbery lips mouthed her shoulder.

Taminisha's view filled with long, serrated fangs. She could see bits of flesh caught in the spaces between them. *Bits of Devinkin.* Her stomach heaved, clenched, and then heaved again. She vomited on the rocks, gasped for air and retched again. Her stomach continued to heave, but she swallowed the bile down.

The monster loomed close.

Taminisha shrank away from the deadly teeth as they brushed her skin.

The colossal mouth hinged open and with his lower jaw, Orunikan scooped her from the rocks.

She shrieked again and again until the burn in her lungs and the lack of breath silenced her.

With delicate precision, the creature held her between razor sharp fangs. The point of each spiny tooth indented her flesh, but did not pierce the skin. Then, with a flick of his head, Orunikan flung her into the air.

She hung suspended over the vast open cavern of the monster's mouth, for what seemed like an eternity, and then she hurtled downwards into the tooth-lined cavity.

Taminisha shrieked.

With a plop, she landed on a rubbery cushion of flesh. The rough bulk immediately moved, and curled around her in a tender, but slimy shroud. The cavernous mouth closed. It became dark—very, very dark.

*Great Ellkii, I'm being swallowed alive. Have mercy on me.* She cringed in the darkness, but Orunikan did not proceed to devour her. Instead, water gushed, and splashed, nearby, and the impetus of incredible speed tightened the tongue against her body. Small rivulets trickled past her into Orunikan's throat, but she stayed relatively dry. Her body burned and throbbed, and blood flowed freely from her wounds. Taminisha's heart beat fitfully behind her breast. A lone heartbeat. Emptiness tore at her, and she did not resist the cloying anguish of incredible loss. *I am dying. We will soon be together again, my love.*

She covered her face with her hands and played the events over and over in her head. *If only I'd stayed as Ellkiiyn. If only I'd known, Devinkin could trans. I should have fled when I had the chance. Oh, Odakan, my love.* Hope seeped away for even as Ellkiiyn, she would have struggled to overcome her injuries, but in her smaller, weaker, sachan body, the massive damage would be fatal. Not that survival seemed relevant, trapped as she was in the lake monster's mouth.

She couldn't understand why Orunikan had not killed and eaten her right there on the shore. Why cart her across the lake? *To store me for later consumption perhaps?* Even that hideous thought failed to rouse her, her body so wracked with torment she couldn't even summon a whimper. She lay still, letting the tortuous throbbing wrap itself around her, as she waited to die.

Everything stilled. Outside her living prison, water lapped with a gentle, languid rhythm. The cold no longer seemed so bad, although the unbearable hurt wracking her body consumed her reason. Entombed in darkness she could see specks of light in the distance where solar rays penetrated through Orunikan's teeth.

The lake monster's breathing snuffled, forcing a breeze over her skin as it moved steadily in and out through the slits at the sides of his throat. Tarlitek had the same slits just behind his sachan ears.

Unable to move, she rested her head and closed her eyes, acutely aware of the slow passing of time.

Unsure of how long she'd lain there, she startled to full consciousness as a soft, whoop whoop noise pulsed around her. Like before, on the lake, the sound appeared to come from both deep in Orunikan's throat, and yet, from outside. Again, the deeper, and the higher, slowly synchronised until the din became a single raucous song right over her head.

The tissue beneath her undulated slightly. She rolled slowly, painfully, toward Orunikan's teeth. Expecting to be submerged in the brackish water of the manawa, she gasped in air before she clamped her mouth shut. Fear sizzled along her skin, and she tried not to let the sobs of despair, that caught in her throat, escape. She didn't want to die, but believed the end had come as she slid toward the rickety wall of enamel spikes. Instead of slamming into the dental barrier however, the flesh she rested on suddenly elevated, and lifted her right over the sharp points.

The bright light disorientated Taminisha and she floundered in a sticky slime filled depression on Orunikan's tongue. Every inch of her body shrieked as the rippling flesh eased her body forward. Just before she slipped over the rounded edge, the flesh lowered with clumsy gentleness to land her with a plop in the mud. Instantly the buzz of kamizee filled her ears. Their savage bites burned into her naked skin, but she didn't have the strength to protect herself from the miniature airborne attackers.

The world stood still as Orunikan stared down at her, and then with a whistle, and a grunt, he turned away, and slid under the muddy water of the manawa.

As the monster disappeared with nothing more than a chain of uneven ripples on the surface, hands—sachan hands, touched her. She cringed away, but the investigation of her body continued. Indignation flared. How dare some sachan maul her body while she struggled in her death throes?

"Leave me be to die in peace."

"You are not allowed to die, little one, after all I've done to rescue you."

She opened her eyes and looked directly up into Tarlitek's amber ones. She could see tears welling at the edges. His exoskeleton flushed a deep greeny-blue.

"Tarlitek," she croaked.

"Say nothing, you're gravely injured. I need to get help."

She moved her head the tiniest fraction to indicate the negative.

"Too late, no helping me."

"No, Taminisha, I will see you survive, it is my duty," Tarlitek replied. "Besides, you have things to achieve yet in your life."

"Jabrikan?"

"I've done my duty as requested despite the fact it mortally offended me to abandon you." Tarlitek grimaced.

Taminisha sagged into his arms. "Nought matters, if the boy is safe."

The blackness came and went. With consciousness came vague awareness of movement, and additional misery where strong arms cradled her battered body. She must have made a slight movement or sound because, each time she surfaced from the darkness.

Tarlitek murmured close to her ear. 'Rest Child, be calm. Hold onto to your life thread."

# Chapter Four

The third time she woke to the same suffering, only different. A faint, but regular heartbeat echoed hers. Steady, warm, loving tendrils curled tentatively through her mind. *Not Odakan—for he lies dead at the castle.* She shrank away from the intrusion wanting nothing of such feelings with her grief for Odakan burning deep in her psyche with its ugly freshness. With her first love extinguished, she did not seek another. However, the insistent beat imprinted on her soul, and she could no longer deny a new soul mate called her. If she survived, she would be compelled to answer its summons.

She stirred. "Tarlitek, someone calls me. I feel it."

Tarlitek smiled. "This is a good thing, little one. Hold onto your life thread. We will soon reach help."

~ ~ ~

Excruciating pain stabbed through her leg, so she stopped trying to move it, and lay still. When the soreness eased, she tried again, this time her head. A harrowing band squeezed her skull until she thought it would cave in on her brain. The blackness rushed in, and she let it claim her.

The next time consciousness came, she just lay there with the soft grasses cushioning her body, and the light warmth of plant woven rugs over her. After a time, she opened her eyes just a slit, and saw a thatched roof. The faint smell of smoke and cooking tainted the air. The murmur of voices, a small distance away, disturbed the quiet. Her head throbbed, and her eyes burnt. She closed them against the discomfort and welcomed the return of the blackness.

Stiffness clenched her limbs, but as she eased her aching body, hands instantly restrained her. Others soothed her hot brow, and wiped her arms and hands with a cool damp cloth.

"Lie still, Child, lie still. Your wounds will not cope with disturbing at this stage." The soft musical chirrup of the words commanded, but soothed, simultaneously.

Taminisha forced her eyes open. The female smiling down at her was a stranger, and strange. She had thin pointy features with a prominent nose, and large round eyes, set wide apart, almost to the side of her face. She had no lashes to shade her extremely expressive eyes; the solid dark irises highlighted by a red ring on the outer edge. Instead of hair, a thick layer of plumage curved from her forehead back over her skull. Delicate downy feathers fluffed around her face softening the boniness of her features into fragile beauty. Taminisha stared in fascination at her first full blood Myattican.

As Taminisha continued to stare wordlessly, the woman bent her head slightly so Taminisha could look directly into one of her eyes.

"I am Shula, Tarlitek's half-sister. Welcome to our home. You're safe with the Myatticans. We will heal you."

Taminisha squeezed her eyes shut for a moment then opened them again as she struggled to see her Tarlitek, and this woman, as siblings. "Shula, thank you for your kindness, but I am beyond even your great healing powers. My wounds are Ellkiiyn sized in my sachan body. Too much."

Shula touched her lips with her finger. "Shush, Child. Drink this then you will sleep and you will heal. Do not worry about anything for now. Tarlitek waits for you outside, and his only message is, 'get well and remember he has done his duty as you requested'."

Taminisha didn't argue with Shula's belief she would heal. She just sipped the sour potion, and lay back with her eyes closed. Nothing mattered if Jabrikan remained safe. As the blackness rolled in, the slightly discordant patter made its presence felt next to her heart. She didn't want it there, calling her, but she didn't care enough to repulse the insistence.

For many solar awakenings, Taminisha slipped in and out of consciousness, only vaguely aware of the passing of time. Shula tended her most with other Myattican women coming and going. Occasionally she heard Tarlitek speak to her, but as she hovered between life and death, wrapped in intense torture, she could not be sure what he said. She could do nothing to help herself as her sachan body struggled under the weight of Ellkiiyn size wounds. As a longer period of consciousness came, she tried to transmogrify. The attempt brought on wave after wave of agony and she slipped back into blackness.

Taminisha opened her eyes. She was alone. With a cautious tilt of her head, she peered out the open doorway, and could just see a solar ray bathed meadow and trees in the distance. Wary of the severe pain it could bring, she moved her limbs a tiny fraction. They hurt, but not with the overwhelming, discomfort of the solar awakenings gone by.

Light, hurried footsteps approached, and Shula's fine boned face came into view.

"At last, Child, you are with us," she said, immediately offering her a sip of potion. With gentle hands, she lifted Taminisha's head slightly off the pillow and placed the cup against her mouth.

Taminisha sipped the bitter brew, screwing her face up at the taste.

"Aha, you must be improving, for you object, for the first time, to my nasty concoction," Shula cackled.

Taminisha tried to smile. "I am better," she croaked. "The pain has eased."

"You are at that. Do you feel well enough to have Tarlitek attend you? He has been beside himself since he brought you to us," Shula chirped.

Taminisha nodded. "I would speak with him. Thank you, Shula, for your care. Without your healing I would be dining with the Great Spirit Ellkii many solar awakenings before this."

Shula laid a gentle hand on her forehead. "You are strong, and you fought the darkness."

"I must survive to re-claim the Guardianship of Aikanshin for my nephew, Jabrikan, and bring justice down on Nyket. In addition, according to Tarlitek, I must answer an unwanted love call that torments me in my grief and suffering." She blinked aware tears had formed.

Shula offered her some water to wash the potion down. "You have much to achieve, but for the moment, your only task is to get well."

"And this, Shula, I will concentrate on."What modicum of energy she had, drained from her body in a rapid flow and she lay back on the pillow with her eyes closed.

When she heard Tarlitek's heavy footfall cross the room and halt by her side, she opened them again. His features were harshly furrowed and his exoskeleton faded to an insipid green. His expression, strained and glum, without his usual wide smile. He looked as if he had aged much in the past phasings. Deep in his rounded amber eyes, Taminisha saw fear.

Tarlitek dropped to his knees. "Little one, I am here. It does my heart good to see you moving away from the jaws of death."

With a massive effort, she reached out and grabbed his hand. "Are you sure Jabrikan is safe?"

Tarlitek smiled. "Jabrikan is hidden. I know where, and he will be returned when the time comes."

Taminisha squeezed her saviour's big hand. "I can never thank you enough for what you've done, above and beyond your duty. In due course you shall be rewarded as is fitting for your service."

He laid one finger on her lips. "Enough about reward, which I do not seek, and more about getting well."

"I feel so helpless. I cannot change my form, and every muscle and bone aches."

"Rest. I will return in a few phasings. I go to survey the aftermath of Nyket's carnage."

"Be careful, Tarlitek. Keep safe."


As each solar phasing passed, sleep came naturally without the blackness. *I am healing. I will live.* Despite the improvement, anxiety plagued her as she waited for Tarlitek to come back.

"Do not fret my brother's safety; he has taken his nephew, Khoury with him. Khoury is half Ellkiiyn."

Despite Shula's assurances, she didn't calm until she heard Tarlitek enter the room.

He knelt beside her. "I have returned, but fear my tidings will cause you terrible distress. Aikanshin has descended into civil war. The loyal Vaprus against the tainted ones and the tainted Khimaeras have the upper hand.

Taminisha whimpered. "Can we do anything?"

Tarlitek shook his head. "The tainted Khimaeras are many, and way too powerful. Besides, you have other pressing responsibilities."

"Tarlitek, I fear, and I fret, for the time I'm well. What is it I should do? Do I just go to my soul mate, and leave this disaster behind me? I am not strong enough to defeat Nyket alone. But how do I go on with life, not knowing, and just waiting until Jabrikan is old enough to reclaim his inheritance?"

"If you are willing to take my guidance, you will concentrate on getting well and finding your soul mate. Now Shula suggests it is time for you to rise from your sickbed, and take some fresh air and solar rays. Gentle movement will be good for you."Tarlitek tucked his hands under her frail body and lifted her.

"Owww," she cried as her injuries were disturbed for the first time in many solar phasings.

"Sorry, little one, I will have you settled outside shortly."

With infinite care, he placed her on an already prepared padding made of grass, and covered her with rugs. Taminisha could see the edge of a forest just down the slope, a spreading stand of thin, straight trees with white trunks. A wide track, roughly carved in the dirt, ran through the middle of the forest and in the distance, she could see water. Female Myatticans moved back and forth in gentle perambulations between the trees, plucking nuts from the branches and picking up seeds from the ground.

Despite her curiosity about those who had taken her in, she needed an answer to her previous question. She gazed up. "Tarlitek, what are you saving me for?"

He frowned. "And why would I not save you?"

"For what purpose have you gone to such risk?"

He smiled a sad, wistful smile. "Do you still feel his calling?"

She paused then touched her chest above her heart. "Yes, I feel him calling me, but why? How dare he call me so soon after Odakan? He does not interest me. I still grieve."

Tarlitek nodded. "Of course you grieve, and he will know what is in your heart. Whatever his reasons for calling, you must find a way to circumvent your antipathy because this is what I saved you for."

"But that does not help Aikanshin or Jabrikan."

Tarlitek smiled. "It will, when the time is right. I promise you."

A sense of peace washed over her as she lay back. Tarlitek believed she had a purpose besides revenge on Nyket. There would be no weakness attributed to her if she just went to her soul mate.

The first time she transmogrified after her illness happened without her consciously trying. The change excited and surprised her. She flapped her wings and stomped her feet.

The terrified Myattican women fled. Their screeches rent the quiet ambience of the surroundings and downy feathers gusted into the air swirling around in the breeze.

Her dance of elation immediately jolted to a standstill as she realised the commotion she'd caused. She hung her head and went to roll only to find fifty large semi-feathered male Myatticans surrounded her. They flapped their huge wings and reached toward her with outstretched talons.

She curled up into a ball, and lay like the dead as they danced around her, squawking.

"Enough, she is a friend. Enough." Shula ran toward Taminisha, shouting and flapping her arms.

Tarlitek bounded right behind her, waving an unsheathed sword. "Back away."

Taminisha lifted her head and peered down at the aggressive creatures. They continued to screech and squawk.

"Be calm," Shula, cried again.

A stunning male with gold and green plumage stepped toward Shula. "Sister, we have been gathering nearby for a while, there has been trouble in Aikanshin. We came to protect you, but I see we have worried un-necessarily." He turned to Tarlitek. "Brother, if I'd known it was you who brought this creature to our home I would not have been so worried." He turned to Taminisha. 'And this is?"

Tarlitek gave a small bow. "Brother Mazin, this is Taminisha, daughter of the late Kititash from her first mating. Tokanin, the second mate of Kititash and his new mate, Oralia, have been murdered by their own son, Nyket, with the help of Devinkin, Oralia's brother."

Mazin's expression darkened. He flexed his broad shoulders and fluttered his wings as if shaking off dirt. "This is not good, Brother, but there is little we can do against Ellkiiyn—even those with diluted bloodlines."

"I would not ask that of you, Mazin. Nevertheless, I do ask for Taminisha to be sheltered here until she can seek her soul mate. The ancient prophecy, as spoken by Etunik before his transformation, warns us a revolt by the Khimaeras would usher in the Era of Darkness and only the Daughter of Kylara can save us. Until Taminisha's new union is made, nothing can be done to stop Nyket."

Mazin studied Taminisha, and then turned back to Tarlitek. "The Ellkiiyn Clans are in disarray. The Ellkiiyn are a dying species."

"No," Taminisha cried, and burst into tears. Large diamond shaped drops fell from her eyes and immediately caused a small lake around the feet of the Myatticans.

"Tamin, either stop bawling or trans to sachan form before you drown us," Tarlitek shouted in romni.

Immediately she flicked a glob of ekta, curled inwards, twisted in a somewhat painful curve and transmogrified into her weaker sachan form.

The Myattican males surrounding her quietly disbanded and went to stand by their partners, their eyes averted until she pulled the habilan over her naked body.

"That is better, little one. You are very imposing as Ellkiiyn."

She lowered her head; tears still tumbled down her cheeks. "Sorry."

Mazin reached out and put a clawed hand on her shoulder. "I did not seek to offend you, but things are not well with the Ellkiiyn Clans. Anarchy is in the air. As the flocks migrate seasonally, we hear stories. The Infernea Ellkiiyn die out because Byneti is dying. His son, Okeyon, has failed to breed again after his young daughter died of the scalinette fever and his son vanished. The Vaprus are in turmoil and the Terraid Guardian ruling Rabikan has kept the clan isolated for years. While Kikishan of Kelkiki, an Aqueena, lost his soul mate and child to the scalinette fever soon after mating. His grief is so deep many say he will never mate again especially now he is passed his prime. With less and less full blood Ellkiiyn breeding, many seek to cross with others. This watering down of the breed does not bode well for the Ellkiiyn Clans with pure blood supreme in most minds and as for the lands of Dykarin the future is dark. The peace we live under now is only because the Ellkiiyn Clans have bonded the species of so many lands into a co-operative existence. Without Ellkiiyn Guardianship there is nothing certain about our future."

"And I cannot soothe your fears, Mazin. With Nyket seizing the Guardianship, my world is in chaos. Despite Oralia's mixed blood status and Tokanin's good standing, the full blood Vaprus would not sanction Aikanshin's mixed bloods having recognition. When Tokanin overlooked Nyket, he reacted with vicious savagery.

"We know many mixed bloods have gone to live under the more tolerant rule of Okeyon in Mitikan," Mazin said.

"Now Nyket has seized control I have no idea what the full bloods will do. I expect civil war will tear Aikanshin to pieces. It breaks my heart." Sick fear formed a lump in her gut at thoughts of the future. Tears welled again, but she swiped them away with her sleeve. *I must be strong.*

Tarlitek and Mazin stood side by side; both men watched her, their faces marred by serious expressions.

"You must answer the call in your heart, no matter if it is too soon," Tarlitek said.

She shook her head. "I have no desire for another—so soon, maybe never. Besides I see no advantage in such a mating for either Ellkiiyn, or Jabrikan and the Guardianship of Aikanshin."

Tarlitek frowned, but laid a gentle hand on her shoulder. "I do not know either. All I can say is you must answer the call. You are the last pure blood Royal Kokoshin Vaprus Ellkiiyn."

"But what does that have to do with anything?" Taminisha tried to keep the frustration out of her tone. "Odakan and I were mated; our offspring would not have been pure Vaprus, but then neither is Jabrikan."

Tarlitek winced at her harshness. "It is prophesised the Daughter of Kylara, the salvation of Dykarin from the Era of Darkness, will be descended from the last pure Royal Kokoshin Vaprus Ellkiiyn. You, Taminisha, are that Ellkiiyn."

She frowned. "What about Jabrikan?"

"He is full blood Ellkiiyn, but not pure Vaprus; his mother belonged to the Infernea Clan. Your mother and father were both full blood Royal Kokoshin Vaprus Ellkiiyn. Their purple blood so dark it appeared to be almost black. Like yours." He pointed at her arm.

Taminisha studied the dark lines where her blood ran under her skin and looked back up to Tarlitek. "But I don't want the responsibility. How will I know what to do? Are you sure there are no others with pure blood?"

"No, you're the only one. Don't worry yourself about such an ancient prophecy for now, what will be, will be. Your only task is to get well."

Taminisha fretted despite Tarlitek's assurances. During the solar phasings, with the others around, she felt strong, but in the long darkness of the lunor drifts, she struggled to come to terms with what had happened. Her grief, deep and dark, weighed heavily on her soul. Her fear of the unknown future seemed even darker, and all the time, the second heartbeat behind her breast called her to a destiny she did not want.

Each solar phasing, as she grew stronger, she practiced transmogrifying. She found this simple enough, but stressed and agonised because she couldn't hold the form for very long. Soreness thwarted any attempts to fly, and ended in humiliating crashes to the hard ground. This she believed would pass as she healed, but her inability to breathe fire, as Ellkiiyn, dwarfed her failure to fly. Without fire, she was not Ellkiiyn. She often found herself dripping with sweat and aware of the pounding beat of her heart as her fear of the future rampaged.

After several failed attempts to spit fire, she growled with ferocious intensity. She stamped her huge feet repeatedly in the muddy banks of the river and ripped mouthfuls of reeds up by their roots. As the sharp spiny ends prickled her mouth, she spat them out and slumped to the ground. *What sort of Ellkiiyn am I, who cannot breathe fire, or soar for hours high in the sky?*

She startled as Tarlitek came up behind her. "Come, this is not the way."

Desperate for comfort she jumped up, transmogrified and sagged into his embrace. "Tell me, Tarlitek, what use am I? I cannot breed unless I can hold my transmogrification, and no Ellkiiyn of worth is without fire." Her voice broke and cracked with self-pity.

He patted her shoulder. "Don't fret, little one, as your health improves your ability to hold your transmogrification will increase. As for the fire, I do not know why this should fail you. But I do have an answer."

She peeked under her eyelashes at him. "And that is?"

"It is time for you to begin your journey. To answer the call that beats deep in your chest."

"But I'm still weak. I'm not ready," she protested, all too aware of the aches and pains still troubling her body, and the grief clutching at her heart.

He waggled his webbed fingers at her. "Now is not the time to wallow in your weakness. Tomorrow we leave."

The Myatticans gathered to wave farewell, and Shula chirruped her sadness to see both of them go. She missed her half-brother during his long absences, and made it clear she'd grown fond of Taminisha by hugging her close to her breast.

They travelled light, so they could move swiftly. As they were both capable of hunting and feeding themselves from the land and the water they took nothing more than bedding and weapons.

"So where are we going?"

"We are going to the Abaye," Tarlitek replied.

"The Fire People?"

"Yes, they can cure your lack of fire."

"But you cannot cross the border." Taminisha grabbed at his arm. "You'll be…"

Tarlitek chuckled. "Evaporated into steam? Maybe. To my knowledge, there has never been a recorded incident of evaporation with a mixed breed before. Especially a mixed breed like me—Orunan shape shifter and Myattican healer. I don't know what my mother was thinking when she jumped into the lake and cuddled up to my father."

Taminisha smiled at Tarlitek's self-deprecating comment. "But you cannot take the risk."

"No, I cannot. Therefore, you will be going alone. You'll be safe, as a fire breather."

Her fear weighed heavier. To go on this journey worried her a great deal, but to go alone, without wise counsel, and a strong arm for defence, terrified her. She no longer felt brave and invincible, even as Ellkiiyn, in the aftermath of Nyket's unexpected insurgency against his father, and his savage attack on her.

Myattican females lived together in small settlements, scouring the lush meadows and forests for seeds and fruit. The women would wave and call greetings as they passed.

Taminisha wanted to stop, but Tarlitek urged her on. Occasionally a flock of migratory males would swoop down low over their heads, and inspect them, but seeing Tarlitek, they merely squawked a greeting, and flew on.

On the first awakening, the manawa lay on their left, with its tidal waters moving sluggishly and armies of whining kamizee biting any exposed skin with a vengeance. By the second awakening, they left the low-lying manawa behind and walked along the banks of a wide, slow flowing, river.

Despite the residual discomfort from her injuries, Taminisha enjoyed walking beside Tarlitek—sometimes in companionable silence, at others, sharing good memories from the past.

On the third solar phasing as the solar orb settled behind the horizon, almost directly behind them, Tarlitek stopped suddenly.

"Here," he said, and pointed to a spot a short distance in front of them. "There is the border. I can go no further."

Taminisha surveyed the area Tarlitek indicated. It appeared no different to any other location in the surrounding landscape—the same bright green, spiky grass and the same towering firnit trees with wide spreading branches. Overhead, the same blue sky darkened, and the same ghostly spheres of the lunor discs glowed in the heavens.

"How can you tell, it all looks the same to me?"

Tarlitek stepped closer to the spot he'd indicated. Steam wafted around his head, his face beaded with sweat, and he fought to breathe as the frills on his gill slits vibrated violently.

Taminisha slapped a hand to her mouth to stifle her cry.

He stepped back. After a moment, the steam dissipated, and his breathing steadied. "Any more questions?"

Frowning in concentration, she stepped forward to where Tarlitek had been. She felt nothing so she stepped farther into the forbidden territory. Still nothing. She spun around to face Tarlitek. "No more questions."

"We'll camp here through the lunor drift, and in the awakening you will go into Abaye," Tarlitek said as he built a small fire.

"But where will I go?"

Tarlitek gave a wistful smile. "Just walk, they'll find you. Ask for Angwye, he's a cousin on my mother's side."

"And they can help me?"

Tarlitek frowned. "If they cannot, then you are unable to be helped."

She snatched at her Rykala locket, twisting it around the chain. *Then what? How can I live without fire or flight? To live such a life would be unbearable.* Afraid she would cry, and embarrass herself, Taminisha proceeded to lay out her bedding.

"I'll get supper," Tarlitek mumbled, as he strode toward the river.

With a tinkling splash, he disappeared. She added more wood to the fire then paced around its meagre warmth, cursing silently the loss of her own Ellkiiyn heat.

Without Tarlitek by her side, the landscape suddenly loomed menacingly around her. Shadows deepened, and objects blurred into unidentifiable foes. The lunor discs had taken solid form and the four small ones had orbited once around the larger Etunik, his wives in their forever spiralling dance, before Tarlitek returned.

On edge, and straining to hear, Taminisha flinched at the faintest shush of the water and crackle of grass that heralded Tarlitek's presence.

He laid a large orrtaya on the fire. The juices sizzled and spat.

Taminisha watched it cook and wondered how Tarlitek could quite happily eat the small gill breather with distant genetic connections to him. To her it would be like eating Potokin, a dwarfed reflection of her as Ellkiiyn. A cold shudder raced over her skin at the thought and she wondered what had happened to her pet.

Tarlitek squatted beside her. She could just make out his smile in the gloom.

"Do not fret the orrtaya, for it is born without a brain, emotions or a soul. It is only instinct and reflexes moving it around the lake."

"It just seems like cannibalism, that's all."

Tarlitek shrugged. "It is, little one, but the Orunan in me dulls the squeamishness that goes with it."

"How do you reconcile your two sides? Myattican, the healer, and Orunan, the gill breather and cold-blooded killer?"

He reached out, flipped the orrtaya over and covered the exposed side with leaves from a baya bush. "I don't, for if I tried, I would go mad. I just live phasing to phasing and gift my loyalty to you, my mistress—

a killer, a communicator and a healer in one devoted servant."

"More than a servant, Tarlitek, you are my friend."

He smiled. "Get some rest you have a difficult time ahead and much distance to cover."

With the solar orb already above the horizon Taminisha still hesitated to cross the border into Abaye. She turned to Tarlitek. "I don't want to go alone."

Tarlitek smiled. "You will not be alone. Feel the heartbeat. Know he is calling. He is waiting."

"Will I see you again?"

Tarlitek smiled. "Yes, for our destiny together is not expired yet. There are times to come."

Comforted by the big man's assurances, she strode away from her only friend, and through the forest in search of the Abaye.

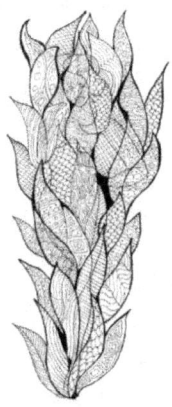

# Chapter Five

Taminisha walked without purpose for a couple of hours, locked in a writhing mixture of self-pity and loneliness. Without warning, the ground disintegrated beneath her feet. She lurched forward and despite extending her hands, she hit the ground hard. She gasped, lifted her head and spat out fine grit and small stones.

The ground beneath her was red, dry and strewn with chunks of loose rock that made the surface treacherous. All around occasional huge jagged monoliths jutted out of the sandy ground to relieve the flatness of the topography. The barren landscape had no vegetation other than shrivelled, stunted, grasses clutching at survival in the shadows of the boulders. The vista appeared inhospitable.

Taminisha could almost feel its rejection of her presence. She climbed to her feet and dusted herself down. For no particular reason her nerves sizzled with unease and she moved forward with wary steps, watchful for attack.

When darkness fell, she curled up under a small overhang in a giant boulder and ate some seeds, nuts and chunks of cold orrtaya before she tried to sleep. Even though Tarlitek had given her the tools, she didn't bother to light a fire. Vulnerable in her sachan body, Taminisha wished she could hold Ellkiiyn form for the whole lunor drift.

Whispers penetrated through her foggy half sleep. A warm glow caressed her face and arms. Close by, soft crackling sounds rose and fell in volume. She laid still, her eyes closed as she assessed the surrounding beings with feelers from her mind. When her tentative probing met with searing heat, she guessed the Abaye had found her.

In one lithe movement, she opened her eyes and leapt to her feet. Just out of touching distance, fiery sachan shapes, that flamed and danced, circled around her. They did not accost her. Taminisha could identify three female shapes, and two males.

She looked directly at one of the females. "I am Taminisha, Ellkiiyn of Aikanshin; I've come to find help."

Sizzling and crackling buzzed in her ears like laughter. Taminisha backed away until she pressed against the rock. The fire people watched her, but made no move to interact.

"Do you understand me?" Taminisha asked in romni, knowing they would understand the universal language of Dykarin. "I have come for your help."

Again, the sizzling sound so like laughter. This time it ended abruptly, and the fire shapes parted their circle.

A fourth female, with pale skin, strong features and glowing eyes, stood just outside the group. She towered over the others and wore a black velvet robe that fell straight to the ground from her shoulders. Shining red and gold flames that appeared to be alive moved with sensuous writhing across the drapes. On her head sat a huge fan shaped crown in golden metal, and decorated with precious gemstones. Long strings of jewels hung down either side of her face and rested on the stiff red collar that jutted with sharp points out over her shoulders.

She held her hands over her head, and clapped twice. A sharp crack and a bright flash that hurt Taminisha's eyes transformed the Abaye into sachan shapes, all dressed in black robes decorated with moving flames.

"I am Izusah, Leader of the Abaye," the tall woman announced in perfect romni. "Why have you come, Ellkiiyn?"

Taminisha bowed slightly to acknowledge the woman's authority. "I have come to the Abaye for help."

"Help? What help can we, the humble fire people, provide for an Ellkiiyn?"

Her disdain cut deep and Taminisha struggled to remain in front of this woman and not withdraw her request and flee back to Tarlitek.

She bowed her head again. "Izusah, Leader of the Abaye, I am an Ellkiiyn in trouble. Tokanin, Regent of Aikanshin, has been murdered by his Khimaera son, Nyket. During the battle for my life, I sustained severe injuries. The Myatticans have healed me as best they can, but I cannot hold my transmogrification, fly or breathe fire. A friend suggested the Abaye may be able to help."

"And this friend?" Izusah asked as she appraised the clearing.

"A loyal friend."

"One of us?"

"No, he is not of the fire people," Taminisha replied. "He told me to ask for Angwye."

A short tubby man with a bald head stepped forward. "I am Angwye. Who has told you to ask for me?"

Taminisha bowed slightly. "Tarlitek."

A wail split the air and one of the females dropped to the ground, her internal glow died to cold black. She writhed in the red dust as if possessed by a jinnexa.

Taminisha stared in shocked silence at the convulsing woman, not believing her words had caused the dramatic collapse, but feeling guilty anyway.

"Jumeeh, Deshikee take her into the cavern and lay her next to Nootau's Child. I will come and deal with her when I have completed my business with the Ellkiiyn," Izusah snapped.

As the two designated Abaye lifted the fallen woman and shuffled away through the rocks, Izusah stood tall and glared at Taminisha.

"See what you've done, Ellkiiyn."

Again, guilt stabbed at her, but she had no idea what she'd done to create such a drama. "But…"

"Izusah, she could not have known unless Tarlitek told her, and he would never shame Clyeva so," Angwye said.

"No, I suppose not. Anyway, the damage is done." Izusah beckoned to Taminisha. "Come, Ellkiiyn, we'll see what we can do."

Petrified she would cause more disaster; Taminisha followed Izusah and Angwye across the flat unrelieved gibber plain in stunned silence. She tried to remember the name 'Clyeva' in relation to Tarlitek, but could not. Yet the dramatic scene made it obvious, even to her, an outsider, that his very name caused this woman such emotional upheaval she collapsed. It would have been useful if Tarlitek had warned her, and she wondered why he hadn't.

Without the slightest signal, the line of Abaye halted.

Taminisha peered over their shoulders. They stood on the precipice of a sheer cliff. She strangled the protest that rose in her throat and wiped clammy hands on her habilan. Her heart pounded with such speed and force Taminisha feared it would explode in her chest. *Do they intend to dump my fragile sachan body into oblivion?* As she glanced around with thoughts to flee, however, the Abaye shuffled forward and climbed in single file down narrow steps carved into the red rock.

With legs still weak with her unfounded trepidation, she stepped down onto the first step. There was no handrail. The steps sloped, and the rough surface crumbled underfoot. Those behind her sighed and whispered with impatience as Taminisha climbed down one step at a time. She clung to the almost smooth rock wall beside her, terrified she would slip and tumble to her death in the canyon below.

Relief rushed over her as they neared the bottom. The Abaye gathered around a large opening in the rock face. There were gasps and cries as they carried the inert woman into the cavern. Those gathered directed hostile stares at Taminisha. Warmth radiated from inside the cavern and she could see a red glow. With each flare of red came a plopping sound.

Izusah and Angwye stood aside and gestured for her to enter. The red glow emanating from the back of the cavern illuminated the area.

As Taminisha moved closer, the plopping sound got louder and more defined. The red glow intensified. Directly in front of her a pool of molten lava boiled and spat.

The woman they called Clyeva lay unconscious next to the pool covered in blankets made from animal furs.

Taminisha retreated several paces. "Is she all right?"

"Clyeva is never all right, but she will be made as well as can be expected. Nootau will heal her," Angwye said, waving at the pool of molten rock. "But more importantly, why has Tarlitek, my cousin, sent you to us?"

"I lost my fire through injury and it must be restored before I can answer my soul mate's call. Tarlitek says this mating is essential to the survival of Dykarin as we know it."

"We cannot help you, Ellkiiyn, the cost is too high. Tarlitek knows this," Angwye growled.

"Tarlitek said nothing to me about a cost. If I can pay it, I will, or something else of value when I can."

Angwye glared up at her. "You cannot pay, Ellkiiyn, for to restore your fire, an Abaye must give up theirs."

Mortification rushed through her. Taminisha bowed her head. "This I am not comfortable asking for."*Why has Tarlitek sent me to ask for such a sacrifice?*

"And so you shouldn't be, because with the sacrifice comes death.

Did you know that, Ellkiiyn? Would you have come, if you knew that's what Tarlitek meant?"Angwye snarled, and spat an intermittent stream of sparks as he paced.

Horror at the reality of what the gift of fire meant stirred nausea in her gut. "I had no idea, Angwye, no idea. I cannot believe Tarlitek sent me here to ask this."

"Stand down, Angwye, you're not authorised to speak such to Ellkiiyn," Izusah said.

"But Izusah…"

"No, Angwye—Tarlitek is your cousin. This question is not a matter for emotion; it is about what Preeya interprets from the embers. The leader made a gesture toward Clyeva.

"No, you cannot ask her that," Angwye protested, his face flushing red.

"If it is the destiny that calls her, she must answer. Do you not think Clyeva will go willingly? She is already lost to us, and most definitely lost to Tarlitek."

Angwye spun away from his leader, and retreated to the darkest corner of the cavern.

"Izusah, I beg you to desist from such talk. I will not take fire from one of your people at such a horrendous cost."

"Shhh, Ellkiiyn, you will not be consulted, and you will have no choice. Wait here. I must consult with Preeya, our oracle. When she speaks, all will obey."

Taminisha sank to the sandy floor as Izusah left. She stared into the liquid rock bubbling in the pool, and silently cursed Tarlitek for placing her in such a position.

Clyeva did not move.

Angwye did not come back.

Others shuffled passed her, but none spoke, or even acknowledged her existence. She wondered if they despised her because she'd asked the impossible.

Hunger gnawed at her gut, and her parched throat prickled and crackled when she tried to swallow. The sulphur emanating from the pool stung her nose and eyes, so she closed them against the discomfort. Soon her head sagged onto her chest and she gave up fighting the fatigue that had crept through her.

"So, you are she?"

The voice, sharp and authoritative, ripped Taminisha from her uneasy slumber.

She jumped and looked up. Just inches from her feet stood an elderly woman, so frail she leaned on Izusah's arm for support. Her skin was dry and wrinkled, her hair, a gray straw-like bun. Untidy clothes hung on her scraggly limbs and torso barely concealing the luminosity beneath, as flames flickered and jumped all over her body.

Taminisha sensed the ultimate authority of this ancient Abaye, and she rose to her feet and bowed her head slightly. 'I am Taminisha, Vaprus Kokoshin Ellkiiyn of Aikanshin, daughter of Kititash. My friend directed me here…"

The old woman held up her hand.

Taminisha's explanation died in her throat.

"So, you seek restoration of your fire breathing power?"

Taminisha scowled. "I came for that, but did not realise, in asking, what it meant."

The old woman gestured with her hand. "Izusah, cut her, and I shall see the truth shown to me in the scattering of the embers."

Izusah seized Taminisha's arm before she could pull it away. Though she fought to free her wrist the leader of the Abaye simply tightened her grip, drew her dagger, and whipped it lightly across Taminisha's skin. Purple blood oozed from the wound.

"Ah! See! So dark, like the lunor sky on Etunik's time of rest. She is the pure blood of which they speak," Preeya said.

Taminisha snatched her hand away. "I am Taminisha, ordinary Ellkiiyn. I have no intention of taking the life of an Abaye to satisfy an almost forgotten prophecy."

"You will, Ellkiiyn. I am Preeya; I decide what will be, here in Abaye. You were right to ask. The balance of power in this world lies in your destiny. You shall bring forth the saviour of the Ellkiiyn Clans; the Daughter of Kylara, the Saviour of Dykarin, and therefore all of us." The old woman peered at her.

Taminisha suspected Preeya sought some contradictory sign or indication she was not actually the one mentioned in the prophecy.

"But Preeya, with respect, I cannot take a gift that costs another's life. I will not."

Preeya stamped her foot. "Enough. Tarlitek did right to send you. It will be done."

"No, I refuse to be party to murder." Taminisha's shout echoed around the cavern.

Those nearby glared in her direction.

"You cannot, Ellkiiyn, retract your request. The embers have foretold your coming, and your need. It must be done."

Taminisha spun away from the two Abaye women. She had barely completed one step when Izusah and Deshikee grabbed her and dragged her deeper into the cavern.

"Secure her," Preeya shouted. "And arouse, Clyeva. We will proceed just before the solar orb settles behind the horizon."

Taminisha wrestled with the restraint, but the women were too strong. Without regard to her comfort, they shoved her roughly into a small room carved in the rock wall and clipped a barred gate into place.

She grabbed the bars. "Izusah, what is this? Let me out. I came of my free will. I demand the right to leave by free will. What you plan is an abomination."

"Shhh, Ellkiiyn," Angwye muttered close by the door. "You cannot stop it now."

"Angwye, tell me what is all this?" Taminisha cried. "I came for help, not to be imprisoned or to do something against my will."

The Abaye smiled. "I am Tarlitek's cousin on his mother's side. I am half Myattican and half Abaye, not that it matters. Clyeva is full blood

Abaye, but when she saw Tarlitek she fell madly in love."

"But…"

"Yes, he is of the water and she of fire. They embraced once in the throes of passion. Tarlitek almost melted and barely survived while Clyeva's fire almost extinguished. She lay close to death for a very long period. Despite it all, they still love each other with a passion bordering on madness. Tarlitek promised never to seek Clyeva out. Unfortunately, for all, Clyeva now lives in a miserable fog, consumed with an insatiable mourning for an unequitable love. She has no desire to live."

"But does she want to be sacrificed for me? I cannot bear the thought," Taminisha wailed.

"To her, you are a link to her beloved Tarlitek. If her fire goes with you, she goes with you, in part, to be with her Tarlitek."

"Great Spirit, I cannot bear it." Taminisha sobbed.

"Nor I, Ellkiiyn, for I am to blame for her love sickness."

"Angwye, please call me Taminisha. I do not approve these actions. If I'd known, I would never have made such a request. Tarlitek must have known, but he did not tell me."

"Maybe Tarlitek sees this as a way to end Clyeva's suffering without her committing the ultimate crime of extinguishing her own fire, and ending her life."

Horror flooded through Taminisha at the cruelty of their situation. Tarlitek had provided an acceptable escape from her life of desolation as an act of devotion. Tears poured down her face and she struggled to breathe air into her constricted lungs.

"Will Clyeva really die?"

Angwye pursed his lips. "For an Abaye to give up their fire is a death sentence, and the ultimate sacrifice. She will be sent away to die alone, but the community will mourn her as a martyr. If she took her own life her very existence would be wiped from the memory of the community."

Izusah walked up with almost silent footsteps. "It's time, Ellkiiyn.

Clyeva has consented. In fact, she is pleased."

Taminisha rose to her feet, struggling against the waves of nausea crashing through her. She tottered on trembling legs toward the opening of the cave.

Clyeva stood there, silhouetted by the solar orb, her fiery red hair swept to the side in tumbling curls revealing the shaved under darkness. A red robe hung around her shoulders, partially hiding her naked body.

She held out her hands. "Ellkiiyn, I welcome thee, and offer thee my fire, for I have no more use for it. I ask, but one thing."

Taminisha stopped in front of Clyeva and took hold of her hands. "Clyeva, I beg you; don't do this."

Clyeva shrugged. "It is now beyond my control, but I welcome this extinguishing as Tarlitek knew I would. It is his gift of love to me, and my gift to you. All I ask is you tell him when your destinies next cross, the fire you hold is mine. Tell him I love him always, and thank him for having the strength to give me this gift of extinguishment. Will you do this?"

Taminisha tried to speak, but the words would not come. She peered deep into Clyeva's dark, almost expressionless eyes. "Yes, I will do as you ask."

Clyeva sighed and smiled.

"I am ready, Preeya." Despite the barely audible voice, Clyeva strode confidently to the stone tables at the edge of the precipice. She took off her robe and climbed naked onto the larger one, stretching out her tall, lean body on the rock table top. The rays of the solar orb transformed her red hair into fire and highlighted the curves of her generous breasts, her taut abdomen and muscular thighs.

The need to escape twinged inside and Taminisha launched herself away from the tables.

Izusah and Deshikee lunged after her latching onto her arms with tight grips. Their restraint brought her to a standstill. With unsympathetic force, they hauled her to the vacant table and heaved her onto the smooth flat surface.

Taminisha writhed and kicked in a desperate attempt to transmogrify, but she couldn't get free enough to curl.

Izusah laid her hand on Taminisha's habilan. The cloth sizzled, and melted under the heat emanating from her palm.

Taminisha cowered against the exposure of her pale pink sachan body to the fading solar rays and those standing on the edge of the cliff. She fought as Izusah and Deshikee wrapped webbing around her limbs to secure her.

Izusah brought a cup of liquid and forced it down Taminisha's throat.

Despite the fact she spat and coughed, the liquid went down, burning her mouth and throat as it did. Almost immediately, the surroundings spun out of focus, faster and faster, until a swirling kaleidoscope of colours encircled her. Nausea sent bitter bile sliding up her throat as she grappled with her bonds. Her limbs refused to obey. Taminisha finally sank into warm, silent calmness.

"Begin the abscission."

Preeya and Izusah moved around and between the tables. Clyeva lay unmoving. Preeya stood over the Abaye woman with a short, curved knife. It glowed red-hot. Preeya brought it down and punctured Clyeva's skin just below her breasts. The smell of seared flesh encroached on Taminisha's senses, but Clyeva did not respond as if she suffered physical anguish.

Preeya leaned over Clyeva and dipped both hands into the wound she'd made. With extreme care, the old woman lifted a small glowing ball out of Clyeva's body. She cradled it in both hands.

Izusah moved beside Taminisha with a similar knife in her hands. As the curved blade came down toward her, Taminisha felt no fear, just acceptance—even when the sting of the blade slid across her ribs.

Preeya hovered over Taminisha before carefully laying the glowing ball beside the wound. In a slow awkward movement, Preeya lifted her hands to the settling solar orb and chanted unintelligible words in a wailing voice. The solar orb flared bright.

Taminisha shut her eyes against the burning rays and kept them closed as the old woman opened up her incision and carefully inserted the ball in the wound. Warmth spread through Taminisha's flesh even as Preeya sutured the gash.

Behind the warm glow, Taminisha felt the strong beating of two hearts.

Izusah appeared, pouring more liquid into Taminisha's mouth, forcing her to swallow by stroking her throat. "It is done, Ellkiiyn. Your fire is restored," Izusah said.

Taminisha's vision blurred. Choking sounds that could have been sobbing came from the table beside her and guilt sliced with more sting than the knife had inflicted. Poor Clyeva. Did she regret her sacrifice as she lay dying, knowing she would never see Tarlitek again? A small distance away, she heard Angwye wailing his grief.

With the terrible deed completed, remorse crushed against her soul. Shame burned beside it. She'd killed another for her own benefit. Taminisha could do nothing about the harm her innocent request for help had done. Her body trembled and she thrashed from side to side. "Please forgive me," she cried.

Darkness crept in and blurred her vision as the vile bitterness of nausea rushed through her. Fear hardened behind her breasts with the awareness of steady hands carrying her. Voices whispered nearby as they placed her on the ground. Silence and coldness enveloped her, chilling all her body, except for the glow of warmth behind her breast. Shadows crept in until only blackness remained. Taminisha relaxed and knew no more.

# Chapter Six

Awareness came slowly to Taminisha. At first a terrible coldness buried in her flesh, then a silence, so heavy it weighed against her chest. Tension gripped her muscles even as her heart raced in her chest. She strained to hear the slightest sound, then lifted her head a fraction and opened her eyes the tiniest of slits. The ground pressed with the stabbing points of rocks against her scales. Her limbs were untethered, but ached with a fatigue she didn't understand.

From her limited view, the clearing appeared deserted. Huge green bulging tiakto with spiny coverings and large boulders loomed beside her. They had tiny brightly coloured blamets in between the spines. The blamets appeared fragile and out of place in comparison with the bulkiness of the plant.

With slow cautious movements Taminisha lifted her head, and surveyed the dry barren landscape. *It seems I'm still in Abaye, but they have abandoned me.* Obviously, the Abaye wanted nothing more to do with her and despite their sentiments being hurtful, and annoying, she understood their attitude. She had taken the life of one of their own. Even if she knew the location of the cavern, she would not be welcome if she returned.

She sighed. Not another single soul knew or cared where she was at this precise moment. Disorientation and loneliness threatened to engulf her, but even as she wallowed in self-pity, the second heartbeat called her. *He cares. He wants me. I will go to him.*

Taminisha rolled over and stood. Her entire body moaned—her Ellkiiyn body. Immediately she grabbed at her throat and sighed with relief as her fingers closed over her Rykala locket. With delicate tugs, she untangled the twisted fibrous flesh of her wings and flapped them.

She lifted her head and spat. Red flame spurted out in a wide stream scorching down one side of the nearest tiakto plant. *Oh, Great Spirit, I have my fire back.* Her breath caught in her chest. Her knees liquefied and she sank back to the ground. Tears filled her eyes as a prickling sensation rushed over her body.

She spat once more exploding a nearby plant into a shower of green sludge. Exhilaration rushed through her as she scurried back from the splatter of mush. *I have my fire back.* The thought hit her in the solar plexus. *Great Spirit, Clyeva has died in giving this to me. Where were the Abaye now? Were they hiding in shame at what they'd done to a lovesick member of their community? Do they feel the shame I do?*

With muscular legs, she stood, stretched and swished her tail. It whistled as it swiped through the air. *I feel good. Better than I have since Nyket's attack. I'm almost whole again, but at an unbearable price. May the Spirit of Etunik curse you, Tarlitek.*

Not sure which direction to take she investigated her surroundings, peering around the clearing, behind the rocks and plants. Nothing moved in the barrenness of the landscape, but she could hear the faint shush of water. She guessed if she followed the sound, it would bring her nearer the border of Fylitia. *I would rather fly over than walk through the spell binder's territory. Just in case they cast a spell and turn me into a green poraka.*

With tentative swipes, Taminisha flapped her wings. At the next downward thrust, she leapt into the air. She hovered just above the ground then crashed. Spitting out dust she straightened her crumpled wings then sat on her haunches fighting back tears. *Why Great Spirit, why can't I fly? Is it some punishment for crimes unknown? If so, I'm sorry. Please restore my flight.* She tried once more, but only lifted a foot from the ground before thumping back down. With her pleas to the Great Spirit unanswered, she sighed, mentally casting aside the melancholy that threatened to engulf her before she formed her habilan and transmogrified.

In the instance of transmogrification her gaze riveted on the faint, pink ripple across her chest. She slid her finger along the faded scar of her sachan body, the only indication she'd undergone an abscission. No mutilation, no bleeding gash, no tenderness; nothing showed to castigate her selfishness in taking the Abaye's life.

Invisible remorse whipped at Taminisha and pushed sobs up through her chest. Tears filled her eyes and poured in salty rivulets down her cheeks. She hung her head and let them flow, releasing some of her despair.

Her tears finally puttered to soft hiccups and, suddenly vulnerable in her nakedness, she hurried over and picked up the fully formed, and almost dry, habilan. With a long, slow puff of warm air she dried the clothing completely and slipped the soft stretchy material over her body.

Powerlessness gripped her. She rubbed her forehead and snorted. Sparks flew. As they sizzled and died to black powder on the ground, she perched on a nearby rock and pondered her situation. *What do I do now? I can't go back, I can't stay here, and I don't want to go forward.* She could do nothing for Jabrikan, or to usurp Nyket, and so she faced the enormity of Clyeva's sacrifice and the obligation to use her gift of fire wisely.

*I must abide by Tarlitek's urging, and seek out the soul mate that still calls me with such loving determination. Later I will reconcile my soul with the sacrifices made, and make peace with the Great Spirit Ellkii.*

After a vigorous mental debate over Ellkiiyn form, or sachan, Taminisha decided on her more fragile sachan form. *I will be less imposing, and more likely to get a positive reaction from others on first contact.* Besides, she didn't fancy pushing and shoving her huge scaled Ellkiiyn body through the vegetation either, knowing she would leave a path of destruction, and reopen wounds in her still tender flesh.

The solar orb hung overhead, but failed to warm the air that blew across the flat, sparsely vegetated landscape. Taminisha trudged on, finding the exercise generated some warmth in her bones. Sadly, it failed to soothe her aching heart and shattered conscience. To feel well at another's expense gnawed at her inner peace, and stoked her anger at Tarlitek's omissions.

As darkness came, she found a sheltered spot beside some tumbled boulders and a stand of tall spiny tiakto. In the shelter of the plants, she transmogrified and curled up, breathing warm air against her body. She slept soundly, knowing she had nothing to fear as Ellkiiyn.

Taminisha woke and stretched as the solar rays warmed her scaly skin. Her very empty stomach rumbled. She scratched her belly with a back claw then lumbered down to the banks of the river. She waded into the slowly running water and sat back on her haunches. With Ellkiiyn vision, she could see plump orrtaya swimming lazily against the undercurrent. She dipped her head into the water and clamped her jaws around the first green body. She ripped the orrtaya in half, and with an uncouth gulp, she swallowed both chunks. Still hungry, she immediately went back for another.

Five orrtaya later, her hunger sated, she splashed water on her face and rinsed the orrtaya scales and taste from her mouth. Using one claw, she picked a few stray scales out from between her teeth then burped loudly. She waded from the water, shook herself then breathed warm air against her scales. Almost completely dry she transmogrified. Her long dark hair hung damp down her back, but she immediately retrieved the habilan she had hung so carefully in a tree, the lunor drift just passed, and slipped it back over her sachan body.

The second heartbeat in her chest seemed stronger this awakening. She spun in a circle trying to get a fix on the direction to travel, first to the right, where the beat diminished, then to the left, where it strengthened.

With one more wistful glance over her shoulder, and a carefully controlled sigh of deep sadness for all she'd left behind, Taminisha hitched up her habilan, turned her back on Abaye, and began to walk toward her future.

A faint whimper scratched against her already twitchy nerves. Taminisha jumped behind the nearest rock. She slowed her breathing to a mere whisper and peered around the edge of the monolith. The low cries of distress came from a short distance away, but she couldn't locate the source.

She inched out from behind the rock, and crept forward. The cries became sobs. Taminisha paused, trying to place the sound as it drifted on the breeze and echoed between the rocks. She stepped forward. The shale slipped beneath her feet, clattering loudly. The noise stopped.

"Who's there? I am Ellkiiyn, and demand you respond."

As her shout faded, silence enveloped her. Even the wind dropped out into stillness.

"Who's there?" She waited for the cries to come again. After a time of absolute silence, Taminisha wondered if she'd imagined the sound, or mistaken an echo from her own rasping breath.

*I'm sure I heard someone crying or an animal, maybe.* After a moment, she resumed her journey, placing her feet with exaggerated care on the uneven ground. Every few steps she paused and listened.

At last, the tiniest cry, muted as if muffled when it escaped, tinkled across the clearing. Taminisha moved confidently in that direction. It came again, very close, vibrated by shaky, shallow breathing. Taminisha slunk around the next rock ready to spring away if the creature concealed there turned out to be dangerous.

Taminisha sagged under the weakness that swamped her. Clyeva huddled by the rock—a pale reflection of the woman Taminisha remembered.

With a hollow faced expression, dark eyes sunken back into her skull and filled with torment, Clyeva hugged herself.

"Clyeva."

Clyeva flinched away as Taminisha reached for her.

"Do not touch me. Go from here."

"You live. They told me you were dead."

The woman glowered up at her. "I will most certainly be dead, soon. You have my fire, and the community have banished me to die. The cold will come soon enough. Leave me be, Ellkiiyn."

"I will not. Why did they banish you?"

"It is the way, so no one has to face the extinguishment of the inner fire." Clyeva's voice came out devoid of animation. "Any Abaye who lose their fire or as it fades in old age, and sickness, they are banished."

"That's awful."

Clyeva joggled her head, her mussed up red curls bounced. "That is how it is and I do not wish it otherwise for I cannot live without Tarlitek, nor can I live with him. Leave me be, Ellkiiyn, go on your journey, fulfil your destiny, or my sacrifice will be for nought."

Taminisha stood in mute indecision, confused, and torn between compassion and reality. Guilt and pride stopped her from just walking away. Even the brutal knowledge that abscission always caused the death of the donor; the need to do something consumed her.

She knelt beside the cringing woman. "Are you hurting?"

The Abaye's full ruby lips puckered into a pout. "No, Ellkiiyn, just cold. Leave me be."

"I can make you warm."

Clyeva gave a weak snort. "I will never be warm again because you have my fire. Soon the cold will come in earnest, and I shall succumb to its torture. And it shall not be worse than the agony that drives a stake through my heart, and soul, every awakening since Tarlitek left."

"Is there no way you can come together?"

A sneer straightened Clyeva's mouth into a thin line. "Only in death."

"Surely this extinguishment does not have to be so brutal, so cruel and so final?"

Again, Clyeva snorted, this time the sound had an edge of bitterness to it. "I want it to be final. Unfortunately, I didn't know it would be this bad. Go, Ellkiiyn, for it will be over soon."

Taminisha stood, and walked a short distance away. She stopped, and turned, taking three strides back to Clyeva's side. "I will stay, until it's over. I cannot bear the thought of you dying alone. No one should die alone, least of all one as generous as you."

A tiny smile curved Clyeva's lips. Small lines formed in the corner of her eyes accentuating the almond shape and the thick dark lashes. "You're kind, Ellkiiyn; I believe my fire has gone to a greater good in you. What do they call you?"

"Taminisha."

"Your wait will not be long, the pain has begun," Clyeva said softly, then doubled over clutching her abdomen.

Taminisha lit a small fire—a token to the darkness consuming the barren landscape. She transmogrified and curled around Clyeva, gently breathing warm air over her writhing body.

Clyeva didn't speak again, but moaned and thrashed about. Her screeches of agony cut through Taminisha's mind. The Abaye woman had lost all her ruddy colour, her exposed face and hands white, the skin almost translucent. Now she sobbed and squirmed. With uncoordinated jerks, she kicked out with her legs, and flailed with her arms. Froth formed at her mouth and her nose began to shed black sooty flakes.

Taminisha fought back nausea. Unable to do anything to help she could hardly bear to witness this horror.

Soon Clyeva stopped moving, and lay silent. She still breathed, but her eyes stared up at the sky, not seeing the sprinkling of stars.

Taminisha leaned close. "Clyeva?"

The dying woman did not respond.

Hot tears filled Taminisha eyes, spilled over, and coursed down her cheeks. Consumed with grief, and guilt, she ached with the unfairness of it all, but even as melancholy clutched at her, tiny fingers of anger wound their way around her soul. *This is not right. Clyeva should not have to die.*

She unwrapped herself from around the dying woman, no longer worried about the lack of warmth, for Clyeva seemed well past feeling, or caring. Taminisha paced back and forth, her Ellkiiyn feet stomped into the pebble strewn dirt. Her claws quickly filled with soil and she lifted one foot up in the lunor light to pick out the small stones digging into her almost transparent claw. Her claws glowed in the silvery light, the dark lines of her veins silhouetted where her deep purple blood flowed almost to the end.

*Blood.*

She leaned over the woman and examined her closely. *She's too far gone to drink my blood. There has to be another way.* Taminisha looked from the Abaye woman to her huge, razor sharp claws. The purple blood flowed rapidly down the claw and back. *If she cannot drink it can I inject it directly into her flesh? Will it still work? Will the blood work at all?*

Taminisha sat back on her haunches then brought her foot up and extended the longest claw as far as it would go. She placed her foot over Clyeva's exposed shoulder, where the skin appeared so thin she could see the shrivelled veins through it. With a swift stabbing motion, Taminisha brought her claw down and slammed it right through the Abaye's thin flesh.

Clyeva's body jagged up at the force then flopped back onto the ground.

Taminisha withdrew the claw.

Without further consideration of the consequences, Taminisha put a second claw in her mouth and bit down hard. "Owww," she howled as pain shot up her arm. Blood spurted out—her rich, dark, purple blood. It dripped to the ground in bloated drops. She pushed the bleeding claw into the puncture wound she'd made.

Revulsion surged through her as the blood began to leak into the Abaye's flesh and she almost pulled the claw out again. It required all her determination to keep it in place. With each throb of her heart, the purple stain spread inside Clyeva's shoulder.

Clyeva did not move. Her breathing remained slow, and very shallow.

Taminisha sensed death close by.

After a while, Taminisha stirred restlessly. Her leg ached with the awkward angle as she tried not to put any weight on Clyeva. Finally, unable to bear the discomfort she shuffled her big body around and managed to lie down beside the ailing woman. The stain continued to spread. With no sign of improvement, Taminisha fretted, even though she'd never been sure there would be one. In fact, Ellkiiyn blood may well kill the Abaye woman quicker than a natural death.

Clyeva's body had a distinct purple hue down to her waist when Taminisha began to feel lightheaded and sick. *Perhaps I'd better stop. How much is too much? Must avoid debilitating my strength because I might need it to defend us.* Besides, the blood exchangement didn't seem to help the dying Abaye.

When she withdrew her severed claw, it kept bleeding. Alarmed by the continued blood loss she held it up and blew on it. "Ouch ouch, ouch," she cried as the flame cauterised the end of her claw. Her whole foot throbbed, but at least the bleeding had stopped.

With nothing else to do, Taminisha lay down and curled around Clyeva breathing gentle puffs of warm air on her. She tucked her aching foot down by her side and tried to sleep, but rest eluded her, chased away by the fear that Clyeva would die while she slept.

Several times during the long lunor drift, Taminisha licked her foot to ease the burning and checked Clyeva for signs of improvement. As soon as the sky lightened, Taminisha went down to the river and fed on fat orrtaya drifting in the warm shallows.

When she returned Clyeva, unconscious and decidedly purple, still clung to life. Her breathing seemed somewhat louder, but Taminisha couldn't tell if the change indicated an improvement or not. She peered closely at the woman. *Should I give her more blood? I have plenty to spare and it's probably too late to do any harm.*

Taminisha chose a different claw and shoved it between her fangs before she could change her mind or contemplate the pain. As the blood spurted from her claw, she stabbed Clyeva's thigh and eased the bleeding claw tip into her muscular leg.

Clyeva moaned and moved her leg slightly against the pain.

*Dear Spirit, she felt that. Is this a good sign?* Taminisha studied the woman's face. She seemed slightly less cadaverous. Maybe? Taminisha sat still, watching her blood flow into Clyeva's leg. The purple stain had spread almost down to her knee and now crept slowly up over her lower abdomen.

Clyeva suddenly roused, coughing and spluttering.

Taminisha inhaled with a gasp and held her breath in anticipation. Her body trembled. All the small scales around her eyes crackled as tears stung her masq. *Great Ellkii, what have I done? Is my blood killing her?*

Clyeva coughed again. A small amount of purple blood dribbled out of the corner of her mouth and down over her jaw.

Taminisha's stomach fluttered as if filled with terrified shawken. She almost ripped her claw out of the woman's flesh, but despite the tremble that rattled through her, Taminisha held the claw in place, praying it was the right thing to do. A stinging tingle seared over her scaly hide and in her chest, her heart raced.

Clyeva took a deep shuddering breath, coughed and slowly opened her eyes. She glared at Taminisha then gazed around the clearing and peered up at the sky. The movement seemed to cause her discomfort and she lifted her head ever so slightly to investigate her leg. Clyeva wailed, and howled as she tried to pull away.

Taminisha held her on the ground with just a fraction of Ellkiiyn weight.

"*Be still, Clyeva. Be calm,*" she broadcast in Ellkiiyn.

The Abaye woman's eyes bulged as she stared up. She grabbed at Taminisha arm. Her lips moved, but no sound came.

Taminisha winced at her own stupidity. *She doesn't understand me.* Other species could not receive or understand Ellkiiyn mind talk.

Clyeva's frantic look darted left and right then back to Taminisha. She lifted her head and peered down at her body. Her eyes rolled back in their sockets and her mouth gaped open before her head hit the ground with a thump.

The slight rise and fall of her chest assured Taminisha the Abaye woman was only unconscious, not dead. *Perhaps I should remove my claw; it might be easier for her when she comes to, not to have my bleeding Ellkiiyn claw embedded in her leg. Dear Ellkii, the purple colour is probably drastic enough.*

With small spurt of fire, Taminisha cauterized her second claw. "Owww," she howled as her claw sizzled. She transmogrified and slipped her habilan on. When she turned back to Clyeva, the woman had come to.

She lay quietly studying Taminisha, her hands covering her mouth. Clyeva lifted her arms and stared at them. "By the ashes... by the ashes of the Fire Nymph, I... I'm purple."

"You are, but you're also alive," Taminisha replied in romni.

Clyeva glowered at her. "I... I wanted to be dead. You have denied me that release." She squeezed her eyes shut, shaking her head. "Now I must live without fire *and* without Tarlitek. I cannot bear the anguish."

"But to be dead is so final..."

Clyeva lifted her hand as if to ward Taminisha off. "And painless."

"Perhaps this is your destiny."

"I do not care about destiny," Clyeva snarled back at her.

"I'm sorry, but I could not let you die."

Clyeva lifted her arms again. "I'm purple. What did you do to me?"

"I gave you my blood. You were dying. I couldn't just sit by and let it happen. I didn't know if it would help, but I had to do something."

"You've selfishly saved me from a death I welcomed, so now what?"

Clyeva's bitter retort hit Taminisha in the gut. "Surely you can go home to Abaye."

"I'm dead to them because I do not have fire."

"Are you sure?"

"I feel the spot inside where the fire once dwelled. It's a cold empty space."

"Then you shall come with me."

"*Then you shall come with me,*" Clyeva squeaked as she surveyed her purple flesh again. She rubbed at the stained skin then jerked her hands away. "And where would that be?"

Taminisha waved her hands through the air. "I'm not sure; I follow the heartbeat that patters in unison with mine. My soul mate calls."

"And this soul mate, would he want an outcast Abaye, a purple one at that, tagging along?"

Taminisha chuckled. "He will take on any entourage I bring, and anyway, the purple is not likely to last. Surely it will fade in time…"

Clyeva stared directly at her. "But you don't know, do you?"

Taminisha pursed her lips. "I'm sorry, but I cannot guarantee it will fade. No Ellkiiyn has shared their blood with an Abaye before. *Great Spirit, what have I done? What if she goes the way of Tolanim?* She stamped down on the ugly thought. She had no proof the gift of Ellkiiyn blood caused mutation and madness.

Clyeva pouted. "You think I should just be grateful I'm alive. Well I'm not."

Taminisha watched her, a sudden chill dancing over her skin. "I'm sorry. I just couldn't walk away and let you die. I don't know what the future holds, but surely it's better than death?"

Clyeva's stony expression made her appear even more haggard. "You've snatched away my one chance at a dignified end. Tarlitek's gift. You repay my sacrifice with a lifetime of torment. The agony of love denied. How could you?"

Taminisha winced, and fiddled with her locket, unsure what to say or do. *Is it so bad, saving her?* She looked away into the distance, not seeing the view. Taminisha wanted to chide Clyeva for being ungrateful, but she knew her revival of the dying woman had been about herself, not Clyeva. She slumped to her knees and picked up Clyeva's hands. "I'm sorry."

"So you should be, interfering where you shouldn't, just because you feel guilty. But it's done."

"So will you come with me, Clyeva? I will see you have a good life... well as good as possible."

Clyeva smiled. "Yes, I'll come with you for I have nowhere else to go."

"Good, then we shall move on when we're ready. I will transmogrify, and you can hop up and ride, until you have your strength back. I just wish my ability to fly would return. The journey would be easier."

"There may be a purpose to your grounding."

Taminisha shrugged. "From you, who does not care for destiny? However, I have given the matter thought and come to the same conclusion. I mean, if I'd flown, I wouldn't have found you, although they placed you right in my pathway to die. Could there be some motive to this?"

Clyeva shrugged. "I don't know, but there is much Preeya, and others know that is not shared."

"Hmmp," Taminisha grunted as they set off into Fylitia.

~  ~  ~

A shiver scuttled across her scales at the subtle change in the ambience. Yet nothing had changed dramatically in the landscape, the wind or the solar rays. Taminisha slowed to an amble making a conscious effort to relax. She peered with concentrated attention through the trees and off into the distance.

Clyeva leaned close to her ear. "I think we've left Abaye."

Taminisha gave a small grunt to indicate she understood, and swallowing down on the quiver in her stomach resumed walking at a steady pace. *I don't like this place. Great Spirit, help us pass through Fylitia undetected. I have no desire to confront a Wheti or a Whydan.*

The second heartbeat tugged at her, pattering and hiccupping. She stopped. Its irregular vibration slightly out of sync with hers strengthened when she swivelled to the left, but faded to the right. She swung to the left; the beat steadied and grew stronger. *"It appears we go this way,"* she broadcast to her passenger.

"Lead the way, Ellkiiyn, and I will follow," Clyeva declared with a flamboyant wave of her hand.

A giggle spluttered up and burst forth, sending ripples of amusement shuddering through Taminisha's body and bringing a sense of calm. At least her companion had recovered enough to make a joke and pretend she understood Ellkiiyn mind talk. *I must remember to speak aloud in romni from now on.*

Taminisha breathed deeply in through her large Ellkiiyn nostrils. The water smelt different—clearer, colder and with a faint tang of firnit tree. A sense of expectation tingled through her.

# Chapter Seven

As they topped the rise, Taminisha saw the glint of solar rays on water. She squinted and made out the iridescent blue waters of Kelkiki Lake. Barely discernible through the forest of giant firnit trees, with their straight trunks, and branches, stark and protruding ribs on a skeleton, the shore appeared to be mostly small rocky cliffs with the occasional pebbly beach. The Aqueena Ellkiiyn held Guardianship over the sprawling Kelkiki Lake and the rich hilly country surrounding it.

Taminisha turned right along the cliff and walked close to the precipice. Clyeva tapped her on the top of the head, and pointed to the beach. Taminisha nodded.

"We'll need to find a way down the cliff. It will be safer to sleep on the beach. Then, in the awakening, we can circumnavigate the lake in the hope of finding your soul mate," Clyeva said.

*"Good idea,"* Taminisha broadcast.

Clyeva tapped her on the head again. Taminisha flinched at the blows and muttered aloud in romni. "Good idea."

Taminisha frowned, already sensing the beginnings of a massive headache that would form when she transmogrified after the Ellkiiyn sized taps from Clyeva. *I won't be fit for anything.* Nevertheless, other more pressing doubts assailed her. She still couldn't fly, and unless she could, there would be no mating. All this; her healing, Clyeva's sacrifice, and her journey, might be to no avail. Where would that leave Tarlitek's assertion she had to fulfil her destiny and save Dykarin?

With barely a rustle of warning sachans rose from the bushes. They wielded spears and axes. Ear piercing yodels shattered the air.

Taminisha reared back.

Clyeva slipped down Taminisha's scaly back and landed on the hard ground with a faint thud.

With a roar and a blast of fire, Taminisha lunged directly at her attackers. Her foot caught in a loop of rope. Instantly it tightened. She jerked sideways, lost her balance, and fell right on the edge of the sheer drop. Taminisha scrabbled with her free feet as she teetered, rocked, then plummeted down the cliff. She bounced and thumped in a downward tumble, bashed violently against the cliff face. Rocks sliced into her hide, dust filled her eyes, and spear tips slid under her scales. Shocked at the suddenness and savagery of the attack Taminisha howled in anger and pain until the force of her crash onto the rocky beach brutally extinguished her noise and breath.

She lay gasping, everything spinning around her. As her equilibrium returned she blinked to dislodge the dirt embedded under her transparent lids. She breathed deeply and howled again, this time spitting fire in all directions. Her ribs hurt, but she rolled over and stood on all fours. As she did, ropes whipped across her shoulders, back and snout. She hunched against them, but couldn't loosen the unyielding bonds. Taminisha strained her neck as far around as she could, searching for Clyeva. She'd vanished.

*With luck, she's just hiding, somewhere safe.* Taminisha focussed her searing attention back on her captors. Her heart raced, pounding blood through her head. She glanced around assessing her foes. Her legs quaked as she struggled to get free. With a deep huff, she tried to roar and breathe fire, but the rope digging into her jaw clamped her mouth shut.

Closest to her, wielding deadly spears were males dressed in long black coats, with dark hair and pale skin. They watched her with dull, expressionless eyes. She'd never seen such as these before—those of the darkness, the Unni of Lycidea. *Surely, this is Fylitia, not Lycidea. Are my bearings so distorted I have come through Fylitia without knowing?* She mentally cast off the jumbled thoughts and uncertainty to focus on her foes.

As she stilled a dozen sachan appeared behind the Unni. Male and female, all adorned in velvet robes that swept the ground. The men wore hats with shawken plumes and the women covered their heads in small beaded caps trimmed with trailing veils. She recognised the Wheti, and Whydan, of Fylitia—feared spellbinders and magic spinners. Chills rolled over her. She battled to draw breath and swallowed convulsively against the dry sourness in her mouth. *I'm in real trouble, but I don't know why.*

Taminisha strained against her bonds, thrashing her huge head around in an attempt to see her captors. *They have no need to attack me. I'm no threat to them.* She desperately wanted to transmogrify and slip from the restraints, but knew her life would be at risk from the spears embedded in her flesh if she were in sachan form.

A large boned woman with white blonde hair tucked under a green velvet cap stepped forward. She exuded authority and rank. "So Ellkiiyn, you have come. Do not expect to leave this place." The woman spoke in perfect romni as her full crimson lips curled up in a sneer.

Taminisha shook her head in denial of the statement. "I only pass through to fulfil my destiny. I have no argument with the Wheti, and

Whydan of Fylitia. Why do you assail me?"

"I am Quanika, and I will change your destiny, Ellkiiyn."

*How does she know my destiny when even I don't and why would she want to change it?* "Why, Quanika? Even I do not know the fullness of my destiny. I do not understand this attack on my person."

"Then I will make you understand, Ellkiiyn. Come." Quanika turned and strode toward the rocky headland at the base of the cliffs.

The black coated men moved in and prodded Taminisha with their spears. She moved to escape the hurt and allowed them to drive her down the beach behind Quanika. The others followed in single file. As she walked, Taminisha scoured the beach and cliffs for Clyeva, desperate to find her ailing friend, fearing the worst.

She didn't expect the Unni to spare her, they killed without thought, but Clyeva's bizarre purple skin might be enough to scare the highly superstitious Unni into leaving her alone. Perhaps Clyeva could make an escape, and be safe.

They stopped on the edge of a deep pool filled with brown water and a surface so still; the reflections mirrored the real thing to perfection. Disorientated by the reflections, Taminisha focussed on Quanika.

The Wheti stood on the edge of the water. She raised her hands high and wide, and began to shout. Long unintelligible words, and sing song phrases, in the language of magical beings. The water swirled and rose, higher and higher until a wall as reflective as the surface of the pool hung suspended in the air.

Colours melted and blotched across the facade before they formed pictures. People running, screaming, and dying. Ellkiiyn battling, a handsome young man, a castle, then a young woman giving birth overseen by a creamy gold Eqazantia, which with a flap of wings and a clatter of hooves, morphflitted into a stunning man with wings.

Quanika shrieked as the young woman perished. In that moment, Taminisha recognised her similarity to the leader of the Fylitia Wheti. Quanika's grief bit deep into Taminisha's chest, throbbing alongside the heartbeat of her soul mate.

The picture changed to a beautiful young woman, a Vaprus Ellkiiyn female with purple eyes and pointed ears. She had no pectenites so Taminisha knew immediately she had tainted blood, but around her neck hung the amulet now dangling between Quanika's breasts. The woman wailed again.

Taminisha's heart jumped a beat then raced, as suddenly she understood. The Daughter of Kylara—this woman would save them all. *I must escape Quanika's trap, and fulfil my destiny.*

Taminisha faced the Wheti. "The Daughter of Kylara will save us all. You must let me go, Quanika, for although your torment is great, and your heart is designing a better path for your offspring, you cannot stop these events. Not even by killing me, for another Ellkiiyn will take my place forging a rockier path than has already been portrayed." All the time she talked, she wriggled her hands and feet back and forth in the bindings.

"No," Quanika bawled. "This cannot be. I cannot bear it." The Wheti turned to the bystanders and raised her hand. "Kill the Ellkiiyn."

Taminisha held up one clawed hand, now loosened from the bindings. "Do not advance, or I shall incinerate you all." Hoping she could deliver on her threat with her mouth still partially closed, she exhaled, sending a small stream of fire along the sand. The Fylitia backed away, but the dark men stood their ground. They did not fear her flames.

She lowered her head, inhaled and blew a deep breath out. Fire raced down the beach, but the Unni were gone before it reached them. Rising in a squeaking black cloud of shikati—Unni of the Darkness transformed, they flew away to hide in one of the caves until darkness came.

One however, stood his ground, in fact, he advanced on her. Taminisha reared back tugging at her bonds. The ropes loosened and fell away. Taminisha breathed in and stared at her foe.

The Unni advanced.

Taminisha spat fire.

The Unni jumped sideways, fell and scrambled up. "Stop! It is I!"

Taminisha choked back her blazing stream. *Clyeva?* Only then did she notice the distinct lavender tinge of the Unni's skin.

Taminisha breathed a huge sigh of relief. *"Clyeva, thank the Great Spirit Ellkii, you're safe,"* Taminisha broadcast silently.

Clyeva pointed. "Not yet, Taminisha."

Quanika stood on the edge of the pool with both hands outstretched in their direction. The waters of the pool gushed down the sand toward them. Clyeva climbed onto Taminisha's back loosening the last ropes as she scrambled up.

"Fly, Taminisha, fly."

*"I can't,"* she broadcast. *"I can't."*

*"Fly, I say,"* Clyeva broadcast in reply.

Shaken by the silent words in her head Taminisha glanced over her shoulder at her friend. Clyeva sat on her back with a squirming shikati in her hand.

The tiny black creature screeched, and snapped with needle like teeth. Spindly legs flailed and lashed with razor sharp claws.

Clyeva held the creature up to the sky. She shouted in Abaye and jerked the enraged shikati back and forth. As forks of lightning flashed and sizzled around them, Clyeva brought the screeching shikati to her mouth and ripped its head off. Blood spurted everywhere as she spat the head out.

Nausea rushed over Taminisha.

Clyeva rubbed the blood over Taminisha's wings squeezing the furry body dry of every drop. "Fly, Taminisha, fly," she shouted.

Taminisha glanced back at the water rushing from the Wheti's scrying pond and flapped her wings. The wind soared under the wide leathery span and she lifted off the sand just as the water spilled into her footprints to make four monstrous lakes filled with venomous water tarqu.

Quanika howled her rage to the sky.

Forks of lightning speared after them. Taminisha ducked and swerved around them as they sizzled and faded into harmless puffs of smoke.

As they left Fylitia behind, exhilaration exploded through Taminisha. *I am restored. I am Ellkiiyn.*

Scarcely able to draw breath above the thud of twin heartbeats in her chest Taminisha dipped and circled in the sky over the lake, surveying the land, searching for the source of the call.

In the distance, a castle stood high on an island in the middle of the wide expanse of water. Off to the left sat another smaller island, clouded in mist and covered in lush oversized vegetation. She felt, even up this high, an eerie aura emanating from the second island.

*"There, Clyeva, is our home. I'm sure of it,"* she broadcast, pointing to the castle.

"Kelkiki, the home of the Aqueena Ellkiiyn. It is reputed to be a dark grief stricken place for many years past. Are you sure?" Clyeva asked aloud right by Taminisha's Ellkiiyn ear.

*"Yes, Clyeva, the heartbeats are almost in unison. Besides, it's not the other surely?"* Taminisha broadcast without thinking.

'No, that's Oventi Rock, the island of no return. We will go to the Castle of Kelkiki, but first I need to tend your wounds and you must bathe. You cannot go to your soul mate with the blood of a shikati on your body or your soul," Clyeva replied.

A wave of sickness and guilt washed over Taminisha. Her flight miraculously restored, but at what cost. Another life sacrificed. It may have been an Unni, but it didn't sit well—the male it had been moments before may have had a mate, children. Fury bubbled inside her at Clyeva's murderous actions. She wanted an explanation once they'd landed.

They flew past her prospective new home. The land spread out for miles, but the island the castle rested on appeared quite small and hilly. The landscape appeared predominately rugged, but green pastures, and patches of dense forest interspersed the rocky outcrops. The

Aqueena had built the castle on the highest point of the island. Constructed of dark gray rock it had three wide towers and two smaller ones. There appeared to be an absence of beaches and, in the deepening shadows of the solar settling, the island seemed formidable and unwelcoming.

A sense of sadness reached out to her. Taminisha shivered, not enthralled by what she'd seen, but her soul mate's call compelled her to come.

As they landed, Taminisha tipped Clyeva off her back and rounded on her friend. *"How dare you kill like that, Clyeva, It didn't have a chance,"* she broadcast.

Clyeva climbed to her feet and stood facing Taminisha. "You needed to fly. Time to remember this world is not the soft one you came from."

*"But, Clyeva, to rip its head of...."* Her stomach gurgled and churned as she recalled the shikati's violent death.

"It's the only way the spell will work; you must use the blood of an Unni of the Darkness turned shikati, but not an innocent shikati. That creature may have looked like a sachan on the beach, but transformed, he would go during the darkness and suck blood to live, innocent blood, sachan children's blood."

*"Children's blood?"*

Clyeva held her hands wide. "That is why the blood is so powerful— it is the blood of innocents."

Taminisha shuddered. *"Do Unni they drink blood in their sachan form?"*

Clyeva blanched. *"No. Only the Unni of the dark arts can transform. Do not fret your shikati, Taminisha, please. Now bathe and prepare or we shall not sleep safe in the castle."*

Taminisha stilled, her mouth sagged open. Clyeva had understood, and replied to her Ellkiiyn mind talk. *But she can't. Surely she didn't. The blood. Great Spirit Ellkii, it's my blood.* She plonked onto her backside and stared at Clyeva.

"Come on; time to ready yourself for your mate. What is this foolishness sitting there gawping at nothing?"

*"I'm not. I'm gawping at you,"* she broadcast in reply.

*"Why for flames sake? Surely you've got used to my purple shade by..."* Clyeva's broadcasted thoughts ended abruptly. "We're communicating—really communicating in *Ellkiiyn mind talk*. Oh Fiery Nymph's eyes, I can hear you speak."

Taminisha grinned. "No, Clyeva, you hear me 'not speak'."

Clyeva collapsed to the ground.

Taminisha closed the gap between them. "You're Ellkiiyn now."

Clyeva laid her hand on Taminisha's snout. "My sister, my friend."

Taminisha peered over her shoulder at the castle rising up out of the ruffled waters of the lake. "Do you think the castle is safe?"

"Do you feel the beat of his heart?"

Taminisha touched her breast above her heart. "It's still strong, calling me. Do you think it is the Guardian or another that calls?"

"It is possible the Guardian calls you, his first joining ended in grief. Now prepare."

Taminisha waded into the lake. The blood of the shikati had set on her wings, tight and constricting. She ducked under and rubbed herself on the rocks and some weed trailing in the water. The weed felt rough and slimy, but it cleansed her scales. Refreshed, she fed herself before bringing a large orrtaya to the beach for Clyeva to cook and eat.

Clyeva immediately screwed her face up at her offering. "I can't eat orrtaya."

Taminisha hesitated, and then she remembered—*Tarlitek. Clyeva loved an Orunan. Of course, she wouldn't eat orrtaya.* Taminisha promptly swallowed the orrtaya whole, and proceeded to blow warm air on her scales. Despite the unified heartbeat behind her breast, she couldn't quite stifle her doubts.

She'd been so sure with Odakan. Their initial mating had been exhilarating. Many passionate, heady and vigorous joinings had followed, but their wish to breed had not eventuated and gradually the urge failed to come. Taminisha had grieved for that failure as she now grieved her dead soul mate.

"Clyeva, I'm not sure I'm ready to join with another so soon after Odakan."

"Odakan is dead. *He* is calling you, but you must go freely, give willingly, or he will kill you in the mating dance."

"If only I could explain."

Clyeva's face paled to almost white. "You have no need to explain. There will only ever be Tarlitek for me, but for you it's different. Love calls you. It is right, and leaves no need or room for explanation in such Ellkiiyn passion."

"I know." Taminisha sat down on the sand and stared at the castle. So close, but now so far. Through the darkness, lights flickered in welcome from the castle balconies.

"If you are uncertain, you must not go."

Taminisha made a sudden decision and stood up. "I'm going to investigate."

"Taminisha," Clyeva protested. 'To do so is not wise unless..."

Ignoring her friend's protest, she rose into the darkening sky on a flap of soft fibrous wings. The lunor discs had just risen behind Oventi Rock and the imposing stone structure of the castle appeared a less bleak now the lunor discs had risen and bathed it in the silvery lunor beams. Air rushed cold and damp past her body as she soared high over the castle. With slow undulations of her wings, she circled back, lower this time.

# Chapter Eight

Her heart hammered, echoed almost painfully by a second thud.

He paced the bailey terrace and peered out over the dark waters before he stared up to the lunor discs. He searched for her. He sensed her nearness, and yet, he had not transmogrified into Ellkiiyn. Tall and solidly built with dark strawberry blond flowing locks, his pectenites protruded from his head in a magnificent multi-spiked crown.

Her body hummed with sexual readiness and her heart thudded. Instinctively, she howled her sexual desire.

He stared up and smiled, but made no effort to transmogrify.

She circled again.

He never took his eyes off her as she floated by. He broadcast his need and desire strongly, but his uncertainty came through above it.

Taminisha swooped close and cried out again, calling him to join her.

He paced the length of the terrace keeping her in sight, but he did not change.

She glided closer, checking the terrace, ready to land. Down she drifted, and with one last flap, her clawed feet caught the edge of the parapet. She jumped, twisted and rolled, before bouncing to her feet. She stood before him in sachan form, naked except for the glint of lunor light on her skin.

He stood at the end of the parapet walk, unmoving, staring, following her every move.

She hesitated then closed the gap between them. His scent, pure Ellkiiyn, her Ellkiiyn, tantalized her. Promising ecstasy, it tugged at her, filled her nostrils and tingled along her skin. With vision enhanced by desire, she studied him—eyes of gold, framed by long dark lashes, sachan skin, pale and clear and a relaxed curve to his wide mouth.

He smiled.

Her heart exploded into a million sparks. She mirrored his smile. His unspoken response surged through her—tender and affectionate. His non-verbal sentiments left her in no doubt about the underlying sexual desire that throbbed through him. Taminisha could not understand why he had not transmogrified and led her into the mating dance.

"You've come, at last," he said. "I am Kikishan."

The deep, husky, timbre of his voice shimmied over her skin and caressed her mind.

He held out both hands. They were large, and fully encompassed hers as she laid them in his grasp. Slight calluses on his palms grazed her skin and she wondered what an Ellkiiyn Guardian would do to get calluses.

She inclined her head. As their pectenites touched, she flinched back as the pure magnetism zapped through her. She gasped, and then steadied herself as she straightened. "I am Taminisha. You called, and I have come."

He stood still, holding her hands and studying her. His broad shoulders were emphasised by the wide collar on his velvet over robe, and his waist, cinched in tight with a carved leather belt. Through the split in his habilen, tight fitting leggings and knee-high boots trimmed with jewels outlined his muscular thighs and long legs.

The air between them vibrated with tension. Taminisha shivered as some ancient instinct called her.

"You're afraid, my heart?"

She shook her head. "I am not afraid, just uncertain. Odakan, my previous soul mate, is such a short time taken the hand of the Spirit. I never expected a second calling. Your call is strong, I feel it, I accept it, I respond willingly, but a tiny part of my heart still grieves my loss."

A soft sympathetic smile softened his expression. "I do not ask you to discard your grief, or memories of your previous mate. I would not. I must admit, Taminisha, I have called you despite feeling I do not have the right. I have previously mated and lost my beloved mate and I have not hungered for a new mate for a long time. When I sensed your vibrancy flickering though your grief, my empathy surged so strong I called you without reservation even though I am much older than you. Since then however, doubts have plagued me—your grief, my age, and the rigours of Kelkiki. I do not want to cheat you of having a younger, more spirited mate, or a better home. This is why I stand before you in sachan form—to give you a chance to consider, or even re-consider."

"To allow such consideration is unprecedented."

He inclined his head. "And is it wrong?"

"No, it is kindness itself. For despite my grief I felt your call, and have responded even with my own misgivings. Now I am here do you doubt the validity of our potential as mates?"

"I do not doubt your rightness as my mate."

"So how should we proceed, Kikishan?"

"Taminisha, if you are willing, we will progress—by our own rules, without fear of the consequences."

She inclined her head. "I would be most happy to do so, but first, I must retrieve my friend, from yonder beach, before she is devoured by wild creatures. Then once she is settled, we shall step into the future together."

Kikishan smiled as he leaned forward, and placed a chaste kiss on her lips. "A kiss to hold your heart in readiness, for me, on your return."

As he stepped back, Taminisha transmogrified and took flight from the parapet. She wheeled into the sky and roared her happiness to the lunor discs. The air shivered as the power of her new love pulsated through her. Its pure force made it easy to banish her doubts and the insidious myths around Ellkiiyn mating. Odakan and she obeyed the rules and still they had not bred. Therefore, with Kikishan, what would be would be.

She swooped toward the beach. The sand shimmered in the lunor light and the waves lapped gently at its edge. Taminisha landed on all four feet with a thud that loosened rocks at the end of the cove. As their clatter faded she examined the area, but the beach appeared deserted.

"Clyeva, it is I, Taminisha. Come out, it's safe."

A tiny patter of sound came from behind her. Taminisha spun around ready to do battle, but sighed with relief as Clyeva emerged warily from the rocks.

"I feared you would not return, and just over the hill I saw signs of habitation."

"Then we will proceed with all haste to the castle as my soul mate has accepted my advance."

"But the mating dance..." Clyeva protested.

Taminisha laughed. "We've decided to make our own rules."

"But..."

Taminisha held her clawed hand up. "It's done. Climb aboard so we can go home."

Clyeva scowled.

Taminisha refused to discuss her concerns and heaved a sigh of relief when her friend did not make further protest, just climbed in silence up onto Taminisha's shoulders. With a couple of flaps, the wind roared under her wings and she rushed forward up into the sky.

Kikishan still waited on the terrace, but since her fleeting visit, he had illuminated the castle from top to bottom. In the big room, behind Kikishan, servants of varying species scurried back and forth with bed linen, loaded trays, and jugs of refreshments.

As Taminisha landed, Clyeva climbed hurriedly down to allow her to transmogrify. Prepared this time Taminisha quickly created her habilan. Clyeva stood silent, her lavender skin pale in the lunor light. Her fear and uncertainty had hardened her expression into a mixture of apprehension and disapproval.

Clyeva's rejection of their plans irritated Taminisha. She wanted her friend to be happy for her; however she staked her claim on Kikishan's heart. She would accept what karma decreed.

Hiding her displeasure, Taminisha stepped forward. "Kikishan, this is, Clyeva, Abaye by birth, my sister by exchangement, my friend by choice."

Kikishan gave the smallest of bows. "Welcome, to Kelkiki Island, home of the Aqueena Ellkiiyn Clan, such as it is in these troubled times."

Clyeva bowed low. "Thank you, Guardian Kikishan. As I am no longer recognised in my own community I am glad of your welcome."

Kikishan smiled. "All friends of Taminisha's will be welcome here." He clapped his hands.

A small male Aqueena Ellkiiyn approached with mincing steps. His masq glittered and kohl outlined his almost orange eyes. A female with short spiky hair appeared behind him. Her masq sat slightly askew on her face and her pectenites were short and very slim. Taminisha guessed her bloodlines were not quite pure.

"Tabro, and Enian, will escort you to your quarters, Clyeva. We will speak further of your future and place here, but for now Taminisha and I must talk. There is much to be determined."

Clyeva snapped a quick glance at Taminisha, and then bowed to her host. "I would suggest there is much to be rectified, Guardian Kikishan, and it is hoped your union will not be at risk because you have both chosen to flaunt the rules."

Kikishan frowned. "I do not like your impertinence, Clyeva, but I will give you leniency because I know you mean the best for Taminisha. Therefore, I will say this just once, Taminisha and I do not flaunt the rules, but simply choose a slightly different path. Our union will not be at risk."

Clyeva looked directly at Kikishan. "Are you sure?"

He frowned. "Leave my presence. I will not tolerate you questioning my authority, or seeding doubts in Taminisha about our mating. The situation is fraught enough already."

As Clyeva walked slowly in the direction indicated, the two summoned Ellkiiyn followed her.

The hairs stiffened along the nape of Taminisha's neck. Sudden heat flooded through her as she tried to clear the lump in her throat. In this foreign environment she had no certainty her friend would be safe. Doubts flared. *Have I made the right decision fulfilling this call? Placing myself at the mercy of a stranger while poor, misplaced Clyeva is even more vulnerable.*

"Kikishan, she is my friend..." Her voice wavered.

"I know, and she will not be harmed, but she must learn not to question me. Times are complicated, and I must, as Guardian, appear strong and in control," Kikishan replied.

Taminisha's uncertainty eased a fraction. "Clyeva means no disrespect, but she fears for our union because our mating dance did not eventuate without first contact as they say it should."

Kikishan smiled. "Come, Taminisha, there is much to talk about." He took her hand and led her into the castle.

They climbed five flights of stairs carved out of gray rock. Scones lit their passage, supplementing the lunor glow that poured in the windows. One glance showed Taminisha they were high up in the bailey. Below the lunor light shimmered on the choppy waters of the lake.

Kikishan paused outside a huge oak door to unlock it and with an over-exaggerated sweep of his arm swung it open. They emerged out onto a huge circular terrace bordered only by a low wall. An ideal location for transmogrification and flight in or out as Ellkiiyn. A low platform occupied most of the space. Kikishan led her to it.

"Sit here beside me," he said, as he patted the stone.

She made herself comfortable, aware as she did, her attraction to this male warmed her from the inside.

He took both her hands in his, turning slightly to face her. "We have much to overcome, Taminisha. The full blood Ellkiiyn is a dying breed here in Kelkiki. I cannot offer you a thriving court or a varied pool of Ellkiiyn females from which to choose friends. Your daughters will get love calls from distant lands by soul mates we shall never meet. Riches, fancy gatherings of the elite, and such, will not soften your life here. Here in Kelkiki you will be building communities, encouraging breeding and the building of Ellkiiyn families. At the same time, you will be fulfilling diplomatic duties to keep the populations around us friendly."

Taminisha smiled. "Kikishan, you are my soul mate, you called me, and I came. To what I came, I did not question, as I do not question it now. Together we will do what needs to be done." She leaned into him and kissed his mouth.

Her lips sizzled with his fiery taste. She breathed in his scent and ached deep inside with the need to be closer to him.

He embraced her, pulling her against the rippled hardness of his muscles barely concealed under his robe. He ran his hands across her shoulders and down her arms before parting her habilan and baring her breasts to his view. Kikishan sighed as he stood and pulled her up with him. Her habilan tumbled to the stone floor. He cradled her face with both his hands, stroking her cheeks with the pads of his thumbs. With a slow descent, he lowered his head and kissed her nose and eyelids before he began to explore her mouth. He stepped back and removed his belt, leggings and boots then took her in his embrace again.

With trembling fingers, she reached up and undid his habilen. With one small push, it slipped from his body and crumpled to the ground. He stood before her, naked, his arousal hard and ready. She felt no shyness at their nakedness totally consumed with desire for her soul mate.

When the urge came, she fought it for a moment, as she revelled in his hands caressing her intimately.

"Do not fight it, my love, come with me," Kikishan murmured against her lips.

His scent intoxicated her, no longer sachan flesh, but the tantalising tang of pure Ellkiiyn—aroused male Ellkiiyn. His skin changed under her stroking fingers. A searing fire ignited in her belly and then she curled and bent in his arms, moulding her transforming body to his.

His claws gripped her as they rose, huge leathery wings beating in unison, back and forth, the motion pushing their heavy scaled bodies together. They rose, long tails entwining, clinging and probing, belly to belly. He held her head to his chest with a tight grip on her pectenites— almost painful, but exquisite at the same time. He thrust at her belly low down at the base of her tail.

She met his thrust with one of her own and his huge prehensile member pushed its way into her. Searing ecstasy blasted through her and she clutched him with clawed hands as they rose twirling, scaly bodies carried by an explosion of sexual need. She growled, and panted, spitting small sparks of fire.

He growled back and thrust faster and harder.

She howled as her whole body vibrated with thunderous undulations.

He repeatedly bashed his body hard against her.

She embedded the claws of her back feet into his sides and dragged him closer.

He growled again this time emitting a long spurt of flame that whizzed right past her face. Simultaneously the hot spurt of his life force raced up inside her.

They twirled slowly now, wings rising and falling with languid strokes as they descended toward the castle, still joined, throbbing rhythmically against each other. Kikishan put his feet to the ground first, easing their landing. Neither could stand and they tumbled on weakened legs to the stone. There they lay, breathing hard, scale against scale, pectenites entangled with pectenites.

Taminisha's body melted into sated softness. She transmogrified without trying, and made no effort to resist, as she lay overcome with exhaustion.

Kikishan pulled away from her. "Are you ready, my love? It is time." He had transmogrified, and still naked in his sachan form, he bent and lifted her from the floor.

Taminisha had no idea what he meant, but really didn't care. She snuggled down against him with her eyes closed. When he stopped, she peeped from under heavy eyelids to find they were inside a huge domed room with wide windows. Kikishan laid her on the huge oval bed covered in velvet blankets and huge pillows.

"Kikishan, where are we?"

"We're in the nesting room I have prepared. The strength of our mating has brought you to the brink. I sense your readiness to breed, my love?"

"I do not know, for I have never bred before despite...despite mating." Heat surged up her face and she buried her head in his chest.

The rumble of his laughter un-nerved her. She stole a quick look at him, shame and uncertainty rushing through her.

"Did your previous mating ever feel like ours?"

She looked away, suddenly reticent. "No. Ours felt deeper, stronger and more explosive."

Kikishan chuckled again. "In this moment, you were ready in a way you've never been. You were ready for *me*."

A blush of shyness heated her face.

He kissed her. "Come." Her mate transmogrified and climbed into the nest.

"Yes, Kikishan, I am ready." She transmogrified and joined him, lying close to her mate and prepare for the birth of the egg that would become her child. It would take only a short time for her body to produce a viable egg, and already she felt a deep ache in her lower abdomen.

Fear nipped at her mind as she faced this unknown. Taminisha settled in the middle of the birthing platform and waited for the birthing of her egg to begin.

Kikishan embraced her, stroking her belly and murmuring soothing sounds.

The ache intensified, her belly rumbled and began to undulate in a similar manner to her climaxes of just a short time ago. A hard lump moved inside her. She parted her legs and with a soft growl, and another push, she made the lump continue its journey to be birthed.

Kikishan massaged her belly and the flesh around her opening.

Each time she pushed, and strained, it slid further toward her opening. She grunted – this time scrunching up against her abdomen as her opening stretched. Kikishan's soft caress eased her discomfort as with a final push and a groan, the egg slipped out and landed with a soft plop on the velvet padding beneath them.

Kikishan growled and rubbed all around her belly, and very quickly her opening shrank back to normal and the pain faded.

She lifted her head to inspect the egg. Large, symmetrical, and the softest blue. Layer upon layer of scales covered the surface, each one with a purple tinge. As expected, the egg took after the father's Aqueena bloodlines, but the strength of her pure Vaprus heritage showed through. Taminisha wondered if the baby would also have a purple tinge.

Protectiveness rushed over her. Inside the blue, and lavender, egg her child developed. In less than sixty awakenings, the baby would hatch. Kikishan and she would share the incubating equally between them, one of them always sequestered in the nest.

Taminisha shivered in anticipation and excitement. With blunt determination she refused to contemplate the notion her child might fail the transmogrifying test on hatching.

This had been the fate of her younger brother. His death had taken the life out of her father and a few solar phasings later he'd succumbed to the winter scalinette virus knowing if his son had been allowed more time, he would have transmogrified successfully.

Despite the intervening years, the horror remained etched in her mind like a black shadow.

"It's exquisite, and our very own. This is a new beginning for the Aqueena Ellkiiyn," Kikishan said.

Taminisha nuzzled the egg and pulled it closer to the warmth of her body. She breathed a soft stream of warm air against the shell before she looked up at her soul mate. "We shall have a beautiful child, the first of many, Kikishan. Now go and announce our joining to all, and please, send Clyeva to me in a couple of hours. For now, I need to sleep."

Kikishan touched his snout to hers, then transmogrified, before he left the room.

Taminisha curled her tired body around her egg and laid her cheek against the shell. Deep in her heart, she felt the tiny heartbeat.

Taminisha sensed Clyeva's presence and pulled herself from sleep. When she opened her eyes, Clyeva startled.

"Taminisha, I have been beside myself with worry, but now, dear friend, I am so overwhelmed by your achievement. Such a perfect egg. I did fear the lack of convention would..." Clyeva flicked her fingers through her hair as if to chase away bad thoughts. "Never mind what I thought. This is what matters."

"Poor Clyeva, it is something you will have to become accustomed to. Kikishan and I will not allow ancient outdated rules of the Ellkiiyn Clans to bind us. We intend to make our own. As you can see, we have produced an heir."

A mix of emotions flittered across Clyeva's face, but she just smiled. "I will leave you to rest. Will you come to me when Kikishan takes over? I have not wanted for anything here, except company. They are wary of the lavender Abaye woman."

Taminisha giggled. "We must find a cure for your condition."

"I would appreciate restoration to my natural colour, although after the first shock I have grown used to the lavender hue, but others find it disconcerting."

Left alone again, Taminisha tried to untangle the myriad of thoughts that filled her mind. It cut too deep to dwell on Nyket's cruelties, but she did fret on Jabrikan.

While she agreed with Nyket's sentiments that all Ellkiiyn should be equal, she could not reconcile herself to the horrendous deaths, and Nyket's ruthless attack on her. Such evil came from within the individual's soul not the fault of tainted blood. Such evil now ruled Aikanshin.

Although Tarlitek had assured her they would meet again, much could have happened in the time since they parted ways. She worried too, about Clyeva, his soul mate. How will he feel about Clyeva's survival? Will he be angry with her for saving Clyeva? Could their love ever be fulfilled?

# Chapter Nine

"It's time for me to relieve you," Kikishan said.

She heard his voice through the fog of sleep.

He nudged against her shoulder.

She opened her eyes.

Kikishan stood beside the nest as Ellkiiyn.

She admired his magnificence—the three rows of pectenites rising from his horny head between elongated ears. A pale gray rippling froxcomb framed his long face and highlighted wide eyes of glowing gold. His blue curling moustache added character to his serious countenance and balanced his features nicely.

Invigorated by the nearness of her soul mate she unwound her body with extreme care, aware she had become stiff and cramped during her confinement. Under Kikishan's watchful gaze, she eased away from the egg and crawled off the nest.

Kikishan touched his snout to hers then climbed into the nest and curled his huge scaly body around their egg. He nudged it tenderly, easing it close to his chest.

A warm rush of love for him engulfed her.

"Go, Taminisha, rest, eat, and explore your new home. I have assigned Enian as your guide. She is not pure blood Ellkiiyn, but very capable. Ask her anything you need to know. Do not fret for I have our child under my protection. Larkin, Adakin and Tabro will be on hand to provide any protection you might need. Larkin is my nephew and almost my twin in looks, and Tabro you met on your arrival. Both are excellent warriors. Adakin hatched in Rabikan, to a Terraid mother and Aqueena father. When Adakin's mother died in a cliff slide her mother blamed Adakin's father for her death. Consumed with terrible grief and no longer welcome with the Terraids, his Aqueena father came home with Adakin. He is young and can be a bit mischievous, and boisterous, but he is an excellent worker and totally loyal to me."

Her sadness must have showed in her expression for Kikishan frowned.

"What is the matter, my love? You seem unhappy."

Taminisha smiled. "Ellkiiyn love is so difficult. I believe we must learn to bond and breed even if not called. Also a reduction on the need for clan purity and *a better way to incubate.*"

"I agree, my love, so if you come up with a solution, tell me, and we shall implement it."

"Too late for us, our plight is now. Our constant separation makes me melancholy, my love. We have not even had a chance to explore each other. The solitude of the nest has allowed confused thoughts from the past to niggle, and I do not know how to make them rest easy in my mind."

Kikishan smiled. "There will be time, soon. I promise we will slay what torments you; together we will free your mind of worry. Now go, enjoy."

She transmogrified into sachan form, pulled her habilan down over her shoulders and tidied her hair around her pectenites. A soft rumble disturbed the quiet.

Her soul mate already slept, cradling their egg, his heavy male breath shuddering out of his nostrils to flow over the fragile shell.

Enian waited for her just outside the door—a tall, athletic female, with short spiky hair, white blond on the top and jet black on the shaved underside. An unusual, but very striking hairstyle. Nothing obvious indicated her cross breeding and while Taminisha wanted to know more, correct etiquette stopped her from asking. *It's not important anyway.*

Enian inclined her head and held out her hands. Taminisha took her hands and touched her pectenites to hers.

"Kikishan has asked me to be your guide, and the source of all knowledge about Kelkiki. It will be my pleasure."

Taminisha nodded her acknowledgement. "Thank you, Enian, for submitting to the request. I will value your guidance in my new home."

"Your friend awaits you in the dining hall, with some impatience. I interpret from her actions she is the nervous sort, volatile, and very protective of you."

Taminisha smiled. "She is volatile, like fire, as all Abaye are reputed to be. I had hoped, with the exchangement, she would develop some Ellkiiyn calmness. It is unfortunate this is not so, and I have not, thanks to the Spirit, absorbed any of her Abaye jumpiness with her gift of fire."

"Abscission? Shouldn't she be dead?"

Taminisha cringed. "Yes. I found her abandoned and dying after the abscission, but I couldn't bear the guilt, so I gave her a transfusion of my blood. Hence the colour of her skin."

"A rare and somewhat risky action."

"I agree, Enian, and I had no idea what the result would be."

"You are close then?"

"Yes."

'Come, I will take you to your friend, and after, we'll go to your rooms. Kikishan has prepared well for your arrival."

As Taminisha followed Enian she tried to memorise the corridors and rooms they transversed, but by the time they entered the dining hall she became thoroughly confused. *I guess it will take time to feel comfortable here.*

Clyeva flew out of the chair and dashed across the room, a creamy veil and gown fluttering out behind her.

Taminisha startled and stepped back. *What in a blue lunor disc is this apparition?*

"What is this, Clyeva?"

"They do not like me," she wailed. "Enian gave me this arrayma to hide myself from staring eyes."

Sympathy washed over Taminisha. *Poor, poor, Clyeva, what have I done to you?* She held out her arms and Clyeva slumped against her, shedding black sooty flakes over her veiling and Taminisha's habilan.

"Has anyone been cruel?"

Clyeva bowed her head. "No."

"Then do not fret, my friend. We will seek a cure for your tainted colour once we've eaten."

"And if there is no cure?"

"There must be a cure." Even as Taminisha spoke, disturbing thoughts of Tolanim teased at her mind.

Enian waited patiently while they indulged in the varied spread of foods.

When they were satisfied, she said, "I know someone in the village who might be able to help. Are you willing to come with me? It will also be a good introduction to the realm. Kilteen is fairly typical of all the habitation on Kelkiki including the population mix..."

A mind-splitting blast of pectenite horns ripped the quiet apart.

Jolted by fear, Taminisha dropped her cup. It hit the floor and shattered.

Clyeva howled.

Three more blasts pierced the air.

Enian scrambled for the door and poked her head out. Taminisha heard her speak before she withdrew back into the room.

"What is it?"

"Adakin advises we have visitors," Enian said. A frown marred her symmetrical beauty and increased the untidiness of her masq. She pursed her full pouting lips into a thin downward arch.

Taminisha read concern in her expression. Foreboding crawled along her spine. *I'm not prepared. It's too soon for me to handle an uninvited visit from outsiders.* "Should we rouse Kikishan?"

Enian frowned and shuddered. "One can never disturb the incubating Ellkiiyn for anything, but death. It will put the child at risk. You are the joint Guardian of the realm with Kikishan now, Taminisha, so *you* must greet and satisfy the visitors."

"How can I, Enian? I know nothing of Kelkiki."

Enian smiled. "Do not worry, my lady. I will be by your side with prudent advice. You can do this."

Taminisha stood taller, adjusted her habilan and smoothed her hair between her pectenites. "I am ready."Her stomach churned. She clutched her locket. *Please don't let my panic show. I must be calm. Don't get flustered.*

Enian opened the door and gestured for them to pass through. "Come, "she said.

Taminisha followed Enian.

Adakin fell into step behind her.

Clyeva scuttled after them.

They hurried along the corridors to a large, luxuriously appointed audience hall. It had two magnificent stone chairs at one end and three low steps at the other leading to huge doors, currently closed against entry.

Enian indicated the chairs. "Take your seat and a couple of deep breaths while I determine the identity of our visitors."

Clyeva sidled up behind the gray stone slab that made the back of the chair. She gave Taminisha's shoulder a light squeeze of reassurance.

Taminisha appreciated her presence. They had already been through so much together. "We can do this, Clyeva...unless it's Nyket."

"He wouldn't dare—would he?"

"I don't..."

The doors burst open. Taminisha jumped at the unexpected clash of metal cymbals announcing the visitors. Tokanin's welcome had been much more subdued.

First Enian, then the male Ellkiiyn, Larkin, appeared at the top of the steps followed by two women. Warriors.

Taminisha instantly recognised them as Viveka. She studied the women so scantily dressed in leather and metal. Intricately patterned black metal masks covered the top half of their faces.

"Oddianna, Leader of the Viveka, seeks an audience," Larkin announced.

Enian gave a discreet nod. Taking her cue, Taminisha stood, and beckoned the warrior woman forward.

"Welcome, Oddianna to Kelkiki Castle. I am Taminisha, soul mate to Kikishan. What do you seek from me?"

Oddianna moved forward with an aggressive stride. The other woman moved in accord, shoulder to shoulder with her leader. Sheathed swords and spears rested diagonally across their backs. Disconcerted by the obscuring masks, Taminisha had difficulty reading their expressions with any accuracy.

Oddianna halted, slapped her right arm across her breasts and bowed. Taminisha also bowed. Oddianna then reached up to remove her mask. Her companion did the same.

Taminisha sighed with relief. They were both beautiful women, with clear olive skin, dark brown eyes and long black hair plaited tightly over their heads and dangling down their backs.

"Thank you for your welcome, Taminisha. This is my daughter, Sharanna. She made a sighting of an unknown on our beach. We are concerned."

Enian walked forward and stood beside Taminisha. She remained silent. Larkin stood directly behind the women, poised in a defensive stance.

"As we should be, Oddianna." Taminisha smiled at the Viveka leader. "Sharanna, please tell us your story?"

Sharanna stepped forward and inclined her head to acknowledge Taminisha's authority. "Two lunor drifts ago I went out hunting along the lake shore. I saw a shadow on the beach and in the rocks. I moved in closer. The figure appeared sachan in body, but shimmered in the lunor light. Like the glow from the dying embers of a fire, but purple. I had come out alone, so I crept away even though there appeared to be only one. In the awakening, I returned to the beach and there were sachan footsteps and Ellkiiyn."

Taminisha cringed inwardly. *By the Great Spirit, I had no idea I committed such a serious transgression by landing on that particular beach.*

"Ellkiiyn never cross our borders without seeking permission and there is nothing in our legends about a purple sachan," Oddianna said, after her daughter fell silent.

Clyeva whimpered.

Enian cleared her throat as she leaned in close to Taminisha's ear. "I think the truth, my lady, and offer of compensation should soothe this ripple."

Relief rushed through Taminisha. *Only a ripple, thanks be to Ellkii. She* held out her hands. "Oddianna and Sharanna, I respect your concern, but I also have a confession to make. The Ellkiiyn footprints on your beach were mine."

Oddianna's expression hardened. "This is most unsatisfactory."

"One moment please, Oddianna, hear me out."

The Viveka women continued to frown, but listened in silence as Taminisha told her story, ending with the successful production of an egg.

"I see, and the purple creature is *your* doing?"

Taminisha waved her hand in Clyeva's direction. "Yes, Clyeva is a harmless, but troubled soul. After having made her sacrifice, I tainted her blood with mine to bring her back to the living. Clyeva, come out and be introduced to our neighbours."

Clyeva stepped into view and dropped her veil.

Oddianna smiled. "What an unfortunate outcome for you, Clyeva of the Abaye, but better than death, I suppose."

Clyeva bowed slightly then stepped back.

"With no war imminent, there is only the issue of compensation for your, albeit unintentional, intrusion into Viveka."

Taminisha bowed her head in acceptance of the Viveka woman's request. "What would you seek?"

Oddianna's expression tightened into a shrewd mask, and her eyes glinted with what Taminisha interpreted as greed.

"I want one solar phasing mining, at your allinik mine. We have urgent need of the light weight metal to make armour for our new batch of warriors. We do not have enough of value to trade to fill this need."

Enian's indrawn breath hissed in Taminisha's ears.

"A solar phasing—from the solar awakening to the solar settling?"

Oddianna nodded. Enian gave a sharp click with her fingers.

"How many miners do you expect to use?"

Oddianna frowned, obviously frustrated at Taminisha's firm stance. Despite her uncertainty however, Taminisha intended to place limits on the compensation.

"I would use fifty of my best," the Viveka woman replied.

Enian gasped again.

Taminisha frowned. "Your request far outweighs my mistaken transgression. You ask too much."

Oddianna glanced at Sharanna. The younger woman's expression tightened slightly before she smiled.

Oddianna turned back to Taminisha. "What do you offer?"

"I offer you the full time between the solar awakening to the solar settling, with ten of your best miners and Ellkiiyn assistance to cart the ore back to Viveka. You will be supervised at all times."

"Fifteen miners, "Oddianna countered.

Enian clicked.

Taminisha stepped forward, and held out her hands. Oddianna took them in a strong clasp.

"We have a deal, Oddianna?"

"We have a satisfactory compensation agreement."

"Make arrangements for its completion with Enian. Larkin will oversee the period of work and I will look forward to furthering our relationship, Oddianna."

"We also, Taminisha. We wish you well with the incubation and hatching."

"Thank you."

The women turned and walked out the door. Larkin followed them.

"You did well, my lady," Enian said.

Taminisha plonked down on the stone seat, exhausted, and trembling with the completion of her first court negotiations. She hoped there would not be many in the near future.

# Chapter Ten

She woke and tried to stretch, but her protective curl around the egg did not allow for such movement. Despite her devotion to the successful hatching of her egg, she fervently wished Kikishan would hurry. Every inch of her Ellkiiyn body ached and she wondered if sachans suffered as much as Ellkiiyn to produce young. They carried them around inside their abdomens, the child swelling the mother's stomach into a huge ball. The mother then had to push the child out of her body through the opening Taminisha had birthed her egg. She cringed with the thought of something alive, and possibly bigger than an egg, using her body in that way. It seemed cruel, and primitive. As Ellkiiyn though, she found the hours alone incubating her egg, and the continuous separation from Kikishan, just as cruel.

Kikishan arrived late. She fretted, not only in her discomfort, but also in concern. The very nature of the incubating period isolated the sequestered prospective parent in the nesting room far from the castle happenings. It unnerved her when she finally escaped, and had to deal with the changes and shifts that had happened while she remained ensconced.

The door flung open and Kikishan strode into the room. He

appeared flustered, and his eyes glinted with orange highlights in his flushed face. "Sorry, my love. Guardianship duties. A stranger has come into the realm and marched up to the castle demanding entrance. He got entrance all right—straight to the dungeons."

"Is he a threat to us, or our child?"

Kikishan transmogrified before he answered. "I don't know. I did not have time to interrogate him. He's not Ellkiiyn." He grimaced as he climbed into the nest and curled around the egg. "Not for the first time I understand why Ellkiiyn do not breed well. It is a tiresome process, and not beneficial to either our relationship, or the building of a strong guardianship."

Taminisha sighed as she transmogrified. "I agree, Kikishan, and I gave some deep thought to how sachans cope, and if it's any better."

"Sachans? You would consider bearing a child the sachan way?"

Taminisha shrugged. "I don't know, but perhaps it should not be rejected out of hand."

Kikishan grimaced. "Considering the burden on you and your body, such a plan will be entirely your decision, my love."

She grinned. "Yes, I would think so too."

"Go now, Taminisha. Do not worry about the prisoner; he will come to no harm confined to the dungeon for a short time. Check him out, if you want though. Tell me what you think?" Kikishan dropped his head and blew warm air on the egg before he closed his eyes.

Taminisha left, so thankful to be free. She stretched, and jumped, to ease the kinks out of her body. Her first needs when exiting the nest were a clean habilan and food. As expected, Clyeva, Enian and Larkin waited for her in the dining hall.

Enian moved restlessly around the room while Taminisha ate. Clyeva squirmed in her chair. Only Larkin slouched against a wall, his lanky body still, except for his gaze. Even with his heavy plait hanging down his back and smaller scales in his masq, he looked so much like Kikishan. The similarity disconcerted Taminisha and she couldn't stop peeping at him while she ate.

113

Perplexed by the two females unusual behaviour she gulped down a final piece of fruit and looked directly at them. "Enian, Clyeva, what is with you both?"

Enian beamed. "I have ordered eqazeen for us—to ride to the village. The purple one is keen to find a cure."

Taminisha grinned. "Ah, I see—our aborted trip from the other solar phasing. Is all this fidgeting because you both wish me to hurry up?"

Enian appeared chastised. "No, of course not, my lady, of course not."

"Yes," said Clyeva.

Taminisha laughed. "Come, I have finished, let's go."


Fresh winds had swept the normal gloom shadowing the castle away. The sky shimmered in a cloudless blue. The waters of the lake were so still and serene the reflection of the castle appeared as a mirror image. A variety of colourful shawken sang in the trees that hung over the road, or scratched in the dirt at the edge of the track.

The lake water lapped gently at the edges of the stone causeway between the castle grounds and the remainder of Kelkiki leaving them with safe passage into the village. Later as the lunor discs rose, swirling whirlpools would gush in and cover the bridge completely, isolating the castle until the awakening.

The village of Kilteen perched between the shore of the lake and the loose shale foothills. A scattered collection of cottages and buildings made up the largest settlement in Kelkiki.

The streets bustled with folk, Ellkiiyn, Viveka, a couple of Myatticans and even more sachans. Some Taminisha could not identify, and didn't bother trying, for it was impossible to know with so many mixed breed bloodlines. Everyone stopped, moved aside, and then watched as they passed by.

The hairs rose on the back of her neck. She glanced at the watchers then directed her gaze away. She grasped her locket in a sweaty hand, finding its cold solidness strangely comforting. It took enormous effort to force her body to relax deep into the saddle even knowing these people meant her no harm. Of course, she should have expected it. After all her new soul mate had been un-mated for a long time, and many wanted to see who'd finally, and unexpectedly, captured his heart.

"I don't like this," Clyeva muttered from behind her veil.

"Don't fret, Clyeva, they're just curious to see who has captured their beloved guardian's heart. Most of them will not even notice you," Larkin said quietly from behind.

Once through the centre of the village it became quieter and Taminisha relaxed enough to enjoy the ride. A short distance down a deserted side road they came to a quaint stone cottage with a thatched roof and bright yellow doors and window shutters.

Enian reined in her eqazeen. "Come, we will speak with Avyvah, she is an ancient. Myattican mother and Fylitia Whydan father. She knows all there is worth knowing about healing."

Taminisha made to follow Enian then realised Clyeva had not dismounted.

An expression of absolute terror twisted her face, eyes wide open and jaw clenched. "I can't do this."

"Yes you can, just get down off that eqazeen."

Clyeva hunched down in the saddle and clutched the reins in a white knuckled grip.

Taminisha stalked toward her and pointed to the ground. "Get down."

Clyeva cringed away.

Taminisha reached up and grabbed Clyeva's hips. With a tug, she pulled her friend from the saddle.

Clyeva slipped into an untidy heap in the dirt unable to support her weight when her feet touched the ground. She sobbed.

Guilt rushed over Taminisha. *I didn't need to be so forceful. Poor Clyeva, she's petrified.* "Sorry, Clyeva. Here let me help you."

Larkin moved up beside them and together they managed to get the reluctant Clyeva onto her feet, and into the cottage.

Avyvah sat in a rocking chair by an open fire. The ancient had shrivelled with age to no more than a skeleton covered in sagging flesh. Her smile showed toothless gums. She appraised Clyeva with rheumy eyes and hooted with laughter.

Clyeva cringed back.

"Ahhh, that is what you get when you determine to cheat death," the old woman cackled. "Sit, all of you. Sit."

As they settled into a variety of worn and ragged chairs Avyvah made tea, an aromatic brew in an old crockery pot. She didn't consult any of them, just poured the brew into cups and handed them out.

Clyeva sniffed hers then placed it on the side table without tasting it.

Enian sipped and squeaked in surprise, scalded by the near boiling liquid.

Taminisha, tentative and cautious, wrapped her hands around the cup and inhaled the fragrant steam before blowing gently on the hot liquid.

Avyvah watched her for a moment then burst into more cackling laughter. "Ah Ellkiiyn, you seek to cool the liquid with your hot breath. It's to be hoped you will have more intelligence when ruling the country."

A flush of heat raced up Taminisha's cheeks at the old woman's gibe. She wasn't used to underlings making fun of her, even if they were right. She glanced at Larkin.

He sat, tense and still, his gaze focussed on her. He appeared ready to issue some reprimand on the old woman if required.

Taminisha smiled at Avyvah, pushing down her discomfort. "You're right, Old Woman, it is a foolish thing, but when one is schooled by an Orunan shape shifter, it is a learned behaviour, at this age, almost instinctive."

Avyvah cackled again. "Good answer, my lady, and I see you hold your temper and are not crushed by the mockery of an inferior."

Taminisha fiddled with her cup before smiling at the woman. "Pure, royal, Ellkiiyn blood does not make one immune to foolishness, Old Woman, or mixed blood free from ambition beyond achievement.

"Ah, you speak now of your step brother, Nyket, son of Tokanin and Oralia."

Taminisha inclined her head.

"But mixed blood does not countenance greed and violence more than pure."

"But rejection and humiliation does," Taminisha answered.

"One cannot choose what life delivers into our hands, but we can choose how we respond to that challenge. There is a thread still to weave in that story, my lady, but not for you to worry about right now. Tell me what you seek?"

"Avyvah, as you can see my friend, Clyeva, is stained purple with my blood after an exchangement. She wishes to have the colour removed."

Avyvah shook her head. "You have both defied the rules of abscission. Only once in all my long life have I seen such a thing. Ellkiiyn rarely share their blood with other species. It's frowned upon. I'm puzzled at Clyeva's survival in any case, and I'm concerned at the possible repercussions, not that I have any idea of what they might be."

Taminisha sat back in her chair, Avyvah's words a warning slap in the face. *Could the horror of Tolanim be one of the repercussions?*

Clyeva held her head and wailed.

Enian leaned forward. "Avyvah, is there nothing you can do?"

The old woman frowned. "What would you have me do? They are both in good health and they seem bonded. Taminisha has her fire, and Clyeva is learning to live without hers. I would suggest, Clyeva, you celebrate your condition. It's a wondrous thing to survive abscission, and carry the blood of your Ellkiiyn recipient. People here will recognise your staining for what it is, and respect you. You must be proud, or you will shrivel and die. Do you understand?"

Clyeva bowed. "I'll try to be proud, and grateful for my life, even if it's filled with a grieving that will never end."

"Grief always comes to those who covet what they cannot have." Avyvah waved her hand in a dismissive gesture. "Now leave me, all four of you, I need my nap."

Summarily sent on their way, they left the cottage, and mounted the eqazeen.

"I suggest we adjourn to the castle. It is getting late and the wind has risen," Larkin said. "I cannot guarantee your safety when the whirlpools rise across the causeway. If it blocks our passage back to the castle you will not be able to return in time to relieve Kikishan."

"Yes, Larkin, it's time to go home. There's nothing more to be achieved here," Taminisha said.

They rode quickly from the village; acutely aware many sets of eyes followed their progress.

A smear of black to the left caught Taminisha's attention. She rotated slightly in the saddle, and stared into the bush, but saw nothing. She followed the others, but couldn't shake the warning tingle along her spine. Taminisha reined in her eqazeen until she'd dropped back beside Larkin. She reached out and touched his hand.

Larkin started, and turned her way.

*"I saw something lurking in the bush. Could we be in danger?"* Taminisha broadcast in Ellkiiyn.

*"It's possible."* Larkin glanced over her shoulder. *"Be ready to transmogrify. I'll take Clyeva. Enian, be aware, we have company."*

Clyeva dropped back. "Are we in trouble?"

*"We are not alone on this road,"* Taminisha broadcast.

Larkin looked at Taminisha with raised eyebrows.

She smiled. "My colour wasn't the only thing Clyeva gained."

Larkin rolled his eyes and glanced at the sky.

"But it only works over a short distance."

Twin roars exploded the silence.

Two blurs of movement, one black, the other gold, slipped through the bushes and into the middle of the narrow road. Two large Felitza blocked their way forward—one jet black and lean, with a long lashing tail. Green eyes flashed in the darkness of the surrounding face.

The other was golden with black spots, and long lanky limbs out of proportion with a smallish head.

Both had bared teeth and twitching whiskers.

The eqazeen sidestepped and jiggled, snorting froth at the predators. Clyeva cried out, her face blanching so pale it hardly had any colour.

Enian fought to control her eqazeen. *"Zynumin. We could be in big trouble."*

Taminisha studied the Felitza prowling back and forth across the road. *"Do we transmogrify, or just run for it?"*

*"Nothing. See, they're morphflitting,"* Enian replied.

Taminisha steadied her breathing, preparing her body to transmogrify. She had dealt with Felitza before; they had a strong predatory instinct even in sachan form. As sachan, she might be vulnerable, but as Ellkiiyn, they would not dare challenge her.

Both animals sizzled and sparked, glossy fur stood on end, ears and whiskers trembled. The air ripped apart under the force of two ear-splitting cracks. Simultaneous flashes of lightning seared the air leaving a sharp, acrid stench in the air.

As the light withered, two males in sachan form took shape. One, tall and black, with a mane of long frizzy black hair while the second had olive skin, short spiky hair, burning golden eyes and black teardrops marking his skin from inner eye to his mouth. They were both stark naked and seemed unconcerned by it.

Clyeva whimpered.

Taminisha relaxed enough to admire their physiques—broad shoulders, defined muscles, long shapely legs and significant genitalia. Their lithe movements were sensuous. Their scent wafted over her. Without consciousness, Taminisha's body responded to the pungent aroma of Felitza pheromones. Desire flared deep inside and for the first time she understood why species came to cross breed.

Larkin rode up beside Enian and Taminisha where he sat tall in the saddle, his impressive crown of pectenites erect on his head. His whole persona crackled with warning. He cleared his throat. "Palakin, this is no way to secure an audience with the Guardians of Kelkiki."

Palakin stared back unblinking. His pupils contracted to small black ellipses in the glistening green of his eyes. He inclined his head in acknowledgement. "Times are such, Larkin, niceties are no longer the rule, but I will, on this occasion, apologise to all of you. Jyquin and I have travelled many solar phasings to make this meeting. We arrived just as you came along the road, and decided to make the most of the opportunity rather than struggle for entrance at the castle. Injudicious of us perhaps, but urgency drove our decision. Under normal circumstances we would have morphflitted and clad ourselves suitably before greeting you."

Larkin grimaced. "Apology accepted, Palakin. Now state your business."

The black man blatantly assessed her. "You are Taminisha, step sister of Nyket?"

"I am Taminisha, soul mate of Kikishan. I have disowned my step brother and severed all links with Aikanshin because of Nyket's betrayal."

A subtle growl rumbled in Jyquin's throat. He drew back his lips exposing his prominent eyeteeth. "You do not have that luxury, Guardian of Kelkiki, you must..."

Palakin swatted him with a large hand. Jyquin hissed and spat at him before he inclined his head in submission.

"Forgive my brother's rudeness. Nyket is terrorising the sachans of Kylara and they flee to the border between Kylara and Zynumin. Some have even breached the Wall of Tennille. It is not safe for them to be in Zynumin, my people are natural predators. For now, our leader Aneverin has forbidden any Zynumin to morphflitt into Felitza form. It will keep the refugees safe in the interim, but we are then vulnerable to attack, and unable to breed with our own kind. It is not a long-term solution. Aikanshin needs its true Guardian."

Taminisha bowed her head in acknowledgement of the big Felitza's assessment of the situation. Distress at the aftermath of Nyket's rebellion trembled through her as a lump of grief and helplessness settled in her gut.

She looked down at the black Zynumin. "Palakin, I fear your journey here has been in vain for I am not the true Guardian of Aikanshin.

Palakin wrinkled his nose as if he'd smelt something unpleasant. "So, Nyket is the heir? It is all we have?"

Taminisha grimaced. "Nyket is neither Vaprus, nor pureblood. As a Khimaera, he cannot legally ascend, even as Regent. The true heir to the Guardianship is Jabrikan, my dead brother's child, but he is too young to inherit."

Jyquin shuffled restlessly. "So you won't help?"He lifted his lips in a snarl.

Taminisha stared directly at Jyquin. "I didn't say I would not help. Only that I did not have a solution to offer right now. Kikishan, and I, are incubating our first child; nothing comes before the successful conclusion to that. Only then will we both be available to negotiate with the Zynumin to broker a solution."

"Aneverin said you would rebuff us, so I will be glad to give him the good news," Palakin said.

"I must make haste to the castle, gentlemen, to relieve my mate. Larkin will see you fed and sheltered. Return here sixty solar awakenings hence and we shall parley."

# Chapter Eleven

Taminisha woke from a short nap on another long solar phasing of incubation duty, to Clyeva screeching outside the door. Other voices rose and fell. Scuffling noises echoed from the corridor. A moment later Kikishan squeezed in the door just ahead of Clyeva. He prevented her from entering by slamming the door in her face.

"Your friend has driven us all to distraction, wailing and crying, but refusing to explain to anyone, but you, what her problem is. For this one phasing, I will be glad to partake in incubating. Go, my love, and sort her out, please."

Taminisha stretched her body extensively as soon as she transmogrified. "I will, my heart, I will." With a wave of gratitude that he had not been angry, she wondered about the cause of her friend's agitation. It didn't take much, for even without fire, volatile erratic mood swings plagued Clyeva—her inheritance as an Abaye.

The instant Taminisha eased herself out of the room, Clyeva latched onto her arm. "We need to talk. We need to talk. Privately. Right this minute."

Taminisha sighed. "Tell me."

Clyeva dragged on her arm. "Come to your rooms, this is not for all ears, only yours."

Enian trailed behind them watching Clyeva with a quizzical smile.

Taminisha did not resist as Clyeva dragged her down the stairs and into her rooms. At the door, Taminisha paused and glanced in Enian's direction. "Please bring a tray to my rooms; only make sure you knock before entering. Thank you."

Enian hurried away.

Immediately the door closed, Clyeva pounced on her. "They have him. Exploding Fire Nymphs, they have him."

"They have who?" Taminisha asked struggling to be interested after the long hours of incubating her egg.

'Tarlitek. Mother of Nootau he's here, in the dungeons."

Clyeva's garbled words slapped across her and Taminisha froze, staring at Clyeva. "Tarlitek here?"

Clyeva nodded.

"It can't be, surely. I left him in Myattica."

"It's him. I know because I can feel him—here... Clyeva slapped her breast. "And here." She tapped her head. She quivered from head to toe. "I feel him, all over my body."

"Tarlitek? Great Spirit Ellkii, of all the good fortune," Taminisha cried.

Clyeva reared back. "No, Taminisha, no. I cannot see him, I love him, but I will burn him, and he will douse me. We will both die." Clyeva bawled, running her hands through her fiery red locks.

Taminisha stared at her friend, trying to comprehend her information. "Are you sure it's Tarlitek?"

"Of course I'm sure, I love him, and he's my soul mate. I felt him, shimmying over my skin, cold and wet. So, I hunted through the castle

123

for him. He's incarcerated in the dungeons."

"Did you speak with him?"

Clyeva hugged herself. "Of course I didn't. We cannot see each other; to get close is to die, painfully. We can never be together. Oh sizzling Fire Nymphs, I wish I'd died, struck dead from the abscission. The pain—to have him so near, and never hold him. I cannot bear it. Why did you not let me die?" Clyeva howled, and choked out great heaving sobs. Soon twin lines of black soot sprinkled down her lavender cheeks.

"Calm yourself," Taminisha admonished, even as she struggled to hold back the tremors of excitement that gripped her. *Could it possibly be Tarlitek? Had he come to find me, or found Kelkiki by chance? I have to know, right now.*

"I can't. An aching void strips me of breath and crushes my soul. The living death of never being able to hold him. To know he is out there alive, and not be able to be with him. I hope you never understand such heartache."

Enian's sharp knock on the door silenced Clyeva, but she did not attempt to hide her sooty tears when Taminisha bade the other Ellkiiyn enter.

"Enian, you have a prisoner in the dungeons?" Taminisha took the tray of food.

Enian placed the bowl of fruit on the table and looked up at Taminisha. "We do. He's been languishing below for a few solar phasings now, Kikishan hasn't had time to interrogate him and nor have you. Nobody has given the guards instructions, so he's been fed and sheltered, but nothing else."

"Take me to the dungeon. It is imperative I see this prisoner." Taminisha snatched up some meat off the tray and put two pieces of fruit in her pockets.

Enian frowned. "Should you not eat properly, my lady?"

"No time for food, take me below, Enian. Clyeva, you stay here and find some control of your emotions before I come back. Do you hear me?"

Clyeva already tried to choke back her heaving sobs, her face smeared with soot.

The tunnels under the castle were low roofed and narrow, and only dimly lit with widely spaced scones flickering in the stale air. They climbed down two levels of stairs, carved directly into the gray rock of the island.

Taminisha shivered in the chilly atmosphere. They negotiated one last corner and came to a dead-end corridor.

Enian pointed to the last cell. "He's in there, but he does not talk."

Taminisha tiptoed up to the barred gate and stared into the gloomy interior. The prisoner sat hunched on a low wooden stool. His clothes were ripped and dirty, and hung on him as if they were several sizes too big. He had a full bushy beard and a shabby cowl over his head that obscured his face.

"Please, I would speak with you?" Taminisha said. "Come closer."

He lifted his head, stilled for a moment, then leapt off the stool and ran with stumbling steps toward her. He lunged at the bars; large webbed hands gripped the rods.

Taminisha startled back, steadied herself then looked deep into his eyes. He brushed the cowl back to reveal the blue-green exoskeleton and the row upon row of spines sticking up from his head.

Her heart somersaulted in her chest. A warm glow of joy flowed through her. "Tarlitek, my dearest Tarlitek, what have they done to you?"

"Nothing bad, just a lack of good food and facilities until I reached here, from Tarneta."

'Tarneta?"

Tarlitek smiled. 'Do not fuss, little one, I will tell all, but please can you get me near some water. I would be most grateful."

Enian moved to her side in one lithe stride. "You know this male?"

"Yes, Enian. This Orunan male saved my life. He is Tarlitek, friend and hallegan to me. Without his quick actions, the heir to Aikanshin and I would both be dead. Let him out."

Enian didn't argue, just signalled the guard to open the door.

It took the two of them to help Tarlitek climb the stairs to the castle.

*"Larkin meet us at the top of the dungeon stairs. I need your help,"* Taminisha broadcast.

Larkin waited on the landing at the top of the stairs for them and led the way to an unoccupied suite in the tower adjacent to the dining hall, and well away from the nesting room.

Even though she didn't need such a precaution, Taminisha appreciated Enian and Larkin's protective instincts. She ordered food, drink, a bath and some clean clothes.

Tabro arrived, his froxcomb bristling and yellow eyes snapping. He shooed the females from the room. "Come back in an hour, he'll be ready for your inspection." He shut the door firmly behind them.

Larkin stayed with his back to the door, his hand on the hilt of his sword, making it clear he had secured the room.

Taminisha giggled and wondered what Tarlitek would make of Tabro; a pure blood Ellkiiyn male with a feminine swagger and a soft musical voice. Tabro had never mated, and now, well past middle age, it seemed unlikely it would ever happen.

Enian and Taminisha returned to wait outside the door minutes before the hour ticked passed. Clyeva refused to come near the tower. Consumed by fear she had closeted herself in her room, curled up on her bed, sobbing black soot all over herself and the linen.

Taminisha understood her absolute terror of seeing Tarlitek, but she fretted for Clyeva's heartbreak and pondered again if the abscission had changed the situation. She would present the idea to Clyeva, if she would only calm down enough to consider the option.

Tabro opened the door. "He's ready for your inspection, my lady."

Taminisha almost pushed Tabro aside as she rushed through the partially open door. There he stood; adorned in fresh clothes, his beard removed and his exoskeleton scraped, and polished. It now shone with a luminous green glow.

"Tarlitek! It's really you," she cried, charging forth, and throwing herself into his arms.

Tarlitek reciprocated her embrace without hesitation. The time for protocol between them had long passed.

"My beautiful, little one, it does my heart good to find you well and safe with your soul mate."

They embraced for a long time. Then Tarlitek put her from him and studied her face closely. "And you are breeding. I see the luminous glow in your eyes."

Taminisha nodded. "We have a beautiful egg. Oh, my dear friend it is so good to see you. I have fretted over our parting every awakening and every lunor drifting. You are well?"

Tarlitek's smile widened. "Of body I am strong as ever, and ready to serve you, in whatever way you wish."

"And Aikanshin, Jabrikan and those we left behind, what of them?"

Tarlitek shook his head. "The realm is in shambles. There are those still loyal to the Kokoshin Vaprus and they fight a guerrilla war, but make no headway. I spent some time with them to get the lay of the land. Of Jabrikan, I heard only whispers on the wind. When I followed them, I found he is safe and grows well. My brother has him well hidden until the time is ripe for his return."

"And we will facilitate his home coming, Tarlitek. You and I."

Tarlitek smiled. "We will."

Suddenly Taminisha grabbed his arms again. "While I'm overjoyed to see you, I'm also angry at you. How could you send me into Abaye in innocent ignorance knowing fulfilment of my request meant an Abaye—and not just any Abaye, but the love of your life would die? How could you send me on such a mission—to sanction, in fact, orchestrate Clyeva's death?" Tears stung her eyes and she stared up at Tarlitek.

Tarlitek's exoskeleton flushed green and the spines on top of his head rattled. He lowered his gaze to the floor. "I sent extinguishment as a gift of love—an honourable escape from our misery."

"You should have told me."

He glowered. "If I had, would you have gone?"

"No, I would not."

"As I thought. Clyeva welcomed it, did she not?"

Taminisha looked at the floor. She shuffled her feet then looked up. "Yes, she did."

A wistful smile touched Tarlitek's lips then faded. Tears glistened in his eyes.

She reached out and touched his shoulder. "Do not grieve, my friend, for Clyeva lives."

She fell silent at the darkness that instantly shrouded Tarlitek's expression.

"Nooo," he bellowed.

"Tarlitek, I have her fire."

He seemed confused. "If she lives, you cannot, and I so wanted her to have release."

"Sit, before you fall, and I will explain. I did not mean to cause you such anguish."

Tarlitek slumped into the nearest chair. His expression stark, his amber eyes dark with confusion. "I sent you there because I knew Clyeva would welcome a death without shame, as I would."

Taminisha sat opposite him, and took his hand in hers. "The abscission with Clyeva was successful and she also restored my flight, but that is a story for another time…"

"Then she must be a living dead… a jinnexa, and I couldn't bear that," he wailed and gabbled through clenched teeth.

"Wait, Tarlitek, hear me out."

He stared at her, shaking his head in denial.

"After the abscission, which shocked me deeply, the Abaye dumped me in the woods. I found Clyeva shortly after. The Abaye left her to die. I felt so guilty…"

"But you shouldn't have. Clyeva would have been glad to exit this life after making her gift."

Taminisha scowled. "I understand your purpose, but I could not come to terms with the sacrifice made. So I gave Clyeva a transfusion of my blood. I didn't know what else to do or even if it would help."

"A transfusion of *your* blood," Tarlitek boomed as his face paled to almost white. The veins in his neck stood out.

Taminisha sat back to escape the fury blasted toward her. "I didn't think about Tolanim at the time, I just did it to save her."

"Has she tried to transmogrify yet?"

Taminisha clenched her hands in her lap. "No, but her skin is tinted purple."

"What? Oh never mind. She must not be allowed to transmogrify."

"Calm yourself. Clyeva has shown no sign of being able to trans."

"Well she can, I'm sure, but what emerges from the change is a monstrous creature with no intelligence, or compassion, just the urge to kill."

"Not Clyeva. Surely it would not happen to her."

Tarlitek nodded, his expression so anguished Taminisha thought he would collapse.

She touched his hand. "Is there anything to be done to protect her, and us?"

He began to sob. "No, she must be executed. My beloved, to have been brought to this after I offered her a dignified end."

"No, Tarlitek, tell me there is another way?"

He shook his head. "There is none. Go now, and see it done."

"No, I will not take the life I saved. I will not."

"You must."

Taminisha stood and faced him. "And where is your evidence? What proof? Even Tolanim is not proof."

"Then what would you call it. When Tolanim received blood by Tokanin's nephew and tried to transmogrify..." Tarlitek paused, and then went on. "He went mad in the process, and killed his mother."

"That does not prove the Ellkiiyn blood caused it."

"It had to be the blood," Tarlitek insisted.

Taminisha glared at her friend. "You don't really know what sent him mad, do you?"

"What else could it have been?"

Taminisha waved her hands wide. "Anything. Just the shock of transmogrifying could have twisted your nephew's mind and soul. You can't blame the drop of Ellkiiyn blood he received from Odakan. Tolanim already stood close to the abyss by his breeding. Your sister, Tamzinat, should have known better than to have mated with one such as Tygram. With her cross blood of Orunan and Myattican and his – well, who would know? Everyone knew he could claim the breeding of at least four species; Myattican, Kylaran sachan, Fylitia and Zynumin."

"Tamzinat loved him, like I love Clyeva. I do not hold it against her for what she felt, but to breed? That reeks of pure carelessness."

Taminisha sensed he'd drawn back from the urgent need to kill Clyeva. Relief flooded through her, temporarily calming her own disquiet. *Have I really done such a terrible thing? Could Clyeva transmogrify?* Determined to keep the subject well away from Clyeva she asked after his two relatives. "Has anyone seen either Tygram or Tolanim since?"

Tarlitek scowled. "When Tolanim killed his mother as he transmogrified, he fled, and Tygram followed him, either to kill him or to comfort him, I do not know. Neither has been seen since."

"I still say the Ellkiiyn blood itself did not cause his transformation."

"You're prepared to take the risk?"

Taminisha stamped her foot. "I am, and so should you. Do you not love this woman? She is your soul mate. How can you talk of death?"

Tarlitek looked at her, unblinking, huge tears rolling down his cheeks. "I love her beyond my own life. This is why I suggested the abscission, for death between us is better than the wrenching torment of being apart. If it were not for being denied a place with the Ethereal Being or the Fire Nymph we would together have found death long ago."

"But, Tarlitek, you have made a life…"

130

He frowned. "Why do you think I became a hallegan? I chose such a dangerous destiny because I hoped to die of misadventure. Instead I have outlived my first charge, Shydee; I've saved you, and Jabrikan, and remain alive, despite my best efforts."

Taminisha stared at her friend, slumped in front of her. It cut deep to see this handsome, intelligent, strong male with a penchant for storytelling and jokes so crushed. She had known of his family tragedy, but never suspected he carried a heart so broken he wanted to *die*.

"My dear friend, what can I say," she murmured as she knelt in front of him. "You are like the brother I lost, and my guardian and saviour. For you to suffer so, clenches my heart."

"There is nothing to be done."

Without resolving the dilemma, Taminisha had to return to incubating. Unable to sleep, she stirred restlessly as her mind grappled to accept Tarlitek's edicts. Tugged between the two of them, she so desperately wanted to overcome the chasm between them. Even her time off the nest became about finding a solution.

# Chapter Twelve

Clyeva refused to leave her rooms.

Tarlitek crept around the furthest corridors of the castle from Clyeva with Tabro as his lookout.

Both her friends were petrified of seeing each other and, at the same time, their hearts cried out for their joining.

Taminisha had told both Kikishan and Tarlitek of her meeting with the Zynumin. Kikishan promised to discuss options with Tarlitek about saving the refugees escaping from Nyket's mercenaries that risked death from wayward Zynumin in Felitza form. She hoped, while she remained in seclusion on the nest, the two most important males in her life would hammer out a plan to present when the Zynumin returned. She lay with her eyes closed in the hope she would drift off to sleep.

She started awake. Blood curdling screams echoed from the main bailey. Fear sizzled over her scales, and her stomach clenched. She curled more firmly around the egg; her first instinct to protect it, but her second urged her to jump up and investigate. She remained motionless, huffing warm air on the egg by her chest in an effort to distract herself from the ruckus outside.

Kikishan would deal with it, unless... a horrible thought knifed through her head. *What if Nyket has come? What if we are under attack?* Her presence in the battle could make the difference between defeat and victory. Again, she forced herself to lie still.

The screeching continued, closer now. A female screech. A single individual screech. There were no distinct sounds of battle. *Clyeva. Great Spirit had she transmogrified?* Taminisha lay there listening; fighting down concern Clyeva had wrecked destruction on the inhabitants of the castle and village.

A door slammed, and silence fell with a mind-numbing heaviness.

Taminisha listened, straining her ears for any sound to give a clue. The silence continued. At last, she lowered her head, nuzzled the egg, and slept.

Kikishan arrived late, flustered and untidy.

"Kikishan, do things go badly?"

He laughed—a loud, raucous, out of control roar of amusement. He laughed and laughed, unable to speak, tears pouring down his cheeks. He slid to his knees by the side of the nest and gulping for air, he tried to compose himself.

Taminisha sat there in silence, astounded at this display of hysterical hilarity from her soul mate.

He gasped, held his ribs and breathed deeply in a concerted effort to calm himself.

"Kikishan, do you wish to share your source of such unbridled amusement?"

"I do indeed, my beautiful Taminisha. Your friend, the purple one,

Clyeva, is such a bubbly little joy. She is right now closeted in her room, under the bed, with the light out, and a guard on the door."

"Why?"

Kikishan smiled broadly. "She decided to take some air along the back parapet walk and wandered along the adjoining bridge, I think by mistake. She saw your hallegan, Tarlitek, pacing the front terrace. They took one peep at each other, for just a second. Clyeva screeched, and ran back the way she'd come. Meanwhile Tarlitek leapt down the stairs two at a time with Tabro galloping behind in a desperate effort to catch him up. Then moments later Clyeva and Tarlitek came face to face on the lower landing from which meeting they both spun around and ran yodelling. Poor Tabro is beside himself."

Taminisha gasped. "Are they all right? Has someone checked on their health?"

"Yes, they're both fine. Larkin told me some of their story…"

"And there were no signs of burns or quenching?" Taminisha could barely lie still as panic exploded through her. "Are you sure?"

Kikishan smiled. "Be calm, my heart, be calm. All is well. Perhaps you can coax them out. Now go stretch your legs, eat and relax. It is my time."

She hurried first to Tarlitek's rooms.

He stood staring out the window, but he turned as she entered.

With nervous anticipation, she examined his face, but found no sign of melting or blistered skin.

"You're undamaged from your unfortunate misadventure?"

"Yes, Taminisha, but I've made a decision. I cannot stay here. Clyeva and I cannot risk meeting again as we just did, and I cannot bear her to be so close, and yet out of reach forever. This time we were lucky, but our encounter only opened up our wounds and fired up unequitable desires. If you choose not to end her life, then I must end my stay in your home."

Taminisha slumped into a chair, fighting tears. "No, Tarlitek, you cannot leave. There must be a way to sort this out."

"There is no way. Try to understand—I am water, she is fire. We will annihilate each other on contact, agonisingly."

As the thought formed, she jumped up. "Wait. Tarlitek, if you could not be together because you are water and she fire, shouldn't that have changed now—with the abscission. She has no fire…"

'Stop. We cannot risk it for even to be in the same room is to cause harm and this time Clyeva may die from the quenching. I will not kill her with my love."

Taminisha grabbed his shoulder. "But there is nothing to quench. Don't you see? There is *nothing* to quench. I have her fire and I stand by you here, now, and you still live."

She saw a flash of hope in his eyes before he extinguished it and pulled away. She grabbed his arm. "Come, we're going to try something."

He pulled back. "It's too risky. A merciful death would be better than the excruciating demise that will be ours if we come together."

"I cannot bear to see the two of you aching with need, and discard a chance. You have to take this chance." Taminisha grabbed his hands and squeezed them hard.

He ripped his hands free of her hold. "I cannot."

"Do not refuse me, Tarlitek. There is nothing to lose. Do you still wish for death?"

"I have no desire for life. Death will bring peace, but to deliberately bring upon my love such agony is not a choice."

"Then I give you a choice, if the worst begins I will deliver a merciful death to both of you, in the instant it is unbearable."

Tarlitek's mouth gaped open. "To kill the innocent brings its own curse. I cannot let you do this thing."

"I didn't say you would die as innocents, only that I would deliver a merciful death. An execution carried out for the protection of my egg is my right as a mother. Even the guilty are still accepted by the Spirit are they not?"

His exoskeleton paled to a sickly green and sweat beaded on his face. His expression became vague, but a light glinted in his eyes that had not been there before.

"Come."

Tarlitek, Larkin, and Tabro followed her.

Larkin touched her shoulder. "Are you sure, Taminisha? I understand she is your friend, but we do not know what happens if the receptor of your blood dies. How might it affect you?"

Taminisha paused in her stride, thinking of her egg. If she came to harm, then what of her egg? She knew Kikishan would incubate it right to the moment of death if he had to, but the thought of her child growing up without a mother, or perhaps as an orphan, horrified her.

Then she glanced at Tarlitek beside her, shook her head, and continued. She had to do this. In her mind, the fulfilment of their love was more important and immediate, than some age-old prophecy.

At the very end of the long parapet walk, which ran along the side castle wall, she stopped. "Tarlitek, stand here. Wait. I will bring Clyeva. Then you walk toward each other. Larkin and I will be right behind you, to do what needs to be done, if the worst happens."

Without waiting for his agreement, Taminisha walked away.

Taminisha burst into the room and Clyeva threw herself into her arms, sobbing hysterically all over again.

"I cannot bear it. So close, but so far." She clutched her breast over her heart, and sank to the floor.

Taminisha pulled at her. "Stand up, and stop this caterwauling. You're ruining my habilan with your sooty tears."

Clyeva climbed to her feet and stifled her sobs. She glared at Taminisha.

"You should have let me die after the abscission." She held out her hands wide. "Look at me. I am Abaye with no fire, no home, no family, a forbidden love in my heart *and* I'm stained purple. What is there for me? You should have let me die. You were selfish to save me."

Clyeva's accusation hurt, but Taminisha accepted her guilt. *Yes, it had been selfish to save the Abaye.* "I'm sorry, but give me a chance to make it right. Tarlitek awaits."

Clyeva stormed forward and beat at Taminisha with her fists, sooty flakes falling down her face. "You refuse to understand. A Fire Nymph's curse upon you for the pain and misery you have wrought. We can never be together."

Taminisha took hold of Clyeva's flailing hands. "Stop. You no longer have fire for him to quench." She touched her chest. "Your fire is within me, so how can you burn Tarlitek; surely it's worth trying to see if you can be together."

Clyeva glared at her. "You ask again what you already know. Do you deliberately hurt me?"

"No, my friend, I want to help you. Please listen to me. Trust me."

Clyeva stared at her, her face darkened to a deep purple hue. "Do you think it's possible?

Taminisha nodded.

"Great Fire Nymph! If only it could be, but the risk to both of us."

"Do not fear, my friend."

"But the agony... you will not be able to stop the quenching and burning should it begin."

"I do not believe it will begin. You have no fire with which to burn him. Now come with me, he will be impatient."

"No. If a toxic exchange begins, you cannot stop it. You should never meddle in things you don't understand. Tarlitek will die in agony. Can you live with that? For I cannot," Clyeva shouted at her.

Taminisha wrapped her arm around Clyeva's shoulders. "I have made provisions for that, and promise an instant death for both of you if it goes badly."

"But..."

"Do not ask questions, just do as I bid."

"You cannot bid me walk to murder my love so cruelly. Not even you, as Ellkiiyn or Guardian of this castle."

"No, I cannot force you. All I ask is for you to trust me."

Clyeva clenched her teeth and curled her hands into fists, as she stood frozen. "I can't, and yet I want this so much. Has Tarlitek agreed?

"He has."

"If I do this please I beg of you, have mercy. Promise me you will not let him suffer," Clyeva pleaded as her anger dissolved in fear.

"I promise."

Taminisha walked toward the door.

Clyeva remained motionless in the middle of the room. "I cannot"

Taminisha frowned. "Just solar awakenings ago you were ready to give up your fire to me and die doing it. Surely to die for love is a more honourable death. I shall see you dead in each other's arms before you suffer. Please, Clyeva, trust me."

Clyeva's shoulders sagged and she held out her hands to Taminisha. They walked hand in hand up the stairs and out onto the parapet walk.

Tarlitek stood beside Tabro. Larkin hovered just behind him. He had his orders, ones he would obey to the letter on Taminisha's signal— Tarlitek must be dead before his body begins to fall from toxic burns. Taminisha would see the same done for Clyeva.

Taminisha hoped with all her heart she would never have to give that signal.

Clyeva stood, paralysed with fear as she stared at her soul mate.

Neither attempted to move.

"Go on, go to him." Taminisha urged her friend forward with a gentle push in her back.

Clyeva took one shuffling step forward, and then stopped.

Tarlitek took two steps.

Larkin stepped up right behind him.

Tabro had retreated to the corner where he stood clutching himself around the chest, his effeminate features contorted into an expression of abject fear.

Clyeva took another step.

Taminisha moved up behind her and touched her briefly on the shoulder. "I am with you. I will not let you suffer."

A tiny squeak of assent squeezed out between Clyeva's clenched teeth. She took another step, a longer, steadier one this time.

Tarlitek approached another two steps.

Clyeva's breath rushed in and out of her lungs. Fear emanated from her.

It echoed Taminisha's own as she perspired, but felt chilled over her exposed skin. She tightened her grip around the dagger to secure it in her trembling hand.

The air whirled around them thick with tension, expectation, and fear.

The parapet walk seemed extremely long to Taminisha as the two lovers closed the gap between them.

Sparks flickered in the air between the two groups.

Clyeva flinched.

"Are you all right?" Taminisha asked.

"Yes, but my fingers are tingling and my skin is shivering," she muttered.

"Another step," Taminisha instructed.

Clyeva obeyed without replying.

The air sizzled and hissed. A mist formed half way between the two soul mates.

"What is it?" Taminisha asked.

"Steam—fire and water," Clyeva whispered, even as she took another step forward. She glanced over her shoulder. "You will go through with it, won't you?"

Taminisha nodded, even as her heart crunched in distress. She clutched her dagger in her sweaty hand.

The steam swirled and thickened.

Abruptly Clyeva picked up her skirt and sprinted toward Tarlitek.

Taken by surprise, Taminisha bounded after her.

Tarlitek immediately broke into a loping stride.

The air crackled between them, but neither slowed.

"Tarlitek," Clyeva shouted as she threw herself into his arms.

"My heart and soul, my love," he cried embracing her.

Steam swirled, hissed, and writhed around them until it consumed them completely.

Taminisha lunged forward, raised her dagger, then froze as the mist obscuring her vision exploded into a million cloudy pieces and dissolved. Larkin too, jerked to a standstill and dropped his dagger. They stood in silent awe beside the couple they had thought to kill and release from agony.

Tarlitek and Clyeva stood unharmed, oblivious to the others, devouring each other with passionate kisses.

Taminisha slowly sank to the ground; her trembling knees no longer capable of holding her upright. Tears welled in her eyes as she watched her two friends share affection for the very first time since they had fallen in love so many years before. She knew then why she had saved Clyeva.

~   ~   ~

The world whirled around Tarlitek, rocking and buzzing as he enclosed his love in a tight embrace.

"My love, my love, we are blessed. From such pain comes ecstasy," Tarlitek murmured in her ear as he nuzzled her neck.

He swept her up into his arms before he turned to Taminisha. "Thank you." His throat cramped as sobs forced their way up. Without waiting for a response, he spun on his heels and carried Clyeva to his rooms.

Every muscle trembled and he struggled to stay upright. With forced concentration, he put one foot in front of the other. She snuggled into his chest and sobbed as she clung to him. Her sooty tears spread in a warm pool against his skin. His groin heated in a way he had not felt for a long time.

*Oh dear Orunikan, I want this female.* He breathed in her scent and swayed under the intoxicating aroma that filled his head. His scales crackled and flexed.

"Clyeva, my beloved, Clyeva."

"Tarlitek, I cannot believe it, yet your arms hold me. I feel your cold shimmying over my skin."

"Your sacrifice has brought us to this."

She stretched up and pressed her lips to his. "Your gift of love," she whispered.

With a booted foot, he kicked the door open then closed it behind them. He gently eased Clyeva's dress over her shoulders and past her breasts and hips. When she stood naked, he scooped her up, laid her on the bed, stood back, and studied her. The soft lavender shade of her skin amused him, but otherwise she looked the same—slim with a generous bust, her red hair tussled and matching the neat triangle at the apex of her legs.

"You are so beautiful, my love," he said. He undid his shirt and slipped his breeches off taking his boots with them. His large hardened member sprang out straight from his body.

Clyeva gasped. Her breasts rose and fell with her agitated breathing.

*I hope she finds my body desirable. As desirable as I find hers.*

She ran her tongue along her lips. "Love me, Tarlitek." Her request no more than a pleading moan.

He moved in and climbed onto the bed beside her. He touched her with his fingertips. The warmth of her body seeped into his flesh. He explored her face, kissing her breathless. As she gasped for air he enclosed her nipples with his mouth, suckling.

She writhed, soft moans slipping from her mouth.

He lifted his head. "I am afraid, my love."

She touched his face. "Why are you afraid?"

"Afraid you won't enjoy me. The chill of my touch, the feel of my member when we join. That my coldness will not satisfy your heat."

"My dearest, from the moment you entered this castle, I felt your coldness against my heat and the ache in my womanhood has been relentless. It is you I want, no other. Love me, Tarlitek, for I cannot bear to wait any longer."

He caressed her breasts then slid his hands between her legs. She moaned and opened her legs to his touch.

"Love me," she whispered.

He moved on top of her and settled against her thighs. Passion stabbed through him, stoking his eagerness to penetrate deep into her heat. He slid his member into her body.

She whimpered and lifted her hips to meet his downward thrust.

He gasped. Ecstasy roared through him, flames of desire lapped at his body where it touched her. Her heat enwrapped him, sending frissons of sensation through his member and into his gut. He thrust again and again and she met him, engulfing him in heat.

She tipped her head back, gasped, then howled. Her muscles clutched his member as he moved. The heat, the tightness and his desire roared through him igniting a throbbing climax. Steam rose as he came. The scent of their coupling tangy in the air between them.

Clyeva shrieked as he buried himself deep. They stilled, joined as one. On a joint sigh, they sagged onto the bed. Sweat poured from his body as he pulled her over with him.

He looked down into her eyes. They flared red. She smiled and stretched up to kiss him.

"I never thought joining could be such divine pleasure."

He smiled. The beating of his heart steadied. The fear she would not enjoy him dissolved. They had their whole lives ahead to repeat the act and enjoy each other. *Great Spirit Ellkii, bless Taminisha for the gift she has given us.*

"We can never repay her," Clyeva whispered.

He looked deep into his lover's eyes. "No, but I will never cease trying."

"Do you think she will mind if we stay closeted here for a while."

"And why, my love, would you want to do that?" Tarlitek inquired even as he tried to refrain from smiling.

Clyeva grinned. "Oh I thought we might join a few times more, just to make sure it works for us."

Tarlitek laughed. "Well we better get on with it then." He ran his hand over her abdomen and between her legs.

She parted her legs as he leaned in to kiss her.

# Chapter Thirteen

The time dragged as Taminisha spent alternate hours managing the realm and incubating her egg. She missed Clyeva's spontaneous energy on her free periods, but she would not make any demands on either Tarlitek or Clyeva as they enjoyed each other for the first time. The only reason Taminisha knew they were still alive after five solid solar phasings closeted in Tarlitek's rooms, were the meals passing from the kitchens to the rooms, and the occasional screeches of desire echoing down the corridor.

She resented being so isolated from Kikishan, always craving his touch, and his companionship. No one had warned her of the hardships the pure blood Ellkiiyn suffered to breed. Kikishan had made it clear he wanted to breed several times. While Taminisha would love more than one child, and agreed she and Kikishan should set a good example for the Aqueena Ellkiiyn, she did not want to spend half her life incubating eggs.

She pondered again, the other way—the sachan way most Ellkiiyn shunned. The way Odakan had been so afraid of, he would not even love her in that fashion. She figured if the Viveka women could carry babies and still live their rugged lifestyle or go to war, then surely she, as Ellkiiyn, would have the fortitude to do this thing. She pushed the debate to the back of her mind resenting that Odakan's fear had left a lasting impression.

Taminisha woke. Something had disturbed her in the silence of the room. She lay still, listening. The faint, but distinguishable, patter of a tiny heart beat, right next to hers, and the echo of Kikishan's. She nudged the egg. The patter quickened. *My baby has its life force.* Joy buzzed through her. *My child is real. Alive.* Until the transition to adulthood, only distance and death would silence the mother and child bond of love. Taminisha laid her chin on the egg and allowed the tiny patter to lull her back to sleep.

Larkin and Enian proved excellent companions, and guides, as Taminisha explored every inch of her island home. One solar phasing soon after the solar zenith she climbed to the terraces above the keep. The whole lake spread out, gray and gloomy, under dark sullen clouds hiding the faint glow of the solar orb.

Consumed with restlessness Taminisha paced the parapet walk to fill in time. Larkin accompanied her.

"Larkin, tell me more about that island out there? Clyeva called it Oventi Rock, and shuddered when she did. I don't understand."*Don't ask me to explain, why the dark and mysterious island draws me like a magnet, or why I feel the need to know its secrets.*

"It has a reputation, even the Orunan do not go there."

"I had a dwarf Tarki as a pet. An ancient and savage creature similar to Ellkiiyn. Tarlitek brought him home after he had been visiting Myattica. He said he found the mother dead on the shore of the lake still clutching the baby, all bedraggled and weak."

Larkin grimaced. "Occasionally we find that type of creature washed up dead on the shore, but they say the island is inhabited by bigger creatures—monsters. I would not go there, my lady."

Taminisha stared at the island. "I have no desire to confront unknown monsters, there are enough in the Ellkiiyn population, but I wonder if my pet Tarki came from the island. I don't know what happened to him after Nyket's attack. I miss him, despite his viciousness, because he could also be very loving."

"They say those who go to Oventi never return. Whether myth or truth, I'm not prepared to say, but I am also not willing to go there just to confirm it. I value my life, alone, and empty, as it is."

Taminisha paused, not sure, if she should comment on his reflection about his life, or not. In the end, she decided perhaps their budding companionship had grown strong enough for her to delve into his privacy.

"And you've not had a mate?"

Larkin turned aside and fiddled with his sword hilt. "No, I've never been called, and considering my mature age, I don't expect I will."

Taminisha heard the wistful longing in Larkin's tone. *Such a shame, a good male gone to waste because a love call did not come; surely Ellkiiyn could form bonds, and breed without the mystical calling.*

Taminisha gazed out at the misty landscape and thought of her child encased in the egg and her mate incubating. She understood the dilemma of the Ellkiiyn Clans.

Concerned she'd troubled the male Ellkiiyn she deliberately twisted around and waved her arm in the other direction. "And these other lands?"

"As you already know Viveka is directly opposite, then your mines, and further behind the mines, is the Land of the Leryi, and further down the lake, of course, you have Zynumin."

"And Conurk?" she asked.

Larkin frowned. "Conurk, the land of the Eqazantia, is on the other side of Viveka and borders Rabikan."

Taminisha peered into the distance. "Do we have exchanges of trade with them?"

"Occasionally, but they have simple needs of food and shelter, and there are problems in the group. Like Ellkiiyn, they do not breed well, and genetic isolation has almost bred the morphflitt ability out of them. If that ability dies, so will the Eqazantia."

Taminisha sighed. "So the Ellkiiyn are not the only ones then."

"No, my lady, it's not just us."

"Well, Larkin, I'd better go and do my bit for Ellkiiyn survival, and relieve Kikishan."

~   ~   ~

When she emerged from her latest incubating stint, she found Tarlitek and Clyeva waiting for her in the dining room. Clyeva charged across the room and into her arms.

Black soot poured from her eyes. "My dearest, dearest friend, how can we ever thank you for bringing us together."

Taminisha hugged her. Her heart somersaulted at the sight of her friends' serenity and big smiles. She looked over Clyeva's shoulder.

Tarlitek smirked and raised his eyebrows.

Heat rushed up her neck and face. "So the last few solar phasings have been enjoyable for you both?"

Clyeva tightened her hug. "Such joy, such pleasure…"

"I'm so happy for you both. Are you ready to get back to work?"

"Whatever you need, Taminisha, just ask. We would both give our lives for you, and even then would not begin to repay your gift."

"Clyeva, just seeing your happiness is all the repayment I need or want. Though your help and loyalty will be appreciated come our hatching event, and when we go to battle for Aikanshin. There is much to be done to stifle this anarchy and the inevitable fall of the Clans."

Tarlitek stepped forward. "I must ask one question, a very important one. If Nyket is defeated, who will become Guardian or at least Regent? Jabrikan is still too young, and you are otherwise occupied."

Taminisha froze. She'd not thought of this dilemma in the sudden early battle they planned against Nyket. She stared up at Tarlitek. "I do not know. I'll need to talk to Kikishan. Perhaps, an Aqueena as Regent?"

Tarlitek frowned. "That might not be any more welcome than Tokanin or Nyket."

"Then perhaps, one of the loyal Vaprus—one resisting Nyket. But that may not bode well for Jabrikan in the future, if they don't want to give up their elevation."

Tarlitek rested his hand on her shoulder. "Let's defeat Nyket first."

Taminisha frowned. Fear spiked through her. *Can we defeat Nyket?*

~ ~ ~

As the last awakening of the incubation period slipped passed, she waited for Kikishan to join her. Custom had it both parents would be present at the hatching. The scales on the egg now shimmered with deep blue, purple and lavender.

Taminisha breathed lightly on the shell. During the last few solar phasings, peeps and squeaks had come from inside the egg and a couple of times the egg had moved after she'd nudged it.

Kikishan arrived. He seemed harassed and tense as he transmogrified and lay down beside the nest. She understood his concern. After all the effort they had already put in, they may still end up without a child. If the newly hatched baby didn't pass the test, it would be Kikishan's task to carry out the execution. Another ancient, misguided, ritual that contributed to the withering of the Dykarin Ellkiiyn. Her heart clenched—for him, her and her own father as she pushed the ugly thought away. She couldn't bring herself to soothe him, or tell him it would be all right. Too much uncertainty clutched at her heart.

They both stared at the egg.

"*It is time, Taminisha. Tap on the shell, and tell our child we are waiting."*

Taminisha tapped gently on the shell with a claw. Immediately a sharp tapping came from within. She tapped again. The tapping got louder from inside the egg, and then stopped. Taminisha nudged the egg. The tapping started again. At the third attempt, the shell cracked at the point of impact and a tiny claw emerged.

Taminisha's hot breath caught in her throat. As they watched, the crack widened, and bits of shell fell away. A whole foot popped out, immediately followed by another. Taminisha hooked back a few pieces of the shell and almost jumped right out of the nest when a snout poked out. As she reached out to make contact with her child, for the first time, the shell exploded into several large jagged pieces and their child hatched.

He sat upright, big golden eyes gazing around. Taminisha's heartbeat quickened and every nerve ending tingled. She tried to swallow, but emotion choked her throat. Her eyes filled with tears. She had never seen anything so gorgeous. So tiny, with a perfectly formed pair of strong wings he flapped wildly; the fibrous membranes so thin Taminisha could see through them. He was a miniature replica of his father, only with a purple belly and edges to his scales and froxcomb.

He squeaked and reached up to her. She touched her snout to his. He sneezed, sending a spurt of flame right past Taminisha's ear. She jerked her head out of danger from the undirected blast.

*"He has fire,"* Kikishan broadcast with a slight chuckle.

The tiny Ellkiiyn wriggled and tottered in the protective circle of Taminisha's body.

They waited. The minutes ticked by.

Their son cried, and rolled over exposing his lavender belly.

They waited. Anxiety needled Taminisha. *He has to transmogrify. He has to. I cannot bear it.*

Kikishan stood up, all the time watching their child. His smile vanished. A dark shadowed expression took its place.

Taminisha watched her mate. A sour taste filled her mouth, but the ache at the back of her throat prevented her freshening it. Chills vibrated over her. She clutched her Rykala locket and pressed it to her chest. Desperate love surged as she leaned down and whispered in her son's ear. *"Transmogrify, baby, transmogrify now."*

The newly hatched Ellkiiyn merely rolled over, and over, then batted the air with tiny feet.

*"Leave the nest, Taminisha. Time is up."*

Kikishan's sharp tones cut through her.

Taminisha glared at him. *"He needs more time. Our son only needs more time."*

*"Get out of the nest, make the rejection complete so I can do what has to be done."*

*"No,"* she hissed as she lowered her snout to her newborn and shoved him so hard the force sent him rolling over several times. He landed with a bump against the edge of the nest. He cried, and came crawling back to her.

*"It's over."*

Kikishan's broadcast sounded as a heavy grumble in her head. Taminisha stood and planted her feet solidly in the nest. Four pillars of motherly flesh now sheltered the baby and a gaping mouth full of teeth and fire defended him.

*"He's had double the time allowed. He is not going to transmogrify now. You know he has to die."*

Kikishan's broadcast scraped across her mind.

*"No. He needs more time, he is but a newborn."*

*"Don't make me fight you, Taminisha, there is grief enough already."* Kikishan's broadcast no more than a mutter.

*"You will have to kill me, before you harm my child."*

*"Our child,"* Kikishan reminded her sharply.

*"Then wait, what are rules. We've broken them before..."*

*"But, if he can't transmogrify, he cannot rule."* Kikishan bared his teeth.

*"But he can live. He could live a good life."*

"*A wasted existence.*" Kikishan roared and charged.

Taminisha met his charge with a blast of fire.

He reeled back, and then lurched forward again.

She lashed out with her tail and caught him in the head.

He halted, shook his head then came again.

Taminisha fought him off repeatedly.

Finally, he stood back, panting and grunting. "*You would consign our son to an empty life?*"

"*Kikishan, no life filled with love is empty. His life will never be empty, I will see to that.*"

"*You will be the death of me.*"

His broadcast thudded through her head.

"*But not...*"

The child's cry split the air, a piercing wail of a newborn babe. Taminisha looked down between her feet. The naked child lay on its back, pink skin covered with the birthing lining of the egg. The delicate sachan features scrunched up into a mask of indignation, legs and arms flailing.

Taminisha leapt from the nest, rolled, and tucked to transmogrify. Not bothering with a habilan, she leaned in, scooped her baby boy out of the nest, and wrapped him in the prepared blanket before putting him against her breast to suckle.

Kikishan sagged to the floor. He sobbed, too traumatised to transmogrify.

Taminisha sat on the edge of the nest and calmly fed her son. "He shall be called Jivinshan and he shall be Guardian of Kelkiki."

Kikishan did not respond to her announcement.

She stood and left the nesting room. Her heart clenched in sympathy for the misery engulfing her sobbing mate as he tried to come to terms with what had happened.

Relief, love and satisfaction roiled through her. She couldn't be angry with Kikishan. He'd only been doing what tradition dictated. As her own father had when he killed his younger son because he failed to transmogrify in the required time. The process had begun as the child took its last breaths, leaving them to offer a half Ellkiiyn, half sachan corpse to Vaprosa wraiths. Her father had never recovered.

Taminisha hadn't known how she would react in the same situation. The risk to her child had always been at the back of her mind, looming like a black cloud dulling the joy of anticipation. Her protective reaction had been instinctive. She still loved her soul mate with every beat of her heart, but her mother's love could not let him extinguish that other tiny heartbeat tapping away beside hers.

She went to Clyeva's room.

"Oh my goodness, he's so gorgeous—a strong, healthy, full-blooded Ellkiiyn."Clyeva held out her arms.

A vague chill shivered over her skin and sweat formed in beads on Taminisha's forehead as the reality of Kikishan's intention thudded home. Her knees strength dissolved and she stumbled.

Clyeva steadied her, and took the sleeping babe. "Taminisha?"

"My son is strong and healthy, but took too long to transmogrify. Kikishan tried to kill him." She paced the room shaking her hands by her sides.

Clyeva stared at her. "You fought him?"

"Yes, I fought him. I could not bear another tragedy like my brother."

"And Kikishan?"

"He's devastated he almost killed his son because of a ritual—a cruel, misguided ritual, when all the babies need is more time."

"Tradition is there for a reason," Clyeva admonished her.

Taminisha dragged on a habilan and continued to pace, grinding her teeth. Her heart pounded as sweat poured down between her breasts. "I know the test is there to weed out those of tainted blood, but it doesn't. Instead it kills pure blood babies as well." She gasped and lowered her voice to a respectable level. "Besides, what if one has a small drop of tainted blood? This does not mean you cannot have a meaningful life—a good life making a worthwhile contribution to our existence." She threw up her hands and inhaled several deep breaths.

"Frightful traditions, killing healthy Ellkiiyn, stunting our population growth, and stopping Ellkiiyn from wanting to breed. No wonder the Ellkiiyn wither to a few 'pure' blood creatures that will die out in a couple of generations. We are killing ourselves. It will have no place in Kelkiki in the future."

Clyeva gazed down at the sleeping baby. "Only the future will reveal the wisdom of your decision."

Taminisha touched her baby's cheek with a gentle fingertip. "He is my son. Regardless, I will always love him."

"And Kikishan? What of your future joining and his attitude to his son—is it salvageable?"

"I do not hold any animosity toward Kikishan; he only did what heritage dictated. As for how he feels about his son, I have no control over that."

# Chapter Fourteen

Kikishan did not emerge from the nesting room for three solar phasing and three lunor drifts.

Taminisha stayed away. She didn't know what to say to comfort him.

Without consulting her soul mate, she assigned Tarlitek as baby Jivinshan's bodyguard, and Clyeva as his nanny. She gave orders no one could go near the child, without her approval, including his father.

On the fourth awakening after the hatching, Taminisha decided enough time had passed. Leaving Jivin with Clyeva, Taminisha sought out Kikishan where he'd found refuge on the parapet walk in the very spot of their first meeting. He leaned on the wall and stared off into the distance, his face haggard and gray.

She waited. He did not acknowledge her presence, continuing to stare unseeing out over the lake, shoulders hunched, hands clenching and unclenching in white knuckled fists.

"Kikishan?"

He did not respond.

She moved close enough to touch him. "Speak to me."

"I cannot."

"My heart and soul, you were only doing what tradition dictated. There is no shame attached to your actions."

He looked at her, his eyes burned dark with remorse. "You fought for him—fought to protect him from me, his father. How can you still love me—consider joining with me, and perhaps birthing another child? The father who would, without question, kill his own son?"

"You were only doing what a thousand generations of Ellkiiyn have done before you. I fought you because I saw my own father kill my baby brother only to have him transmogrify in death. He needed time. My father never recovered, as I believe you would not. Our son, Jivin, *lives*, and we will *both* love him until death takes us."

Kikishan threw himself into her arms. "My heart, my love, yes! Together, we will love him and each other, no matter the circumstances."

He kissed her, a lingering, thoughtful exploration of her mouth. His arousal pressed hard against her softness.

Her heart beat faster as the tingling warmth of desire spread through her body. She moved closer to him moulding her body to his hard, muscular frame—rubbing her hips against his hardness. The closeness she had desired since their first meeting called her.

The closeness Odakan had forbidden. A sliver of doubt cooled her heart and desire and she went to pull away, afraid of rejection.

At her slightest movement, Kikishan encircled her body with strong arms then lifted her from the ground.

She snuggled close as he carried her into his rooms and set her down by the bed.

With tentative tugs, he loosened her habilan. His fingers trembled. As he slid it from her shoulders, he marked each inch of flesh exposed with a fiery brand from his mouth.

She shivered as he kissed her cleavage and moaned as he cupped the fullness of her breasts. Tremors of arousal vibrated through her body at his feather-light touch brushed her skin with tenderness.

He stroked her skin, pushing the robe to the floor. She stood before him, naked and vulnerable, in her sachan body. He studied her form appreciatively then with a flick and a tug, disrobed his own body.

Taminisha admired the sculptured beauty of his male sachan form. Hard in contrast to her softness, chiselled where hers curved and his manhood, a large silken rod that throbbed with desire as it protruded from the thatch of blond hair that trailed up to his navel. She reached out and touched his flesh—hard and hot under her fingers.

He groaned.

Liquid warmth swelled between her legs, bringing a pulsing ache of desire deep inside. Taminisha waited for the urge. It did not come. She stilled, expecting Kikishan to pull away.

Instead he stepped closer, easing her down onto the bed until he crouched over her. With one knee, he eased her legs apart and moved between her thighs. With gentle strokes, he touched her in the warm, moist apex of her legs.

She shuddered as a firestorm of sensation blasted through her. Soft moans escaped. A maelstrom of heat pooled where his hand caressed her sensitive skin, exploring its folds and crevasses. She lifted her hips to meet his touch. "The urge has not come," she whispered.

Kikishan grinned. "It does not matter. I shall love you the sachan way."

Anticipation sizzled over her skin. "You are willing?"

"I certainly am. Now sshh and enjoy."

He removed his hand and lowered himself over her, his swollen manhood pressing between her lips.

She craved his penetration, so she clutched his buttocks and pulled him closer.

He lowered himself.

As his manhood slid inside stretching and filling her, an exquisite vibration powered through her. She arched to meet him.

He sank deep inside, then thrust rhythmically; each time he filled her body a rush of heat pounded though her. He moved faster and faster.

She gasped as her body shuddered under an onslaught of throbbing ecstasy that swept her over the precipice into a swirling climax. Holding him close and deep as her bones softened and every nerve ending sizzled with awareness she gasped and moaned her release.

He grunted and howled as his seed burst from him.

His heat flooded through her.

They collapsed onto the bed, sweat glistening on their skin, sexual tension melting into satiation as they gasped for air to ease their exertion.

Kikishan eased himself to one side and lay on his back beside her.

Taminisha stared at the ceiling above, her body soft and relaxed except for the occasional hum of sensation that radiated from between her legs. She pressed her hands to her cheeks feeling the heat infusing her skin. Her mouth curved into a smile as she cuddled into her lover. She pressed her palm to his chest and slid it over his skin. "So that is the sachan way?"

Kikishan chuckled. "It is, my love. And what do you think of the sachan way of breeding?"

"Amazing, mind blowing. I'm stunned. Why don't Ellkiiyn *always* do it in their sachan form?"

"Because it comes at a price. Although unlikely, if you breed in the sachan form you will have to carry the child in your body as it grows and then push it out through the opening where my seed went in. I have been told, on good authority, 'childbirth' is not something one would want to go through willingly."

"And yet sachans do it all the time."

"They do," Kikishan replied.

"But the Ellkiiyn way is hard too. It takes both parents with long hours on the nest and forced separation. That's not easy either."

"Indeed it is not, but at least the parents share the responsibility. The sachan way, the female carries the entire burden, and the pain."

"Ah, but the pleasure. So exquisite, so wondrous."

"Yes for you, and for me too. Shall we do it again?" Kikishan already leaned closer to her.

She stared at her lover. "Again, so soon?"

"Ah yes, my love, another advantage of doing it in sachan form is for pure pleasure alone. No waiting many solar phasings for the female breeding cycle and the urge to inspire a joining."

"Mmmm, I could get to like this, very much." Taminisha whispered as Kikishan began to stroke between her legs.

~  ~  ~

Jivin as Ellkiiyn screeched and jumped into his father's arms as the pectenite horn blasts shattered the peace and quiet of the castle.

Kikishan hugged Jivin before handing him to Clyeva. "Transmogrify, Jivin and behave yourself for Clyeva. Your mother and I have important business to conduct."

Jivin grinned, then obeyed his father.

Clyeva cuddled him and he gurgled and waved his tiny fists toward her face.

Taminisha smiled to see her son trans with such ease. He made it clear every solar phasing he hated the helplessness and vulnerability of his sachan form and preferred to spend his time as Ellkiiyn, scurrying around the castle, leading Clyeva on a never ending seek and find chase.

Kikishan held out his hand to Taminisha and together they hurried to where the Zynumin, Palakin and Jyquin, waited for them in the audience hall. Larkin and Adakin waited just behind the Zynumin while Enian took her place behind the thrones.

The Zynumin were in sachan form and dressed in brief loincloths that showed most of their muscular legs and chests. Palakin wore his hair loose and it hung half way down his back in a black cloud of frizz. He smiled, but it did not transform his serious expression and his green eyes, with a small black iris in the centre, remained half closed against the solar rays streaming into the room. Jyquin watched them approach from orange eyes filled with suspicion, a spear held tightly in his right hand.

Palakin stepped forward the moment they entered the room. "You told us to return after sixty solar phasings. We have come as requested. I hope you have had a successful incubation." He inclined his head to Taminisha as a sign of respect.

Taminisha stepped forward. "Thank you, Palakin. We have indeed had a successful incubation. Our son Jivinshan is strong and healthy. This is my mate, Kikishan, Guardian of Kelkiki."

"I am pleased, Guardians of Kelkiki, things have gone well. Now, we seek your help. Nyket is still rampaging out of control in Kylara. Refugees flood across the border. Our leader, Aneverin, currently holds the Zynumin in check, but soon they will throw off his will and morphflitt anyway. Such action will bring a bloody massacre of innocents. We need to drive Nyket out of Kylara, and the sachans out of Zynumin."

"Kikishan, can we provide assistance?"

Kikishan smiled. "Of course we will, although I know little of Aikanshin to develop strategies."

"We must speak with Tarlitek, he is not Ellkiiyn, but he knows Aikanshin even better than I do," Taminisha said.

Immediately Tarlitek entered the room, tension sharpened the air. Taminisha sensed the apprehension emanating from the two Zynumin and understood their concerns. Even this strong species had issues with the larger Orunan from the manawa along the lakeshore bordering some of their land. Their encounters with Orunikan had always been disastrous for the Zynumin even in their Felitza form. Life became hard when the hunter became the hunted.

Tarlitek respected their uneasiness and stayed on the far side of the table. The others gathered around and with a map designed by using various items around the room. Tarlitek created the basic structure and Palakin used more items to explain what had happened.

Soon they all had a clear idea of what the campaign would entail. By the time the solar orb settled behind the horizon, they had a battle plan hammered out.

Although Taminisha had expected to remain at the castle, she wrestled with disappointment once the decision became final.

Larkin appeared only slightly disgruntled he would also remain at the castle to guard Taminisha and Jivin.

All Ellkiiyn, full blood or not, and battle trained others would be leaving in a few solar phasings to drive Nyket from Kylara and retake the throne of Aikanshin. They planned to attack Nyket from two fronts using the strengths of each species to bring him down.

With the conference over, the Zynumin went out to hunt and feed while Kikishan and Taminisha retired to their rooms. Jivin had been grizzling with hunger for some time and latched onto Taminisha's breast as soon as she offered it.

"Clyeva, go and spend time with Tarlitek, for he shall be gone soon along with the rest, and then we shall be alone to bide the castle."

Clyeva pouted. "To be parted after such a short time together cuts deep, but we shall bear it together, you and I."

Taminisha smiled as her friend exited the room. To see her and Tarlitek together gave her immense joy. Two lovers once destined to be apart despite their passion for each other burning so strong, hot and fierce. In spite of their obvious bond, she wondered again, how two such different entities had become so drawn to each other it bordered on madness? She touched the faint mark on her chest just below her breast and thanked the Great Spirit again for the abscission.

~ ~ ~

Tarlitek waited for her, naked, and ready with the hot passion of anticipation. Clyeva immediately dropped her robe and walked into his embrace. He kissed her, biting her lip as he pulled her roughly against his hardness. He pushed her back onto the bed and lifted her legs in the air as he stepped between them. Without a second of hesitation, he thrust his manhood deep into her moist burning hot interior.

As she placed her feet on his shoulders, he stroked her body, massaging her breasts, all the time shoving his hardness deep in her flesh. Clyeva groaned as an icy coldness flickered through her body. Steam rose between them, hot and fragrant with the scent of their coupling. Tarlitek sank deep and grunted. Clyeva couldn't stifle a raucous whoop of ecstasy as the coldness of his life force evaporated inside her, sending sharp waves of exquisite pleasure shuddering through her body. With a billow of steam, she roared over the precipice and sagged, limp and sweating, underneath his weight. Tarlitek rolled onto his back, taking Clyeva with him. She snuggled close, holding him inside her.

"Ah my fiery one, my heart and soul, we have the most magnificent gift, you and I, and we will celebrate it every solar phasing and every lunor drift when peace is restored."

"Tarlitek, my love, please return to me unharmed."

He kissed her nose, and eyelids then lingeringly caressed her mouth. "I will, never fear. We have too much to lose now."

Clyeva sighed. "If only we could breed…"

Tarlitek touched her lips with his finger, silencing her words. "Do not wish for what you can't have, it is bad luck. Be grateful we have each other. Besides, you have Jivin and there will be others, I'm sure. Please, do not give up what joy we have to crave something that cannot be."

She sighed again. "I know. It's not that I'm ungrateful, for I am not, but a child—I see Taminisha nursing Jivin and my heart aches."

"When I come back, we will go and seek a child, Myattican or Abaye mix maybe, to adopt. There are always abandoned babies with mixed blood. My sister knows about a place where mothers abandon mixed blood newborns all the time. They get limited care from those willing. We will choose a newborn to raise as our own."

Clyeva kissed him with a fierceness that reflected the love she felt afresh in her heart for this man of the water, her lover and her true love.

~ ~ ~

Jivin fell asleep with her breast still in his mouth. She eased him off and laid him in the cradle. With undying adoration, she ran the tips of her fingers over his tender skin and rosebud mouth. Her heart exploded with love for her child. With one lingering look at her son, she turned and walked into her lover's embrace.

He hugged her tightly. "You are not pleased with the outcome of our conference?"

She relaxed against him. "I am pleased Aikanshin will be freed, but I'm anxious for you, my love, and sad to be left behind. I knew it would be, because I have a child to nurture and protect, but I wish to be at your side, to protect your back. You will come back to me, Kikishan? We've had so little time together to strengthen our bonding, and I do not want my son to grow up without his father."

He kissed her lightly several times. "I will return safe, then we shall live long lives in peace."

He led her to the bed, and disrobed her. As she went to climb into bed, he patted her buttocks. Fire flared inside and raced through her body as she swayed her bottom at him. Despite her blatant invitation, she squealed when he stepped up behind her and slipped his manhood between her legs. He thrust hard and fast and she rocked back and forth to meet him. Devoid of tenderness, their coupling had a silent desperation for closeness, before miles and conflict parted them.

Her body growled hungrily as he sank deep, the embers of passion burst into flames sending heat rampaging through her body. She cried out a primeval call of pleasure and pain. He quickened his thrusts, their bodies slapping together as sweat glistened on their skin. She cried out again, and would have collapsed with satiation except Kikishan held her pinioned on his manhood. Now he grabbed her hips and held her buttocks pressed hard against his body, his member fully buried in her flesh. He grunted and bellowed as he climaxed, releasing his hot fluid deep inside her. After a moment of stillness, they collapsed together onto the bed. Kikishan dragged the covers over them and in moments he was asleep. Taminisha lay in his arms and wondered how she would face it if this was the last time they joined. *Rot in Orunikan's gut, Nyket for what you have stolen from me.*

~ ~ ~

Kelkiki's ragtag army gathered on the shore of the lake in the solar orb awakening mist. All Ellkiiyn with flying capacity had transmogrified and as many as possible of those who could not fly had climbed aboard.

Those who could not find a place on Ellkiiyn backs embarked on boats. The strongest at the oars and a canvas sail ready to deploy at the first sign of a breeze. Tarlitek gave orders to those travelling by water while Kikishan hurried the others.

Taminisha stood quietly at the water's edge absorbing the bustle, and fighting melancholy thoughts. She squeezed her son tight against her breasts. Clyeva stood well back from the gentle lap of the water determined not to go closer for fear of what might happen, but needing to catch a last glimpse of her lover.

Larkin helped Enian heave bundles of weapons onto the boats. The big male Ellkiiyn had handled his exclusion with grace and acceptance.

Taminisha watched the two Ellkiiyn together. They made a handsome well-matched pair. Despite the fact, Enian had a drop of tainted blood; she wondered why a love call had not come for them. She determined to talk with Kikishan about the subject after they had defeated Nyket. If more Ellkiiyn mated, despite not finding a *true* soul mate, it would increase their chances of surviving as a species.

Fervently she wished the conflict over, and called on the Great Spirit Ellkii for the safe return of all she loved and ruled. A weight settled in her gut and tight bands of trepidation wrapped around her heart. She had no idea what they would find on arrival, but she knew without a doubt, Nyket would be merciless toward all those who opposed him.

As the solar orb peeped over the horizon, the boats shoved off, and sailed swiftly down the dark, still waters of the lake. They would take a wide berth of Oventi Rock, and steer directly to the manawa of Orun. The flying contingent would land on the beaches between Zynumin and Kylara.

Kikishan and Palakin had decided a two-pronged attack would be the most effective, but Taminisha thought to see everyone, en masse, charge Nyket's strong hold, and annihilate him.

Taminisha and Clyeva moved back as the Ellkiiyn flapped their wings—the motion generated a swirling wind, which kicked up sand from the beach, and bent the trees and grasses. As they rose into the pale solar awakening sky Taminisha walked back up the path to the almost empty castle.

Times were going to be hard without Kikishan and the others. They had enough bodies of various breeds for a limited guard through each solar phasing, but Taminisha doubted she would feel safe until her soul mate returned.

She had grown so used to the beat of Kikishan's heart next to hers as time and distance separated them and the two beats became slightly discordant, fatigue wavered through her, contaminating the sense of hope she clung to. She would know immediately if anything happened to him. In one way it comforted; in another, it terrified her.

The climb to the nesting room for one last glimpse of the warriors before they faded out of sight seemed unbearably hard, her legs heavy, her steps slow. Clyeva hurried right behind her. They stood together at the window, holding hands, Ellkiiyn and Abaye, watching until they could no longer see anything of the motley army charging into battle.

Jivin's squirming roused her from the misery engulfing her. Welcoming the distraction, she walked across to the nest and laid him on the silken padding.

He kicked his legs and gurgled unintelligible sounds. His bright yellow eyes snapped and sparked as his gaze followed her agitated pacing back and forth.

Taminisha gazed at him and her heart swelled with love. She moved closer, studying his features. He had pale skin like his father, but a shock of dark hair like her. His chubby baby fists beat the air as he tried to rollover. She smiled at his efforts. Suddenly he transmogrified into Ellkiiyn.

Clyeva squealed. Taminisha jumped back then stared at her son. He gazed back at her, knowing intelligence in his eyes.

"Jivin," Taminisha, warned, not wanting to transmogrify to control her baby son.

As Ellkiiyn, he was three times the size of his sachan body. He flapped his wings and walked toward her with unsteady steps on the soft surface. He squeaked and blew fire across the bed.

Taminisha held up her hands to ward off the heat. "Jivin, no fire."

He giggled then dropped to his knees before transmogrifying easily back into his sachan form.

"Sizzling Fire Nymph, should he be doing that so often, or at all?" Clyeva gasped.

Taminisha struggled to form the words as she watched her child. Her mind already searched for ideas to deal with a situation that could so easily get out of hand. "I don't know. I didn't expect he could change back until he reached sexual maturity, but he does it all the time." Taminisha glanced out the window hoping and praying to Great Ellkii they would be victorious in this needless conflict. Her heart ached. "Please come back to me, my love, I need you."

165

# Chapter Fifteen

Kikishan kept his eyes on the water passing beneath him. The ten fully armoured warriors in sachan form on his back weighed him down and he fought to keep enough altitude. All had come to fight the evil Nyket through loyalty to him as Guardian of the Aqueena clan and Kelkiki. He wanted to do them proud and secure a resounding defeat. Part of his heart remained at the castle with his soul mate, and son. It would be difficult to keep his mind concentrated on the battle ahead when his heart and thoughts were back home with the family he thought he would never have.

The solar orb dropped below the horizon. The beaches below were crowded with more than a hundred Zynumin, all in sachan form. As he came into land, Kikishan immediately sensed their restless desire to morphflitt and hunt. The smell of fresh meat in the form of sachans just on the other side of the bushes made it even more acute.

Vulnerable Kylarans—real sachans, with no magic whatsoever. In fact, they scorned magic of any form and scorned those of their own who bred with other species. They had not asked for help with Nyket, and Kikishan wondered if they would accept it from a motley collection of cross breeds, magic spinners and morphflitters, including himself.

As soon as his feet touched the sand, his passengers jumped off. With a flick of ekta, he created a habilen and then transmogrified to his sachan form. He needed to meet the Zynumin on equal terms.

Even as Kikishan pulled on his garment, a tall, thickset man strode forward. He had piercing eyes of gold, prominent ears and short spiky hair. "Welcome, Kikishan, to Zynumin. I am Aneverin."

Kikishan bowed acknowledgement of the greeting. "Together we will defeat this terror," he said. "The other half of my warriors have gone by boat through the manawa."

Aneverin frowned. "The manawa is unsafe."

Kikishan smiled. "Normally yes, but my people are led by a half Orunan named Tarlitek, who is loyal to my soul mate; he saved the heir and rescued her from death when Nyket pounced."

"He will protect them. Come, we must consider tactics." Aneverin gestured for Kikishan to accompany him.

The big Zynumin led Kikishan to a large cave well back from the beach. A number of Zynumin females and children, all in sachan form, gathered in the shadowy back.

As the leaders settled down to talk, a half-grown black Felitza bounded up, all gangly legs, flashing green eyes and unretracted claws. Sparks flashed and he morphflitted as he reached the entrance.

"Aneverin, Father, sachans are coming. They're armed!"

"Phelix, you have broken the rules. Go to your mother," Palakin growled.

The child hung his head. "Sorry. I got excited and lost control."

A large black female hurried forward, snatched up the child and dragged him to the back of the cave. She cuffed him first, then stroked and kissed him.

Palakin jumped up, and strode to the entrance. Four other male Zynumin gathered right behind him. "It is unwise for you to be here, Kylarans, very unwise. The Zynumin are edgy, and keen to hunt."

Kikishan and Aneverin moved closer to hear the exchange.

"I know, Zynumin, but I seek your indulgence. I am Kiet, leader of the refugees sheltering under the Wall of Tennille. We heard rumours you are going to fight Nyket."

"You have heard correctly, Kylaran," Palakin replied, in his accented romni.

"We want to help. I know you consider us puny and weak, but another sword may make the difference between victory and defeat. It is our land after all, occupied by evil."

Aneverin stepped past Palakin, and faced the sachans. "I am Aneverin, Leader of the Zynumin. We cannot guarantee your safety once we morphflitt, a sachan is a sachan, but the extra armed bodies will be to our advantage. You are welcome to share the risks of this battle."

Kiet bowed low. "We understand and respect the nature of the Zynumin, and we thought to all wear red armbands or shirts to differentiate ourselves. At least you will know which sachan to kill."

Aneverin smiled. "You have planned well, Kylaran, I will advise my people. During this lunor drift, we will hunt on the Leryi side of the mines so stay under the shadow of the Wall, and you will be safe. Gather here in the light of the awakening for battle."

Kiet bowed again before he spun around, and walked swiftly toward the Wall of Tennille.

In the shadows of the solar orbs settling, Ellkiiyn hunted in the lake for orrtaya, feeding themselves first, and then bringing back extra for those who could not hunt so easily. Even some of the Zynumin satisfied their hunger with orrtaya

Cradling a full stomach, Kikishan sat back and observed. The way so many of the inhabitants in Dykarin had come together in such a wave of goodwill and desire to free the land from the scourge of Nyket filled him with pride. Kikishan vowed he would do more for Dykarin, and the unity of the lands when they had defeated Nyket. He would do more than just bring the withering population of full-blooded Aqueena Ellkiiyn back to ultimate strength.

Taminisha would support him when he called for changes to ritual and protocols not in the best interests of Ellkiiyn, especially the transmogrifying rules for newborns. A shudder surged afresh at how close he'd come to slaughtering his own son, a perfectly healthy full blood Ellkiiyn. He surveyed those around him and wondered how many here had killed their offspring because of a minute or two delay. If the Ellkiiyn Clans were to survive in the ever-changing world of so many species, much of the law needed revision and he would see it done.

The lunor drift stretched interminably as he thrashed back and forth on the hard ground, missing with a desperate craving, the warmth of Taminisha's body. Even though he could feel her heartbeat in his chest, it provided only a modicum of comfort. He wished he could feel his son's, but only mothers sensed their children.

As the pale glow of the solar orb awakening lightened the skies above Dykarin, the army gathered. All in sachan form: Ellkiiyn, Zynumin, the Kylarans, and others of many breeds and cross breeds. It amazed Kikishan how similar they actually were in sachan form, as they stood side by side ready to strive for a common goal.

He wanted peace throughout Dykarin and vowed to achieve it through all species finding common ground and respect for each other. He sighed because no answer came easily to him on how to accomplish his goals.

On Aneverin's signal, they surged forward, Zynumin morphed and loped through the forest and over the wall, Ellkiiyn transmogrified and flew in the direction of Kylara, and sachans marched shoulder to shoulder in an impenetrable line. The battle for Kylara and Aikanshin began.

~ ~ ~

Loneliness gripped Taminisha more solidly as each solar phasing and lunor drift passed. A despondent quiet hung over the castle as thoughts of the battle troubled those left behind.

Larkin paced the castle at all hours, always ending up on the balcony, watching out over the lake. Taminisha guessed he wanted to hide the disappointment at his exclusion from the battle and wished he would desist, because he had failed miserably.

Taminisha sympathised with him, as she also hated having to stay behind. Nothing came to mind that would provide a welcome distraction, so she left him to his pacing, and concentrated on her son.

Although she'd been shocked at her baby son's ability to transmogrify, she now spent time encouraging him to do just that. Clyeva also immersed herself in Jivin's care, and tried not to show how much she fretted for Tarlitek. Taminisha sympathised. Clyeva had no way of knowing how Tarlitek fared. Through the long periods of darkness, they clung together in the dark with baby Jivin cradled between them.

Seeking to lift her negative mood, Taminisha planned a new garden based on Aikanshin's carefully manicured grounds with lots of water features. She brought in some gardeners from the village, and she supervised its construction.

Clyeva watched with interest, but kept her distance from the ponds and rivulets, although repeatedly assured Taminisha, Tarlitek would love it.

As the time passed, her minor irritation grew as she watched Larkin pace around the garden area, up the stairs, and onto the bailey parapet walk, and back again. Unable to bear his constant movement, she decided to confront him about his edginess. She walked quietly up behind the big blond Ellkiiyn where he stood on a rock staring out over the lake toward Lycidea.

"Larkin, you seem troubled? Do you so resent being left behind?"

He started at her first words then faced her. "I do not resent being left behind, my lady, it is an honour to guard you, Clyeva and baby Jivin."

"Then tell me what ails you? You're driving me crazy with your restlessness and you keep watch on the sky to the lunor rise instead of the direction of the battle."

He hung his head; his rugged, angular features coloured a rosy pink. He pushed his long fringe back from his face. "I am being called, my lady, I feel her heartbeat in my chest."

Excitement sparked through her. "That is wonderful, a soul mate at last."

He frowned. "It is not wonderful. It's the wrong time, and wrong place. My duty is to you, and your son, at this time, not to a joining with my soul mate."

"But Larkin, it is such a beautiful thing to be called and of course the mating dance..." Heat rushed up her face in response to Larkin's obvious embarrassment. She looked out over the lake to break the tension between them, but by the time, she looked back at him, a cold lump had settled in her gut. "Oh Spirit, if you are successful, and breed, you will be incubating." Taminisha's words spluttered into silence. *Curse on the Ellkiiyn breeding cycle. Why is it so complicated?* However, even considering the difficulties she did not even contemplate denying Larkin.

"Now you understand why I'm not happy. I need a nest. I don't have approval from Kikishan for space and time off, and there is only me to guard you, the babe and Clyeva." Larkin slumped down onto a nearby rock. "We must complete the mating dance on first contact to secure our bond. If circumstances are not right for breeding in that first coupling and conception is withheld by my soul mate, we might never

171

breed."

"Never breed?"

"Yes, Taminisha, that's why I worried so much about you and Kikishan, in the wake of your unconventional meeting," Clyeva said from behind her.

Taminisha glanced toward Clyeva and back to Larkin. "To be honest, I do not believe such Ellkiiyn fables and myths, but I will not see you denied a chance of the happiness I hold. Preparations must be made just in case there is truth in the myth."

"But, my lady, she is very near. I feel it. I will not leave you unguarded."

"Ah, but Larkin, when you're incubating, your soul mate will be there to guard us, will she not?"

He scowled. "I do not know her credentials. How can I leave you in the care of a complete stranger?"

"Do not fret, Clyeva and I are not helpless, and she is your soul mate, so surely her loyalty lies in conjunction with yours."

"I suppose so. I just feel my responsibility heavily."

"Follow your heart, Larkin, you may only ever get one call. We will manage."

"And a nest?"

"Would it bother you to use Kikishan's nest?"

"No, I would be honoured."

"That's settled then," Taminisha said.

While she put up a calm front, Taminisha played over in her mind the worse outcomes. As time passed, she lost her appetite and spent hours pacing, unable to settle to any one thing. She made an effort to appear unruffled, but found herself jumping at the slightest sound or unexpected touch.

The thought of having a strange Ellkiiyn in the castle near her son filled her with a deep sense of protectiveness. With Kikishan gone she already had difficulty sleeping at all during the lunor drift, then struggled to stay awake during the solar phasing. When the stranger came, she would have to be on guard, all the time.

Larkin paced the parapet walls, from awakening to lunor drift and onwards. His incessant movement drove all in the castle to distraction.

Finally, Taminisha heard the whoosh of leathery wings beating in the air. She looked up. A huge red Ellkiiyn swooped and soared around the castle towers.

The red Ellkiiyn cried out, and Larkin answered her call.

Even as Taminisha watched, they rose together, twirling and entwining.

Tails lashed at each other, claws clutched at scaly skin. Flashes of fire lit their entangled bodies, sparks flying for many feet. Larkin bit hard on his soul mate's neck. She writhed and howled and then Larkin wrapped his tail around her lower body and roughly penetrated her.

There appeared to be none of the tenderness Taminisha remembered between her and Kikishan and she hoped both experienced the ecstasy she felt when her soul mate first joined with her.

Both Ellkiiyn howled again as they spun in a slow spiral, Larkin determinedly thrusting, while she clutched him with her claws and teeth. Sparks flew and fell sizzling to the parapet walk moments before Larkin and his soul mate glided down into the nesting room. As the sparks died on the cold rock, silence fell.

Taminisha walked inside where Clyeva waited with Jivin. A blood curdling howl ripped the silence to shreds. Several grunts and groans followed. Then silence fell again.

As she nursed Jivin, Taminisha couldn't decide if the turbulent joining of Larkin and his soul mate repulsed her or sparked unrequited desires. Either way, their display of intimacy had opened up a deep chasm of loneliness inside her. She missed Kikishan so much as she faced another long lunor drift alone.

Even before she opened her eyes, nausea twisted through her. Her stomach churned and her mouth watered. She jumped out of bed, raced for the waste bowl in the corner of the room and vomited, twice. She gasped in air, rinsed her mouth and crawled back into bed glad the disgorging of her stomach contents had improved how she felt. Jivin stirred between them and she offered her breast in an effort to settle him.

Clyeva stirred. "Are you all right?"

"Not really, Clyeva, I've thrown up. Must have been the orrtaya I ate for my solar settling repast. Nothing to worry about. Go back to sleep. It's early yet."

"Well that'll teach you to eat a gill breather, albeit a small one," Clyeva muttered.

Taminisha smiled at her friend's resistance to eating the same species as her lover, even though he cheerfully chomped on his own genetic kin.

Larkin appeared as they were taking their awakening repast, the restlessness gone, and a big grin on his handsome face still covered with awakening beard growth. "We are incubating. My beautiful, beloved, Ulyana. Our joining... so amazing. Exciting, and volatile, just like her."

Taminisha noticed the scratches on his face and the restricted way he moved. "I am glad for you, but assume you need some tending."

He blushed. "It's just a few scratches. She's very passionate."

"Clyeva will tend you, and then I suggest you take it easy until you return to the nest."

"Thank you. I hope you will like Ulyana and in time she will become a treasured part of this family."

"She will," Taminisha assured him as she left to feed Jivin.

Ulyana turned out to be a stunningly beautiful female in her sachan form, big bust, green eyes and long red hair. Her significant rack of curling pectenites displayed her pure Infernea bloodlines. She had a wide-open smile and a slightly apologetic demeanour as she held out her hands. "My Lady of Kelkiki, thank you for making me so welcome. Larkin tells me it's a difficult time for you. I'm sorry to crash in like this, but when the mystical urge came over me, I could not resist. I have never called another before."

Taminisha took her proffered hands and leaned in slightly. The touch of their pectenites, light and brief. "Call me Taminisha, and yes we do welcome you, Ulyana. Congratulations on your joining and incubating. It is an exciting time."

Ulyana smiled. "I'm so excited. It's hard to wait for so many solar phasing to see our child. Larkin has explained I must be of service to you when not on incubating duty. He says you're building a garden by the lake to replicate your home, and I must supervise the workers."

Taminisha nodded. "Yes, and keep a watch for any who may approach. We do not know the outcome of the battles yet."

"I am at your service, my lady," the beautiful Ellkiiyn said, as she bowed low.

Ulyana made herself useful, befriending the remaining servants and helping where needed, always pleasant and smiling. Larkin strode around the castle on his periods off with a huge grin on his face.
Except that she missed Kikishan with a relentless primeval ache, life in the castle had settled into a smooth enjoyable routine.

Taminisha began to relax. Though still wary of Ulyana she hoped they could become friends in time. They had one thing in common missing from her friendship with Clyeva was the Ellkiiyn experience of motherhood.

Twenty solar phasing into the incubation period Taminisha noticed Ulyana appeared tired and when Clyeva took Jivin upstairs for his afternoon nap, she pointed to a shady spot just out of the way of the gardeners.

"Sit with me, Ulyana, you look tired."

She smiled and immediately sank to the grass. "Thank you,

Taminisha. I would welcome a break. I am finding incubation very stressful."

"It is a hard time."

"Yes, I get lonely on the nest and do not find it easy to sleep. You have made me very welcome, but it is still not home."

Taminisha touched her shoulder. "I understand. I also found it lonely, both on and off the nest."

"Why does it have to be so difficult?"

Taminisha shrugged.

"And I worry about the hatching. I fret my child will not pass the test. I could not bear it, my lady if…"

Again, Taminisha touched her shoulder. "The rule is tragic. My brother failed, and my father killed him but even as he died, he transmogrified. I believe sometimes babies need more time."

"But the rules."

"Ulyana, the hatching is between you and Larkin—a minute or two extra would not be a crime. No-one is ever going to know."

Ulyana sat back and stared at her.

Taminisha squirmed under her scrutiny. She did not intend to tell her Jivin had failed, but she could not bear the thought of an executed baby.

"You advocate flaunting the rules."

Taminisha shook her head. "That would not be flaunting them, just extending them."

Ulyana smiled. "You have soothed my fears. I really don't think Larkin could do the deed anyway. He's such a softy. So caring and patient."

"A good mate."

"Excellent."

"I really miss my mate, Kikishan."

"Larkin told me your mate has gone to do battle with a rogue Ellkiiyn."

"Yes, he wishes to free Aikanshin and Kylara from the tainted

Khimaera, Nyket."

"What are Aikanshin and Kylara to Kikishan?"

"He's doing it for me."

"Because Nyket is a mixed blood?"

The sharp edge to Ulyana's tone scraped along Taminisha's nerves. She sat straighter in the chair and faced Ulyana squarely. "No. Because he has no right to rule Aikanshin, he is not Vaprus."

Ulyana relaxed back in her chair her expression softening. "I understand, but I do hate the thought of mixed bloods being so rejected."

"I agree, Ulyana. They should be treated equally, but this battle has nothing to do with that." Tension gripped her. Taminisha did not like the tone of Ulyana's inquiries about the conflict and the reasons behind it. She would not understand—she was Infernea.

Ulyana smiled and glanced up at the castle. "Enough of such unpleasant subjects. Tell me, Taminisha, will you and Kikishan try to breed again as you already have a son and heir."

A shadow of tension remained, but Taminisha tried to relax with Ulyana's rapid change of subject. "I know Kikishan would like more children. I'm not sure. The incubation process is so unpleasant."

"I want a son to..." Ulyana stared out over the lake for a moment then turned back to Taminisha. "Not that he will be heir to anything, of course, but I'm sure his father would be pleased."

"I'm sure Larkin will be happy as long as the child is healthy."

Ulyana climbed to her feet. "Of course, we both will. Come, Taminisha, the workers are finishing for the phasing and soon I must relieve Larkin."

Taminisha watched the red Ellkiiyn stroll toward the castle suddenly not sure if she liked Ulyana or not.

# Chapter Sixteen

Taminisha looked up into the sky. The pale blue expanse called her. She needed to fly.

She sought out Clyeva. "I need to get away for a short time will you please put Jivin down for his nap?"

She handed Jivin to Clyeva and headed up to the parapet walk. She wanted to stretch her wings, to fly and soar, and feel the heat of the solar rays on her flesh, but most of all she needed to escape the confines of the lonely castle.

On the bailey terrace, she ducked and rolled. Shock shuddered through her as she crashed into the parapet with a thud. She sat still trying to work out what had happened. Her shoulder ached and a spot on her head already swelled into an egg-shaped lump from contact with the stone. *What in the name of Spirit? This has not happened since Shula healed me. Am I ill? I don't feel ill.* Taminisha glanced around to see if anyone had seen her and let out a huge sigh. No one had observed her failure, so she promptly rolled and tucked again, pushing away the embarrassment.

Thud, she hit the rock wall.

She climbed to her feet, still in her sachan form. *Why haven't I transmogrified?* She stood still studying the wall. *Do I try again?* This time she squatted, tucked and rolled. This time she didn't hit the wall quite so hard.

She scrambled to her feet and clutched the wall for support. Sweat beaded on her skin. Blood pounded in her head as she opened her mouth in a silent scream. When her tension eased, she snapped her mouth shut and swallowed against the sting in her throat. Nausea washed through her and she dropped her head to the cold stones. As the heat in her face cooled, she pushed herself upright and walked inside using the wall to steady her wobbling steps.

She came face to face with Clyeva on the landing. Taminisha ducked her head down determined not to reveal her state of mind to her friend.

Clyeva paused. "I thought you were going for a fly?"

"I changed my mind; I'm going for a walk on the shore."

"Do you want company? Jivin would like the fresh air."

"Thanks, but I would rather be alone for a while," she replied, knowing very well Clyeva did not want to go to the lake.

Clyeva rested her hand on the banister. "I wish they would come home."

"So do I," Taminisha replied as she hurried down the stairs.

Taminisha fretted in silence, not only about her inability to transmogrify, but also about the other changes to her body—the fatigue, the mental confusion and the emotions racing back and forth through her mind bringing an erratic beating of her heart. However when sickness woke her every awakening for the next ten, she finally accepted something terrible ailed her. She needed advice. With efficient swiftness, she fed and settled Jivin then hurried to find Clyeva.

"I need to talk to you."

"So, you're ready to tell me now."

"Tell you?" Taminisha exclaimed.

"Yes, about your sickness. You think just because you've been ever so discreet, I haven't noticed. I'm not stupid you know."

"Oh Clyeva, I'm so scared. I can't transmogrify, and I can't keep food down, not just in the awakening, but right through the solar phasing and sometimes in the lunor drift. I'm tired, tearful and confused. I don't know what's wrong with me. If I die will you promise to care for Jivin?"

"Taminisha, you're not going to die, you're just with child."

"What? No. Ellkiiyn do not get *'with child'*."

Taminisha's screech drowned out the cackle of Clyeva's laughter.

"You did join with Kikishan in the sachan way, did you not?"

Heat rushed up Taminisha's face. The sachan joining seemed so much more intimate, and private. "Yes we did—a number of times. I found it the most amazing, intimate, exciting experience." *The closeness of the joining, the tenderness, and the pleasure with no waiting for the urge.*

Clyeva burst out laughing. "Yes, it is all that, Taminisha, but it also comes with a risk. If you can't transmogrify it means you are too far along. You must now carry the child to full term, and give birth to it the sachan way."

You mean I'm incubating in the sachan way?" Taminisha touched her stomach. "That I have a child inside me." Her heart raced and she struggled to draw in breath. Her skin tingled.

"Yes. A living babe. You will feel it move soon."

"I can't have a babe in the sachan way. I've heard it's a terribly dangerous process, and excruciatingly painful to birth a live babe," Taminisha blurted out.

Again Clyeva laughed. "It's not dangerous with the right care, but yes, it is painful."

Taminisha sank slowly into a nearby chair. "Great Spirit, what have I got myself into?"

'You'll survive; thousands of females do it every year."

'But Kikishan is not here?" Taminisha wailed. "How will I manage without my mate?"

"It does not matter. There is no need of your mate now he has placed his seed inside you. And a good thing too," Clyeva declared. "You could not incubate an egg alone; it would kill you, almost sixty phasings alone on the nest."

"So what now?"

Clyeva leaned over and hugged her tightly. "Nothing. And I suggest you don't tell anyone else just yet."

Taminisha frowned and chewed on her bottom lip. "Why?"

"Because it makes you vulnerable, carrying a babe, and also, let's not take the shine off Larkin and Ulyana. There will be plenty of time for your news after their babe has hatched."

Taminisha rested one hand on her flat stomach and wondered what it would be like when the child grew, making it swell. A squeaky giggle bubbled up. She tugged at her hair and then tucked it behind her ears. She'd seen plenty of sachan women, heavy with child, but had never really thought about it in regards to herself.

"You have got yourself into the Fire Nymph's flame, *haven't you*?"

Taminisha couldn't meet Clyeva's gaze and stared at her hands as she clasped them on her lap. "Yes. Please don't abandon me, my friend, despite my carelessness?"

Clyeva stepped up behind her, laid both hands on her shoulders and squeezed. "Never, my friend."

~ ~ ~

Kikishan examined the decimated battlefield. The most recent battle had been another victory for their motley army. The Zynumin had taken the lead, terrifying into retreat most of Nyket's cross breed army. No one wanted to be prey for the big Felitza.

When the enemy huddled behind roughly built defences or natural landscapes, Kikishan and his Ellkiiyn would dive-bomb them. Those that could sprayed flames, while others dropped rocks, hot oil or nets onto them. When the nets entangled them, the Kylarans and any cross breeds raced in, and secured them and their weapons. Most surrendered without resistance to be imprisoned on a rocky outcrop in the centre of Menishin Lake.

Kikishan suspected they had not encountered the main army yet because they were fully occupied fending off Tarlitek's larger contingent trying to take Aikanshin Castle. He believed if they could reach the castle and combine, they could win this battle.

At last, the Ifaseeti Falls were in sight. The army gathered in the shadow of the cliffs just far enough away to avoid the spray from the gushing falls. Aikanshin Castle rose up into the clouds that swirled around the summit of the mountain. The bridge across the falls and the surrounding agricultural land appeared deserted by the inhabitants of Aikanshin.

Word came just on the settling of the solar orb. Tarlitek had retreated having taken a severe beating from a well-trained contingent of new renegades unexpectedly swooping to swell Nyket's diminishing ranks. All parties agreed a joint attack on the castle would begin at first light and would be their best opportunity for victory.

With the camp heavily guarded, Kikishan retired for the lunor drift. Constantly tired and very aware of his advancing years he snatched what sleep he could amongst the horror. Battle after battle, and food snatched when and where he found it sapped his strength, as did always remaining as Ellkiiyn. Because there were very few creatures willing to attack a full blood, adult male Ellkiiyn, he felt safer. However, despite the reassurance of his imposing form, he slept lightly.

The shush, and whoosh, of air and the splash of waves on the shore penetrated his sleep. He lifted his head. They were there. Ellkiiyn, in many colours; red, purple, and green of the full bloods, and others, of garish splotched or muted colours that revealed their mixed blood.

Kikishan rose, and bellowed a warning, even as one red Ellkiiyn latched onto his back with razor sharp claws. He bellowed again, this time in hurt and rage.

The camp came alive. Warnings and orders rang out, and weapons rattled. Those who could change into larger creatures did and went into attack, while other smaller species set about attacking the invading Ellkiiyn in packs.

The vulnerable sachans fled. They could do nothing against the onslaught of such huge savage creatures. At least one hundred Ellkiiyn swooped and dropped, killing sachans with one blow and slicing Felitza fur from their bodies with vicious slashes. They bellowed battle cries, and blasted the camp with fire. Trees exploded. Living creatures flamed and burnt with agonising screeches. The offensive continued with merciless savagery. The dead dropped, and the injured crawled away to hide.

Kikishan writhed and twisted. He lashed with his tail against the Ellkiiyn clinging to his back. The red Ellkiiyn blasted the top of his head with fire, and Kikishan bawled at the harrowing agony. He ducked and rolled, forcing his foe beneath his greater weight.

The red Ellkiiyn let go, but spun around in an instant, sinking its teeth into Kikishan's leg.

The bones in his leg crunched under the force of the clamping jaws. The leg gave way under him, but he swung around and lashed out with a blast of flame.

It hit his assailant right in the face, melting the Ellkiiyn's eyes, and twisting his pectenites. The red Ellkiiyn gave a bloodcurdling screech and collapsed, writhing on the ground.

Another larger foe dived in to take the injured Ellkiiyn's place. This time it was a blotchy purple Vaprus Khimaera, with twisted undersized pectenites, and a sneer curling his lips.

Kikishan charged his enemy, rearing up on his hind legs, clawed hands slashing through the air. He missed the face, but latched onto the neck dislodging a multitude of misshapen pale purple scales. Kikishan twisted his head around and bit deep into the muscular structure of his opponent's throat. He tasted foreign blood. He dragged back, tearing the flesh from the Ellkiiyn's neck. Blood sprayed all over Kikishan and the ground.

The Khimaera screamed, but no sound came out. Terror filled the purple eyes even as they glazed over.

The body went soft in Kikishan's grip and he let the corpse thud to the ground.

Kikishan spun around to face another, muddy brown, much smaller Ellkiiyn. His new enemy struggled to hold form and Kikishan suspected she had less than a half Ellkiiyn blood. He breathed a stream of fire at her.

She coughed, howled her rage then spiralling down she landed on the ground even as she transmogrified. Another blast of fire and the sachan form collapsed in a blaze of red.

Moments later a huge black Felitza pounced on her and tore her throat out.

Nausea rushed over Kikishan at her sudden dispatch.

Finally, the marauding Ellkiiyn began to retreat, many losing form and hollering for rescue before they dropped into the lake. Those of Kikishan's army still able chased them half way across the lake before they too retreated to tend injuries and re-group. Few slept through what remained of the lunor drift that followed the attack.

The solar orb barely showed above the horizon when they began their push forward to Aikanshin Castle. Those who could fly carried those who did not. Kikishan called his warriors and they followed him through the dark sky into the cloud obscuring the turrets of the castle.

He swooped high over the battlements then glided down into the writhing tangle of bodies, Ellkiiyn and sachan, swords flashing, spears flying and bodies falling. He unloaded his passengers and they immediately transformed or waded into the melee. Kikishan rose, circled, and then swooped over the parapet walk seeking the most beneficial way to strike.

From aloft, he saw a lone Ellkiiyn, secluded from the battle, but watching the action closely. He showed no intention of participating. A Terraid Khimaera within significantly, deformed pectenites, and shabby uneven scales. The part blood Ellkiiyn glared up at him.

*So this is the tainted one who hurt Taminisha, and instigated this slaughter. I will deliver her vengeance.*

Kikishan landed with a thud.

"This is not your conflict, Ellkiiyn. Since when does our kind fight our own, in support of mere sachans? We are Guardians and we shall rule. Be gone, Ellkiiyn." The green Ellkiiyn waved him away with a clawed hand.

Kikishan stood taller and puffed his chest out as he spat fire within inches of the Ellkiiyn's feet. "I am Kikishan, soul mate of Taminisha, and champion of the true Guardian, Jabrikan. This is my conflict by right of joining with Taminisha, whom you, Nyket, dispossessed of her home and caused her grievous harm."

Nyket laughed, bending double with the strength of his amusement. "So she lives. What a shame, now I will have to deal with her as well as this shambles. Go from here, Kikishan, before I kill you."

Kikishan did not wait for further exchanges. He reared up and spat a wide stream of fire.

Nyket jumped back, flicked his wings and rose above the fiery blast. Nyket came at Kikishan, head down, claws out. His charge hit Kikishan in the chest.

They grappled each other, claws slashed, and tails bashed against the other's flesh. They rolled—one on top, then below. Fire spewed in all directions.

Kikishan freed one back leg and swung it down hard, right across Nyket's stomach.

Nyket snarled as he fell back on the stone floor.

Kikishan leapt on top of him, clawing and slashing. He opened his mouth, crunched down on Nyket's deformed pectenites, and jerked vigorously. Several pieces broke off in Kikishan's mouth. Kikishan spat out Nyket's pectenites and bit again.

Nyket roared as he bit down on Kikishan's other leg. Blood spurted all over the stone floor.

Kikishan rested on his tail and pummelled Nyket with his hands alternately snapping at his extremities and spitting fire in his face.

Nyket let go and tumbled across the stones. He moved slowly, his eyesight damaged and blood pouring from his head. He tried to rise, couldn't, and roared his fury as he struggled to hold his Ellkiiyn form.

Without warning, a weight hit Kikishan's shoulders. He fell face first onto the stone floor. Claws raked down his back opening up his scaly skin from shoulder to tail. He screeched and gathered his strength.

The attacker flew off, rolled in mid-air and came at him again.

Blood poured from Kikishan's wounds. Blackness hovered at the outer edge of his vision. His back legs crumpled as agony tore along his back. He staggered as he glanced up at the large green Ellkiiyn bearing down on him from the sky. His strength drained away. *I must flee now or die as I stand.*

His promise to return to Taminisha jolted him into action. He leapt into the air sweeping his huge wings up and down; slapping his opponent off course for the few seconds it took him to get airborne. He rose into the sky, struggling to gain altitude. Kikishan flapped his wings just managing to stay aloft, flying crookedly.

The green Ellkiiyn circled him. A screech came from behind him.

He swung his head around to see Enian and another small Ellkiiyn pull his foe out of the sky and back into the throes of battle. He grunted in agony as he tucked injured legs up close to his body. *Dear Great Ellkii, protect, Enian. It will be my shame if she dies to save me.*

He could see the battle now. The sheer numbers of opponents had already overwhelmed his army and the loyal Vaprus Ellkiiyn they had come to support.

Nyket had recruited reinforcements, Ellkiiyn mercenaries, and cross breed misfits ready to fight and kill for the best reward. The rejected ones with tainted blood, just like Nyket himself, had risen up to wreck their own form of revenge on those determined to keep the species pure.

Below him, Kikishan could see remnants of his rag tag army retreating from Aikanshin Castle. He searched for Tarlitek, but could not find him or any of the Ellkiiyn close to him. He drifted, losing height. Blood poured from his wounds leaving him light headed and fatigued. His wings still rose and fell, but with great effort, sluggish and wobbly.

*I will never make it back to Zynumin.* Cold shivers danced over his scaly skin. With convulsive gulps, he tried to swallow against the ache at the back of his throat. *This is it. I'm sorry, my love, I have failed you.*

He glided for a moment ready to surrender to death, but the slightly discordant beat of Taminisha's heart called him. *I cannot abandon her and our son. I cannot.* With a grunt, he forced his wings to undulate and scanned the land beneath. *If I can just land. Please Great Ellkii find me a place to land.* The thought of dying in the air and tumbling into the lake terrified him. As he continued to scan the murky waters of the manawa, he calculated Myattica would provide the first solid landing opportunity and much closer than Zynumin. He tilted right and glided slowly down.

A flash in the corner of his vision caught his attention. A faded red, almost pink Ellkiiyn, and another, blue larger one. He glanced sideways and sighed with relief. *"Enian, my friend."*

She came close, and then slid underneath him. His body bumped into hers. The strain of staying aloft receded as she lifted and guided him. The lake shore loomed closer, and they slowly glided down.

Kikishan landed with a clumsy thump, Enian right beside him as he fell to his knees, drained of strength.

In a rush of wings, the other Ellkiiyn landed beside him.

*"Help me Nysiah; we have to stop the bleeding before he gets too weak to recover,"* Enian broadcast in Ellkiiyn as she transmogrified to her sachan form and grabbed some leaves from the nearest baya bush and pressed them on the wounds. The blood kept pouring out.

Kikishan's strength slipped away. Blackness hovered. "Go Enian, to safety. I am for death. Tell Taminisha I love her."

"Nooo," Enian howled.

"Shush that racket, Ellkiiyn. You'll have Nyket's henchmen down on us in seconds," a female voice chirruped.

Kikishan lifted one lid and peered in the direction of the voice. A youngish, fine boned woman with sharp angular features and wide set eyes bustled toward him. Dressed in a long flowing skirt in earthy tones she appeared to flutter across the sand. Lime green and yellow feathers covered her skull. He recognised her as Myattican.

"I am Shula. Tarlitek told me of the battle. He asked me to watch for the injured and offer healing. Now stand aside, Ellkiiyn. I will save your Guardian, if for no other reason than he is soul mate of Taminisha, and friend of Tarlitek."

Kikishan sighed and let his eyes close. Blackness hovered around his mind as voices discussed his health. Gentle hands touched his scaly Ellkiiyn skin.

~  ~  ~

The solar orb awakening signalled the imminent hatching event. Larkin rampaged around the castle overcome with anxiety. With Ulyana on incubating duty, Larkin had nothing to keep him occupied. He paced, back and forth, past the nesting room door then marched up and down the parapet walk. He even went to the lake and back.

Even Taminisha had trouble settling. Anticipation prickled along her skin. Excitement for Larkin and Ulyana, subtly suppressed by anxiety. After her own experience, she would not feel calm until they confirmed their child had transmogrified satisfactorily.

Taminisha watched him from her room. "Did Kikishan suffer so much angst, Clyeva, when we were about to hatch?"

Clyeva laughed. "He did. So much torment." She pointed to Taminisha's stomach. "I think this is a better way to go."

Taminisha frowned. "But what happens to the test of transmogrifying?"

Clyeva smiled. "Well that's just it, my dear friend, there will be no test. You will have to wait until puberty to be sure and by then it is too late to kill a beloved son or daughter."

"Oh," Taminisha said, unable to find further words to express her thoughts.

As the solar orb settled toward the horizon, Taminisha and Clyeva waited in the dining hall as Larkin joined Ulyana for the hatching. Even the non-Ellkiiyn inhabitants of the castle walked more quietly, spoke in whispers, and kept glancing in the direction of the nesting room.

Taminisha fed Jivin then she and Clyeva alternated between rocking the baby to sleep and pacing the room. Jivin had already settled for sleep when a howl of elation reverberated around the castle.

Worry slid from Taminisha's shoulders. It had gone well. They hurried to the dining hall. Larkin and Ulyana appeared, in sachan form, with a tiny pink-skinned babe in Ulyana's arms. She had tears in her eyes, and Larkin danced around her in excitement.

"We have a daughter," Larkin announced. "She has red hair like her mother and is such a cutie."

Taminisha and Clyeva gathered around the happy parents, and cooed and clucked over the tiny babe, who did indeed look like its mother with wispy red hair and startling green eyes."

"And her name?" Taminisha asked.

"We have called her Aiyana," Ulyana said quietly.

~  ~  ~

Larkin and Ulyana were besotted with their daughter. Even Jivin, when laid next to her, reached for her and gurgled baby sounds. Despite the constant worry about the outcome of the battle for Aikanshin, the time passed pleasantly enough with the two babies, the garden completion, and the mild weather.

When her condition began to show Taminisha told Larkin and Ulyana first, then allowed it to become common knowledge in the castle. News of her condition caused much curiosity, and some derision. Very few knew of Ellkiiyn who had given birth in their sachan form.

Ulyana seemed most disconcerted by Taminisha's condition, and watched her closely.

Being with child only bothered Taminisha, physically, in minor ways and she grew used to her misshapen body. She revelled in the sensation of the babe moving inside her. She already felt closer, more bonded with the child than she had with her egg. Even when the nudges inside her abdomen gave her discomfort she remained delighted with the process of incubating a baby the sachan way. She talked to the child, stroked her belly and pressed lightly against the bulges.

Ulyana watched her so closely sometimes Taminisha squirmed.

Finally, as her bulk grew, and she reached the last fifty solar phasings, Taminisha wished it would arrive right now as she struggled with the hugeness of her body, although the thought of the birth terrified her. Clyeva encouraged her and warned the child could arrive at any time from now on.

~ ~ ~

Torn from a deep sleep, Taminisha leapt out of bed. She checked on Jivin and satisfied he slept safe she rushed to the door.

Clyeva pushed through as soon as she opened it a crack. "That noise, what is that terrible noise?"

Taminisha had already guessed and went to the window. High above the castle two Ellkiiyn were entwined in a mating dance. Sparks flew. Ulyana dominated the copulation with claws and teeth. Ulyana bit hard on her mate's snout.

Larkin screeched again, this time in distress. In response to her roughness, he rammed his prehensile member hard and deep into her opening.

She cried out and beat her wings in a frantic rhythm.

They dropped swiftly from the sky.

Larkin gave one more thrust and an agonised bellow before he pulled away from his soul mate.

Taminisha pulled back from the window as they dropped with thuds into the nesting room. She would have been embarrassed to be caught staring at what should be a private act of exquisite pleasure. This time she doubted either felt much pleasure.

"So they're joining again?" Clyeva asked.

Taminisha pulled her head inside and closed the shutters. "It appears so."

"Such passion. Let's hope it does not result in a breeding."

"I doubt it. It's way too soon and not every joining results in an egg."

"Well if it did Ulyana would have a big job on her hands, incubating with such a young babe. Then like you, coping with two young ones."

"I know, Clyeva. I'm not overjoyed with my situation. I would have waited a year or two I think."

"Ah yes, but Ulyana has a choice. In the sachan way it just happens."

As they ate their awakening repast, Larkin appeared. Bites and scratches marked his body and he seemed very tired and grumpy. He held a wailing Aiyana in his arms.

"What in the Spirit's name do I do with this?" he shouted above the child's wailing. "Her mother is incubating a second egg and no longer has milk or time for her first child."

Taminisha didn't hesitate; even though she disapproved of Ulyana allowing herself to breed without making provision for her first child, she would never see the babe go hungry. Larkin handed her over and Taminisha put Aiyana to her breast. Her own milk had reduced considerably as her sachan condition advanced, but Clyeva assured her at almost a year in age Jivin would thrive on the milk of bovinites.

191

Several herds were kept by the village council to provide milk for any who couldn't provide sustenance for their children. Taminisha had already arranged for three to be brought up to the castle along with a herder and milker to care for them.

As the warm milk filled her empty stomach, Aiyana quieted.

Larkin sank into a nearby chair and watched his daughter suckle at Taminisha's breast. He directed a glowering look over his shoulder. "I said no, but Ulyana insisted. She had an urge." Larkin flushed red. "I offered to satisfy her needs the sachan way, but she refused."

"Never mind, we'll manage and I pray every solar phasing the conflict will soon be over." Even while Taminisha reassured him she worried about the incubating and the outcome of the conflict.

If their offensive failed, Nyket might come hunting her. She quivered with a wave of fear. How could she defend herself and her new child from such an attack from Nyket when she could not even transmogrify? She would have no chance in her sachan form of fighting off a male Ellkiiyn, even a shabby one like her stepbrother.

The next awakening Ulyana appeared, bright and bubbly. She took it for granted Taminisha had fed her daughter. However, on advice, milk would not be available for much longer; she went ahead and obtained two more bovinites to provide milk for her tiny babe.

Clyeva made it clear she didn't approve. She thought the child far too young.

Taminisha did not share her black thoughts with Clyeva not wanting to magnify her disapproval. *By the Great Spirit Ellkii, your first responsibility is to me, both of you. In this time of conflict, more consideration would have been helpful.* Taminisha felt abandoned by Larkin and her resentment ate away at her trust in the blue Ellkiiyn's commitment.

# Chapter Seventeen

Fourteen solar phasings into the new incubation period they rose to find the castle engulfed in a red haze. Everyone coughed and gasped. A few of the cross breeds had to go down to the village for the clearer air.

The mist made Taminisha's eyes water and her nose burn. She kept Jivin's face covered with a fine cloth to filter the air, as did Ulyana for her daughter. Despite these precautions by the next awakening both babies were red faced and coughing nonstop.

Taminisha's heart weighed heavy in her chest, and chilly tremors raced over her skin. The mist hung above the towers and wafted through the corridors on the settling breeze. Jivin wouldn't feed and by the evening, he had become quite lethargic. Aiyana fared modestly better. Taminisha paced from one child to the other. Her knees trembled and her head throbbed.

Clyeva announced she would go to the village and consult the old woman, Avyvah. She insisted on going alone convinced Taminisha and the children would need Larkin at the castle.

Time dragged as Taminisha paced the parapet walk watching for sight of Clyeva. The solar orb had almost settled behind the horizon by the time she spied Clyeva urging her eqazeen up the track to the castle. Taminisha returned to the bedroom just as Clyeva hastened along the corridor.

Larkin hurried on her heels.

"Avyvah gave me her best recipe. Although she says it is not the time for such fevers."

"Regardless we have to give the children something to help them breathe."

"She agreed. I have most of her supply of the danika plant, but we need to mix it with the blood of a shikati then made into a steam for the babies to inhale. We have to find our own shikati."

Larkin frowned. "A shikati—that means a trip to Lycidea." He shivered and wrinkled his nose.

"Well, I'm going. I'm the one who can catch the shikati," Clyeva announced.

Taminisha nodded her agreement. The thought of handling one of those blood-sucking vermin upset her stomach. "You will have to take her, Larkin. Ulyana is incubating and I'm useless. I can't transmogrify or fly."

*I can barely walk, never mind about flying. My waddle is so bad anyone would take me for a guarvee not a sachan or Ellkiiyn.*

"I have no problem with flying to Lycidea. We should be back shortly after lunor disc rise," Larkin said. "Will you be all right, Taminisha, here by yourself?"

Taminisha tugged her habilan closer around her. "I'll be fine. You won't be gone long."

Larkin glanced at the sky. "As soon as it is dark we shall be off."

A shiver of unease whispered across Taminisha skin as she watched them soar into the lunor drift gloom. The servants had retreated to their quarters or the village for their rest and Ulyana remained sequestered in her nest. The castle echoed with emptiness just like Taminisha's soul.

 Even Kikishan's heart beat beside her own, brought no comfort. She worried about her son as he struggled to breathe, and lay lethargic in her arms, the fever burning in his body and sapping him of life. Even Aiyana had deteriorated in the last hours. They both whimpered and stirred restlessly

Taminisha laid them side by side in the big cradle. A terrible weight of responsibility for both children burdened Taminisha and a flash of anger sparked at Ulyana for placing her in this position.

Taminisha soon tired of pacing with her bloated body so she curled up in the middle of her big bed and hugged the blankets around her to ward off the physical cold, and the emotional emptiness. In an attempt to distract herself, she worked on a new cloak to welcome Kikishan home. With the quiet surrounds, she soon became absorbed in the creation of the intricate pattern that would tell the story of their mating.

A faint shuffle disturbed the quiet. Then silence. A sharp click on stone. Taminisha stared at the closed door. She laid her hand protectively on her belly and carefully slid out of bed. Both the children slept soundly even though Jivin snored slightly through his congested airways. She tiptoed to the cradle and stood in front of it, watching the door.

Again, the soft shuffle and a click of claws on rock.

*Surely, Larkin had not returned so soon. Had something happened to them? Who else could it be, but them?*

Fearing then for Ulyana's safety she stumbled to the door and threw it open. "Larkin, are you..."

Ulyana loomed up in the doorway as Ellkiiyn. She blasted fire through the opening. Taminisha's habilan caught alight. Taminisha shrieked as she ripped it off and threw it to the floor. She couldn't transmogrify or spit flame to defend herself. She backed away, panting out short breaths of hot air. The room reeled, receded, and then swung back into focus. Blood pounded in her ears.

"Ulyana, what is this?" she shouted. "What is this?"

Ulyana laughed, transmogrified and charged at the door.

Taminisha slapped at the door in an effort to close it.

Jivin squealed.

Taminisha backed up.

Ulyana followed her, pushing through the doorway before she transmogrified to Ellkiiyn again.

As she pushed the timbers of the tower roof upward with her shoulders, she lashed out at Taminisha with clawed feet.

Taminisha whimpered as one claw sliced down her bare shoulder and arm. She clutched her injured arm and retreated.

Ulyana laughed as she pulled her lips back from pointed Ellkiiyn teeth. "Nyket will rule here soon. My soul mate."

"But Larkin's your…"

Ulyana cackled, and then screeched with laughter. "Larkin is my twin sister's soul mate. Gullible male so easy to fool; he wanted a soul mate so badly. Well he'll never get Nysiah, for she's dead." Another crack of maniacal laughter sliced through the air.

Ulyana lunged.

Taminisha grabbed a spear off the wall, with a sudden burst of action, and stabbed toward her attacker. The thrust didn't come close. Sweat beaded on her skin and she tightened her grip with clammy hands. Struggling to remain upright she shouted, "You will not harm the babies. You will not."

"Ha, only yours."

"Never." Taminisha lunged again with the spear.

A rush of wind gusted past her face. A screech shattered her hearing and she tipped off balance with a weight on her shoulder. She glanced sideways. Jivin, as Ellkiiyn perched precariously by her face claws digging into the flesh of her upper arm.

"No, Jivin love," she cried.

Ulyana swiped massive claws within inches of her son's face.

Taminisha reached up to snatch him to safety.

He sidled away and spat a stream of flame directly into Ulyana's face.

The red Ellkiiyn swiped at her face then charged.

Jivin spat again.

Ulyana shrieked as the fire caught her directly in one eye.

Jivin clung to Taminisha's shoulder and spat repeatedly.

Ulyana staggered sideways swiping at singed scales and her blistered eye lids.

Careful of her son Taminisha gripped the spear tight and charged. The sharply honed barb hit Ulyana in the neck, the special hardened metal cracking open her red scales. Red blood squirted out onto the floor.

Ulyana screeched, stumbled, and flailed the air with her claws as her knees buckled.

Taminisha backed away.

Jivin clung tenaciously to her shoulder. His grip weakened as his baby strength faded.

Taminisha swept him off her shoulder, kissed his snout, and dumped him in the middle of the bed. Cursing her swollen belly, she stretched up and ripped a second spear off the wall. Holding it with both hands, she charged again at the disorientated Ulyana.

The red Ellkiiyn fell to her knees. Her eyes were red and blistered from Jivin's blasts of fire, but they still sparked fury. Her tail continued to lash the floor.

Taminisha ran as fast as her burdened body would allow, and rammed the second blade deep into Ulyana's neck just below the other.

More blood bubbled out. A huge pool of crimson flooded the floor. Ulyana blindly flailed the air with razor sharp claws.

Taminisha retreated and searched for another weapon. She tore a bar from the cradle and faced her foe. She paused.

Ulyana wavered where she kneeled, fluid poured out of her eyes.

Her sight obscured by milky blisters. "I have failed. I'm sorry, my love." Ulyana gasped for breath. Her head drooped. She searched for the floor, and then crumpled.

Taminisha stood motionless, the stake held out in front of her.

Jivin made tiny screeching noises on the bed and Aiyana stirred.

It seemed to take forever, but finally Ulyana laid her head down and closed her eyes.

Dull cramps grabbed inside her abdomen and Taminisha flinched. Their presence sparked trepidation. She tried to ignore them. With one eye on the unmoving Ulyana, she snatched up Aiyana and Jivin, still in Ellkiiyn form, and scuttled from the room. She put them on the floor long enough to lock the door behind her and prop a chair under the handle.

Grabbing up a screaming Aiyana under one arm and tucking the bulk of Jivin's Ellkiiyn body under the other she carried both squirming children and waddled as fast as she could toward the nesting room. Sometime during the terrifying climb up the stone staircase, Jivin transmogrified. She sighed with relief as he weighed a lot less in sachan form. With the extra burden and her huge lumbering body, she could barely drag her legs up to mount each step. Her back ached.

The door to the nesting room stood open; she went through and staggered to the empty nest.

She laid the children on the soft padding and went back to lock the door. She inspected the room and saw the precious egg smashed against the wall. The beautiful blue shell had disintegrated into a dozen pieces and in the middle of the inner filling laid a baby Ellkiiyn, no bigger than Taminisha's hand. It did not move. Her heart clenched and a burning anger speared through her. *How could she kill her own child? Why had she even bred again? Poor Larkin, how will he bear it?* Her hands trembled as she swept up a spare habilan hanging on a chair and laid it over the mess.

Her stomach churned.

She raced to the nearest container and vomited into it, sullying the large fragments of shell stored there.

Both children howled.

Taminisha tamped down her dismal thoughts and stumbled back to the bed. She had no bovinite milk, so she put one child to each of her almost dry breasts and lay back against the pillows to wait for help. What insignificant amount of milk she had seemed enough to ease their immediate hunger and as they quieted, she laid them together and threw a rug over top to keep them warm.

The cramping in her lower abdomen intensified. Dull aching cramps came and went every few minutes. With the discomfort still bearable, she crawled under the covers and tried to rest her body in preparation for the labour to come. Dread held her muscles tense. Her mind sparked with alertness as she listened for further attack, or the welcome sound of Larkin and Clyeva's return.

Ulyana was either, already dead or fatally injured, but Taminisha had been too afraid to confirm it. Horror seeped through her at the horrendous deed Ulyana had committed. A terrible suspicion filtered into her mind. Ulyana loved Aiyana, the child of her soul mate. The child of Nyket. Poor Larkin. Taminisha had no doubt Ulyana had duped him, but never the less, both deaths would devastate him.

As she lay there she realised the mist had cleared, the children already breathed easier. In the clarity of hindsight, she suspected the whole thing with the mist had been a ruse to get her alone.

Ulyana had planned all along to take over control of Kelkiki in Nyket's name while they were vulnerable.

Taminisha moaned as her heart clenched against the vicious torment of betrayal. With a rush of dismay, she realised Nyket didn't just want Aikanshin, but Kelkiki and probably all the lands in between. He planned to rule the whole of Dykarin with a savage dictatorship.

Tears filled her eyes and slipped down her cheeks—for herself, her children, and those who would suffer in the future. Those who were gone were best out of it.

The pains grew more severe making her whole abdomen harden.

She curled up in a foetal position and tried to muffle her cries.

The children slept on.

Taminisha rubbed her belly as Kikishan had done when she laid her egg. When that failed to ease her pain, she climbed out of the nest and walked, slowly, half-bent while she massaged her back as best she could.

As each contraction clutched at her she paused and tried to breathe in slow breaths. When it passed she walked again. An icy cold gripped her, so she pulled on another habilan. Round and round she waddled, at times staggering, staying close to the nest just in case she collapsed under the appalling pain wrenching through her.

Through one of the open arches, she watched the lunor discs rise, and sobbed as she scanned the sky through tear-filled eyes for any sign of Larkin's return. Foreboding speared through her. Maybe Larkin would not return with Clyeva. If he had been part of the plot, Clyeva might be dead, drowned in the lake or broken on the beaches of Lycidea. *Great Spirit Ellkii! Such a betrayal would be more than I could bear. Dear Clyeva, I need you, come back safe.*

Taminisha walked until she could no longer manage. Her knees shook so badly they would not hold her upright as cramp after cramp ripped through her.

Clyeva had explained what would happen to her body and sort of what to expect but her friend had been rather skimpy on the amount of pain involved and the time it would take. She had told her when delivery of the baby drew close she would feel the desire to push. Clyeva had assured her she would recognise it when the time came.

Taminisha assumed it would be like birthing an egg. Taminisha hunched on the edge of the nest, and watched the lunor discs drifting across the sky. The agony of the birthing process held her trembling and incapacitated. Fear of the unknown confused her thought processes. Sweat poured from her brow. Sickness roiled around the sting of terror in her gut. *I can't do this on my own. Clyeva come back to me. Help me.*

Another greater fear hammered at her. Even with Ulyana dead, she remained petrified her thwarted efforts were not the end of the plot to take Kelkiki Castle. Were there other mixed blood Ellkiiyn just waiting to pounce? Advancing on the castle right now, as she lay trembling in agony?

Taminisha tried to gather her thoughts. *Where are you, Clyeva?* The locked door would hold them for a while, but not long enough. She glanced around the room but saw nothing suitable to use as a weapon. She sagged back; tears stung her eyes and blurred her vision.

Her physical helplessness as she prepared to birth her child had stripped her abilities, her strength and her independence away taking her courage with it. *I never want to feel so vulnerable again.*

She wondered briefly how soon her transmogrification ability would be restored. At least, as Ellkiiyn, she had a chance to defend herself, and the three babies.

The five lunor discs had risen to their full height when the urge to push took control of her body forcing her to bear down. Taminisha squatted by the nest using it to lean against and pushed. A scream ripped from her throat. She choked it back as the whoosh of leathery wings, and the thump of landing feet reverberated through the castle. Taminisha clamped her mouth shut determined to remain silent until she confirmed it was Larkin and Clyeva.

"Taminisha, where are you?"

Taminisha cried out. "In the nesting room, come quickly. Clyeva, for Spirits' sake, help me!"

Taminisha grunted as nature forced her to bear down. A howl of agony ripped from her throat. She grunted and groaned.

"Great Fire Nymph, you've locked the door! Unlock it."

"I can't."

"Break it down, Larkin."

Two great thumps and a sharp crack brought hurried footsteps and Larkin and Clyeva to her side by the bed. They stared down at her.

Larkin frowned. "Where is Ulyana, the egg?"

Despite her misery, Taminisha couldn't stop from glancing at the rug.

He followed her gaze and glared at the rug-covered mess by the wall before he knelt beside Clyeva.

Clyeva lowered her head and peered between Taminisha's legs. "Keep pushing."

Taminisha pushed down when the compulsion came. The place between her legs stretched and expanded until she thought it would burst. The agony, the tightness and the relentless cramp in her abdomen were unbearable. She wanted to die.

"Push, girl, push. Nearly there," Clyeva cried.

Sweat poured from her body. A guttural cry ripped from her throat.

Both babies, already woken by Taminisha's first cries, began to wail.

Taminisha pushed again and felt something happen, break or ease. She pushed again.

"Your babe is here love, relax, you've done your job,' Clyeva said.

Bathed in sweat, her knees shaking Taminisha slid slowly to the floor. Her purple blood pooled around her. She felt another uncomfortable twinge, and more mess eased out between her legs. This time a mixture of blue and purple—the blood of the child, and the mother.

Taminisha wanted to move away, but she didn't have the strength. She shivered. Her legs trembled, and her body ached.

The baby let out a loud squeal. Clyeva held out the squirming child wrapped in her cloak. Taminisha took the bundle in her arms as tears poured down her face. She had a daughter. As the child sought the breast Taminisha stroked her downy head and let her suckle, totally exhausted, but elated. With no debate this time about the right to live, she could relax and fall in love with her daughter.

Whether her child could transmogrify into Ellkiiyn, or not, would be something for the future. Taminisha thought about Kikishan, and her heart cringed at the fact he could not share the miracle of her birth with her. She knew he would not realise he had another child unless he came home safe.

"She needs a name, but it seems wrong to name her without her father."

Clyeva paused in the process of cleaning up the birthing mess. "She should be named, Taminisha, for without a name, a stray jinnexa could possess her."

Taminisha hugged her baby closer to her breast. "Then I shall name her after Kikishan's beloved mother. He cannot be dissatisfied with my choice." She kissed her daughter's downy head. "I name thee Millinsha, after your paternal grandmother."

"A good choice," Larkin stated as he paced the room with the older children in his arms. He kept glancing at the blanket-covered mess.

Taminisha knew he wanted answers. Those answers would hurt and confuse him, but he had to wait. She needed only a short time to celebrate her joy before she faced the horror in the corner of the room. Staying quiet, she lay back and kept her eyes closed.

Clyeva efficiently cleaned up all evidence of the birth then signalled Larkin to carry Taminisha and her new child to her own room.

"No, Clyeva, the guest room," Taminisha mumbled. "It must be the guest room."

Clyeva frowned, but silently waved Larkin back the other way. She followed with one child under each arm, both wriggling and howling in frustration and hunger.

With Taminisha settled, Larkin went down to prepare milk for the two older children.

Clyeva fussed and fretted around her and the baby. She wanted to know what had happened, but had the good sense not to ask questions until Larkin returned. With the children suckling, and finally quiet, Larkin faced her.

"Where is Ulyana? Did you break our egg?"

Taminisha flinched but looked directly at Larkin. "I'm sorry, but Ulyana is dead. I killed her defending myself."

Larkin glared at her. "She would never have left the egg."

"She broke the egg, and came to kill me and Jivin, also maybe Aiyana. She was Nyket's soul mate not yours…"

"No. I heard the heartbeat; I still hear her heartbeat…" He fell silent as the magnitude of what he'd just said struck him. Ulyana's death should have left an aching hole nothing could fill.

"How?" he asked.

"She has a twin, but Ulyana claimed Nyket had killed her. Perhaps this twin is your true soul mate."

Larkin studied his daughter. "What about Aiyana? Surely that had to be genuine?"

"Are you sure Aiyana is even yours?" Clyeva asked bluntly. "Ulyana birthed that egg immediately after you joined, but she could have mated another and held the birth back until she arrived at Kelkiki."

Taminisha remembered the eggshells she'd seen. Larkin came from the same bloodline as Kikishan so they should have been a clear deep blue. The fragments in the tub had been the colour of the lake waters, blue-green on the outside, but red on the inside.

"Of course she's mine. Ulyana and I joined."

"But …"

Taminisha touched Clyeva's arm, and shook her head. Clyeva fell silent despite being obviously unhappy about the situation. At that moment, Taminisha could not bear to destroy Larkin's hope for the future.

"Larkin, go now, and secure the castle. Prepare the armoury, add extra guards to the parapet walk, I fear further trouble. Also send the servants here for instructions."

Larkin scowled. "I will see my mate's body first."

"No Larkin, Clyeva will see to all that, and then when she is laid out ready for Spirit you can mourn her and your child. Now go, do as I instruct."

Larkin glared at her, but she saw the tears in his eyes as he walked away to do her bidding. She wished to spare him the ugliness of his soul mate's damaged body. No father needed to handle the corpse of his child amongst the mess of the egg sack. There would be time enough for his expressions of grief when the bodies had been prepared.

As the door shut behind him, Clyeva stepped forward. "Who is the father of the babe?" she asked pointing at Aiyana."

"I cannot say for sure, but, Ulyana claimed Nyket was her soul mate and the father of her child. From the egg fragments in the nesting room, I would believe her claim. Aiyana is Nyket's."

"Then she must die."

"She is, but an innocent babe. Look at her," Taminisha said, pointing at the sleeping child.

Clyeva did, and tears poured down her face.

"Could you murder this child?"

Clyeva winced. "No. But she is Nyket's."

"Yes, by genetics, but she will be Larkin's by nurture. He will bring her to adulthood in the right way."

Clyeva shrugged. "Perhaps she has a part to play in destiny."

"Maybe. Now go and prepare the bodies. My room will become Ulyana's tomb. She is of Infernea, but we cannot burn her in the castle nor shift her until we have help. At least Larkin can mourn her and the child."

For two solar phasings, Larkin sat in solitude by the body of his mate and child. Then he came to Taminisha.

"I cannot mourn longer when my heart beats for another. It is time to seal the room," he said.

"And Aiyana?"

A shadow of sadness darkened his face. "I suspect Aiyana is not of my bloodline, but I love her, and will raise her as my own. It is not for me to direct her destiny."

Taminisha nodded. "You have made a good decision, Larkin, and soon your soul mate shall find you and you will know love."

"I shall pass Ulyana's Rykala locket to Aiyana, for no matter how evil, I believed Ulyana loved her daughter."

"Yes Larkin, I believe she did." Taminisha didn't comment on the fact Ulyana loved her daughter because she was the child of her soul mate, Nyket.

# Chapter Eighteen

The first beaten and wounded began to arrive six solar phasings later. Their stories of the battle were stark and gut wrenching. They had freed Kylara, at least temporarily, but had not been able to defeat Nyket. Everyone talked in horror of the attacks by the swarms of mercenary Ellkiiyn. No one knew where they had come from or where they went after the battle.

Tabro arrived. He had no news of Kikishan, but advised the boats would arrive within the next few solar phasings. He had also found a mate of his own kind; a little brown Ellkiiyn, who appeared even more effeminate than Tabro. Ikaya had significantly tainted blood, but Taminisha figured it didn't matter, as they could not breed anyway. Tabro broke down in tears as he related the terrible battles and the injuries that maimed or killed.

"Taminisha, they came, silent in the darkness, with scales all colours of the rainbow, some full blood, but most obviously carrying tainted bloodlines. My dear sweet Ellkii, they came again, and again. The viciousness of the attacks were unprecedented, no mercy shown for any, no prisoners taken. Indescribable, my lady, and then we attacked the castle..." Tabro broke down in tears.

"Tabro, go and rest. Is Enian back?"

Tabro's expression crumpled and tears trickled down his cheeks. "I last saw her at the castle."

Adakin arrived with several of Kikishan's mixed blood Ellkiiyn in sachan form on his back. He carried a deep slash to his back leg and, once he crash-landed on the rocky shore of the lake, they could not move him.

Taminisha hurried down the narrow stone steps to him. Her breath squeezed tight in her lungs. Surely, Adakin had news of the battle.

"Adakin, tell me of Kikishan," she pleaded as the two Myattican Ellkiiyn cross breeds tended his wounds.

"I saw him leave Aikanshin Castle, but he carried horrendous wounds inflicted in his one on one battle with Nyket."

"*He fought Nyket*? Great Spirit, how did he survive? I know he lives because I feel him here." Taminisha touched her left breast.

"He fought well, my lady—with so much tenacity, despite the odds against him.  As he fled, he must have realised he wouldn't make it to Zynumin, and I saw him change direction and glide toward Myattica. Enian and another Ellkiiyn assisted him. He would have surely landed safely. Adakin shrugged. "But I do not know how the Myatticans would have received his uninvited visit."

"They would care for him, Ellkiiyn, do not doubt that," Sadrina snapped as she dressed Adakin's wounds.

"Ouch, Sadrina. No offense meant – but we are an impressive creature to be just dropping by, especially in this time of strife."

"I know, Adakin, but my people are used to us."

Adakin blushed, knowing his words had unintentionally hurt

Sadrina.

"And Shula is Tarlitek's sister and Mazin, his brother. I am sure if Kikishan has landed he will be restored to health," Taminisha said quietly. "He should not have tackled Nyket alone. Nyket is not only young, fit, and battle trained, he is ruthless." Her heart clenched. She took a deep breath and held it. Faint, but definite, her soul mate's heartbeat fluttered beside her own.

Over the next few phasings several other Ellkiiyn landed with thuds and skids on the shore, many of them grievously wounded. Ellkiiyn sized wounds that would kill them if they transmogrified to sachan form. Sadrina, and her mate, Takash, hurried from one to the other instructing the smaller less capable souls how to help the wounded and the dying.

It broke Taminisha's heart to see so many of her people hurting so badly. As she turned away, Avyvah arrived. Four younger women carried her along the beach on a litter.

Taminisha bowed slightly to her as she climbed off the litter.

"I have come to help. I have brought my two daughters and my granddaughters. We will do what we can."

"Thank you, Avyvah, for caring."

The old woman gave a toothless smile. "If he should come, we will all suffer, and life will not be as it should. If it comes to pass, I for one will be glad to meet death in the near future."

"We cannot be defeated, Avyvah. Nyket's rule would be intolerable."

"And wither the true blood Ellkiiyn to the detriment of all of us," the old woman said. "It is written. Only the Daughter of Kylara can bring restoration."

Fear shuffled across Taminisha's skin. *The Daughter of Kylara.* She had no idea what it all meant, but she feared for her future, and that of her offspring, at the whisper of her name.

"We will fight to survive, Avyvah," she replied.

The old woman bowed her head. "And so you should, my lady," she mumbled.

Taminisha stayed silent as she walked away, unable to find the words, or the strength to refute the old woman's predictions.

Every chance she got Taminisha scoured the sky for any sight of Kikishan. His slightly discordant heartbeat confirmed he still lived. She tried to keep occupied with her children and the management of the realm, but it failed to distract her completely.

Jivin had grown so much. He walked, giggled and spoke some words in sachan form, and transmogrified at will. He preferred Ellkiiyn form because it allowed him more freedom and more maturity in his interactions with the world. Millinsha fed and slept just as a sachan babe should. She already smiled and cooed when paid attention. Taminisha wondered from time to time if her tiny daughter could transmogrify, but didn't worry too much because she just loved her so. Clyeva doted on her and insisted in calling her Milli, saying the name suited her cheekiness better. Taminisha soon found she used the nickname more often than her full name.

In the end, Larkin didn't really grieve for Ulyana.

"I feel a heartbeat of a slightly different tattoo beating in my chest since Ulyana's death. It's very similar, but softer, less sure," he said as he left the tomb for the last time.

His willingness to move forward relieved Taminisha's guilt to some extent. "So you can tell the difference?"

"I feel a fool for being duped."

"I have no idea how they did it, but obviously it seemed very real to you at the time."

Larkin touched his chest. "I will make absolutely certain next time."

Unsure of when that would be, he threw himself into being a doting father and Aiyana provided joy to everyone near her.

Jivin and Aiyana played together all the time. They only quarrelled if Jivin transmogrified in the middle of a game and scared her. She did not attempt to copy him. Taminisha wondered about the child's ability considering her father had tainted blood. She kept her concerns to herself, not wanting to upset Larkin's hard-earned serenity.

The solar orb had not peeped over the horizon yet, but Taminisha gave into her restlessness. Desperate for his comfort, she'd convinced herself during the lunor drift Kikishan's heartbeat felt stronger than before. After feeding Milli, she paced the parapet walk. A movement in the sky caught her attention; she ran out onto the terrace and peered through the soft translucent awakening light. A smudgy block of colour against the sky—a blue, darker than the sky, with a touch of red. *Could it be?* She clutched her heart aware in that instant of a stronger beat completely in harmony with her own as the smudge became more defined movement approaching the castle. She stared out over the lake. Now she could make out two, no, three Ellkiiyn. The biggest appeared to struggle, only staying in the air with the support of the second blue one. She could just make out a faded red Ellkiiyn, trailing alongside. Fear flared in her breast. She did not want another red Ellkiiyn in her home. She paced, wringing her hands and staring at the Ellkiiyn in the sky. As the solar orb awakened and lit the sky with bright light, she could see clearly.

"Kikishan, my heart, my soul," she cried.

A shout went up from below. Others had seen them. Larkin took off from the adjacent parapet walk.

Clyeva raced into the room. "I have the babes, Taminisha, go. Go greet your soul mate."

Taminisha didn't even glance over her shoulder as she tucked, rolled and with a strong downward movement of her wings she took off from the parapet. As she soared toward the group, she cried out.

Kikishan lifted his head and howled in reply.

As she got closer, Taminisha could see clearly Kikishan laboured under terrible half healed injuries. Taminisha cringed at the sight. Tremendous great slashes down his back and both legs seemed crippled and tucked up near his abdomen. Taminisha spared only a brief glance at the smaller, paler Ellkiiyn. There would be plenty of time for introductions when she had her soul mate safe.

Enian struggled to sustain her flight and support Kikishan so Larkin eased himself in beside Enian.

As he took the weight, Enian eased out. She faltered and sank before she steadied.

Taminisha eased herself under Enian and together they flew to the castle.

Even with Larkin's bearing most of his weight Kikishan thudded heavily on the terrace after just clearing the parapet. He lay there calling for Taminisha, but making no effort to rise or transmogrify.

Already transmogrified she threw herself down beside his head and wrapped her short sachan arms around his huge face. She kissed his snout.

"My love, you are home. I will make you well again," she sobbed against his scaly skin.

"We lost, my love; Nyket is terribly injured, but alive. He called in mercenaries; we had no chance against these trained killers. I'm sorry, I've failed you," he whispered.

"No, my love, you have no need to be sorry. Kylara is free again, and even if Aikanshin is still in Nyket's hands, I believe Aikanshin will be free in time. For now, you must heal."

"The boats are coming." The cry came from the shore of the lake.

Larkin immediately took off and made a low sweep, then again, before he returned. "Our boats have many injured. However, Clyeva, I see Tarlitek is at the helm of the last boat. He is well."

Clyeva burst into sooty tears. "Great Fire Nymphs, he has come back to me."

"Go Clyeva, see Tarlitek, and then treat the wounded. I can manage here."

Clyeva fled with a transmogrified Larkin right behind her. Enian transmogrified into sachan form and limped over to Taminisha's side.

"I think he just needs rest and food. A Myattican female called Shula healed him as best she could. She sends her greetings to you."

Taminisha sat back on her heels already seeing the familiar stitching on her mate's scaly skin. He would scar as she had, but it would not matter. She looked up at Enian. "Thank you for bringing him back to me. I hear there were some fierce battles and Nyket survives to rise again."

Enian scowled. "Kikishan almost annihilated Nyket. They were both on their last when a renegade Ellkiiyn flew in and jumped Kikishan. The renegade's claws ripped Kikishan's back open before he could throw him off. By then Nyket had run for shelter. I attacked his foe until he broke free, but we had to fly away to survive. There were too many of them, all trained fighters."

"Perhaps we were somewhat naive going into this battle. Nyket is determined to conquer, and plenty of mixed-blood Ellkiiyn support his sentiments. He would have had plenty of recruits for reinforcements. Never mind, Enian, you and Kikishan, have come home, safe."

"We will know better, next time," Enian muttered.

Taminisha did not want to think of next time, but she knew already there would be one. She appraised the smaller Ellkiiyn standing off to the side. Taminisha started back from the familiar features. She jumped to her feet and pointed at the young woman with the red hair and green eyes. "Lock her up, she's a traitor. One of Nyket's spies."

"Taminisha, no," Enian scolded as she moved between them. "This is Nysiah; I rescued her from Nyket's clutches."

Taminisha advanced. She pushed Enian out of the way and stood toe to toe with Nysiah. "I know who she is. She is twin sister to Ulyana, murderess, conspirator, and Nyket's soul mate. I shall see you dead like her. You will not harm my babies!" Taminisha raged, right in the cringing female's face.

Nysiah dropped to her knees, huge sobs buffeted her shoulders. "I am not her. Ulyana shamed me with her evil, unwise choices."

Fury surged through Taminisha. She refused to accept the sister had not colluded in the plot. "Your twin deceived Larkin. I don't believe she could do this without your assistance. The subterfuge of the love call. How?"

Nysiah shrugged. "I am not sure, but Nyket kept me in chains, dosed with a potion that drained me of bodily strength and mental focus."

"Really. To what end?"

Nysiah peeped up at Taminisha. "They took my free will. I do not know how Ulyana tricked Larkin."

Taminisha stepped back a pace. The desire to spit fire at the kneeling woman threatened to overtake her. She bit it back. She dredged up a shred of her natural compassion. If Nysiah had been Nyket's victim, shouldn't she feel sympathy for her, not hatred? She sighed. The betrayal ran too deep making it hard to move on. Surely even Larkin would reject this Ellkiiyn's call of love. "Liar. Your sister's guilt is yours."

"You cannot just pronounce guilt. Yes, she is Nysiah, but she has done no wrong," Enian asserted.

"Yes, Taminisha, she has done no wrong." Tarlitek echoed Enian's words from the doorway.

Taminisha ran into Tarlitek's arms.

He hugged her tight before easing her away. "Nysiah saved my life. She is Nyket's victim also, and she is Larkin's true soul mate. All this you will have to accept."

Taminisha pointed to Nysiah, "Her twin sister came here on the pretext of being Larkin's soul mate. She then tried to kill me, and my son. She killed her own child conceived with Larkin."

"You can't blame the sister."

"Maybe, but I do not want her around the babies. I do not, I cannot, trust her."

Nysiah remained on her knees, tears coursing down her cheeks as they squabbled over her.

Enian stepped forward. "Obviously there are things to be sorted, and I understand your distrust, Taminisha. I am sure Nysiah is willing to be confined to her room with a guard for the time being—until things are clearer."

Taminisha glared at the pink Ellkiiyn. "The dungeons."

Tarlitek frowned. "Taminisha, please. A tower room in the bailey will do. And a double guard."

Sobs cramped her ribs behind her fury and confusion, and uncertainty swamped her. With her fear for Kikishan eating at her, she didn't have the strength to fight their resistance to her orders. "Fine, but if anything untoward happens to the babies, you will all pay with your lives."

Tarlitek and Enian both inclined their heads in acceptance of her edict.

Enian took Nysiah's arm and led her away.

Taminisha dropped to her knees by her soul mate, laid her head on his shoulder and sobbed until she could cry no more. She didn't hear Tarlitek leave the terrace or Tabro enter.

Sometime later, her child's cry cut through her lethargy like a honed blade. She lifted her head and listened. *Milli*. She climbed to her feet struggling with the stiffness. Taminisha felt so torn, she wanted to be by her soul mate's side, but her child needed her.

Kikishan stirred a fractionally in his drugged sleep, but didn't awaken.

She smiled at Tabro. "Take care of him, Tabro; I will return soon, my daughter needs feeding."

Tabro frowned. "A daughter ?

Taminisha smiled. "Yes the sachan way."

Tabro's frown dissolved into a wide grin. "Well I never—a daughter for the Guardian the sachan way. I shall not move, my lady, until you come back."

She entered the room to find all three of the children red faced and screaming. Jivin stood up in his cradle, bouncing up and down as he bawled tears streaming down his face. Aiyana had pushed herself up against the bars of the cradle and she waved her clenched fists in the air wailing in high-pitched cries. Milli whimpered in her cradle, still wrapped tight in her blankets.

Taminisha hugged Jivin and Aiyana as she passed, promising them food. She picked up Millie and put her to her breast, just as Larkin barged through the door with warm bovinite milk and a young female Ellkiiyn called Flatasha.

Larkin gave a bottle and Jivin to Flatasha, and then sat down next to Taminisha on the edge of the bed. He cuddled Aiyana as she fed. He didn't look toward Taminisha, as he began to speak. "I know Aiyana is not mine. I know you, and Clyeva, have had doubts. I know. I saw the eggshell even though Ulyana tried to hide it. It appeared to be blue, but I could see the green tinge. I got distracted when Aiyana transmogrified and since then I have talked myself into believing I fathered her. I had a Terraid mother so I justified the colour. I know, and now accept Ulyana had already joined with another before she arrived here. I suspected it, but I fell so madly in love. Not with her, in reality, but the idea of having a soul mate, and a family. I'm not young, and I thought I had no chance to breed. I'm sorry I put you, and Jivin, in danger."

"Larkin, you were not to know Ulyana deceived you. In the end, it won't matter if Aiyana is your bloodline or not, she will be your daughter, she is your daughter.

"I hope so."

"Just one question, Larkin, I need to know. What did Aiyana look like as Ellkiiyn – normal, and did she transmogrify in the required time?"

Larkin blushed bright red.

Taminisha knew the answer.

"Larkin?"

"She seemed normal as Ellkiiyn, even red like her mother, but her eyes weren't quite right. We waited, and when she didn't transmogrify for quite a while, I tried to end it, but Ulyana threatened to cut my throat if I touched her. Now I could not, because I love her."

"Larkin, promise me one thing. Love your daughter with all your heart, but she must never answer if called by a Guardian. Imprison her if you have to. She is of tainted blood."

216

"But Ulyana was full blood," Larkin protested.

"That may be, but her father isn't."

"Her father? You know this?"

"I suspect, but do not trouble yourself."

"You will not tell me, so Aiyana is never to know her true bloodlines?"

"It is best if she does not. In fact, it is critical she does not know. She must always believe her bloodline is yours."

Larkin cuddled his daughter closer to his chest. "And later, if she transmogrifies, and her paternal bloodlines show?"

Nausea gathered in her gut. "Even if she shows her father's bloodlines, it will not reveal his identity, only his tainted blood. You might have to take the blame if it shows."

"I can bear such an insult to save my daughter upset," Larkin said quietly.

Taminisha smiled. "I hope in the future there will be no shame to tainted bloodlines. Such things have to change if the Ellkiiyn Clans... or even we as species are to survive. Now we must never speak of this again."

Taminisha laid Milli back in her cradle, her eyes already closing in sleep.

The door opened and Tarlitek entered.

"Your son is a strong, Taminisha. I hear from Clyeva he transmogrifies at will."

She grinned. Her son's ability amazed all in the castle. "He does, but come, meet my daughter."

Tarlitek glanced over her shoulder, and then looked at Larkin still nursing Aiyana.

He seemed startled. "But how..."

Taminisha chuckled. "I carried, and birthed her, the sachan way. I didn't even know I carried a babe until after you had all left. With it already too late for the Ellkiiyn way I had no choice and I didn't mind really."

"Well you are a clever little thing, aren't you?"

"I am," Taminisha said with a smile. "Now Tarlitek, you have news of Jabrikan?"

Tarlitek nodded. "He is safe in Tarneta. My cousin, Tahir, a three quarter blood Vaprus Ellkiiyn Myattican cross has him disguised as his nephew. He makes jewellery under Tahir's supervision and studies Ellkiiyn law."

"This is good news. When the time is right we will install him in the role of Guardian."

"By the way, I have something for you." Tarlitek reached into his pocket. A high pitched screech burst out. Tarlitek yelped and ripped his hand out of his jacket. A very angry Tarki clung to his thumb.

"Potokin!" Taminisha lunged forward her hands held out. "I never thought to see you again. Thank you for bringing him back to me. Come to Mamam, my pet."

"Sharp-toothed, and decidedly ungrateful fiend," Tarlitek grumbled as Potokin released his thumb and leapt the space between them to land on Taminisha's shoulder. "Never did take to the animal."

She smiled at her indignant hallegan and hugged the Tarki to her breast. A sense of contentment seeped through her. Her life was complete. She rubbed her face in Potokin's gritty skin. He wriggled closer. "Where did you find him?"

"Jabrikan had him, but Tahir said the little monster fretted so badly they feared for his wellbeing so I brought him back with me."

"Thank you, thank you. I've really missed him. He will be a good guard for the children when they're moving around."

"You're going to trust that bad tempered beast around the children?" Tarlitek screwed his face up in disapproval.

Taminisha stroked Potokin and smiled. "Yes, I am. In addition, I'm releasing both of you from duty forth with. It is time you and Clyeva have some time together. I will tend Kikishan through the lunor drift, and Flatasha can be nearby for the children.

Taminisha returned to Kikishan's side and there she stayed for ten solar phasings, feeding, warming him and bathing his wounds. She only left his side for the short periods it took to manage the realm, and be with her children.

At first, she didn't know what to do about or with Nysiah. She pondered on the whole debacle through the long hours with Kikishan. Ulyana's acts had destroyed what minute trust she'd retained. She finally had to admit she could not blame Nysiah for Ulyana any more than any could blame her for Nyket's actions. It didn't seem fair to keep her locked with such revengeful determination. Besides Larkin's moping around made him next to useless. She guessed his need to join with his soul mate tortured him; the persistent heartbeat beside his own must be driving him crazy. Apprehension shadowed her thoughts and remained like a misty wraith around her final decision. She had to give Nysiah a chance.

Still uneasy, Taminisha called him to her. "Larkin, despite my misgivings I'm going to release Nysiah into your care. You are a loyal member of this household, cousin of Kikishan and good friend to me in hard times. You deserve the blessings of a mate—this time, a true soul mate."

Larkin fell to his knees. "My lady, you are compassionate and wise. I will always remember your kindness, and be here to help you in times of need. I assure you, Nysiah will also be loyal to you. I promise if there is any doubt I will kill her myself."

"Well off you go and enjoy your love for the first time. And Larkin, the nesting room is free, if needed."

As the lunor discs rose in the darkness of the sky, Taminisha heard the cries of Ellkiiyn love. She glanced up to the sky and saw Larkin and Nysiah twirling in the passionate throes of the mating dance. She watched for a moment as the big blue Ellkiiyn took his smaller mate gently in an embrace of clawed arms and penetrated her. She cried out in ecstasy and a shower of sparks engulfed them.

Taminisha put her head down and closed her eyes, finding the tender consummation of their love too intimate to watch. She snuggled close to her soul mate and prayed soon they would bond again in either Ellkiiyn passion or the tender, enthralling sachan mating act.

On the long lunor drifts she lay on the terrace with him, she transmogrified to be more comfortable and to supply some additional warmth to her ailing mate. They talked for hours, each relating their adventures, hurts and fears of the past solar phasings.

Kikishan could not get his head around the concept of Taminisha birthing their child the sachan way. Repeatedly, he expressed his amazement and pride that she achieved it successfully on her own.

Taminisha cried when he told her with great sadness the changes wrought on Aikanshin by Nyket and the subdued way the population lived from phasing to phasing afraid to protest any cruelties or tried to escape to Kylara or Myattica in the search of dignity and freedom.

At last, Kikishan had healed enough to transmogrify.

Tarlitek and Tabro helped him inside.

"Rest, my love, finally in the comfort of your own bed."

Kikishan held out his arms to her. "Come to me, Taminisha. Lie with me so I can wrap my arms around you."

Taminisha snuggled close to her mate, but she couldn't settle. There were too many uncertainties, too many unanswered questions. "What of the future, Kikishan, my heart? Will Nyket come; will he try to destroy us?"

Kikishan shook his head. "I do not know, my love. It is my shame I did not kill him at Aikanshin, as I should have. We will have to be forever on guard until we can gather a greater contingent of warriors and mount another offensive—a successful one this time."

"Jabrikan must be installed as Guardian. It is his right."

Kikishan gave her shoulder a gentle squeeze. "He will be, Taminisha. Now bring me my children. I would meet my youngest, and wish to see how Jivin has grown in my absence."

As he lay on the bed, Taminisha brought Jivin in first.

The child immediately transmogrified and flew around his father's head. After three circuits, he lost control and crashed into the pillows. He giggled and transmogrified back to his sachan form.

"Da, Da, I fly. See, I fly," Jivin shouted. He looked up at Taminisha with a cheeky grin. "I do fire for Da?" he asked.

Taminisha waved a finger at her son. "No Jivin. No, my sweetness. Da is unwell. No fire this time."

Jivin pouted, then giggling, he promptly plonked onto his father's chest and hugged him tightly, nuzzling all over his neck and face.

Kikishan hugged him back, tears filling his eyes.

Leaving the two together, she went and collected Milli from Flatasha and returned to the bedroom.

As Kikishan looked up his face transformed. He held out his arms for his daughter. As Taminisha placed her babe into her father's arms, Milli promptly squealed and clutched Kikishan's nose in one of her chubby fists.

Kikishan kissed her.

She squealed again, kicking her feet with enthusiasm. Sparks flashed, and Milli transmogrified to Ellkiiyn for the first time. The child cackled with laughter and spat a tiny stream of flame straight at her father's face.

Kikishan bellowed as the flame caught his eyebrows.

Taminisha leapt forward and patted the smouldering hair out. She immediately started to laugh as her daughter bounced up and down in her father's grip laughing hysterically at what she'd done.

"Ooops. Our children seem precocious for their ages," Taminisha said.

Kikishan laughed. "So it seems, my love." Then his laughter melted into tears as he held his son and his daughter in his arms. "Taminisha, we are the luckiest Ellkiiyn I know. A son and a daughter in just over a year. We are truly blessed by the Spirit and our love for each other."

Taminisha climbed onto the bed and lay close to her mate letting the two children climb all over them. *Yes, but for how long?*

# Chapter Nineteen

The calm continued through several solar phasings. Injured warriors continued to arrive at the castle.

After lengthy discussion with her and Tarlitek, Kikishan began preparations for a future battle. He instructed the blacksmith to make more weapons and all the youth of the village, regardless of their breeding to undertake training by Adakin and Tabro so they could fight alongside all Kelkiki Ellkiiyn.

Kikishan kept Larkin busy with preparations. Everyone knew of his growing melancholy because he and Nysiah had joined on two occasions now, but had not bred either time.

Taminisha sympathised with their sadness, but considering the uncertainty of the future, thought it might be for the best. Taminisha tried to shut the ultimate goal from her mind and concentrate on raising her children, but the undercurrent of war eroded any peace she could find.

Taminisha stood on the terrace enjoying the beautiful evening and the stunning vision of the solar orb sinking behind the waters of the lake. So peaceful on the surface, yet under the water were carnivorous Orunan and the ultimate killer of Kelkiki Lake, the gill breathers' monstrous deity, Orunikan.

Oventi Rock brooded, eerie in the distance. Whispered about and referred to as the island of no return it piqued Taminisha curiosity. She believed Potokin had come from the island, and his viciousness alone strengthened her belief in the myth.

She started as a hand touched her shoulder and spun around directly into Kikishan's embrace. They had not been able to join in any form for a long time. Suddenly Taminisha felt the spark, the need to transmogrify, the primitive pull of passion between them. She tried to pull away. With war imminent, it would be foolish for them to mate, but Kikishan felt it too. The passion exploded and dragged them both into Ellkiiyn form.

*I must resist. Must hold back. Now is not to time to breed.* She fought against the breeding urge, but already changes within her body had begun, instigated by the depth of their shared love.

With a sweep of leathery wings and a spring from muscular legs, they rose together into the darkness. The passion gripped them and they held each other tightly. Kikishan sought her opening with his prehensile member. They were both more than ready for this joining. He thrust deep inside her and she roared as a rush of pure ecstasy flooded through her.

His legs clutched her sides and she pressed ever nearer to his scaly belly. She wanted him deep inside her. They writhed and twisted, growling and roaring. Taminisha cried out as the height of her desire speared through her. She crashed her belly against his, feeling his hardness thumping into her. He roared and thrust. On that last plunge, his hot seed spilled inside her. They slowly floated down to the terrace only pulling apart as their feet touched. They transmogrified together and lay in each other's arms on the cold stone, revelling in the glorious satiation of their joining.

Two awakenings later Taminisha felt a familiar ache in her lower body. She tried to ignore it, but the nesting urge became too strong. She went to find her soul mate.

"Kikishan, I fear I am going to birth an egg. I know it's the wrong time. What shall we do? Incubating will leave us vulnerable, but I can't face the thought of smashing our egg like Ulyana did, and I don't think to carry the child in the sachan way is going to be any safer."

Kikishan smiled. "Come, Taminisha, I have refreshed our nest. We will do what we can for this child. With no sign of Nyket, we may still have time. Rumours have it he is still in his sickbed. It is less than sixty solar phasing to hatching. Come."

Taminisha followed her soul mate to the nest. She didn't feel comfortable about bringing an egg into such an uncertain world. With great difficulty, she stamped down her doubts.

He waited for her in the nest and they curled up together. As the ache in her belly increased, Kikishan massaged gently to ease the discomfort.

This pain could not be compared to the agony of birthing a child in the sachan way, and an hour later they sat back to admire their beautiful blue and lavender egg.

Taminisha immediately curled up protectively and breathed warm air over it.

Kikishan lay for a moment to watch her then he transmogrified and left her to rest.


Taminisha spent most of her time off from incubating playing with the children and watching the sky. Two solar phasings later, when she saw a group of warriors arriving in a boat, she left the children with Clyeva and raced down to the beach. Two half-blood Ellkiiyn led the group; many of whom had injuries that permanently disabled them. Taminisha arranged care and shelter for them before she called the two Ellkiiyn into the meeting hall.

"Tell me, Rabyan and Kyden any news you have of Nyket and the rebels?"

Rabyan frowned. "My lady, he prepares for war. He plans to come here then on to Rabikan. He believes his soul mate, Ulyana, has taken possession of this castle."

"But she is dead. Does he not notice the absence of her heartbeat?"

Rabyan smirked. "He's a tainted one, a Khimaera, like me. I only feel my soul mate's heart beat when I'm in close proximity. I suspect he suffers from the same defect."

"I didn't realise. Rabyan, please don't refer to yourself in such demeaning terms. You are Ellkiiyn even if not full blood."

Rabyan inclined his head and smiled.

"He intends to rule all of Dykarin with an iron fist. Kylara is on its knees, and they, and the Zynumin, are almost ready to surrender, unequivocally. The Orunan will fight him to the death of their species. He has hundreds of mixed blood Ellkiiyn, mercenaries ready to kill for reward." Tears filled Kyden's eyes. "The Prophecy of the Ancients of Dykarin is upon us," he wailed.

"Kyden shut your mouth."

"Let him speak, Rabyan, for he is right. The Era of Darkness is here. Our only hope is the coming of the Daughter of Kylara. We must prepare to fight for our lives. Larkin, go fetch Tarlitek."

Taminisha offered the Ellkiiyn refreshments as they waited. Tarlitek strode into the room with Larkin, Enian, Adakin and Tabro right behind him.

"Nyket is coming. He thinks Ulyana has control of the castle. We need to be ready for him. Tarlitek send out messengers to Viveka, Conurk, Rabikan, Lycidea, Fylitia, Abaye and the Land of Leryi. Use half-breeds—get the message out the Era of Darkness has come to Dykarin. Evacuate all women and children of Kelkiki to the smaller villages on the furthest borders of Kelkiki."

"The messengers will never make it in time."

"I know, Tarlitek. We'll have to hold Kelkiki on our own until the reinforcements come. Larkin come with me." She dismissed the others.

She headed for the old nesting room not even pausing to see if Larkin followed her. It only took a moment to unlock the door. She slipped inside. Larkin almost stepped on her heels as he squeezed through the gap behind her.

"What are we doing?"

"We need to hide the evidence of Aiyana's birth. Here." Taminisha grabbed up the bin in which she had vomited so many solar phasings ago.

"What are you doing?"

"Larkin, we need to swap the blue shell from the broken egg with the green shell. Nyket has to believe Ulyana killed his child or he will hunt you to the ends of Dykarin to get Aiyana back."

Larkin stared at her blankly.

"Nyket is Aiyana's father."

Horror at this new knowledge shadowed Larkin's face. "Nyket?"

"I'm sorry. I never intended to tell you, but perhaps it is best for you to know and guard against. Now carry that bin to my old room.

The air in the room smelt stale and unpleasant as they crept across the tomb. Taminisha glanced briefly at the embalmed body of the red Ellkiiyn in the middle of the floor. A shudder of remembered terror shivered over her skin. She pushed the memory aside trying to focus just on the unpleasant task she must complete.

"Help me," Taminisha urged as she hastily gathered up the pieces of blue shell from around the now embalmed body of Larkin's child. She put them aside and replaced it with the greener coloured shell.

Larkin helped her; tears welled in his eyes as he did so. By the time they had finished the gruesome task no one could tell a blue egg had originally encased the dead baby.

Together they shoved the blue eggshell into a sack and Taminisha carried it under her robes up to the door of the new nesting room. "I shall mix these with Jivin's shell and we can then add more blue egg fragments to it after the new baby hatches. No-one will ever know."

"What of Aiyana? If she has such evil flowing in her veins, is she not a risk for the future? She is not pure blood either so could evil come out in some way?"

Taminisha frowned. "I don't know. Only time will tell, but I believe if you love her and bring her up right, the best you can, she will overcome any evil infiltrating her blood. You love her; she has no need to be evil. Now promise me when Nyket comes, you will take Nysiah and Aiyana, and flee to Rabikan, or even to the Infernea Ellkiiyn colony, Mitikan. Nyket must never get his hands on her."

Larkin frowned. "I will do as you bid, even though I protest at abandoning Kelkiki in its hour of need."

"Do not stay and fight, promise me."

"I promise, Taminisha. What of you, your children and Kikishan?"

"I do not know. We have an egg to incubate, but it may yet be lost."

"Do you think to flee if Nyket overwhelms the castle? They say hundreds of mercenary Ellkiiyn will come."

"No. We cannot flee for it will only bring Nyket down on Rabikan or Mitikan. We have to make a stand here."

~  ~  ~

Each solar phasing she had to incubate left her physically, and mentally drained. So isolated from the goings on in the castle, and vulnerable, all the time on edge, listening for sounds of attack. She missed her children while incubating but knew Clyeva made the perfect nanny for them and she now had Flatasha to help when needed.

Potokin came with her every time she had to incubate, cuddling up to the egg, chattering and whistling to it. Without Potokin's company, she would have gone mad. It made Taminisha smile and time pass faster. The savage creature's show of tenderness for the egg surprised her for even with the children he could be rough and spiteful.

Jivin loved Potokin, but did not tolerate being bitten and would cuff the diminutive Tarki solidly. If Jivin got upset, he would transmogrify into Ellkiiyn and tussle energetically with the now smaller Tarki until he rolled over in submission. Even after their conflicts though, Taminisha never saw any hostility. Jivin and Potokin seemed to have respect for each other.

Each time she changed places with Kikishan he updated her on progress. Messengers had returned from Viveka with Oddianna and Sharanna bringing two thousand Viveka women to swell the ranks. The Fylitia Wheti and Whydan, declared they would stay neutral therefore would not help.

Tarlitek had sent a young man of three quarter Orunan to the gill breathers in the mangroves and Orr himself had appeared at the edge of the lake. Tarlitek and Orr had conversed for a long time, and Tarlitek seemed pleased when he came away.

"Are they going to help us?"Taminisha asked as he entered the castle.

Tarlitek jumped when she spoke, not realising she'd been observing him. "To some extent, Orr is willing to arrange for Orunikan and his larger brethren to capsize the boats and kill those that enter the water for any reason. Other than that, they will not get involved."

Taminisha shrugged. "Such help is better than nothing."

"They are close to Aikanshin and concerned what Nyket will do to retaliate if we should lose."

"I understand. To lose is unthinkable, but I cannot envisage otherwise. The Era of Darkness is truly upon us and all Dykarin."

Tarlitek frowned. "To be honest, I saw what Nyket had rounded up as his army. I do not see us winning. I would like to see you, the children and Clyeva leave. Flee to Myattica, Shula will make you welcome."

"But Tarlitek, my presence would bring Nyket down upon them. They are pacifists and would have no defence against Ellkiiyn, or even the others of mixed breeds. I could not do that to them."

Tarlitek bowed his head. "I understand. And yes, in that case, you have no choice, but to make a stand here."

"Again, Tarlitek, I ask you to forsake me if the situation is dire. Save my children, Jivin and Milli and the third if it lives. Promise me, you, and Clyeva, will take them, and flee, hide them, protect them."

"I will, Taminisha. It is my solemn promise on the Great Spirit Ellkii." Tarlitek reached up, and clasped the red gemstone hanging on a thong around his neck. He pulled it off and tied three knots in its length. "One for each child, to keep them close to my heart as it is not the Orunan way to gather ones offspring close."

Taminisha stepped forward and took hold of his hands ignoring the tears streaming down her cheeks. "Tarlitek, you do understand what I am asking. You and Clyeva will be hiding, or on the run, until they reach adulthood. If Nyket knows they are alive he will hunt you to the ends of Dykarin and farther."

Tarlitek nodded. "I understand what you ask, little one, but as long as I have Clyeva, it will not matter, and it is you who gave her to me. This sacrifice is but a trivial one, besides I have learnt to appreciate the bond between parent and child from loving you and your children."

Taminisha stepped forward and embraced Tarlitek. He hugged her back. Her heart ached as she sobbed her heartbreak onto his shoulder.

As time slipped by Taminisha became more and more reluctant to do her stint incubating despite the commitment they had made.

Even Kikishan now expressed his concern about their choice as they changed places.

She settled in the nest, Potokin curled around the egg, muttering to it and stroking it tenderly. Taminisha smiled. The Tarki's actions were so endearing. With his strong attachment to her egg, she wondered if he could have true affection for the tiny Ellkiiyn growing inside. With the babe half way grown she knew in another twenty solar phasings it would survive outside the egg if forced to. She fretted about the future, for even if this child survived, what then? If they defeated Nyket, all would be well, if not, the future would be bleak, both short term, and long term. Taminisha nudged her egg and sighed.

~   ~   ~

Once Taminisha had settled with the egg, Kikishan joined the watch on the keep terrace. The Viveka women had arrived early in the solar phasing and they rested in the central hall of the bailey he had converted to a dormitory. Grateful Clyeva had taken on the full care of Jivin, Milli and Aiyana, Kikishan expressed his appreciation, despite the fact he still had trouble accepting her outspokenness.  He wished Taminisha could be at his side. Her presence made him feel stronger, more assured. At least Larkin, Adakin and Enian were in constant attendance, with Tabro and Ikaya not far behind.

Nysiah made herself useful, providing food and guidance for the Viveka women and helping Sadrina tend any of those with lingering injuries. Kikishan didn't feel any animosity toward the pink Ellkiiyn, but some of Taminisha's mistrust had impressed upon him, and he refused to let her near the children. Far below the gray castle walls, he could see Tarlitek pacing the shoreline of the lake, watching the waters for any sign of boats.

The solar orb settled behind the mountains and a thin white mist drifted in and then settled over the water. With hardly any breeze, the water of the lake lay mirror smooth. The unwary would have no idea of the dangers that lurked beneath the surface. Even now, large gill breathing Orunan cruised through the waters between Kelkiki Island and Oventi Rock.

Kikishan paced as the sky darkened, and the biggest of the five lunor discs, Etunik, glowed in a huge silvery orb with the tiny satellites of Sarilan, Soralan, Sariada and Saritan twirling around him, blinking in the shades of the clans. As Etunik rose higher, a wide path of silvery lunor light flowed across the lake to Oventi Rock.

Kikishan shivered.

Larkin came and walked beside him. "Do you think we have a chance of survival?"

Kikishan took a few more steps, his head down. He suddenly halted, and peered across at Larkin. "I don't know. We are as ready as possible, but until we see the size of his army, I cannot say how we'll fare. Promise me, dearest cousin, if anything happens to me you will keep Taminisha and the children safe."

Larkin inclined his head. "I promise, cousin."

Kikishan felt somewhat easier having that promise, even though he had no idea where Taminisha would be safe.

More creatures arrived at the castle over the next few solar phasing, half-breeds, mostly from Viveka, Kylara and a few Zynumin even, though Aneverin had already surrendered to Nyket in a misguided attempt to protect his people.

With defeat inevitable Kiet had determined to surrender because if the conflict continued, the displaced sachan from Kylara would flee over the borders and become fresh meat for the Zynumin when they morphflitted and hunted.

No one quizzed the new arrivals and all who came were welcomed.

Tarlitek continued to patrol the shore of the lake with anyone who had Orunan blood.

Ellkiiyn patrolled the turrets, terraces and parapet walks of the castle and, every two hours, pairs would fly off and circle the perimeter almost as far out as Oventi Rock.

Taminisha and Kikishan continued to alternate the incubating. As each solar phasing slipped by, both of them became more unsettled and fretful, trapped by their loyalty and love for their egg.

Kikishan heard them coming. The steady swish of leathery wings through the quiet lunor drift. He went out to the parapet walk. Hundreds of Ellkiiyn silhouetted against the lunor discs, spreading across the sky in a mottled mass of colour, scales, and claws.

On the lake, boats left a silver trail of broken lunor light on the water. The sound of many pectenite horns blasted repeatedly in warning.

Kikishan stared at the invaders. "We are lost. Overwhelmed. Great Spirit Ellkii spare Taminisha and my children."

His small army gathered on the walls and the beaches. They would fight to the death out of loyalty to him, and for the preservation of the Aqueena Clan.

Kikishan, Larkin and Enian transmogrified and took to the sky. Everywhere Ellkiiyn lifted off and went to meet the enemy head on. A maelstrom of Ellkiiyn surrounded them, claws slashing, teeth crunching and chomping, and tails whacking. There would be no surrender, no sanctuary, and no quarter given.

Kikishan howled as a set of claws slashed open the old wound on his back. He twisted and lashed out at his attacker. His claws caught flesh; he tugged, ripping the flesh free. Blood spurted, blue and red. He swung his head and clamped giant jaws tight on a smaller Ellkiiyn's head. He bit down hard and bone crunched.

The smaller red Ellkiiyn howled and when Kikishan let him go, he fell out of the sky and landed with a splash in the lake.

The water frothed and swirled. Orunikan leapt above the water and snatched up the hapless Ellkiiyn in his great gaping mouth.

Kikishan turned away and gulped back nausea at the thought of falling in the lake. He soared upward and viewed the battle before picking out his next opponent, a large brownish Ellkiiyn. With a spurt of speed, Kikishan flew upward and then rotated nose down and dived. He hit his target in the middle of the back. Kikishan heard the spine snap.

The fatally injured Ellkiiyn dropped into the lake, howling in agony and anger. As his body hit the lake a dozen large Orunan surrounded it. The water frothed and surged, staining brown with blood and within minutes only a twisted skeleton remained to sink below the surface.

Kikishan shuddered and launched back into battle.

A sudden weight on his back forced him downward. Sharp claws dug in between his scales tearing his tender flesh and making his gaping wounds bleed even more profusely. He roared his agony and spat fire as claws and teeth attached to the softer underside of his body.

He plummeted.

Even with powerful thrusts of his wings, he continued to fall, unable to hold the weight of two full-grown Ellkiiyn hanging off him.

He writhed and twisted, but could not free himself. With gnashing teeth, he bit and slashed, but he couldn't quite reach the vulnerable bits of his opponents. Closer and closer to the water they dragged him.

He increased his twisting and jerking until finally, he managed to get his claws into the leg of the Ellkiiyn on his underside. He dug them in deep then swiped with the other foot. Finally, barely a foot above the water, his claws on the other foot caught in the softer scales of the groin. He sank them in deep feeling the leg bone in the hardness of muscles.

The Ellkiiyn screamed and twisted to escape, but the three of them hit the water together.

Blackness hovered on the edges of Kikishan's sight, but he saw Orunikan, the gaping open mouth and the lines and lines of teeth as the lake monster crunched down and gulped.

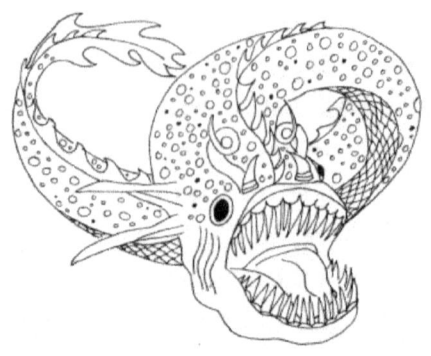

# Chapter Twenty

Tarlitek saw Kikishan fall, dragged down by the weight of two Ellkiiyn. The moment Kikishan hit the water Tarlitek howled. Orunikan would not be selective.

Only one Ellkiiyn rose above the water.

Tarlitek grabbed a big half breed Ellkiiyn Orunan and pointed. "Go Daleti, go kill that bastard flying away. You have time enough to transmogrify and kill him."

"It shall be done, Tarlitek. Kikishan only ever showed me kindness. If I die remember me to my mate." Daleti transmogrified.

With an enormous downward swipe, Daleti lifted off the ground.

Tarlitek strained against the blast of air.

Daleti soared. After a short pursuit, the big blue Ellkiiyn got close enough to latch onto Kikishan's killer. He closed monstrous jaws across the middle of his tail. Jaws with incredible strength of his mixed blood—a miniature Orunikan with wings. Immediately Daleti closed his jaws, green blood spurted all over him.

"Yes. Bite him again my friend," Tarlitek yelled as he faced an attack from a male of indeterminate breed. He slashed his sword taking his foe's arm off at the shoulder.

The cross breed yelped and flew at Tarlitek.

Tarlitek didn't hesitate, but opened his mouth and bit into his opponent's other shoulder, ripping the arm free of the socket.

His foe fell and lay writhing on the rocks.

Tarlitek didn't even stop to finish him off. But risked a quick glance at the sky in time to see Daleti and the other Ellkiiyn nose-dive toward the water. Tarlitek turned away and charged a diminutive Ellkiiyn struggling to transmogrify. He grabbed its partially formed wings and tugged the leathery webs so violently they ripped away from the skeletal structure and the Ellkiiyn fell screeching to the ground.

Tarlitek slashed with his sword and took the head off at the shoulders. He could have bitten, but already struggled with the nasty taste of his last foe and the bits of scale between his teeth.

He surveyed the scene. Grief and rage thrust through him. He waved his fist to the sky as his spines vibrated and clattered. *This is not a battle. It is a massacre. Time for me to fulfil my promise.*

He battled his way toward the steps of to the castle. Every step hard won with another dead foe.

The spinning flail crashed into his head. His brain vibrated against the inside of his exoskeleton. Tarlitek clutched his head as he staggered under the blow. He steadied and swung his sword in a wide arc. His attacker bellowed and dropped his flail and shield. Tarlitek slashed again and again until he flayed most of the small green Ellkiiyn's chest and shoulder open.

His foe collapsed to the floor emitting guttural cries for mercy. Rage blasted through Tarlitek. He snatched up the abandoned flail and whipped it over his head in an arc before he slammed it onto the creature's head. The Ellkiiyn fell with a thud. Tarlitek turned away and continued to climb the stairs.

His head throbbed. Sparkling lights and flashes obscured his vision. Nausea roiled in his gut. He grabbed the wall, leaning heavily. His knees sagged and he hit the ground with a jarring thud.

The world spun around him as his cold blood pounded behind his exoskeleton. He reached up to his head and it came away smeared with blood. He wiped his hand on his tunic before he crawled one step at a time toward the castle. *Sorry, little one, I have left it too late. I have failed you, as I never have before.*

~    ~    ~

Taminisha started awake. The harsh blast of the horns had penetrated her incubating stupor. Every nerve sizzled, her stomach churned.

Potokin hissed and curled tighter around the egg.

She writhed inside with indecision. To be trapped while the battle raged or consign her baby to death. Torn between maternal love, and the need to fight for survival she stirred restlessly. Even now, as she looked at her beautiful dark blue and purple egg, an immediate warm buzz of maternal love raced through her.

At almost the same moment, she could only sense two tiny patters beside her own heartbeat. Kikishan's had fallen silent. Huge sobs ripped through her. With her soul mate dead Taminisha knew she had to save her children, the ones already born. She tried to lift Potokin away from the egg.

He screeched and clung to it, his claws scratching the surface. He chattered frantically then bit hard on Taminisha's hand.

"Fine, you ungrateful fiend, stay!" she cried, as she turned away from her egg. She transmogrified on the run, and dragged her habilan over her head. Her breast ached as her heart rent into pieces: for her lost love, her abandoned egg and all that would be wrenched from her. She hurried through the deserted corridors, to Clyeva's room and found her dressing the children in warm clothes.

"Clyeva?"

Clyeva dropped the clothes and grabbed Taminisha. "The castle is falling to Nyket. Our Ellkiiyn have been overwhelmed. Enian is dead;

Larkin has returned wounded. He is leaving with Nysiah and Aiyana for Rabikan. They will try to bring help. Two Ellkiiyn mauled Kikishan and pulled him into the lake. They do not know if he lives."

Taminisha shook her head. "Kikishan has taken the hand of spirit. We must flee."

"Your egg?"

"I've left it. I couldn't bring myself to smash it, but the child will die by tomorrow," she said almost choking on her words as her prediction stabbed deep into her soul. She grabbed up Milli.

Clyeva snatched Jivin from the floor.

Fear stalked them.

Taminisha glanced repeatedly over her shoulder.

They hurried out the door, down the corridor and across the bridge between the towers. They entered the second tower, where they could take off.

Nyket pounced. Although in sachan form he had three Ellkiiyn with him, nasty motley looking mixed bloods.

Taminisha screamed and backed away.

Nyket swaggered toward them. "Ahhh, Taminisha, you seek to flee my company again. Shame on you."

"Let us pass, Nyket. We are no threat to you."

He laughed and pointed at Jivin. "He is. Full-blooded, Aqueena Ellkiiyn just like his father."

"Leave us, Nyket. He's only a baby."

"Ah yes, my dear, but babies grow up, and grown up babies seek revenge. They want to inherit their father's realms. Just like me and if they don't get it they take it with bitter revenge. I came to secure Ulyana's hold on Kelkiki and see my child, the future Guardian. However, as I closed in on the castle I felt a hole in my chest where her heartbeat should have begun to patter. Then I knew someone had murdered my soul mate and child. Did you kill her?"

Taminisha lifted her chin and stared directly at her enemy. "Yes, I killed her. She would have killed my child, just as she killed yours. She killed him."

Nyket leapt across the gap and grabbed Taminisha by the throat. "She would never, never kill our child. How dare you say such a thing?"

The tightness of his grip numbed the feeling in her arm. She held herself stiff in his grip. She dragged air into her lungs through her restricted airway.

"I dare, because it's true. She realised her mistake when she joined with Larkin."

"No," Nyket bellowed.

"I can show you, Nyket, your child, dead in its shell," she croaked out against the pressure of his hands.

Nyket shoved her hard. She fell, landing on her side with Milli still clutched in her arms.

"Trans you idiots and take the children to the dungeon," Nyket roared.

"No. Leave my children be, you monstrosity. Khimaera. Cross breed," Taminisha bellowed as she tried to back away.

But Nyket held her arm in a vice like grip. "Take them."

The two guards stepped forward. The larger grabbed Milli from Taminisha's arms even though she kicked his legs and slapped at his face. Taminisha tried to hold the child close to her breasts. Unfortunately, the guard had hold of the baby's lower body and tugged relentlessly. Milli writhed and screamed. Petrified she'd hurt her child Taminisha let her slip from her grasp. The lanky guard with the ochre coloured hair snatched Jivin from Clyeva's arms and followed his larger companions across the bridge. The third guard hovered uncertainly nearby.

Jivin yelled out and kicked against the constraint. "Mamam, Mamam, Clyvee."

Taminisha sagged, the fight in her draining away. *Where are you, Tarlitek? You promised to save the children.*

Nyket stepped forward and grabbed Taminisha's hair, dragging her up from the floor. "You will show me," he bawled as he began pushing her toward the bridge.

"No, not that way, this way." Taminisha pulled against Nyket's brutal pushing and shoving. Her heart thudded, drowning out the petite beats of her children's. Deep inside, she cried for her lost love. Nothing mattered now, except the children. She hoped Tarlitek still lived and would again obey her, and save the children. With one last desperate effort, she broadcast in Ellkiiyn. *"Tarlitek, save my children. You promised."*

Nyket grimaced as he picked up the silent plea. "You're wasting your time, that scaly gill breather is already dead. There is nobody to help you, or save your children."

Her plea had been for Clyeva still crouched trembling on the dark walkway, the one who could hear her cry, and would see it done if possible. With her children safe, she could die happy, for without Kikishan, she had nothing else to live for—especially under Nyket's rule.

She halted at her bedroom door, and then took the key from around her neck.

Nyket kept a tight grip on her hair and arm.

The restraint not only controlled her movement, but it stopped her tucking and rolling to transmogrify. Taminisha unlocked the door, but paused before entering. "Nyket, are you sure you want to see this? It's not pleasant."

"Show me," he growled, and pushed her through the barely open door.

She heard him gasp in a deep breath that caught in his chest with a hiss. *Good, he was shocked, hurting even.*

"I told you it wasn't pleasant."

He shoved her from him. "You didn't say death caught her during transmogrification. Because of her intent, Spirit wouldn't accept her."

"No, Spirit wouldn't, that is why we interred her here." It pleased her, in a macabre way, that his lover's ungainly body and the knowledge Spirit would not accept her had shocked him.

"And the child?" Nyket asked.

Taminisha pointed to the smashed egg hidden under its shroud. "Spirit wouldn't take that either."

Still holding her in a clawed grip, Nyket marched her across the room. His hand on her shoulder trembled as they halted by the edge of the shroud.

"Lift it up," he said as he pushed her toward the shroud.

A stinging burn ripped through her gut. Nausea threatened. She hesitated. *Would her subterfuge hold up to scrutiny?*

Nyket shoved against her shoulder. She leaned down and lifted the shroud. A wave of sadness washed over her at the sight of the tiny embalmed body in the middle of the egg fragments. Her child would be the same soon, and she could do nothing to save it.

He growled. "Cover it," he said as he swung away and vomited on the floor.

She laid the shroud back down. 'It had no chance, Nyket. She abandoned it to kill me."

"So you tell the truth, it's dead. I don't believe she killed it, and now someone will have to provide me with a replacement."

"What?" Taminisha exclaimed.

"I need a child to inherit. There is no point in fighting for control and guardianship if I do not have an heir with purer blood than mine. My soul mate is dead, so I will use someone else's soul mate." He glared down at her. "And I figure you'll do with your purer than pure purple blood."

"No, Nyket, no. We're siblings!"

"We're not. Our bloodlines do not intertwine."

"Don't do this evil, please," Taminisha pleaded. Her inner body recoiled from the thought of Nyket touching her intimately.

Her fate appeared to be far worse than any she had imagined. Death would be more welcome than mating with Nyket. At least the chances of breeding were slight, for she did not love him, and very few Ellkiiyn could breed without love. Bile rushed up her throat, and she swallowed hard pushing her revulsion down.

"Royden, install the Lady of Kelkiki in the dungeons, the low ones, not next to the children. She and I have business to conduct when I've finished cleaning up here."

*No, no, no. To come to such an abomination.*

"Yes, Guardian Nyket."

Taminisha flinched. *How dare he call himself that? He is not the Guardian of Kelkiki. He is not the Guardian of anywhere.*

Taminisha dragged her heels, kicked and shrieked, but nothing stopped the inevitable arrival into the lower dungeons. Her captor shoved her into in a small dank cell. As the door slammed shut with a clang, she collapsed to the floor, and buried her face in her hands. Her throat burned from her raucous protests, and bruises already showed on her legs and arms from resisting her captors. She had nothing left beyond outward displays of grief; Taminisha sank to the floor in a crumpled heap. The cold seeped into her body and she let it come.

~   ~   ~

The guard's huge fingers dug into the flesh of Jivin's arm. He cried out. "Mamam, Mamam, Da, help me, help me!"

His cries echoed along the corridors, drowning out the wails of his baby sister. Although totally petrified he decided he would not let these nasty Ellkiiyn hurt him and Millinsha. He would get free and find his Mamam.

Without a thought of the consequences, he tucked his head and curled his legs. *Yes, I change. I am Ellkiiyn.* It hurt to do it with the guard holding his arm, but in his sachan form, he would be too immature and puny to fight back.

He flapped his wings and pulled free of the guard's cruel hold. He spat a stream of fiery flames straight into his face. The big male bellowed his agony.

Instantly two non-Ellkiiyn males appeared from the dark doorway and crowded the corridor in front of him.

Jivin spun and swooped as best he could in the confined space. He darted in, and slashed with his razor, sharp claws slicing one of the guard's cheeks open.

The half-breed Lycidean, with his black hair and strange white skin clutched his torn face with one hand and slashed through the air with his sword in the other.

The blade whistled passed Jivin's wriggling tail. He tucked it in under his belly and circled to land on the back of the Lycidean. He snapped, with strong jaws filled with sharp baby teeth, at his head and shoulders. Blood spurted from the puncture wounds and the male dropped to his knees, his sword clattered loudly on the stone floor.

*I did. I did. He broken.*

Jivin pushed off, and spat again, setting the other guard's hair alight.

The male dropped to the floor and rolled back and forth screeching.

Jivin flew up to the ceiling, twisted then dived for a new attack. He didn't see the net and hit the obstacle at speed. His claws and bared teeth caught in the fine mesh. Panic speared through him. *Need get out. Get free.* He tugged and twisted, and flapped his wings, but the mesh closed over him, around and around until he dropped to the floor with a painful thud.

He crawled along the floor, but the movement only tightened the mesh and entangled him more. He clenched his jaw, whimpering and shaking his head. His legs shuddered. Desperate to escape he tucked his head and did a clumsy restricted roll immediately transmogrifying back to his sachan form. Now he could free his hands and feet, but before he could escape, the two uninjured guards pounced on him, wrapped the net tighter, and carried him after the guard holding his sister.

He slumped; his little body throbbed with Ellkiiyn sized hurt from his injuries. Shame burned through him. Tears stung his eyes. He blinked them away. *No cry. I big boy. Be brave like Da.*

Without freeing him from the net, they threw him into the cell where his sister lay on the floor wrapped in her blanket, sobbing at the full force of her immature lungs. By the time Jivin untangled himself he realised they were not alone. The half-blood Ellkiiyn Flatasha, who sometimes helped Clyeva, sat weeping on the only stool in the space. Behind her in an untidy stack were some of their clothes and a supply of milk. Jivin sat on the floor for a long time trying to comprehend what had happened. "*Help me, Mamam. I frightened.*" He broadcast then began to weep.

~   ~   ~

Awareness nudged at her—the coldness of the floor and the dank air cloying her nostrils. She lifted her head and listened with her mind. "*Jivin.*" Silence. "*Jivin, baby.*" Silence. Tears filled her eyes. She brushed them away. Numbness hung heavy behind her breasts.

She glanced around her prison. The reality bit deep. An icy lump sat inside her where Kikishan's heart beat used to be as she struggled to breathe. Her stomach churned, and she swallowed against the dry sour taste in her mouth. The tiny patter of her children's heartbeats beside her own gave her hope. While they lived, she would fight for their survival. Taminisha no longer cared who held the Guardianship of Kelkiki or of Aikanshin. Nyket could have it all for she wanted no part of it. All she wanted now was her babies in her arms and peaceful sanctuary.

The guards muttered together down the corridor expressing their disgruntlement with being assigned guard duty when the rest of the contingent had headed down to burn and pillage the village and gather any valuables they could find. A guard appeared every now and then and glanced absently into her cell, but Taminisha suspected he didn't really see her as he made his inspection.

"*Jivin, baby, answer Mamam.*" She broadcast again well aware any nearby Ellkiiyn could hear her plea. She didn't care.

Footsteps and the rattle of keys from the corridor disturbed the gloomy quiet. She cut off her broadcast and emptied her mind.

Nyket appeared at the door, splattered with blood and sweat beading on his forehead. His eyes sparkled with satisfaction. He unlocked the door and prowled toward her. She scrambled to her feet, but he came close and leaned right into her face. "You are finally mine, Taminisha—the purest of all blood to meld with mine. You will conceive my child, my mixed blood child."

"I will never be yours, Nyket, and I will never conceive your child."

He surged forward and grabbed her chin, lifting it sufficiently so she looked directly into his eyes. "You *are* mine, and you *will* let yourself conceive."

Taminisha wrenched her chin from his grip. "No—never."

He sidled around her now, touching her breasts and buttocks with light strokes.

She stood immobile.

He moved back in front of her again, leering. "Not even for your children, Taminisha?"

Her gut hardened into a frozen lump and her lungs clamped on the desire to scream. She clenched her hands, forcing them into her sides so she didn't pummel his face into a bloody mess. She tried to swallow, but her mouth and throat were so dry she had to force saliva to form.

Nyket raised his eyebrows at her silence.

Her breath choked in her chest and she forced her throat to move. "Spare my children and I will do your bidding."

"I thought so. I'm keeping them safe just in case I needed leverage. Would you like to see them?"

Taminisha's knees gave way and she dropped to the stone floor. Oblivious to the pain of the connection she shuffled forward grabbing at Nyket's clothes. "Bring them to me, Nyket, they are but babies, and need their mother. Show me they're alive, I beg of you!"

Nyket stepped back pulling his clothes free of her clutches. He signalled one of the guards. Taminisha waited, her heart barely beating in her chest, air hardly moving in or out of her lungs. She clenched her hands together, wringing them into tortured, shapeless flesh. Her knees creaked under the pressure of the stone as she wavered between hope and despair. She heard footsteps coming down the corridor.

She saw them.

Jivin hobbled held by an Ellkiiyn with a collar and chain. Flatasha trailed behind them. She appeared terrified as she stood still and straight, clutching a whimpering Milli in her arms.

Taminisha held her arms out. "Come to Mamam, my darling children." Great lung torturing sobs burst out and tears flooded her cheeks. "My babies." She beckoned them.

Nyket put out his hand to prevent them moving any closer.

"So, you've seen. You want them to stay alive?"

"Yes, Nyket, please do not hurt my children. I will do anything you want, just don't hurt them."

Nyket laughed as he waved the children away.

"That's more like it. Now this is how it's going to be. They will stay alive and you will submit to joining with me and allow yourself to be ripe for conception. If you falter the first time – the youngest will die. If you fail, then the boy will die."

"And when I birth a child? What of them, after you have what you want?"

Nyket guffawed. "Maybe I will keep them for my amusement, maybe I won't. Maybe if you birth me a son I will let some Ellkiiyn family adopt them—they'll be young enough to forget their true Mamam."

"Nyket, give me some guarantee you will spare them."

He laughed again. "You are in no position to negotiate, but do as I want, and we'll discuss it further."

"And how will I know you've kept your side of the bargain?"

"I don't have to prove anything to you, but I will for the good will. When you conceive you shall see them, when you birth you will see them again. After that, I do not promise anything."

Taminisha knew she'd made a fragile deal with evil. The dismal thought tugged at her mind. Perhaps it would be better if they died now, rather than later, because that would be their ultimate destiny. She sat back on her heels, drained and broken. Tears ran down her cheeks.

Nyket laughed. "It won't be so bad, Taminisha. You can shut your eyes and pretend it is Kikishan. At least your unwelcome spawn gets to live a while yet. Now stand. The guard will escort you to your room. You will bathe in readiness for our joining."

# Chapter Twenty One

Clyeva crept across the walkway. She could hear the battle on the lower level of the castle and could see the hordes of creatures locked in combat on the shore of the lake. She could see Kikishan's motley army had retreated toward the cliffs or further up toward the water.

The water of the lake swirled and rippled in the lunor light. Any who entered the water would not come ashore again.

Clyeva had heard Taminisha's silent plea to Tarlitek, and instinctively knew Taminisha meant it for her because Tarlitek could not hear Ellkiiyn mind speak.

She crouched in the shadows until Nyket and Taminisha had disappeared across the bridge and into the corridor leading to Ulyana's tomb. Clyeva covered her face and moaned. Alone in the midst of the battle there was little she could do. With no weapons, and no clue if Tarlitek still lived, any attempt at a rescue of the Jivin and Milli would only result in her own death. *I have to get out of the castle and find*

*Tarlitek...*Her thoughts faltered. *If he still lives? My love please be safe. Come to me, for I am nothing without you. What should I do? Stay, go, hide?* Her options scurried around in her head.

She peered up and down the bridge. It remained deserted. The wrench in leaving the children tore through her. *Dear babies. Clyvee loves you.* She climbed to her feet and stumbled from the bridge calculating the shortest way from the castle. Lethargy dragged at her. A searing sting twisted in her gut as she fought back the tears stinging behind her eyes. She muttered tearfully to herself. "I have no choice. Nothing I can do. Sorry, Taminisha, dear friend I fail you."

A thought formed. *Perhaps not.* A tingle raced over her skin. She licked her lips and clenched sweaty palms together. The egg. She could save the abandoned egg. *This I can do.* Through the silent mind communication, Clyeva had sensed Taminisha's guilt about her egg. Suddenly her thoughts focussed. *Yes, this I can do.*

With the decision made her strength revived, the fog cleared from her mind. The only thing she could do without reinforcements. Her stomach quivered and churned. She hesitated, straightened her shoulders and continued. *If there is any chance, I have to save it.*

With cautious steps, she sidled down the passages toward the nesting room. Taminisha had left her egg, but it hadn't been long, maybe it remained viable. With only fourteen solar phasings to hatching, the baby might survive with care. Clyeva could not let it die. A tragic death in such circumstances would rip an even greater hole in her own heart, where she already mourned for her childless life.

She opened the door to the nesting room and stopped.

Potokin stood on his hind legs and rolled the egg ever so gently across the floor toward her, chattering and cooing to it. He hissed and squeaked when he saw Clyeva and tried to roll the egg in the other direction.

"Potokin, give me Taminisha's egg." Clyeva reached for it.

Potokin hissed and spat at her.

Clyeva pulled away.

"Potokin, Taminisha is in trouble, she can't come back for the egg. It will die without care."

The Tarki glared at her, his arms protectively around the egg's girth.

"Potokin, I'm not going to harm it. I want to take it before Nyket comes and breaks it. I want to see if we can save the babe. Help me, Potokin." Clyeva dropped to her knees as she pleaded with the Tarki, not knowing if it even understood her.

Potokin watched her, tipping his head from side to side.

Clyeva doubted it comprehended her explanation, but she knew the creature had some intelligence and thought being soothing may convince him to give the egg to her.

"Come on Potokin, it needs to be kept warm. You're not big enough to keep it warm, but you can help me. Come on, let's save your Mamam's babe."

Potokin's glare softened and he rolled the egg toward Clyeva.

She held her breath. *He seems to understand. Will he bring it all the way to me? Come on, Tarki, come to Clyeva.* As soon as he got close enough she reached down to pick it up, wary the Tarki would attack her, but he didn't.

Clyeva wrapped her arms as far around the egg as she could and scooped it from the floor. She tucked it inside her robe. Her hands trembled. The egg was heavier than she expected and so large it stretched her flowing over robe to the limits of its seams.

Potokin squeaked, scuttled across the room, scrambled up Clyeva's leg and burrowed under the short hem of the over robe. His sharp claws dug into her flesh and Clyeva flinched, but didn't drag the creature away as it settled just under Clyeva's breasts and curved around the egg.

She supported the egg with her arms, as she lumbered along the corridor. She leaned against the wall and took the steps that led outside one at a time. The weight of the egg pressed on her chest and cramped her breath making every movement awkward. Clyeva didn't know where to go. *I need somewhere safe, but where? I need to hide. What of*

249

*Tarlitek? How will he find me?* Not for the first time, she wished she had Ellkiiyn echoing heartbeats to guide her on her mate's condition.

As she made her way through the castle, she saw the dead and injured. She flinched away and sidled around the bodies keeping out of reach of hands grasping for help. She gasped back a sob when she came across Enian's Ellkiiyn body disfigured by multiple wounds and her wings crushed and broken.

Clyeva crept down the back corridors, hiding and dodging any creature, friend or foe. She knew of a back entrance once used by prisoners to escape when they worked in the garden. Kikishan had told her of it when Jivin had disappeared on one of his escapades.

In the darkness of the corridors, Clyeva stumbled on the uneven surface. Each time she did the tiny Tarki dug its claws into her flesh to secure itself, and squeaked softly in admonishment of her clumsiness. Clyeva concluded Potokin had a reasonable intelligence in his uncivilised head.

"Sorry, Potokin, your Mamam's egg is big and heavy, and it's dark."

The Tarki squeaked in response.

Suddenly Clyeva felt glad she wasn't alone with her burden.

As she neared the entrance, the acrid smell of burning stung her nose. She crouched in the darkness of the entrance and peered out the opening. The glow from the lunor discs and the fires burning on the beach bathed the landscape in a flickering light. Nothing moved out here in the wildness behind the castle, but she could hear the sounds of battle ringing in the still air.

Clyeva weighed up the risks of crossing the exposed ground between the castle and the scrubby forest by the lakeshore, or staying put. The open ground seemed safer than the castle in the long term. For once Nyket's army had cut down all of Kikishan's warriors they would scour the castle for survivors and put them to the sword. She prayed for Tarlitek and hoped he remembered his promise to Taminisha, but Clyeva suspected he would not leave the battle until the final defeat or had fallen to a stronger foe.

She eased out into the open, every cell of her body on alert. Once out of the castle, she stumbled down the steep slope on an over grown path that led toward the village, praying to Spirit to keep her balance and hold of the egg.

People shouted and screamed in the distance.

Being encumbered by the egg left her vulnerable. She had no weapon to defend herself with either. Her heartbeat clattered. She scanned the surroundings. Nothing moved. She gritted her teeth and took a dozen steps. The breeze shushed through the leaves. She froze. Listened. Glanced behind her. Nothing moved. She walked on.

As she neared the lake, she saw people hurrying down the road away from the castle and across the already flooded causeway toward the village. Cries of distress and urgent calls of warning echoed on the breeze.

Clyeva debated whether she should join them or keep hidden. Attracted by the thought of company in her fear she decided to join the fleeing castle staff. She hefted the egg higher and stepped out from the concealing bushes.

As she moved from the shadows two Ellkiiyn soared out of the sky and blasted the lines of fleeing creatures with flames. They fell, hollering and burning, or ran shrieking with flames gusting out behind them until they too finally fell to the ground.

Clyeva shuddered, nausea stinging her gut. She shrank back into the bushes and tall grasses and stood hidden, unsteady and trembling. She looked down at the egg. *This egg leaves me vulnerable. I cannot run. Perhaps I should have left it.* Her chest tightened and she struggled to swallow. *How can I even consider such a thing? It is Taminisha's. She never abandoned me.*

She needed to go to the lake. If he had survived, Tarlitek would gravitate to water, especially if he sustained significant injuries. With a shake of her head, she pushed away morbid thoughts. *He will survive. He will come to me. To our special place. I will go there. He will remember. He will know.*

The weight of the egg dragged heavier and heavier as she fought to keep hold of it. Unable to encircle it completely with her arms it slowly slid downward. She stopped every few steps to hitch it up and tuck her hem under to secure it. Petrified of dropping the egg she picked her way slowly through the trees and over rocks until she could see the lake.

All the time, she could hear screams and battle calls coming from the castle. As she made her way through a large scattering of boulders, the water lapped on the shore and made her nervous. She hated water.

Their secret place wasn't far from the castle, but around a cove and behind a rocky point. They had sheltered there once from a sudden rainstorm. Tarlitek had lit a fire and they had mated on the dry sand while the deluge fell outside. They had often retreated to their secret hideaway to mate with abandon and loud cries of passion not possible in the castle.

The narrow, secluded beach appeared deserted and quiet, but Clyeva did not intend to expose herself. She crept through the bushes along the edge of the cliff rising above the lake.

Burdened by the egg she placed one foot on a secure spot then peered through the dark for the next. All the time the water lapped at the rocks just inches away. She flinched as each wavelet surged between the stones. Her heart jumped and spluttered. Sweat beaded her skin as she fought the urge to run.

At last, Clyeva made out the darker shadow of the partially concealed opening of the cave. She clutched the egg, dashed across the sand and without pausing slipped inside. The egg slipped down her thighs. She gripped it tighter and hobbled, half bent over, to the deepest corner. On a deep exhale, Clyeva sank to her knees letting the weight of the egg rest on to the sand. She continued to breathe deeply trying to calm her erratic heartbeat. She desperately wanted to message Taminisha with Ellkiiyn mind talk, but knew other Ellkiiyn would pick up her broadcast.

Potokin wriggled.

She lifted her tunic up exposing both the egg and the Tarki.

He grumbled and snuggled closer to the egg.

Her fingers trembled as she outlined each scale. Taminisha's Vaprus heritage showed in the purple edges to the blue scales. She leaned closer. No sound came from the egg. Disappointment washed through her, but refusing to let go of hope Clyeva assessed the egg and how best keep it warm.

In almost total darkness, she twisted a strip of material from the bottom half of her skirt into a sling.

Potokin watched her as she stripped and put the sling over one shoulder and tied the ends around her waist. The lunor drift air caressed her bare skin with icy fingers. She shivered and hurriedly pulled her clothes back on.

Rising to her knees, she manoeuvred the egg into the makeshift sling with Potokin still clinging to the shell. After adjusting her clothes to fit around the bulge she huddled down on the sand, curled herself around the egg, and buried her feet under the sand.

Potokin muttered and whistled in her ear, but she didn't mind, at least she wasn't alone.

From here, she couldn't hear the sounds of battle and she had no way of gauging the progress of the battle. Despite her frustration with the uncertainty, fear of detection and leaving the egg unattended kept her from checking the situation. The sand felt damp against her skin and the draught wafting in from the lake caressed her with icy fingers.

She mourned her loss of fire, for before the abscission, she had never been cold, but then she had not had Tarlitek either. Her heart stirred with a deep ache. *How will I go on without my beloved? Where will I go?* Unanswerable thoughts taunted her. Seeking comfort, she pulled the egg closer and laid her head on the shell and she made a futile effort to sleep through the long cold darkness.

As time stretched out, her stomach growled with hunger.

"You know what, Potokin? If I'd known we would end up here, I would have brought food," she mumbled absently to the small but fierce creature hiding in her over robe.

He chattered back at her then let go of the egg. With a wriggle, he scampered from under her clothes and out of the cave.

Panic at losing her only company whipped through her. "Potokin come back! Please don't leave me alone."

He ignored her strangled plea, and as the scrabbling sounds on the rocks faded, there were no sounds except the lap of water on the shore.

"Fiery blasts of the Nymph, you rascal. Why did you leave me? Why did you leave the egg?" Clyeva muttered, overcome suddenly with the desire to cry. She choked the sobs down, afraid to give into her grief, and shock, in case it overwhelmed her. Someone might hear her loud, uncontrolled sobs from around the cove.

Then, through the dark silence, she heard sounds of movement. She shuddered and huddled lower. *Dear Fire Nymph let it be Potokin.* A splotch of shadow moved amongst the rocks, and seconds later Potokin danced right up to her feet. The Tarki gurgled and hissed at her as he dumped his burden on the sand. Clyeva leaned forward and scrutinised the items—nuts, fruit and the cone shaped shells of the fresh water matian.

"Food. My goodness, Potokin! You're such a clever little creature. Is this for us to share?"

The Tarki waggled his head and chattered madly. He grabbed the shells and opened each one with a razor sharp claw. He handed every second one to Clyeva. She shut her eyes and gulped. Her stomach churned at the taste of the shelled orrtaya, but she fought to control her revulsion because she needed the sustenance. He cracked the nuts, and held up the fruit in one hand and the nuts in the other.

"Thank you. I'm sorry I didn't like you before. I thought you were just a savage little creature."

Potokin looked up at her, his head on one side. He chattered with several, short, sharp bursts before he resumed eating.

Clyeva sighed satisfaction warming her now she'd made peace with the Tarki.

When they had consumed all the food, Potokin ducked his head under the hem of her over robe, climbed up inside the sling, and hugged the egg tightly. Clyeva wrapped her arms around the egg again, hugging it close as a sachan would her belly swollen with child.

As she lay there, she wondered if they were wasting their time trying to save an Ellkiiyn egg abandoned by its mother. Could they even give it enough warmth to ensure the viability of the baby? Left unwarmed for that short time might have killed the babe already.

Just before the solar awakening, she decided she would stay only a couple of solar phasings waiting for Tarlitek, and then she would move on. If he hadn't come by then he would be either dead, or a prisoner of Nyket. She needed to leave the Kelkiki, but where did she go. Even her own people would not have her, and anyway, between her and safety lay the water of the lake.

*Would the Orunan shape shifters recognise me, if I called them as Tarlitek did? Would they help me across the lake or eat me as an exotic snack? Besides where would I go—no one wants me, even my own people?*

Potokin hissed in her ear.

She flinched, and then listened.

Footsteps, soft crunches on the sand, coming closer—slow and stealthy.

She froze.

Concealed in the darkest corner perhaps they wouldn't be seen. As Clyeva cringed back against the rock, a damp chill crept around her neck and the tips of her fingers and nose cooled. A familiar and welcome moist caress.

She sat up with a start. Her heartbeat hiccupped and raced. "Tarlitek?"

"Clyeva," he breathed and went to snatch her into his embrace. "What the Spirit?" he gasped, and stood back. He stared at her in the darkness before reaching out and touching the lump of her abdomen. "What have you done?"

"Taminisha abandoned her egg. Potokin had it. I retrieved it, and Potokin and I are incubating it."

"In the name of the Fire Nymph, the Spirit Ellkii and anyone else who will listen, why are you doing that? The babe would be dead."

"I had to give it a chance. It's Taminisha's baby, and yes I do know there is not much chance of it being born alive, but please don't tell me I can't." Tears filled her eyes. She so wanted this.

Tarlitek kissed her on the cheek. "My dear, Clyeva, I would not tell you no, firstly because it is Taminisha's egg, but it is not my right to deny you. I know how much you want a child to love. All I worry about is your heartbreak if the child inside is dead."

Clyeva stroked the bulge made by the egg. "I know the risk is high, but I will be relying on you to mend my broken heart."

"And I will, my love. And where is the Tarki?"

Clyeva patted her shirt.

Tarlitek raised his eyebrows. "That's risky."

"No, he's being gentle."

"Mmmmp. I don't believe it."

Potokin hissed from inside the shirt.

"All right, Tarki, but don't you draw blood from my lover."

Potokin hissed again.

Tarlitek sat back on the sand. "Now, we have to make plans to escape."

"My love, you're injured."

He touched his exoskeleton. "My head hurts like Orunikan's bite, but the rest are only scratches."

"What's happened at the castle? Nyket dragged Taminisha off to show him the dead baby, and the children were sent to the dungeons. Did you try to rescue the children?"

"We are defeated. Nyket has control of the castle. All Kikishan's Ellkiiyn are dead or those capable have fled into hiding. I expect Nyket will hunt them down. I feared being captured if I went near the dungeons. All I know for sure is Larkin, Nysiah and Aiyana fled early, on Taminisha's instructions. Nyket will abuse Taminisha, and I can do nothing to change that. He will want a child to replace the dead one. I do not know why he didn't kill the children immediately. He has no use of them and Jivin will grow up to be his greatest threat. Perhaps he has a tiny twinge of compassion after all. And while they're alive, I will try to rescue them."

~ ~ ~

Tarlitek and Clyeva huddled in the cave knowing Nyket's victory over Kelkiki would be complete—an utter annihilation of the Aqueena Ellkiiyn and subjugation of the remaining population.

"We have to leave this place, before we are found. It will do no good to anyone if we are executed," Tarlitek said.

"But the children," Clyeva cried. "What about the children? We cannot leave them to their fate."

"I cannot openly fight Nyket, he is Ellkiiyn and there are too many others. We will need to be cunning. We must retreat to safety so we can plan for the future and the rescue of the babes."

Clyeva sobbed. "Those poor babies."

Tarlitek kissed her soot stained cheek. "Do not cry, my love. If he hasn't already killed them, he won't. Perhaps murdering a child is beyond even his evil. Now stay here, I'm going to call the Orunan."

"Water? Never. I cannot do this. Please do not ask me to go out on the lake."

Tarlitek frowned. "I understand your fear, but there is no other choice."

Clyeva shuddered and clutched the egg more securely. She flinched at the sharp sting of Potokin's claws sinking into her flesh.

"You will not have to get wet. I'll find a way. Do not fret, all will be well."

As he disappeared through the cave opening, Clyeva laid her head on the bulge of the egg, and sobbed for her lost friends, the entrapped children, and her own fears.

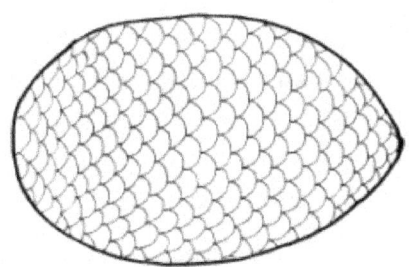

# Chapter Twenty Two

Tarlitek crept around the rocks on the shore, keeping to the shadows. Sounds of battle still came from the direction of the village, but all seemed calm at the castle. He sent a silent prayer to Spirit that Taminisha did not suffer too much, and Nyket would not slaughter Jivin or Milli before he could rescue them. Either he didn't have it in him to kill them, or he had some purpose in keeping them alive in the first place. Tarlitek hoped that purpose would keep them safe for long enough.

The castle walls rose with a formidable steepness into the dark sky. His cold Orunan heart with its soft Myattican centre had shrivelled to an empty shell. The colossal pain inflicted by this carnage sinking deep through his Orunan psyche and singeing his soft Myattican centre.

The bitter taste of defeat and loss stung Tarlitek as he squatted at the edge of the water. He leaned forward and dipped his face slightly under the surface. He lowered his lids to protect his tender Myattican eyes from the cold and blew bubbles. A short spurt, then two long spurts before he lifted his head and tapped the surface of the water five times. He squatted at the edge of the water, the gentle lap of the waves wetting his buttocks as he waited. Etunik and his wives had already fallen to the horizon and soon it would leave the lake in darkness. He hoped it would be long enough to conceal their escape.

A moment later, the water rippled with the slightest splash. A head broke the surface, then another right beside the first. He stayed still, watching them approach.

"Greetings, Brother Tarlitek, you called."

"Greetings, Kalonia. I did call, and thank you for your response. You are no doubt aware of the troubles that have come to Kelkiki."

"We are aware, Brother," Hauk said softly. "Why have you not simply changed and escaped."

Tarlitek frowned. "I couldn't, for I have my mate, Clyeva. We will need a boat. We have an unhatched egg belonging to the Guardians. He is dead, she is prisoner."

"An Ellkiiyn egg. Why?" Kalonia asked the spines standing up on her head clicking with the distortion of her frown.

"My mate believes she can incubate it. She is Abaye, but Taminisha saved her life with Ellkiiyn blood after an abscission."

Hauk cleared his throat with a rasping crackle. "You plan to bring an Abaye, even an extinguished one, on water?"

"She will come, if you are willing."

"Of course we're willing, Brother Tarlitek," Kalonia said. "Be here when the lunor discs sink behind the horizon. It will give us just long enough to be on the lee side of Oventi Rock before the awakening of the solar orb. I assume you're going to your mother's people."

"I am, but I intend to sneak back, when I see Clyeva safe, to rescue the children of Kikishan and Taminisha."

Hauk cleared his throat again. "We'll help you, whatever you do, but we consider you're a fool to even consider such a rescue, in a castle full of Ellkiiyn. Besides, by the time you return, the children are sure to be executed."

Tarlitek shrugged. "Maybe." He stood and stepped back into the shadow of the nearest rock. When he glanced at the water again, he saw no sign of the Orunan.

Clyeva had control of herself by the time he returned to the cave. It eased his angst. He had an overwhelming respect for his soul mate. She had endured much, become strong in the face of adversity, and yet retained her compassion for all. While the abscission had taken her fire, it had not tamed her volatile nature or her fiery passion in the bedroom. Sadly, Tarlitek's own breeding made it difficult for him to cope with her volatility at times.

While he feared she would fail with the egg, and be heartbroken, he admired the way she wanted so desperately to give the unborn Ellkiiyn a chance of survival.

She looked up as he entered. "So you've made the arrangements then?"

He nodded. "When the lunor discs sink we shall go. Hauk and Kalonia are bringing a small boat. Your feet will remain dry, my love."

She tried to smile, but only managed a faded version of her usual sparkling grins.

Tarlitek understood how petrified she must be. He sat beside her, and laid his arm around her shoulders. She leaned into him, both arms hugging the egg close to her body.

Claws sank into his thigh sending a stinging pain ripping across his flesh. Tarlitek stifled a yelp as he grabbed at his injured leg.

"What in the name of Orunikan." His hand closed over the silky skin of the miniature Tarki. "Potokin, you scaly monster, do that again, and I'll leave you behind."

Potokin pulled himself free of Tarlitek's grip and jumped to the floor. He ran with mincing steps to the cave opening, and stood staring out, his front foot raised and pointing.

Tarlitek crept up behind him, and peered out. He couldn't detect anything at first, and then he heard muffled voices and the soft clink of metal on metal. He ducked back down into the deeper shadows and waited.

Potokin did not move, just stood there, pointing.

261

Tarlitek saw them highlighted by the silvery light of Etunik.

A huge black male covered from head to foot in shining armour. He held a wide bladed sword in his left hand.

Beside him, walked a smaller man. His skin so pale it almost glowed against the shiny black armour. His long black hair dangled down his back and a mask covered half his face.

Tarlitek shivered. A full blooded Lycidean—a blood sucking monstrosity. If the Lycideans had joined Nyket then he could expect the Fylitian Wheti and Whydan had also sided with him. He feared Nyket's subjugation of Dykarin would be total.

As Tarlitek watched, the two warriors walked slowly along the sand. Their presence so far from the castle disturbed him. Obviously there would be no safe hiding place in all of Kelkiki. They must make their escape to Myattica this lunor drift or all would be lost.

Not willing to begin a conflict he might lose, Tarlitek stayed still, and watched.

They didn't seem in any hurry.

Etunik and his satellites dipped toward the horizon, and Tarlitek glanced in the direction of the lake. He sensed Kalonia and Hauk nearby, but the surface of the water laid still and silent.

A sudden scuffle by his knees startled him. He looked down.

Potokin had vanished. A fleeting shadow scurried between the rocky outcrops.

Then nothing. He scanned the area. Nothing.

A flash of movement caught his attention.

Potokin leapt from the top of the rock straight at the black warrior's throat. The aggressive Tarki latched onto the soft exposed neck flesh with sharp claws and bit deep and hard.

Blood spurted onto the white sand staining it red.

The man tried to yell, but no sound came out of his mouth. He clutched his throat trying to stem the bleeding as he staggered to his knees.

Tarlitek charged forward, his dagger sliding between the ribs of the other male, right level with his heart.

The man gurgled and dropped to the sand, dead.

The black man clawed at Potokin, trying to release his grip. Potokin sank his teeth in deeper, clamping his jaws tight before he braced his back feet on the man's chest. With the full force of his muscular body, he jerked and tugged. Large chunks of flesh came loose. Potokin threw them over his shoulder before he bit again.

Tarlitek ducked as a piece of bloodied flesh flew in his direction then he leapt forward. He rammed his knife into the black male's stomach. He stabbed repeatedly until the man sagged to the ground, his eyes glazed in death, his mouth slack and his trousers wet with his own urine.

Potokin danced on the sand before he scurried back into the cave and up Clyeva's robe.

Tarlitek scanned the lake. The silver pathway of lunor light on the water had faded and he knew it wouldn't be long before his escape arrived. He grabbed up the Lycidean's battle pack and riffled through the other warrior's clothes removing a dagger and dried baya nuts. He left the bodies where they lay planning to dispose of them as they left, and hurried back to the cave. He shoved the extra supplies into the pack and dropped it on the sand.

He hugged Clyeva. "Not long now, my love."

"Tarlitek, why has everything turned out so badly? Have we angered the Spirits so much they would wish this upon us?"

"Don't think that. You will only cause yourself misery. Besides, it is Nyket who has angered the Great Spirit Ellkii; we have only reacted to ensure our survival."

"No, not that Tarlitek, us. Taminisha saving me, it goes against the laws."

"Only of the Abaye, and this is bigger than that. Now prepare yourself, and your burden, I hear movement on the water." Tarlitek scanned the beach for movement. A gentle ripple on the water the only indication of his siblings' presence. He signalled for Clyeva to come.

Together they scurried across the sand barely bothering to stick to the shadows. The bodies of the warriors lay on the lakeside of the rocks and Tarlitek rolled them into the water far enough so they would float. By the solar awakening, there would be no bodies and the perpetually hungry Orunan would appreciate the snack.

The bow of the dingy slid well up on the dry sand before coming to a standstill.

Clyeva eyed it suspiciously, as she sidled up to it.

Tarlitek helped her climb into the boat because her burden made movement difficult. He didn't want her to falter, or accidently come into contact with the water.

"Hauk, Kalonia, my partner, Clyeva.

Hauk examined Clyeva. "You wouldn't know she was Abaye—she's purple."

Clyeva blushed. It had been quite a while since anyone had commented on her skin tone.

Tarlitek shivered with sympathy for her, and glared at Hauk.

The Orunan shrugged, unable to empathise.

"Ellkiiyn blood exchangement. There is no cure," Tarlitek muttered as he climbed in beside Clyeva.

The two Orunan gathered up the towing ropes and began to swim with long swiping swishes of their tails, moving the wooden boat through the water quickly, and quietly.

~ ~ ~

Clyeva gazed back at the castle. It loomed, dark and haunting; the only illumination came from the dying glow of the fires. To the left the village still burnt. Such murderous destruction of a peaceful land that had become her home broke her heart into multiple pieces. She clutched the egg, and mourned for the two baby Ellkiiyn left behind. She had so loved them both and Aiyana, despite her bloodlines. She gazed up at the sky in the direction of Rabikan and wondered if Larkin had his family to safety. Clyeva silently called on the Spirit Ellkii that Nyket would never find out he had fathered Aiyana, for if he did, then they would never be safe.

Shrivelled with fear, Clyeva sat hunched on the wooden slat that served as a seat and hugged the egg. She couldn't even look at the water sliding past the boat; even the shallow slop in the bottom frightened, and repulsed her.

She shuddered as they sailed through the deep shadow cast by Oventi Rock. Clyeva stared out over the water to where Oventi Rock brooded in darkness.

Tarlitek squeezed her hand hard. "Soon we will be safe."

She smiled at his assurances knowing to reach safety they first had to circumvent the Rock, with its swirling rips and hidden reefs. Logically, with Orunan, they should be safe, but Clyeva didn't feel safe.

"I'm going to help them get past Oventi before the solar orb awakens or they will see us from the castle. We will have no chance if they follow us," Tarlitek whispered in her ear.

Clyeva had only seen her soul mate change shape once, and it terrified her, as he did, in his Orunan form. He stood and stripped off. As he stood there, she couldn't help but admire his naked sachan form, muscular shoulders and torso, narrow waist and long legs. His creamy skin shimmered with green iridescence matching the elegant exoskeleton cradling his upper face. As his body responded to her appreciative gaze, he slipped over the side of the dingy.

The movement rocked the open craft enough to make Clyeva cling to the sides, and stifle a shriek. Potokin squeaked a protest at the clumsy rocking movement even as she grabbed the egg, and resettled it against her body.

"Shhh, Potokin."

She shut her eyes as Tarlitek splashed slightly in the water, and when she opened them, he had shifted into a fully formed Orunan gill breather. The only prominent changes to his handsome features were a large set of pointed teeth, and four matching long slits on the edge of his armpits matching those on his neck. His long muscular tail undulated up and down just below the surface. The way Tarlitek moved so gracefully in the water made it instantly obvious he felt far more comfortable in, than out.

She looked over her shoulder to see Kalonia and Hauk moving with the same graceful strokes, and she couldn't help but wonder if Tarlitek would have been better off if she had died. Her death would have allowed him to grieve then move onto mate with one of his own kind and produce offspring. He said it didn't matter because Orunan abandoned their spawn as soon as they were born.

He told her he struggled to understand the family bonding of his mother's people, and the lifetime commitment of Ellkiiyn parents to their children, or sachan for that matter. Not that he didn't care about people, or children in particular, he just couldn't quite comprehend that sense of ownership parents often had over their children. She supposed this is why he failed to understand her grief at not being able to have his child.

A blood-curdling howl floated across the water. Clyeva hunched down lower, but glanced under her lashes in the direction of Oventi Rock. No one had ever returned from there, they said. Rumours abounded about the huge creatures that roamed the jungle covered island, the swamps infested with huge taraqu that could wind around a full-grown sachan and strangle him to death.

Potokin wriggled and squirmed across Clyeva's body and down passed the egg. He popped his head out under the bottom of her robe.

The howl came again, louder, longer, and higher pitched this time.

Potokin climbed onto the seat and stood upright, his front claws grasping the wooden side of the dingy. He sniffed the air, and scratched his back feet across the seat, then sniffed again.

Another howl reverberated across the water.

Potokin lifted his head toward the sky and howled in answer. Clyeva swung her hand around and over his mouth to silence him. He bit her hand drawing blood and immediately howled again.

A high pitched howl echoed the Tarki's. Potokin responded again.

"Shut him up, Clyeva," Tarlitek grunted from beside the boat.

"I can't, he bit me when I tried."

"Potokin shhh, you'll wake the castle," Tarlitek growled.

The Tarki swivelled around, screwed up his fine boned face and spat in Tarlitek's direction before he howled again. He received a response once more. As the last howl faded Potokin jumped back on Clyeva's lap, pushed his way back into the sling, and curled up around the egg.

"What the Orunikan's bite brought that on?" Hauk spluttered as he moved through the water.

Tarlitek smiled. "I found him on the lakeshore years ago; I suspect he comes from Oventi. Maybe he's communicating with his own kind."

"Well I hope they don't take it into their monstrous heads to come retrieve him."

"That might be a problem because I don't think Potokin wants to leave the egg," Clyeva said.

"Well if they come for him, they can have him, and the egg, if needs be," Tarlitek grumbled. "I do not want to die right now. I have children to rescue."

They sailed around the far end of Oventi Rock just as the solar orb rose. The three Orunan towed the boat into a sheltered cove and in under some eroded cliffs. Here they stayed right through the solar phasing.

Tarlitek shared the hunt for food with his kin someone always guarding the boat. Even Potokin gobbled down some raw orrtaya while Clyeva made do with some nuts and fruits courtesy of the dead guards.

At last, the solar orb disappeared, and darkness fell. Etunik hadn't risen when they set off and Hauk assured them they would be safely on Myattican shores before it did.

They moved swiftly around the island's shore, and then with a sudden spurt of speed, they hurtled across the lake to the shore of Myattica.

Clyeva watched the horizon with a quiver in her stomach and a prickle across her scalp as the glow increased behind the hills. She glanced back toward the castle, but Oventi Rock blocked her line of sight. They were just pulling the boat up onto the sand when the Etunik peeped above the horizon.

Tarlitek transformed back to his sachan form, got dressed and helped Clyeva climb out of the boat onto the dry sand.

By the time she'd steadied herself and adjusted the egg, the boat had vanished, and the lake appeared deserted. Not even a splash showed her where Hauk and Kalonia had gone.

They hurried up the sand and slipped in between the trees just as the lunor beams lit the beach in silver gossamer light.

"We did it, my love. Do you want me to carry the egg?"

She clutched the egg closer to her body. "No, I'll do it."

Tarlitek nodded. "Let's find Shula."

Darkness shrouded the Myattican settlement. Tarlitek navigated through the village to his sister's hut and tapped softly on the door. A squawk and a flutter came from inside and Shula appeared, her eyes still glazed with sleep.

"Dearest Brother, thank the Great Spirit you are safe." She threw herself into his embrace. "I so feared for you. Mazin told me of the slaughter at Kelkiki."

Tarlitek held her tight. "It is indeed a slaughter." His voice vibrated with his distress.

Clyeva suspected his croak came from pushing sobs down so they didn't escape.

"Shhh, Brother. Everyone sleeps. Come inside, so we can talk."

Tarlitek held out his hand to her. "Come Clyeva."

She followed her lover and his sister inside.

Shula studied her.

"This is Clyeva, my soul mate."

Shula's eyes popped wide open. "But how Brother, she is fire."

Tarlitek shook his head. "It is a long story for another time, Sister, but Taminisha brought us together and we are forever indebted.

Shula paled. "Taminisha and Kikishan? Are they safe?"

Tarlitek's expression darkened. "No."

Tears glistened in Shula's round eyes as she glanced at Clyeva. "And you're breeding, Brother?"

Clyeva cringed, and Tarlitek burst into laughter.

"No, Sister, we are not, but we have rescued Taminisha's unhatched egg."

"An Ellkiiyn egg? Great Spirit. Come Clyeva, welcome, and put your burden there by the fire."

Clyeva found it difficult to explain her need to protect the egg and her hope it would hatch.

Shula seemed to understand. Together they made a nest and Shula showed Clyeva how to provide warmth by heating rocks and placing them under the nest coverings.

All the time Potokin clung to the egg. Nothing could lure him away. The Tarki howled and screeched hysterically if anyone dared try to lift him from the shell.

Shula used a slim bone instrument to listen for the babe's heartbeat, but the thickness of the shell blocked out any sounds of life.

Potokin continued to chatter and whistle to the egg. Clyeva watched his devotion and prayed to the Fire Nymph and the Great Spirit Ellkii this indicated the child still lived. With no way to tell if the babe inside had survived the journey, it would be an uneasy wait until hatching.

~   ~   ~

Tarlitek wandered restlessly around the settlement, talking to this one and that one about escape plans for the children, but nothing seemed to gel. Tarlitek fretted. Time passed quickly, and he had failed to devise a plan to rescue the children. Three solar phasings after their escape and he didn't even know if they were still alive. He kept hoping Nyket, despite his previous murderous actions, didn't have the level of malice it would require to murder tiny babes.

No one seemed willing or able to help. They feared the Ellkiiyn, in particular Nyket. So far, he had left the Myatticans alone, and they wanted it to stay that way even though they now harboured several hundred refugees.

Tarlitek wandered down to the refugee camp and walked through the narrow spaces that served as paths between makeshift dwellings. He stared into every face, searching for someone familiar. Someone who might help him attempt the impossible.

As he walked, his spirits dropped even more. The majority of the refugees were women and children, or injured warriors crippled beyond usefulness on a battlefield. Tarlitek grappled with his dilemma, but nothing would solidify into a workable plan.

"Come on, Warrior, give us some food. Any will do."

"One orrtaya will feed a family."

"Please, Warrior."

Three tiny urchins surrounded him, tugging at his clothes, begging for food. They were Ellkiiyn children in ragged habilens, their pectenites not yet formed. He tried to ignore them, but his heart ached for they were only babies, and obviously hungry.

"Hey you lot, leave the Warrior alone," a young voice scolded.

Tarlitek glanced at the boy who'd spoken. He gasped then clutched his chest as his heart lurched painfully. "Jivin, by the Spirit, Jivin how did you get here?"

The boy sneered at him. "I'm not Jivin, I'm Kashwen."

"Kashwen?" Tarlitek repeated. "But you look so like him."

"He looks like whom?"

Tarlitek turned slowly to face the woman who had spoken, reluctant to take his eyes off the boy that could be Jivin's twin. "He is identical to a child I know, Madame."

"What child and what's your interest?"

The harshness in the woman's voice, and the glum expression on her face cut through his tough gill breather skin. He considered shying away without replying. Instead, he steadied himself and looked directly into her eyes and her unspoken challenge. "He looks like the child of Kikishan, the Guardian of Kelkiki and my interest is that of a family friend."

"Ha, the dead Guardian you mean?"

The whip of her nastiness lashed at him. "Yes, the dead Guardian."

"Not that I had anything against Guardian Kikishan, my mate died in the battle to save Kelkiki. My animosity rests on his uncle, Mekkan. My son is his offspring. Took me by force, he did and I had to birth him the sachan way. Destroyed me it did. They said he was mad from the scalinette fever at the time. No excuse, I say."

The shock of her statement slammed into his chest. His heart faltered, and then raced, as he gasped in huge breaths. Kikishan's uncle fathered the child, Kashwen. He looked again at the embittered mother. "You are full blood Ellkiiyn?"

"I'm Islantina, full-blood Aqueena Ellkiiyn. So the boy's pure, if that's what you mean."

Tarlitek nodded.

"You can have him if you want. I have no love for the boy. What'll you give me in exchange?"

The idea whipped at his mind. *Could he? Would he dare? What about the child?* A life in prison would be no worse than life on the streets begging and picking pockets for any scrap of food. He probably wouldn't reach adulthood anyway, dead of starvation or exiled as punishment for his petty crimes. His mind whirled. The pros and cons slammed at him. Could he do this? Guilt seared. Rejection of the plan hovered, but he inhaled deeply and sighed the breath out. If he had an escape planned before Kashwen reached adulthood and became a threat to Nyket's rule he could tolerate the guilt.

"So you'll sell him to me?"

"If you pay the price," the woman snapped.

The children stopped mucking around and stood watching them talk. Kashwen seemed wary, but sidled closer to his mother.

"My offer is this; I will support you, and your six children, until you mate again, or for life. I will give you food and shelter. My sister, Shula, will find you gainful occupation here in Myattica. Life won't be luxurious, but it will be adequate."

The thin, dishevelled woman gaped at him then smiled a cunning, satisfied smile. "I agree to your terms." She smiled at Kashwen. "So, at last he has brought some good to his mother, instead of misery and shame."

Kashwen glared at her, spun on his heel and took off down the road; his bare feet pounded on the dirt road stirring up a cloud of fine white dust.

Tarlitek leapt into motion and thundered after the child. He caught up to him well before the end of the row of dwellings and grabbed him by the threadbare collar.

"Whoa boy, you aren't going anywhere," he growled.

"Let me go. Let me go, charlatan, monster, scaly head!" Kashwen yelled as he flailed with his fists and kicked vigorously with his bare feet.

Tarlitek laughed. "Calm down. Abuse will get you nowhere; my orrtaya scales are very thick. You are mine now, do you understand? Your mother has sold you so she can feed your siblings and herself."

"Ma! Ma!" Kashwen cried.

Tarlitek carried him back to where his mother stood.

She appeared unmoved by his distress, her expression sour and cold.

"Madame, tell your son his fate."

"Why? You've already told him," she snarled.

"He needs to hear it from you, Madame, so he knows he's not welcome to return to you any time soon. It will make my job easier," Tarlitek said, as he set the boy's feet on the ground.

The boy made no further attempt to run away. Just stood hunched miserably, his gaze lowered.

"Kashwen, listen closely. I have sold you to this male Orunan called Tarlitek. He has use for you, I don't know what, but with so many mouths to feed and no mate, one less will be a blessing."

Kashwen gazed up at her. "But Ma, it wasn't my fault."

Islantina frowned. "That may be so, son, but your presence here reminds me every moment of the shame your father wrought on me. It is better you're gone."

"Ma, I love you," Kashwen wailed.

"Take him, Orunan, take him now," Islantina said.

Tarlitek saw her eyes fill with tears, and knew she did have a heart after all. Nevertheless, she'd made a deal and the boy would serve his purpose very well. He took the boy's arm in a slightly gentler hold.

"Come on, Kashwen, we have things to do."

"Ma, Ma, please don't do this. Ma," Kashwen bawled, struggling to pull away from Tarlitek.

When his mother didn't reply, simply turning away, and gathering her other six around her, he stopped fighting his destiny, and walked obediently beside Tarlitek, his head down, tears wetting his cheeks.

Tarlitek felt for him, and by the time he got back to Shula's house, a terrible guilt preyed on his soul for what he planned to do.

Clyeva pounced on the boy as soon as they entered. "Jivin, by fire and fury, it's you!"

Kashwen pouted. "I'm Kashwen and I'm his now," he mumbled pointing at Tarlitek.

"What is this, Tarlitek? Who is this child, and why do you have him? He's not happy. What is going on?"

Clyeva's words batted at him.

His guilt swelled into an unbearable lump. "I need you to listen to me. I have a plan, but you must let me speak before you judge."

Clyeva looked from the boy's tear-stained face to her mate.

Tarlitek knew her disapproval would be enormous, savage even. He became defensive before he began to speak.

"Shula, take the child, see him bathed and fed, but do not let him out of your sight. Boy, remember your good behaviour buys food and accommodation for your family for life. You run and they starve, understood?"

The boy bowed his head, but remained silent.

"Tarlitek, that is so cruel," Clyeva protested loudly.

"Shhh, Clyeva," Tarlitek hissed.

They watched as Shula disappeared outside with the boy.

"Tell me what thing you have done, what is this plan that involves a child, a baby."

"You see he looks just like Jivin, yes?"

Clyeva nodded.

"Well, he's actually the spawn of Kikishan's Uncle Mekkan, a nasty piece of work. Not only did he force himself on the child's mother, but also he tried to usurp a very young inexperienced Kikishan when he first became Guardian. He refused to give up the elevation that came with being Regent so in the end Kikishan killed him." Tarlitek explained the history, trying to pave the way for his plan.

"But what is your need of him?"

"Do not be mad at me, but I intend to exchange this unwanted child for Jivin..."

Clyeva leapt up from her chair. "How could you propose such an evil thing? To sacrifice one child, for another? How could you?"

Tarlitek stared at her. "Then what do you propose. If I rescue them, we will have Nyket chasing us forever after. Their deaths would be inevitable along with ours. We will have to leave Myattica and where would we go? None would give us sanctuary. This way he will never know. Jivin will have a chance to grow up and reclaim his throne."

"But Tarlitek, that poor child. Nyket might kill him."

"Yes, Nyket might, but I don't think so. If he has not already executed Jivin and Milli, I don't think he will. It won't be until they're older and he perceives a threat to his rule. Of course, if he has already killed Jivin and Milli, I will bring him back."

"That's monstrous."

"Maybe, but workable, and let's face facts. Kashwen will soon die on the streets anyway. He is so malnourished that although he's five, he only appears the same size as Jivin. He's starving, as are his six siblings and his mother. This way the six and the mother survive with a good life and she no longer has to see the face of her rapist in her son's features."

"In theory—but such an ugly plan—cruel, cold, ruthless. For Fire Nymph's sake, he is but a baby."

"I know."

"On our love, Tarlitek, come up with another plan. One I can accept."

Sooty flakes scattered down her cheeks.

Tarlitek slumped to the floor. Disgust burned through him. *Am I that cold of heart, devoid of soul? No, I cringe, but have nothing else."*

He touched Clyeva's shoulder.

She flinched away from him.

"I'm sorry, my love, I have no other plan that will not bring Nyket's wrath and mercenaries upon us and any who help us."

"Well, say you do this horrendous thing, how are you going to manage it, and if you do, how will you reconcile your soul with Spirit?" Clyeva said.

"I don't know yet how I'm going to accomplish the rescue, but as for reconciliation I have no need, for Orunan have no souls," Tarlitek said quietly.

"No, Brother dear, but Myatticans do."

A shudder pulsed through him as he stared back at Shula.

"Fire and brimstone, what a horrendous plan," Clyeva wailed, pacing the room.

Tarlitek grabbed her shoulders and peered down into her face. "Then you suggest we leave Jivin and Milli to die, or rot in the dungeons. Do you not want to save them?"

She choked back sobs. "No, my love, we must save them, but it seems so cruel."

"It is, but these are cruel times," Tarlitek said.

"And what about Milli?"

Tarlitek stroked her cheek with one finger. "Do not ask, but know I will make arrangements. I will bring *both* Taminisha's babies home to you."

Shula touched his shoulder. "Tarlitek, in the lack of another plan, can I suggest you take Khoury with you. As half Ellkiiyn and half Myattican, he could infiltrate the castle. He could watch over the boy and snatch him to safety if Nyket threatens his life."

Tarlitek inhaled deeply then let the air out on a soft whoosh. "For a male to have such a sister is a blessing. Thank you, Shula, you ease my self-condemnation." He faced Clyeva. "My love, can you reconcile yourself to such an arrangement."

She looked up at him. "Only just, my love."

"Then it shall be. Summon Khoury."

# Chapter Twenty Three

A solar phasing later, Tarlitek waited on the edge of the forest for darkness to fall.

Khoury lounged against a tree whittling on a small piece of timber a wide grin on his face.

Even though the youth appeared level headed and keen to leave home, Tarlitek worried at his nephew's eagerness to take on the mission. As an Ellkiiyn mixed breed he couldn't migrate with the Myattican males as his size alone would cause an uproar in any settlement they visited. He had voiced his resentment for the last year as the natural restlessness of the Myattican males consumed him. Tarlitek silently sympathised with his dilemma.

Kashwen sat by his feet flicking his hands through the fine yellow sand. He'd shown no interest in his fate, still reeling from his mother's betrayal. He listened obediently when Tarlitek had drilled him in the details he needed to know about the Guardians of Kelkiki. He had merely nodded when Tarlitek had outlined the future, explaining, despite his imprisonment, he would receive food and clothing, and possibly training in Ellkiiyn law. More than he would ever hope for on the streets or in his mother's dubious care.

Tarlitek promised his protector would ensure he received the best care and if Nyket suddenly decided to execute him Khoury would snatch him from the castle and transport him to Myattica. The boy had an obvious intelligence, and being older than Jivin, he had better communication skills.

Kashwen looked up. "This child, Jivin is more important than me because he is the Guardian's heir."

Shame heated his Orunan coldness. He looked the boy directly in the eye. "Yes. If he lives he will restore Kelkiki to its true state and help bring peace back to Dykarin."

The boy sighed. "I suppose this is my karma for my father's crimes. I accept my burden."

Tarlitek patted the boy's shoulder. "You are a clever and brave boy, Kashwen. Jivin will reward you when the Era of Darkness is passed."

"I hope."

Despite the boy's apparent acceptance of his fate, guilt plagued Tarlitek.

With a slight splash, the shadow of the boat appeared by the rocky point at the end of the cove. Tarlitek took Kashwen's arm and walked toward it.

Hauk pushed it onto the sand, "Greetings, Brother."

"Greetings, Hauk," Tarlitek replied as he lifted Kashwen into the boat. "Has Kalonia managed to secure what I requested?'

Hauk grimaced. "She had no problem, many young die at birth or soon after in these terrible times."

"They do. Nyket has much to answer for," Tarlitek said as he stripped, waded into the water and transformed.

With the lunor discs resting behind the horizon, and a blanket of cloud shrouding the landscape, a deep darkness concealed their movements. With a light load and two strong swimmers, they made good time across the lake, easing into the concealed cove behind the castle. Khoury glided beside them just above the surface of the lake. He had nothing to fear from Orunikan in the company of two gill breathers.

Kalonia emerged from the rocks in her sachan form, a tiny bundle in her arms.

"I have what you requested. It's Aqueena Ellkiiyn, more than half blood, I think. The mother died trying to incubate it alone after her mate died in the attack on the castle and this..." She held out a small flask. "Just a drop or two, and they will both sleep through one solar phase and one lunor drift."

"Ah, that is for the best, the mother will not mourn her lost child," Tarlitek said as he took the flask of potion, and then held his arms out for the pitiful bundle Kalonia held. He opened the wraps and peered down at the tiny face of the dead babe. It appeared almost full blood Aqueena Ellkiiyn and perfect to replace Milli. He carefully tucked the corpse in his coat.

Tarlitek turned to help Kashwen out of the boat. "I don't know how long I will be, or even if it can be done. Will you wait for me—a couple of solar phasings?"

Khoury transmogrified, and waited in silence.

Kalonia had already waded into the water keen to transform to her gill breather body, and Hauk rested his muscular tail on the sand as he floated by the boat.

"We will wait, Brother, or if anything goes wrong, call us if you can," Hauk replied.

"Thank you," Tarlitek said quietly, and then trudged up the sand with Khoury and Kashwen trailing behind.

The castle walls came right down to the beach on this side. There were tunnels dug out of the coastal rock that went all the way into the dungeons. The opening came out in the cellars, which had allowed supplies to come in and out during sieges of past eras. He entered now into total blackness. Kashwen baulked at the darkness.

Tarlitek took his hand and pulled him forward. "Kashwen, do not be afraid, it's only the dark."

"But bad things come in the dark," he whimpered.

"You have me, Kashwen, now let's move on, and you must be very quiet, or we shall all die," Khoury whispered.

Kashwen pouted. Tarlitek could feel the weight of the boy dragging on his arm as he reluctantly followed in his footsteps.

He heard the guards long before he reached the dungeons. They were arguing about the lateness of their evening rations, and in the distance, he heard the cry of a baby. Milli, he assumed. The cold of the tiny corpse seeped into his flesh, and even though he didn't believe, he whispered a blessing on the dead baby as he moved deeper into the tunnels.

At last, he could see a light glowing from one of the cells and he could hear a childish voice complaining about his lack of food. When he heard a woman's voice soothing the child, he halted. *By Orunikan, they had a nanny.* The one scenario he had not thought of, or factored into his plan, but of course, someone had to care for the baby. *My lack of fore thought, by Orunikan, will foil the plan. I'm a careless Orunan fool.*

He backtracked to where the guards sat grumbling about the lack of food. He could see the keys hanging from the big black guard's belt.

Kashwen touched Tarlitek's shoulder, and held out his hand for the flask Kalonia had given him. Tarlitek tightened his hold on the bottle, but the boy just indicated again that he wanted it. With no other plan coming to mind, Tarlitek laid it in the boy's palm.

He heard footsteps and signalled to Kashwen someone approached along the corridor. Kashwen's hand closed over the small container, and he vanished, slipping in and out of the shadows like the spirit of the dead.

The serving boy came around the corner.

Tarlitek saw him stumble then scrabble to regain his balance without spilling the food. There was a rattle of metal plates and a splatter of wine, but the boy stayed upright.

He continued on past Tarlitek's hiding spot to where the guards waited.

Tarlitek looked down at the slight touch on his arm. Kashwen stood there holding out the half-empty flask. As Tarlitek took the bottle, Kashwen indicated the guards would soon fall asleep. Despite Tarlitek's close observation, he had not seen the boy administer the potion. He guessed the life on the street had forced him to hone his sleight of hand as part of his survival skills.

They waited silently in the corner, listening to the males gobble down their food. Tarlitek heard the door of the children's cell clang. His angst slipped away at the unexpected bonus to his plan that the serving boy had delivered the drugged food to them as well.

With all of them asleep, there would be no risk of the nanny screaming or Jivin shouting in excitement and revealing his presence.

With the tray empty, the boy walked jauntily past, though he did hesitate at the spot where he tripped, and peered around before he disappeared up the stone steps.

It wasn't long before the conversation from the guards became stilted and slurred. Soon it faded out altogether.

Tarlitek peered around the corner. They all slept, one lying down, the other two still sitting upright their chins on their chests.

Kashwen darted forward, and without even the slightest jingle, he had the keys in his hand. Tarlitek patted the boy on the back and the three of them made their way to the children's cell.

All inside slept soundly.

Tarlitek opened the door and slipped inside. Tarlitek lifted Milli out of the nanny's embrace and laid her in the cradle; he pulled out the corpse of his coat and slipped it between the woman's arms. A wave of sympathy washed over him for the trauma Flatasha would endure on waking.

He scooped Jivin from the floor and Milli from the cradle then stepped out of the cell. He laid the children down on the stone outside the door and leaned closer to Kashwen. "Your sacrifice for the good of

Dykarin will always be honoured. Your family will be well catered for."

Tears filled the child's eyes and ran down his cheeks. "You're not really going to leave me are you?"

Guilt stabbed at him piercing his cold Orunan heart. "Yes, I must take the children before I am seen because Nyket knows me. Khoury will remain here in the castle. He will see you are cared for."

"I don't want to do this. What if Nyket kills me?"

"Kashwen, I don't think he'll do that. Cold blooded as he is, I don't think he will kill you as long as you pretend to be the Guardian's son. See, he hasn't harmed these little ones. Khoury, will watch over you and rescue you if need be. It's the best I can do."

"I don't want to do this."

His pleas cut through Tarlitek with the sharp sting of a knife, but he'd made this plan and he couldn't let his soft Myattican side stop it from succeeding. He reached out, pushed the boy into the cell with the sleeping nanny and the dead baby, and hastily pulled the door shut. He held out the flask. "Take a sip, Kashwen, and sleep. It won't be so bad when you wake.

He tugged his necklace with the big red lake pebble from around his neck and ran his fingers over the three knots. "Here, take this and give it to the Lady Kelkiki, when you see her. Don't lose it for your life may depend on her getting it. Make sure to call her Mamam. She will know you are not Jivin, but she will understand my message.

"What if she doesn't?"

"She will."

"Don't leave me here," Kashwen pleaded.

"I'm here, Kashwen. I will join the guards and you will see me every solar phasing and lunor drift. Drink some potion and sleep."

Almost blinded with tears, Tarlitek scooped up Taminisha's children and hurried down the corridor. He glanced over his shoulder, just once, and immediately wished he hadn't. Kashwen stood at the barred door, his tiny hands clinging to the bars, his face white and tear stained. "Take care of him and yourself, Khoury."

Khoury nodded. "Never fear, Uncle, all will be well."

Tarlitek turned away feeling like the monster worshiped by his people. Had his Orunan side overwhelmed his mother's gentleness? He hoped not. However, considering what he'd just done, he questioned it. Did one child have more value than another? He couldn't answer that question, not right now, anyway, and maybe never.

He hurried through the corridors and down the tunnels, the sleeping children heavy on his arms and back. He paused in his shuffling run to catch his breath, and heard sounds echoing in the tunnel behind him—Kashwen, wailing for him to come back. The plaintive sound cut through his determination and stabbed deep into his soul. Even his Orunan detachment cringed at what he'd done and Tarlitek almost retraced his steps, but he hardened his heart. He knew for Jivin and Milli would never have a chance to grow up to right the wrong of Kelkiki if Nyket ever found out someone had rescued them.

The boat lay abandoned on the sand. The waters of the lake were still and dark. A thick mist wafted over the water, right up to the castle walls and Tarlitek grateful for its concealing curtain. He paused in the lee of the cliffs before he hurried to the water's edge. He laid the unconscious children in the boat before he squatted in the water, ducked his head under the surface, and blew a series of bubbles. He barely had his head back in the air and Hauk and Kalonia bobbed up beside him.

He stripped and waded deep into the icy water before he transformed. With the three of them towing the wooden boat, it scudded across the surface of the lake. He didn't want to spend any time trapped in the lee of Oventi Rock with the children so they skirted Oventi by staying in the shallows along the Abaye coastline. Any attack at this stage would be a disaster because Tarlitek knew he could not hide in Abaye, or ask their help because of Clyeva. A desperate need prodded him—a need to get back to Myattica and settle with Clyeva to raise the children. The cold hard lump beside his heart would be his constant companion until he saw Kashwen safe. He hated himself for what he'd done, and hoped Clyeva would forgive him in time.

~   ~   ~

Taminisha paced the room, anger boiled inside her, stoked by a terrible grief. She could do nothing to end her torture. With her children alive, she had something to live for at least, but for how long, she didn't know. She stared out the window across the lake and wondered if Tarlitek and Clyeva had survived. Shut in the room she had no way of finding out. No one spoke to her.

Even though she knew Larkin had escaped with Nysiah and Aiyana, she did not expect him to bring reinforcements. She didn't care so much for herself because with Kikishan dead nothing, but her children mattered.

She believed if Tarlitek had survived, he would fulfil his promise and rescue her children. Nyket had ignored the purple Abaye woman when he'd captured Taminisha, and the children, but others could have captured or killed her since.

There would be no escape from her comfortable prison, but she would do anything to keep her children alive. She did not doubt Tarlitek would keep his promise if he could. She clung to the tiny patter of their hearts echoing faintly next to hers. She shied away from the thought of her abandoned egg and the dead babe.

Nyket would come to her soon, and she had to prepare her mind to allow herself to ovulate. She knew he would mate with her in sachan form because her lack of love and desire for him would nullify the Ellkiiyn urge to mate and breed. Besides, his tainted blood probably prevented him from completing the mating dance as Ellkiiyn.

It pleased her that the sachan way made conception harder and the incubation longer. She wondered briefly how he mated with Ulyana. If sachan form then Ulyana would have transmogrified immediately to delay the production of the egg until she reached Kelkiki and joined with Larkin.

Nyket came and yes, he took her in the sachan fashion. Taminisha cringed against the burning pain as he thrust into her repeatedly. She stayed silent while he completed the act then she lay on the bed and cried as he walked from the room.

After he left, she washed herself thoroughly, feeling sick at the smell of his sticky life force. He came again early awakening, often ripping back the covers and waking her. Already aroused, his swollen member sticking straight out in front of him he did not pause to arouse her. She lay back and opened her legs.

"Ah you are such a good mother. What you will do for your children," Nyket scoffed.

"Only for my children."

He laughed as he climbed on top of her poking roughly with his hard member. She cringed against the agony as he shoved himself into her. He didn't take long and when he finished he climbed off and admired her naked body.

"So beautiful, so alluring. I will be back often, for I desire you, almost as much as I desire a child."

"Nyket, I want something from you."

"Really, besides my joining? What more could you want?"

"I want my children to live in comfort, not in the dungeons. They are children; they need fresh air, solar rays, training in the law of Ellkiiyn."

"Ha, you ask far too much, Taminisha besides there is no 'law of Ellkiiyn' anymore only the law of Nyket. Be grateful they still live."

She let the tears fall then, so he could see, but she didn't ask again.

~ ~ ~

Nyket shuddered with anger as he left Taminisha crying on the bed. He didn't know what to do with the children. He'd acted atrociously toward others in his climb for power, killing and maiming any who opposed him, and some who didn't.

He acknowledged his vicious streak and greed for power, but somehow he couldn't quite come at killing babies. The thought sent a shiver of disgust over his skin and yet he despised his weakness. It created a problem, for they grew up, and then sought revenge. He paced the keep terrace staring out over the lake without really seeing it, as he sought a solution to his dilemma.

The blood-curdling scream came repeatedly, echoing up the stairs leading from the dungeons. Nyket spun around. The scream came again. He hurried down the steep stone stairs as another scream scraped along his spine. The guards huddled inside the children's cell around the screeching nanny.

Nyket walked over and slapped her across the face. Her hollering died in her throat as she gasped for breath.

"What is this ruckus about?" Nyket shouted.

The woman held up the baby still wrapped in its blanket. "She's dead, gone in her sleep. Millinsha is dead," Flatasha cried.

Shock thumped into Nyket. He gasped as he looked at the infant. The tiny face had become blue in death, the rosebud mouth open, eyes closed. The boy crouched in the corner of the cell, his chubby face white, and pinched, around his masq. Tears trickled down his cheeks.

"On the wrath of the Spirit, couldn't you even keep a baby alive, you useless female," he yelled, and slapped the nanny again.

Nausea washed over him. Why had the child died? Now what did he do. Her living children kept Taminisha pliable. He glanced toward the boy. Did he just kill him now, or did he let him live? Nyket looked again at the tiny corpse then glared at the cringing boy. "Curse the Spirit, I cannot," he muttered even though he knew in time it would come back to haunt him. "You there." He pointed to the orange Ellkiiyn Myattican cross breed standing silently to one side. "Get me Dynatina and Adielan, here, now."

Nyket stayed in the cell beside the sobbing nanny until the older couple appeared.

"Dynatina, Adielan, you will take this child, settle in the northern tower and raise him. Feed him, educate him and let him play in the solar rays. Everything you would do for your own grandson, except he is never to be unattended or leave the castle. If he escapes, I will kill you, your two children and your grandchildren. Do I make myself clear?"

They bowed.

"And you—what's your name?"

"My name is Khoury, my lord."

"It's Guardian Nyket to you. You'll guard the child with your life through solar phasing and lunor drift."

Khoury bobbed his head. "Yes, Guardian Nyket."

"Go now and take him with you. He snatched the wrapped corpse from Flatasha and shoved it in Dynatina's direction. "Arrange for the baby to be offered to Spirit as appropriate. Her name is Millinsha. In addition, you will not talk of this, ever. When instructed, you shall present one of your granddaughters and the boy to his mother, Taminisha."

"The boy's name, Guardian Nyket?"

"I don't know, ask him?" Nyket snapped as he swung around. With a savage thrust of his blade, he ran Flatasha through the chest.

The nanny never made a sound as she died, and slumped to the floor.

Dynatina walked toward the child. He cringed into the corner.

"What is your name, child?' she asked.

He looked up at the woman. "My name is Jivin," he said.

# Chapter Twenty Four

Shula and Mazin met him as they pushed the dingy up onto the beach. Jivin stirred, but didn't wake. Mazin picked him up and slung him over his feathered shoulder. Shula held her arms out and Tarlitek handed her the unconscious baby before he pushed himself back into the water intending to feed before he transformed.

Clyeva didn't like orrtaya, especially freshly dead, and raw. Out of respect for their love, Tarlitek would forgo it mostly, but at times like this, he made the most of getting a feed of his favourite delicacy.

Mazin and Shula began the short walk back to the settlement, but Tarlitek easily caught up with them as they laboured under their burdens. He immediately took Jivin from Mazin as they walked together through the gloom of the forest. The solar orb had risen well above the horizon by the time they entered the settlement.

"You have the babes? My love, you've rescued them!" Clyeva cried as she took Milli from Shula just in time to see her open her eyes.

The baby immediately began to cry.

"I'll get food," Shula said hurrying away.

Clyeva smiled her thanks to Shula. "Did you see Taminisha?"

Tarlitek frowned. "With such a limited time to make the exchanges, I could not look for her."

"And the boy, Kashwen?"

"He cried when I left him, but Khoury will watch over him."

"And what if Nyket kills this child? And what of Milli's substitute, is she to die too?"

Tarlitek pulled his fiery mate and the now quietly sobbing baby into his embrace. "Milli is dead as far as Nyket knows. There is only Kashwen, and for him I cannot guarantee anything."

Clyeva wept on Tarlitek's shoulder. "So cruel, the world is so cruel."

She didn't pull away until Shula arrived with the milk taken from their bovinites. Clyeva began to spoon it into Milli's mouth. She spat it out and cried. Clyeva spooned more warm milk in and finally Milli took it without protest.

"Mamam. Mamam," Jivin screamed as he woke up.

Clyeva handed Milli to Shula and snatched the boy off the floor where Tarlitek had laid him.

"Shhh, baby, shhh, Clyeva is here. Do not be afraid, Clyeva is here."

The child looked up at her before he buried his face in her shoulder and began to sob, his tiny hands clinging to Clyeva's hair and neck. "Clyvee, Clyvee," he cried, again and again.

"Come, baby, take this, it will fill your tummy." Clyeva perched Jivin on her knee.

Tarlitek held the bowl of mushy stuff close and Clyeva spooned the warm food into Jivin's mouth.

"Where's, Mamam? Jivin saw her, she is crying. Jivin cry too, bad Ellkiiyn hurt Jivin. Jivin make fire hurt bad Ellkiiyn."

Clyeva cuddled him. "You made fire?"

Jivin nodded and smiled. "Jivin make big fire at bad Ellkiiyn. Where's Mamam?"

"Your Mamam is at the castle. A bad Ellkiiyn is making her stay there," Clyeva soothed.

"I want Mamam, Clyvee. I want my Mamam."

"Dear baby, she cannot be with you right now. You will have to make do with Clyvee and Tarlitek, and Milli is here too," Clyeva said gently rocking the child.

"All right. Will Mamam come soon?" Jivin asked.

It took an enormous effort for Clyeva to keep her voice steady, and sobs choked in her throat. "I don't know, Jivin, I don't know."

Jivin tucked his head down when offered more food. Clyeva hugged him and rocked gently back and forth. The child's eyes closed, he put his thumb in his mouth, and moments later, he fell asleep.

~ ~ ~

Nyket came every awakening for fifty solar phasings.

At the end, Taminisha knew she carried his baby in the sachan way, and she cried herself to sleep. She intended to tell Nyket when he next came in the vague hope he would stop assaulting her while she was with child. She had submitted to his demands without complaint and she intended to press hard to see her children.

Taminisha woke with a start. Sweat beaded on her skin. She scanned the room for the alien presence. She sank back on the pillows and stilled, filled with a sense of trepidation. Something was wrong, different, missing. On the next breath, realisation shot through her. She coughed and gasped as the silence by her heart seared through her. Nothing, but an empty shadow where her children's pattering should be. A hole, wrapped in a pulsing throb—alien, but familiar. She jerked upright in the realisation the only heartbeat beside her own was the child she carried!

The intrusion worried her less than the absence of the others. Icy paralysis gripped her. Tears welled, but she wiped them away, venting her torment with a silent scream in her mind. *My babies, dear Spirit, my babies are gone.* Her whole body vibrated, her heart splintered. She choked on each breath. Shudders of grief consumed her.

Sometime before the solar awakening, she harnessed her grief and flexed her resolve. Nyket's murderous actions had released her from the obligation to survive. She would extinguish herself and give no apology to the Great Spirit. She huddled on the bed raking through her options.

When he walked in dressed only in his under robe already sexually aroused, Taminisha sighed.

"You are tired, my lady. Too tired to service me?"

"Nyket, I have conceived. In just over one hundred and sixty solar phasings, you will have your child. Please leave me alone."

"Dear Taminisha, it doesn't work like that. I have come to enjoy our joining so much I plan to continue until I grow bored, or you're too big to handle it."

"Fine, Nyket, whatever you want, but you promised I could see my children when I got with child I want you to honour that promise."

"Ah yes, the children. Well turn around and bend over. I'm going to take you like a creature of the field does and, when I'm finished, I will bring the children to you," he replied.

Taminisha shuddered, but took up the position he requested. He had never bothered with preliminaries so Taminisha had taken to using some salve to ease his brutality. He strutted up to her and forcing her legs apart, he shoved his swollen member inside her. She lay her head down and bore the thrusting and the discomfort until he'd finished. She stayed kneeling in the position until he left the room then she dragged her aching body from the bed.

With the water remaining in the wash jug, she doused her body and wiped his presence away with a well-soaped flannel. The coldness eased her irritated flesh and still damp she drew a fresh habilan over her body. She wrapped a shawl around her shoulders and eased herself into the rocking chair.

She suspected she waited in vain. The stillness in her chest, the aching empty hole, told its own truth. Nyket's lack of concern at her demands sliced through her. *What by Spirit, did he plan to do? No Jivin, no Milli then there would be no unborn heir. She vowed revenge in the only way open to her. I will unburden myself of this child.*

It took so long, she had almost given up hope when she heard footsteps, and a child's high piping voice.

"Where are we going, Dynatina, where are we going?"

"We're going to see your Mamam, you remember that pretty lady in the painting?"

"Yes, I remember."

The door opened, and a woman entered. She had a swaddled baby in her arms and she gently pushed Jivin forward. "Go hug your Mamam, there's a good boy," she instructed.

Taminisha felt no heartbeats in her chest even with the children in the room. Her mind riled against the confusion flooding through her. *How can this be? I see my son, but do not feel him. Did the new child block the touch of the old? Is it because I carry the sachan way?* She swallowed hard forcing the lump almost choking her down into her chest. Her hands trembled.

Taminisha studied the woman who had brought the children. She didn't know her. She wondered what had become of Flatasha. This woman appeared barely Ellkiiyn. *"Bring my daughter here please."* Taminisha broadcast the instruction kindly, when instinct urged her to grab the babe and hold her.

The woman ignored her, pushing the boy forward.

Temper flared. *"I want my daughter."* The woman still did not respond. *Oh, Great Spirit she's so diluted she can't broadcast. What an ill-fated choice for my children.*

Taminisha looked directly at the woman. "Please bring my daughter to me."

The woman grimaced. "She's sleeping, and I'll not have her woken. Hug your son, my lady, and be grateful."

Taminisha sensed mixed emotions in the woman's tone—

resentment, anger, guilt. She couldn't be sure.

"Mamam, I've missed you," Kashwen cried as he jumped on Taminisha's lap.

Taminisha looked down at the child on her lap as he reached up to hug her.

Shock bolted through her. The features were so similar, the mouth, the eyes and the hair, but something in his expression, the tilt of his head and his smile. This was not Jivin. Her gut somersaulted, and hot bile seared her throat. Tears welled in her eyes.

She stiffened, made to push the child from her lap and opened her mouth to howl, but something in the child's expression made her hesitate. With a sharp click of teeth she bit back her protest and allowed her shock and horror to strangle in her throat with just a squeak. She softened back into the chair.

The child cuddled closer and laid his head on her shoulder.

After several deep breaths, Taminisha managed to overcome her antipathy toward the child and wrap her trembling arms around him.

She cleared the lump in her throat. "Jivin, my darling, you have grown so much since Mamam last saw you. Such a big boy."

"I am big, Mamam; Dynatina takes me to the garden and by the water," the child replied.

"I am so glad you've come to see me, Jivin," Taminisha murmured, and hugged the boy close to her breasts, forcing herself not to recoil at his touch.

She felt something warm and hard slide down her cleavage. She peered into the child's face.

He smiled back at her and leaned in very close as if to kiss her. "*A gift, Mamam,*" he broadcast softly as he glanced over his shoulder at the woman waiting, then back to Taminisha.

"*Shhh.*" Taminisha broadcast as fear stabbed through her.

The child grinned. "*She cannot hear.*" Without warning, he kissed her cheek. "*From your Orunan friend. He said you would understand.*"

"Enough now, Jivin, it's time for you to nap," Dynatina said.

The child slipped off Taminisha's lap and stood by her side.

"Please let me hold Milli, before you go. I beg of you." Taminisha had to know.

The woman came forward and placed the baby in Taminisha's arms. "She is growing well, my lady. You can be proud of such a beautiful child."

Taminisha lifted the rug and looked down at the pale face of the sleeping babe. It was not Milli. She cuddled the mixed blood child in pretence of acceptance, then after a moment's hesitation, she handed her back to Dynatina.

"Yes, I am proud of my children, Madame. Care for them well."

The woman took the boy's hand and walked out of the room, locking the door behind her.

Vomit rushed up her throat. She spewed onto the floor by her feet. Wave after wave of tremors shuddered through her. *What kind of fool do you think I am, Nyket? What sort of mother—to think I would not know? To not recognise my own children.* She sat shuddering, unable to rise from the chair. Tears poured down her cheeks and fell, unheeded, from her nose and chin.

He had taken her only meaning, her only purpose to stay alive. She grasped her Rykala locket and prayed to the Great Spirit Ellkii to take her.

Still shaking, she pushed to her feet. Nyket would come again. She had to decide what to do. To stay silent, or to challenge him, demand an explanation. Her stomach lurched again as the smell of her vomit wafted. She found a cloth and knelt to wipe it up.

The click and rattle startled her. She checked the door. It remained closed, but a foot from her knees sat a smooth, rounded, red Orunan gemstone—Tarlitek's gemstone. After he had retrieved it from the bottom of the lake, deep in the shadow of Oventi Rock he had placed it around his neck on a piece of thong; the one he had so lovingly tied a knot in each time she gave birth. *"To keep them close to my heart,'* he'd said, *"for it is not the Orunan way to value your offspring."*

The stone hung on that thong, three knots tied in its length—each one bigger than the last.

She held it in her palm. Her fingers trembled as she ran them over the leather feeling each knot. Hope flared. Tarlitek's stone. The knots indicated her children, and of course Aiyana. She tried not to think of the egg she'd abandoned. If things had gone differently, she would have had three children, one to match each knot.

She looked up at the door. The other child, so like Jivin he could be his twin. *How? Who?* Part of her rejoiced in the message. Could Tarlitek have rescued the children? Taken them to safety. What did this mean for the other Jivin and Milli? She hugged herself as her mind grappled with conflicting thoughts. Had Nyket knowingly foisted these substitutes on her after her children vanished? Alternatively, had he been fooled by a clever ruse?

She stroked the pebble. The substitute child could have only come from Tarlitek. She shuddered as comprehension formed. Tarlitek had replaced her babes with others to gift them the freedom and safety they needed. But what price? What of the boy, who looked so like Jivin, only a mother would know the difference? Where had he come from? Why did he not protest? *Why? Why? Why?* There were no answers.

She sat back clutching the stone over her heart. The heaviness of uncertainty held her immobile. If Tarlitek had taken her children and replaced them with others, they could now enjoy a freedom she had never envisaged. Contentment flowed through her. She knew nothing of the substitutes except they would die if she exposed the subterfuge to Nyket and her beloved children and friends would lose the freedom they now had. It ripped her to the core knowing she would never see any of them again, but that they lived swelled her heart so much she feared it would explode. Either way she could now end her life and prevent the birth of the monstrosity, she carried.

# Chapter Twenty Five

A drawn out ear-splitting screech broke the silence of the sleeping household. Clyeva leapt out of bed to find Potokin attacking the egg with his claws and teeth, scratching with a furious intensity.

"Potokin, no," Clyeva shouted and sprinted to the nest. "No, Potokin, do not hurt the egg!"

The tiny Tarki glanced up at her, screeched and resumed scratching the egg. He held it close in his arms, and pummelled the shell with his back claws fully extended.

Clyeva wasn't game to put her hand in to grab the Tarki knowing his claws would slice her flesh to the bone.

"Tarlitek, Tarlitek, Shula, Help! Potokin's gone mad!"

Tarlitek appeared in the doorway.

Potokin screamed at him, spitting and howling in between scratching the egg.

Shula staggered from her bed. She took one look at the egg and the

Tarki and lunged forward onto her knees. "Help me, Tarlitek, help me! The Tarki is trying to break the egg. Maybe it's too weak." Shula reached in.

Potokin spat at her and ripped again at the egg.

Tarlitek grabbed up a cloth and threw it over the frantic creature then grabbed him with both arms. The Tarki kicked and shrieked, but Tarlitek held him close to his chest, his arms wrapped tightly around him. "Quiet, Potokin, quiet. We will help. We will rescue Taminisha's baby. Be calm."

Potokin continued to kick and howl.

Tarlitek pulled the rug off the Tarki's head so he could now see, but held the rest of his body in a vice like grip. "Stay calm, you crazy creature. We will help."

Clyeva knelt by Shula. She could hear faint peeps and whistles coming from inside the egg. Shula snatched up a digging instrument and scratched on the shell. Almost immediately, a faint scrabbling noise answered her sounds.

Potokin screeched again, but Tarlitek held him.

Shula grabbed up a delicate saw with fine sharp teeth. She began to saw. The tool cut a deep gouge in the shell. Shula kept sawing.

Potokin stopped struggling, and began to whistle and chatter.

Tarlitek knelt down to bring the Tarki closer to the egg.

"Careful, Shula, don't hurt the babe."

Shula ignored Clyeva's warning.

"Don't worry so, Clyeva, Shula knows more about eggs than most," Tarlitek assured his mate.

Clyeva felt silly then. "Of course, Myatticans have shawken heritage and birth their young in an egg. Sorry, Shula."

Shula chuckled. "I understand. This is *your* baby. Of course you're worried."

"Do you think it will all right? I mean the egg has been through so much."

"Listen. Can you hear that?" Shula put her ear to the egg.

Clyeva leaned forward. She could hear the faint scratching and mewling of the baby within. As Clyeva sat back anxiously,

Shula sawed some more.

With a sharp crack, the egg split on the saw line into a jagged opening. A tiny, blue, clawed foot poked out. It wriggled.

Clyeva's heart stopped, thumped frantically, then beat evenly again. *Oh Spirit, Taminisha's baby is alive. My baby."*

Potokin leapt out of Tarlitek's arms and scrambled right up to the egg, whistling and chattering.

The baby Ellkiiyn inside the egg chattered and whistled back.

Potokin inserted his claws in the opening and, with extreme gentleness, eased the edges of the shell apart.

None of those watching attempted to interfere with the Tarki's ministrations.

Another leg popped out.

Clyeva thought her heart would burst with love and pride as a tiny snout appeared, followed quickly by a tiny Ellkiiyn face.

As Potokin spread the shell apart, the baby climbed out, and stood tottering on all four feet as it tried to untangle its gossamer thin blue wings from the gooey shell lining.

"Fire Nymph, oh Spirit, it's alive. Taminisha's baby is alive. Tarlitek, we have a female baby."

Potokin hissed and glared at Clyeva before he wrapped his scaly arms around the baby Ellkiiyn.

Tarlitek laughed. "I think you will have to share, my love, Potokin has staked his claim."

Clyeva leaned toward the Tarki. "We have a child, Potokin, for without you rescuing the egg, the child would be dead."

The Tarki chattered happily, and proceeded to lick the baby clean.

"How long before the babe should transmogrify? Should we worry if she does not?"

"Transmogrify, or not, Clyeva, by Nootau's extinguishment, I am not going to kill that baby, after all we've been through. We'll take what we have, and be grateful it lives. Now, my love, what are you going to name her?"

Clyeva stared at the blue Ellkiiyn. "I think with all that has gone before, Shydia would be appropriate after Taminisha's older brother."

Shula and Tarlitek both smiled.

Clyeva leaned forward to the Tarki. "What do you think, Potokin, shall we name *our* baby Shydia?"

Potokin peered up at Clyeva, chattered, then leapt onto her shoulder and whispered excitedly in her ear before smooching up and down her neck and through her hair.

Clyeva giggled at the savage Tarki's rare show of affection, and apparent approval. "So Potokin, Shydia it is. My goodness," Clyeva cried, as baby Ellkiiyn Shydia transmogrified into her sachan form.

Clyeva scooped her up just as Jivin stumbled up to the nest. "Look, Jivin, you have a sister."

He rubbed his eyes, yawned and screwed his nose up. "Another one?"

Clyeva laughed along with Tarlitek and Shula, but this birth brought deep concerns to mind. Clyeva knew the limitations of her own life span, and bringing up three Ellkiiyn children would have its challenges. In their sachan form they grew swiftly and matured faster than true blood sachans, but as Ellkiiyn they matured physically much faster still.

Their life span could be anything up to five hundred years. Clyeva fretted for with all her Abaye frailties, and short life span of only fifty years. Would she live long enough to raise the three children to an age where they could be independent? Tarlitek would live longer than she would by thirty years or so, maybe more if he took after his mother's Myattican side. A purebred Myattican could live to one hundred and fifty years, barring accidents. She sighed and choked back sobs. She would never regret taking on the task ahead and together, her and Tarlitek would face the future, and do the best they could for the three orphans.

Tarlitek and Clyeva sat outside in the last of the solar rays with Shydia and Milli lying together on a blanket. Both girls thrived and young Jivin had become an active adventurous child, full of confidence as he played with the Myattican children. They squealed, and ran in mock terror when he transmogrified by accident or sometimes on purpose. Tarlitek had warned him not to, in case he squashed someone because as Ellkiiyn he was already as big as a sachan adult.

They heard him long before they saw him.

"Am not, am not. I Jivin. Don't call me that. Not Kash... Kash..."

Tarlitek leapt to his feet and strode down the slope. Jivin appeared—dirty and bloodied, his clothes torn, and his hair tousled. Tears poured down his cheeks. Five boys chased him, waving sticks and carrying rocks.

"Ma doesn't want you, Kash. Ma gave you away, and glad to get rid of you. Can't come back, Kashwen," the biggest boy yelled.

"Tarlitek, Tarlitek," Jivin yelled as he staggered up the hill, a few feet ahead of his tormenters.

Tarlitek walked passed Jivin as he ran into Clyeva's open arms. He held up his hands. "Back off, boys. He's not Kashwen, he's Jivin. You don't want me speaking to your Ma, do you?"

The five boys stopped and stared at Tarlitek.

The older boy screwed his face up. "You're the gill breather who took Kashwen away. Why did you take him?"

Tarlitek grimaced at the boy, all his buried guilt rushed to the surface of his cold Orunan brain. "None of your business, boy. Be warned if any of you hassle Jivin again, I'll have you removed from Myattica, and your rations will cease. Understood?"

The boy flushed red. "How do you know about our rations?"

Tarlitek pointed back toward the refugee camp. "I know, because I provide them. Now go home, all of you."

The boys scuttled away.

Jivin peeped through his hands. "They call me Kash...wem? I not der brudda. I son of Taminisha and Kikishan of Kelkiki. I will be Guardian of Kelkiki when I growed up, won't I, Tarlitek?"

Tarlitek settled comfortably back in his seat and pulled Jivin onto his lap. "I'm going to tell you something important, Jivin, and I want you to remember it."

Jivin tilted his head to one side and waited.

"You are the son of Kikishan and Taminisha and *will* be Guardian of Kelkiki in time, but I do not want you to ever say it aloud again. Ever. Not even to me, Clyeva or your sisters."

"Why dis bad?"

"Because there are those who wish you dead, Jivin, along with your sisters. If you ever want to be Guardian of Kelkiki, you must stay alive to grow up. Do you understand?"

"Mamam and Da not coming see me?" Jivin asked, his childish voice trembling with unshed tears.

"No Jivin, they are not."

The boy nodded. "Who Kashwem?"

"Kashwen is a boy who looks just like you. He is a very special boy, your cousin, and I will tell you his story when you are old enough to understand. His existence gives you your freedom, and in the future, if he lives to grow up, you will reward him."

Jivin slid from Tarlitek's knee. "I hungry, want food please."

Clyeva stood. "Come child, I will get you food."

As she turned to go inside Tarlitek met her glance. He shook his head just a little.

Clyeva felt a cold chill whisper across her body. The years to come would not be easy for any of them.

~ ~ ~

Whichever guard watched her, their gaze never left her for a moment. If Taminisha picked up anything to use for self-harm, the guards snatched it from her fingers before she had even given its potential a second thought. Undaunted, she waited, and watched, for her chance, resenting her burgeoning belly full of Nyket's child.

Her first chance came as she entered the last forty solar phasings before the child could be born. A new female guard came and went. Taminisha admired her long luscious hair, often worn up in a swirling bun and held in place by metal combs. Taminisha eyed those combs with serious intent. One would do to slice her wrists, during the dark hours, when the tired guard quite often slept while on duty.

Taminisha stood by the barred window, and watched the solar settling. She heard a child's voice below, and leaned over to see. Below she could see the boy who called himself Jivin, playing with a smaller female child. They might have been her children, but she knew they were not.

The thought of Tarlitek and Clyeva raising her children somewhere safe had kept her sane during her imprisonment and Nyket's vicious rutting. Believing sometime in the future, Kikishan's bloodline would hold sway in Kelkiki again gave her hope for the future, regardless of her destiny. She thought often about Jabrikan too, and prayed to the Spirit that he grew strong and wise, so he could claim his realm when the time came.

A hand latched onto her arm. "Come away from the window. Guardian Nyket would not like it."

As the guard tugged her arm, Taminisha collapsed to the floor, with a distressed cry, pulling the smaller bodied guard down with her. As the female tried to stand up Taminisha ripped a comb from her hair and tucked it into her cleavage.

"Up you get. I hope that didn't hurt the child. I have never dealt with anything as fragile as a sachan pregnancy," the woman grumbled, as she struggled to lift the unresisting Taminisha from the floor.

Once standing, Taminisha held her swollen belly with both hands, and groaned. She bent over slightly and hobbled to the bed. The guard flushed red and tried to help her.

Taminisha shrugged off the female's helping hands and crawled onto the bed, crying. The guard stood back watching her, not at all sure what she should do.

Moments later the kitchen servant entered with Taminisha's food. The guard handed her the tray.

"Please sit up and eat, Taminisha – there is some herbal tea, hot and sweet, perhaps that will help your shock of falling."

Taminisha glared at the woman, but sat up and drank her tea. She stayed on the bed for the rest of the evening, and simply pulled up the bedclothes over her clothed body as the air chilled. She refused to get undressed under the guard's watchful gaze.

The guards changed places. The lunor drift guard, an older Ellkiiyn Unni cross breed; always fell asleep, snuffling and snorting through his shift. Taminisha thought it amusing he couldn't stay awake. She wondered if he could transmogrify to Ellkiiyn form or transform into a blood sucking shikati, and hoped he could do neither. If he could smell her blood when she slashed her wrists it would attract the Unni in him, and wake him enough to interfere with her intent.

The larger lunor disc, Etunik, and his four satellites, were sinking toward the far horizon by the time the male guard slept. He snored, and snuffled, his head lolled back in the chair.

Taminisha pulled out the comb and, without hesitation, sliced the flesh of her arms open. She clenched her teeth against the pain that stabbed through her as purple Ellkiiyn blood poured out of the jagged gashes.

Determined to speed the process she rolled over and let her arms hang over the side of the bed. She laid her head on the pillow and watched her blood flow in a stream onto the floor, where it pooled, before it spread silently across the floor like a cloud across the sky. Soon it reached the guard's boots and parted into two streams, flowing around the obstacle, and then rejoined on the other side.

The world spun, confusing her brain function. Nausea washed over her. The child in her belly tumbled and kicked, repeatedly. A vague sense of guilt stabbed at her about causing an innocent such distress. For the sake of the future, they both had to die.

Besides, this child should never have been bred to become a part blood Ellkiiyn carrying her pure bloodlines. Conceived through force and humiliation the child would follow its father's example of ruthless cruelty to many, and the subjugation of all Dykarin. The thought horrified her.

Chill fingers of fatigue crawled over her skin; she sighed and closed her eyes. Death crept closer, slowly. Darkness hovered around the edges of her consciousness, as her lungs refused to draw in air. She tried to lay still and silent, petrified of discovery before she had achieved what she desired.

Barely conscious, Taminisha heard the snort that rumbled from the guard's nose. She heard the chair jerk and creak. With a deep grunt, the guard jerked awake just before the chair crashed over. He thudded to the floor. With another grunt, he rolled over and tried to stand. He slipped in the blood and crashed to the floor. The Unni in him identified the wetness as blood in an instant. He scrambled up bellowing for help. "She dies – the lady dies. Get help." He dropped to his knees beside her and began to bind her arms.

Taminisha fought his grip, pulling her bleeding arms free. She tried to kick him, but her belly got in the way. Anger surged through her as she tried to gather her thoughts and move her dying body away from his intervention. Then there were more hands on her, binding her arms, holding them up. She coughed and spluttered, then vomited on herself.

"Get blood, purple Ellkiiyn blood," someone shouted.

Time passed for Taminisha in semi-blackness, penetrated by voices, and hands grabbing at her. She sensed an Ellkiiyn looming over her. Then an incredible burning in her arm. She felt the spurt of alien blood spread from the centre pain, the heat of it flowed down her arm then across to her heart. Her heart thudded, faltered, then beat on, strong and steady.

"Fix it, by the curse of Etunik, you accursed idiots. Stop the bleeding. Save her, and the child."

Nyket's shouted orders shattered her resistance and she lay there letting them save her. *No good fighting, too late. Death is receding.*

She kept her eyes closed, but tears squeezed out from under her lids and rolled down her cheeks. She sensed Nyket's face close to hers. She could smell him.

"If you have hurt the child, Taminisha, I shall kill your son, do you hear me. I shall kill your son."

Knowing his threat to be empty, Taminisha wished fervently for death. "No, Nyket, spare my son."

Time passed. Taminisha didn't bother to count each solar phasing as she drifted in and out of consciousness. Finally beginning to revive she tried to roll over. Her arms dragged behind her movement. She rolled back. Her arm flopped to the bed. Chains rattled and the cuffs cut into her flesh. She tried to sit up but couldn't manoeuvre her bloated body without leverage. She tried to move her legs. The effort tightened the manacles around her ankles.

She lay back on the mattress, her mind and body numb. Emotion drained from her as she stared at the ceiling, seeing nothing.

~ ~ ~

When her labour first started, Nyket decreed she would stay in chains for the duration. Despair rushed over her. Right through the solar phasing and into the lunor drift, she suffered the pain of contractions with just a guard watching over her. She couldn't walk or roll over. As the pains increased, she groaned and grunted, writhing continuously to find some relief.

Nyket came to the doorway. "Shut up your whinging, and birth my child," he shouted at her.

Taminisha lifted her head slightly, panting under the effort of sachan birth. "To Orunikan with you, Nyket. Do you have any idea what's involved in birthing a sachan babe?"

He shrugged. "I don't much care, as long as it's alive."

She glared in his direction just before another contraction ripped through her body. When it passed, he still watched her.

"That is just the beginning. I cannot birth this child alive, unless I have help, and I cannot do it in chains."

Nyket shrugged again. "What help? Ellkiiyn birth themselves pretty much."

"You Khimaera, you half brain," Taminisha screamed at him. "Have you ever seen a sachan birth?"

Nyket screwed his face up. "No."

"Well now is your chance. You can deliver the baby. I'll just push it out of the hole from whence it went in. *You* can catch it and clean up the blood and birthing mess," Taminisha shrieked.

Nyket squinted at the apex of her legs. He coloured vaguely green and the scales of his untidy masq seemed to lift and curl slightly at the ends. He spun around and strode from the room.

Taminisha howled after him. "Get me a sachan female to help, or lose your child."

Less than an hour later, two sachan females entered the room. They cringed back, and the younger one had tears on her cheeks. Nyket stood behind them.

"They call themselves dyinyahs; they claim to birth all the sachans in the village."

Nyket retreated and stormed from the room.

"My lady, we heard you were close to birthing, so we came to the castle to offer our services. Your soul mate always showed Avyvah respect, and kindness. I am Avyvah's granddaughter, Tensa. She died in the troubles."

"I'm sorry your grandmother is no longer with us, Tensa, and I am so grateful for your assistance and kindness. I cannot offer you reward. As you can see, I am prisoner of Nyket."

"We understand, my lady, now let's see to you," Tensa replied in romni.

As her labour progressed to the pushing stage, Tensa summoned

Nyket and demanded her release. "You have to release her, my lord. She cannot birth safely in chains. Your baby will be at risk."

"I will not risk the babe, here, release her, but guards will be outside the door," Nyket replied, throwing the key at Tensa.

"My lord, she is in labour, and not capable of running away," Tensa scoffed.

Taminisha lay in agony on the bed and she cried out in relief when her hands were unchained.

"Now push, Taminisha, push this babe into the world," Tensa encouraged.

Taminisha bellowed in her efforts as she pushed. She sank back on the bed as the discomfort eased. As the next cramp clutched her, she pushed again. Taminisha felt the baby's head pushing between her legs.

"By the Great Spirit, the baby is not moving," Tensa cried.

Taminisha looked at Tensa, confused at her claim.

"You do not want this child birthed alive, my lady?" Tensa whispered.

Taminisha nodded. "It should never have been conceived."

Tensa gave a half smile and waved the other woman toward the door. "We need more water, we need help, the child is stuck."

Together they both hurried from the room.

Taminisha eased off the bed and squatted on the floor. She pushed hard. The babe's head stretched her opening wider. She endeavoured to stay upright as the agony ripped through her. She clutched the bed and pushed again. The baby slipped out and Taminisha collapsed with a thud to the floor. The child lay still between her legs, all covered in the birthing fluids. He didn't cry.

Taminisha grabbed him around the throat and began to squeeze, tighter and tighter.

She gazed into his face, all blue and scrunched up. He looked so like Jivin. Her chest clenched, sobs choked up her throat. She removed her hands and sat still, filled with horror at what she'd attempted.

The baby didn't move.

Guilt sliced through her. She grabbed up the child and shook it. Then tipped it upside down and slapped its buttocks and back.

It hung lifeless from her hand. Panic scrambled through her. *Great Ellkii what have I done? Murdered my own child.*

She brought it to her face, covered the tiny nose and mouth with hers, and blew. The chest rose and fell. She blew repeatedly. Finally the baby squirmed, gasped and mewled. Pink colour replaced the blue. She stroked its downy head, tenderness washed over her. *How could I want to harm you, baby? Poor baby, I didn't mean it.* Tears poured down her cheeks. She put the baby to her breast. It latched on and suckled.

"You left her alone, you fool, you imbeciles," Nyket yelled from the doorway.

As he burst into the room, Taminisha didn't even look up as she continued to nurse her son.

Nyket grabbed the child, and pulled him away from her, thumping Taminisha in the chest as he did so.

The baby wriggled and cried its lusty bawling filling the room.

"I have a son. He will be called Perrok."

"Give me my babe, Nyket. He needs his mother."

Nyket stared at her. "He is *my* son."

She held out her hands, even as guilt gripped her.

Nyket scowled at her. "He is the son you never wanted, and now you can't have him."

Taminisha shrivelled inside. She dropped her hands into her lap and glared up at Nyket. "I want to see Jivin and Milli. You told me I could see my children when I gave birth."

Nyket smiled. "I'll take you to see your children, before I kill you. Get yourself cleaned up ready to take the hand of Spirit."

Tensa crept forward. "Come, my lady, I will help you." Tears ran in rivulets down her cheeks.

Nyket strode from the room, the baby screaming in his arms.

"I couldn't do it, Tensa."

"I know, my lady. You don't have evil in you like that one."

Numbness flooded over her. She sat, motionless, a great rent in her heart. She welcomed death, a cure to the great hole inside her, the coldness, and the deadness where once Kikishan's heartbeat had livened and warmed her. Where once the love and hopes for her children lived. Now a great nothingness resided.

Jivin and Milli, perhaps alive somewhere, were beyond her reach while Nyket lived. Her egg abandoned to wither and the son, the tainted son, would be raised with his heart set against her, and filled with malicious cruelty.

Her heart beat slowly as she went through the motions of getting dressed under Tensa's gentle ministrations. Clean and dressed, she sank onto the bed, hands in her lap, head bowed ready to face death.

She heard his footsteps and sensed his presence beside her. She sat motionless.

"Get up." He grabbed her arm in a savage grip and dragged her to her feet. She didn't resist. "Move it, I don't have time or patience for this. I have a world to conquer, and a son to raise."

Taminisha put one foot in front of the other. He pushed her forward.

Childish voices trilled in the distance. She roused. The solar orb shone, and the garden smelled of perfume and cut grass.

She stood at the bottom of the steps. Four children skipped and danced around. The dark-haired boy turned to look at her.

He paused, and then smiled. He held out his hands as he raced toward her. "Mamam, Mamam."

She studied him. This child may not be her son, Jivin, but something inside her stirred as the boy threw himself against her.

She rested her hand on his head. "And what of my children?"

Nyket laughed. "Well you can take him with you if you like. Wouldn't want you to be lonely. Besides, the Kikishan Aqueena bloodlines must end here."

Rage exploded inside her. She bit down on it. "And my daughter?"

The boy pretending to be Jivin gazed up at her. "Milli died, Mamam. I cried lots and lots."

She glared at Nyket. "You murdered a defenceless babe."

"I did nothing of the sort. The female child just died."

Grief slammed into her. She had known the baby displayed to her on the brief visit had not been Milli, but she never conceived of the idea Milli had died.

A maelstrom of emotions swirled through her, extinguishing the despondency. She surveyed the garden. Four children and one orange skinned mixed blood Ellkiiyn guard in sachan form.

She snatched up the boy's hand, bounced once, and rolled. For a moment his weight dragged on her then he rolled beside her.

The orange Ellkiiyn stepped forward, pushed the three remaining children through the gate and slammed it shut.

Nyket snatched up a metal garden stake. The orange Ellkiiyn lunged and hit Nyket in the shoulder as he flung his makeshift weapon. The stake wobbled and lost its momentum, but it caught Taminisha in the shoulder ripping the flesh open before it fell to the ground.

She rose as Ellkiiyn and roared her rage with a blast of fire. Nyket hollered as the flame caught him in the chest. He doubled over and staggered backward. "Guards, guards. She escapes."

With a swipe of her front leg, she sliced Nyket's shoulder and back open.

He crumpled.

She leapt forward.

Nyket rose to his knees, snatched up another stake with his uninjured hand, and threw it.

It pierced her shoulder and hung in her flesh wobbling with its cut off momentum. Taminisha squealed and leaped back.

"Fly, Mamam, fly," the boy yelled as three more guards appeared.

They struggled to get the gate open. The orange Ellkiiyn guard just stood and watched.

She scooped the child up and tossed him over her shoulder. He clutched her pectenites to secure himself. With a flap of wings, Taminisha lifted. Dropped. Lifted again. Throbbing from her damaged shoulder pounded through her as she brought both wings down. She caught the wind and soared.

She bellowed as the bones in her shoulder crunched. She could barely lift her wing. Wind whipped across her face. A green Ellkiiyn slammed into her side. She wavered, dropped, gathered her strength, and pushed upward.

Fire seared along her side. She blasted back catching her attacker on the softer underbelly. He screeched. She blasted again. He transmogrified and plummeted toward the lake.

Another latched onto her tail. She swayed erratically under the weight as she jerked her tail from side to side, but couldn't dislodge the burden.

"I'll get him, Mamam."

A shower of sparks stung a path along her back. The red Ellkiiyn hanging onto her tail howled. A flash of orange zoomed in from the right and latched onto her attacker's tail. The red Ellkiiyn writhed and released its hold. The orange Ellkiiyn hovered in the sky.

Taminisha gained height then drifted sideways and tilted to one side. She lost height. Each uneven flap of her wings sent her off balance. She stretched her wings wide to catch the draught rising from the lake. She glided. The lake lay below, calm, serene and dangerous.

A screech behind her scored her nerves. She glanced over her shoulder. Nyket had transmogrified. Despite his tainted Khimaera shabbiness, he gained on her. She flapped her wings, and howled as agony stabbed though her.

The boy slipped. She snatched at him as he floated passed. However, he tumbled and rolled out of her reach. He transmogrified right in front of her snout.

"Turn, Mamam. Together we will blast him."

She twisted her body, bringing her tail down.

Nyket zoomed closer.

She blasted a stream of flame.

Nyket roared as he recoiled from the flame as it caught him in the face.

The boy dived at Nyket's face and blasted in his ear.

Nyket bellowed, swerved and plummeted toward the lake. He hit the water as Ellkiiyn, sank then surfaced. He floated for a moment then leapt free of the water spearing through the air directly at her.

She blasted again as she turned away. She missed.

The boy blasted and hit Nyket right in the nostril. Nyket swiped his snout, snorted and gasped.

Taminisha flew, but tracked to the right, toward Fylitia.

The boy grabbed her injured wing and tugged.

She skewed back onto a straight path.

Nyket charged from the side.

The orange Ellkiiyn dived down and slammed into Nyket's abdomen.

He grunted and spat, but his blast just singed her belly. She screeched, rolled, spun and began to drop.

She tried desperately to flap her wings, but the left one refused to do more than vibrate.

The boy latched onto her snout and tugged.

Nyket rammed her from the side.

She slewed and rolled, dropping out of the sky. Faster and faster.

Nyket pulled away. With a slow flap of wings, he suspended himself in the air. He tracked her glide. He made no effort to stop her.

The unknown orange Ellkiiyn latched onto her with his claws, flapping and straining to keep her in the sky.

"*Who are you?*"

"*I am Khoury. Tarlitek sent me to guard the child.*"

Emotion choked through her. She spread her wings, steadied, and floated on the air currents. Not enough to stay in the air. Swiftly she lost altitude. Below she saw green. Rich lush jungle. She fought against the downward motion. Oventi Rock loomed closer and closer. The child in Ellkiiyn form buzzed around her head.

"*Mamam, save yourself, please fly.*"

*"Fly, Taminisha, for Spirit's sake."*

*"I cannot. Tarlitek has my children?"*

*"He does and your egg."*

She gasped. They had saved her egg. Her heart fluttered and warmed. She could die at peace. *"Tell them all I love them."*

She peered into the boy's eyes and shook her head. *"I cannot do this anymore. Fly little one. Fly. Save yourself. Go with Khoury."*

The young Ellkiiyn screwed up his face. With the softest of touches, he landed on her head and curled his claws around her pectenites. *"I will not leave you, Mamam."*

Khoury tried to dislodge the child, but he clung to her. As they neared the lake, Khoury hovered beside them. He could not prevent her heavier body plummeting downward.

Oventi Rock loomed large. She could see the individual leaves on the plants, the glint of water and shawken flitting through the foliage. She closed her eyes and waited for impact.

Her body ripped through the foliage, tearing branches, scattering the shawken, and shredding leaves. Her massive body slammed into the ground. The tremendous force of the collision expelled the air from her lungs. Agony consumed her, blackness hovered and she let it come. As the world faded, she heard the boy sobbing in her ear.

The End.

## REALM & SPECIES APPENDIX

**The Dykarin Prophecy series**

**Continent of Dykarin**

Dykarin is a large continent inhabited by many species. In their true form, they are very different, but in their sachan (human form), they are remarkably similar. While it is frowned upon to breed offspring, between species, it is common. These offspring are mostly accepted by those of their mixed heritage. The Ellkiiyn are an exception to this acceptance.

**The Ellkiiyn**

There are four clans of Ellkiiyn (Fire breathing, flying Dragon shape shifters able to transmogrify from (human) sachan form to Ellkiiyn at will.

As the dominant, longest lived species, they have been the benign Guardians of Dykarin for centuries.

Blood purity is highly valued. Those with a mixed species/ heritage are scorned, and discriminated against. They are called Khimaeras, or the tainted ones. Their mixed blood is evident in malformed pectenites, untidy scales and other deviations to Ellkiiyn appearance.

Each clan has their own distinctive pectenites (horns or antlers) and colour of skin and scales. In sachan form they retain the antlers and a pattern of scales on their faces called a masq.

They are telepathic between themselves, but also verbally communicate in the universal language of Dykarin called Romni.

They have highly developed hearing and sight, breathe fire and can stay aloft and cover miles on a single flight.

They worship the Great Spirit Ellkii.

Mating, is usually instigated by a rare mystical calling felt between potential soul mates, and they bond for life. If parted by death often a surviving partner will die of a broken heart. Most Ellkiiyn never receive the call, so never mate, or have offspring so the population is withering. Ellkiiyn can breed in both Ellkiiyn form by laying a single egg with sixty solar phasings (days) incubation by both parents or in sachan form taking nine months and birthing the same as sachans (humans). Making love in their sachan form happens, but most do not want to risk getting pregnant like a sachan does. Cross species, breeding is in sachan form.

### The Four clans:

### Aikanshin

The Vaprus or Air Clan is Guardian of Aikanshin. The largest of the land occupied by Ellkiiyn since the demise of Hawakati Clan (Silver).

Currently the Vaprus are the dominant clan. The castle of the guardian is on Aikanshin Island set in the middle of the Aikan River at the top of the gigantic Ifaseeti Falls that flows into the Menishin Lake. The climate is a warm misty, muggy sort of climate with heavy vegetation and rich lush pasture.

The Vaprus in Ellkiiyn for are purple skinned and scaled and have two sets of pectenites (horns) one straight and one curving with two points.

They dispose of their dead at the Stones of Kannia on the mountain peak behind the castle. The Vaprosa wraiths claim the body. If they do not accept the deceased, the body is thrown off the falls and consumed by the Orunan monstrous deity, Orunikan.

- Tokanin: second mate of the late Kititash. He is Terraid and as such can only be Regent for Jabrikan, Kititash's grandson until he comes of age.
- Oralia: Tokanin's 2nd mate. She is of Terraid/Fylitia mixed blood. Most refrain from calling her a Khimaera out of respect for Tokanin.
- Nyket: Tokanin and Oralia's son.
- Taminisha: Kititash's daughter from her first mating
- Jabrikan: Guardian Apparent and son of Shydee (deceased) and Taminisha's nephew
- Odakan: Taminisha's soul mate and Tokanin's nephew
- Devinkin: Oralia's brother. Of mixed blood
- Shydee: Deceased brother of Taminisha

## Kelkiki

The Aqueena Clan or Water Clan's leader is Kikishan, Guardian of Kelkiki. Kelkiki is a vast, but mostly mountainous land. Kelkiki castle is set on an island on the edge of a huge lake called Kelkiki Lake.

The Aqueena Ellkiiyn have blue skin and scales with multiple pectenites of varying lengths in a crown like structure. Guardian Kikishan is a mature widower struggling to bring prosperity to Kelkiki.

- Kikishan: Male Aqueena. Guardian and Taminisha's second mate.
- Larkin: Male Aqueena. Kikishan's cousin
- Adakin: Male Terraid/Aqueena. Kikishan's loyal warrior.
- Enian: Aqueena/Viveka. Warrior.
- Jivin: Full blood Ellkiiyn of Aqueena and Vaprus heritage. Taminisha and Kikishan's son.

- Millinsha: Full blood Ellkiiyn of Aqueena and Vaprus heritage. Taminisha and Kikishan's daughter
- Shydia: Full blood Ellkiiyn of Aqueena and Vaprus heritage. Taminisha and Kikishan's youngest daughter.
- Kashwen: Male and full blood Ellkiiyn of Aqueena heritage. Kikishan's cousin. Son of the late Mekkan, Kikishan's Uncle.
- Islantina: Female and full blood Ellkiiyn of Aqueena heritage. Kashwen's mother through rape.
- Tabro: Male full blood Aqueena. Gay and Ikaya's mate.
- Ikaya: Male of Terraid/Infernea and Viveka heritage. Gay and Tabro's mate
- Sadrina: Female Aqueena/ Myattican. Healer
- Perrok: Male Terraid/Vaprus/Fylitia heritage. A Khimaera. Taminisha and Nyket's son.
- Avyvah: Female Fylitia/Myattican/sachan heritage. Old woman with healing and future telling skills.
- Tensa: Female and Avyvah's grand-daughter

**Mitikan**

The Infernea Clan or Fire Clan and Guardians of Mitikan. Mitikan is the second largest of the Ellkiiyn realms, but also the most inhospitable – cold, snow and ice with volcanoes bursting through the planet's surface with short times of light and long times of darkness.

The Infernea have one set of pectenites, long, slim and spiralling with red skin and scale and blood. Their Guardian, Okeyon, is troubled having lost his daughter to the scalinette fever and his son has disappeared, possibly kidnapped.

- Okeyon: Guardian. He is a great believer in equality for all. Rise and fall on own hard work and merits.
- Ulyana: Female full blood Infernea. Nyket's true soul mate, Larkin's temporary soul mate and mother of Aiyana
- Nysiah: Female full blood Infernea. Ulyana's twin sister and Larkin's true soul mate. Her color has faded because of trauma.

**Rabikan**

The Terraid or Turf Clan has guardian ship over the smallest area of land called Rabikan. Rabikan is a flat island with extremely rich pastureland, and small lakes teeming with orrtaya (fish). Climate is temperate. Terraid Ellkiiyn have one set of tall, straight, slim pectenites.

- Trayet: Terraid. Guardian. Dictator. Does not encourage outsiders. Does not believe in 'love calls'.
- Jycosa: Female Terraid. Adakin's soul mate
- Tehya: Female Terraid and Jycosa's sister
- Rynkari: Male Terraid, friend of Tehya.

**There used to be a fifth clan, the Hawakati, Ellkiiyn of Salt Water— considered to have died out long ago**

**The other realms making up the Continent of Dykarin:**

**Sachan Realms (mortals or humans)**

1. **Kylara**: inhabited by sachans. Anti-magic, Christian type religion, speak only Romni the universal language of Dykarin. They live in various size settlements and rarely mix with other species.
2. **Tarneta**: Have no magic, but tolerant of it and outsiders. Nature based religion and speak Romni only.
3. **Zalemia**
   Gypsy people. Speak Romni and their own language of Zal
   Magic in small ways such as predicting the future.

**Non-Sachan Realms**
**Myattica – Shawken (Bird) like humanoids.**
The women live in villages with the children. They are more human and do not have wings. The males are migratory with wings. They have

healing abilities, are vegetarians, with a non-violent culture. They lay eggs to breed.

- Shula: Female Myattican and Tarlitek's half-sister
- Mazin: Male Myattican and Tarlitek's half-brother, Shula's brother
- Khoury: Male Myattican/Ellkiiyn cross breed (A Khimaera, but he does not identify as Ellkiiyn) Tarlitek's nephew

**Orun –Merman/mermaid like gill breathing shape shifters**

Live in the lakes, rivers and manawa (mangroves). As Orunan gill breathers, they range from small mindless, soulless creatures to large intelligent shape shifters. In Orunan form, they are aggressive, ruthless killers and can strip a large creature down to a skeleton in a very short time.

In sachan form, they have a chitin exoskeleton and scales over the forehead and the top and side of the head. Gills are in side of neck behind ears and in armpits. Eyes are rounded and water proof. They have long spiny Mohawks. The ears as part of the exoskeleton protrude in a fin-like shape from the side of the head.

They eat orrtaya, which is cannibalistic, but also eat other small amphibians, insects and water grasses.

Worship Orunikan – the water monster.

Speak romni and own language.

- Tarlitek: Male Orunan/Myattican cross breed. Taminisha's Hallegan (body guard)
- Hauk: Male Orunan
- Kalonia: Female Orunan
- Orr: Leader of the Orunan
- Orunikan: monstrous deity of the Orunan

**Zynumin**

Shape shifter—they morphflitt (change) from sachan to felitza (big cats).

Hunt live prey in felitza (feline) form and live in prides with one dominant male.

- Aneverin: Dominant Male of Pride, Cougar
- Palakin: Male black panther
- Jyquin: Male Cheetah

## Viveka

All female community. Sachan form and only speak Romni. These women are stunning, but fierce, warlike, strong and athletic.

When they wish to breed, they leave the community and find a temporary mate. Usually choosing a sachan male, but may breed with an Unni or Fylitia male. Occasionally with a Zynumin male, but the risks can be high of becoming prey. Male issue are abandoned, given to the sachan father or offered to sachan couples for adoption.

- Oddianna: Leader
- Sharanna: Oddianna's daughter

## Fylitia – Spellbinders and magic makers.

Females are referred to as a Wheti and a male as a Whydan. Can speak most languages, tell the future, commune with the dead and move items by telekinesis, lay curses and control the elements. They are not able to change shape.

- Quanika: Leader of the Wheti.

## Abaye – Fire People

Fiery and volatile. Worship the Fire Nymph through the volcanic pools that bubble up from the volcano, Nootau. They are not able to change shape, but can be sachan with or without flames.

When fire inside is extinguished they die. To do anything to extinguish the inner fire before its time will result in a sudden execution in the boiling lava pools and inability of the Fire Nymph to accept your soul. On rare occasions, an Abaye can give fire to someone through abscission. They will die as a result, but be known as a martyr.

- Clyeva: Female Abaye, Tarlitek's soul mate
- Izusah: Leader of the Abaye
- Preeya: wise woman, oracle
- Angwye: Male Abaye and Tarlitek's cousin on mother's side and Clyeva's friend.
- Jumeeh: Female Abaye
- Deshikee: Female Abaye

## Lycidea –Unni

Pale skin, dark expressionless eyes, long dark hair, body piercings and tattoos. Wear black clothes with metal adornments and boots.

Can transform into shikati (bats) many of whom are blood-sucking creatures preying on innocent sachan children.

Ruthless killers with no empathy for others. They have a treaty with Fylitia.

They only speak Romni.

## Land of Leryi

Small monkey like creatures living in small troops – dominant male is leader

Intelligent, verbal, gentle, environmentally aware

Soft white fur, lavender eyes and prehensile tails

Vegetarians

Telekinesis & Clairvoyance

## Conurk

Inhabited by Eqazantia

Shape shifters—changing from winged sachan form to winged horses

Palomino colouring with creamy to white manes and tails.

Nurek the lead stallion

# GLOSSARY

| Dykarin Reference | Real World Reference |
| --- | --- |
| | |
| Allinik | Bronze |
| Ekta | Silicone-type substance |
| Ellkiiyn | Dragon-like shape-shifters |
| Eqazeen | Horse |
| Felitza | Large cats such as cougar, panther or cheetah |
| Habilen/ habilan | Male/female stretchy robes made with Ekta and Ellkiiyn saliva |
| Hallegan | Bodyguard |
| Khimaera | An Ellkiiyn cross-bred with another species |
| Lunor discs | Moons |
| Lunor drift | Night |
| Morphflitt | How the Zynumin change shape |
| Orrtaya | Fish |
| Pectenites | Ellkiiyn horns or antlers |
| Sachan | Human or mortal |
| Shawken | Bird |
| Shikati | Bats |
| Solar Phasing | Day |
| Solar settling | Sunset |
| Solar Awakening | Dawn |
| Tarki | Small aggressive dinosaur like reptile |
| Transmogrify | How Ellkiiyn change shape |
| Unni shikati | Vampire bats |
| Wheti/Whydan | Female Sorceress/male Sorcerer |
| Poraka | Frog |
| Dyinyahs | Midwife |
| Tarqu | Vipers |
| Danika | Herbal plants with healing properties |
| Jinnexa | Demon |
| Guarvee | Duck |
| Waylia | Jasmine |
| Froxcomb | Frill |
| Solar zenith | Midday |

| Baya | Palm-like tree with broad edible leaves |
|------|------------------------------------------|
| Kamizee | Mosquitoes |
| Arrayma | Garment similar to a niqab or burka |
| Abscission | Detachment of a natural part of a plant or person |
| Tiakto | Cactus |
| Blamets | Flowers |
| Ikter | Silver |
| Entresol | A mezzanine floor |
| Eqazantia | Shape-shifter winged horses |

# Collect your FREE GIFT of the 44 page

# Dykarin Prophecy Colouring Book

Discover the magic of Taminisha's story and the characters who share her world: the good, the bad and the uniquely different.
Get to know them and learn to love them as you indulge in the calming influence of colouring in the Dykarin images brought together by Emily for your enjoyment.

**CLICK ON OR SEARCH THE LINK BELOW**
**TO COLLECT YOUR FREE PRINTABLE COPY.**
**https://dioniemcnair.wixsite.com/dykarinprophecy**

# OTHER BOOKS BY THIS AUTHOR

*Writing as EMILY TYLER (Fantasy)*

    THRONES OF ANNATICCIA series

    BOOK 1 - Savage Betrayal

    BOOK 2 – Retribution and Restitution

*Writing as Dionie McNair (Young Adult)*

    THE ABRASAXON'S DAUGHTER series

    BOOK 1 – The Scorpion's Heart

    BOOK 2 – Curse of the Chakka Chakka

    and

    Finding the Upside of Down

*Writing as Cassandra Hawke (Romance/Erotic Romance)*

    Demolition of the Heart

    Deathly Embrace

    Blood Ties a Broken Heart